THEMATIC CATALOGUE
OF THE WORKS OF
GIOVANNI BATTISTA SAMMARTINI

GIO. BATTISTA S. MARTINO MILANESE

MORI L'ANNO 1775 17 GENN. D'ANNI 74

Giovanni Battista Sammartini. Anonymous eighteenth-century oil painting.

THEMATIC CATALOGUE
OF THE WORKS OF
GIOVANNI BATTISTA SAMMARTINI

ORCHESTRAL AND VOCAL MUSIC

BY

Newell Jenkins

AND

Bathia Churgin

Published for the
AMERICAN MUSICOLOGICAL SOCIETY
by
HARVARD UNIVERSITY PRESS
Cambridge, Massachusetts
London, England
1976

Library of Congress Catalog Card Number 73-81672
ISBN 0-674-87735-7

Printed in the United States of America

7/25/77 Ka

To Jan LaRue
in appreciation of all the years
of patient and wise counsel and friendship

ACKNOWLEDGMENTS

We wish to acknowledge our great indebtedness to Professor Jan LaRue of New York University for the vast store of information he has so generously shared with us, and for his invaluable guidance, suggestions, and ever ready personal concern in the progress of our work.

Our special thanks go to the following persons for their extensive help and advice with numerous problems of research: Professor Guglielmo Barblan of the Conservatorio "Giuseppe Verdi," Milan; Claudio Sartori of Milan; Günther Rhau, former director of the Amerikahaus in Giessen, Germany; Dr. Martin Cremer, formerly of the Westdeutsche Bibliothek, Marburg; Vladimir Fédorov of the Bibliothèque du Conservatoire, Paris; François Lesure of the Bibliothèque Nationale, Paris; Paters Johann Baptist Bolliger and Kanisius Zünd of the Abbey of Einsiedeln; Dr. Alexander Buchner, the late Dr. Emil Hradecký, Dr. Milan Poštolka, Dr. Oldrich Pulkert, and Dr. Milada Rutová of the Národní Muzeum, Prague; Dr. Cari Johannson of the Kungl. Musikaliska Akademiens Bibliotek, Stockholm; Herr Kern and Klaus Häfner of the Badische Landesbibliothek, Karlsruhe; Dora Coggiola of the Biblioteca Civica A. Mai, Bergamo; and Dr. Jan Olof Rudén of the Universitetsbibliotek, Uppsala.

We are grateful to the following librarians for sending us valuable information concerning various Sammartini collections in manuscript and print, and for allowing us to examine and microfilm materials in their libraries: Dr. H. Zehnter of the Universitätsbibliothek Basel; Professor Vincent Duckles and Mrs. Judith Hudson of the University of California at Berkeley Music Library; Dr. Heinz Ramge of the Staatsbibliothek der Stiftung Preussischer Kulturbesitz, West Berlin (formerly Westdeutsche Bibliothek, Marburg); Dr. Karl-Heinz Köhler of the Deutsche Staatsbibliothek, East Berlin; Johann Philipp Hinnenthal of the library formerly at Schloss Rheda, Bielefeld; Professor Napoleone Fanti and Sergio Paganelli of the Museo Bibliografico Musicale, Bologna; Mr. Lawrence G. Mowers of Isham Memorial Library, Harvard University; Sven Lunn of Det Kongelige Bibliotek, Copenhagen; Herr Koch of the Hessische Landes- und Hochschulbibliothek, Darmstadt; Dr. Ammann and Dr. Helmut Deckert of the Sächsische Landesbibliothek, Dresden; Professor Salvatore Pintacuda of the Biblioteca del Liceo Musicale "N. Paganini," Genoa; Dr. Volker von Volckamer and Count Richard Wedel of the Oettingen-Wallerstein'sche Schlossbibliothek, Harburg; Pater Paulus Niemetz and Alois Niemetz of the Abbey of Heiligenkreuz; Hermann Lang of Abbey Lambach; A. Hyatt King and O. W. Neighbour of the British Museum, London; Madama Isabel Niño of the Biblioteca Nacional, Madrid; Professor Adolf Trittinger of Abbey Melk; the late Professor August Halm of the Bayerische Staatsbibliothek, Munich; Dr. Erich Thurmann of the Universitätsbibliothek, Münster; Professor Anna Mondolfi of the Conservatorio S. Pietro a Majella, Naples; Professor Brooks Shepard, formerly of the School of Music

Library, Yale University; Peter Benedikt Kuen of Abbey Ottobeuren; Mme. Yvette Fédorov of the Bibliothèque Nationale, Paris; Mons. Sabatino Ferrali of the Biblioteca Capitolare del Duomo, Pistoia; Dr. Preindl and Hugo Angerer of the Fürstlich Thurn- und-Taxissche Hofbibliothek, Regensburg; Signorina Emilia Zanetti of the Conservatorio Santa Cecilia, Rome; Dr. Rolf Dempe of the Mecklenburgische Landesbibliothek, Schwerin; Paters M. Grebenc and Stefan Köll of Abbey Stams; H. Watkins Shaw of St. Michael's College, Tenbury; the late Francesco Piovesan and Dr. Mario Messinis of the Biblioteca del Conservatorio "Benedetto Marcello," Venice; Dr. Hedwig Kraus and Dr. Hedwig Mitringer of the Gesellschaft der Musikfreunde, Vienna; Dr. F. Grasberger of the Nationalbibliothek, Vienna; and Dr. Paul Sieber formerly of the Zentralbibliothek, Zürich.

For kind assistance we extend our thanks to the many other libraries listed in this catalogue. We also gratefully acknowledge the numerous replies to our requests for information from libraries in Europe and the United States not listed in this volume, since those collections contained no relevant Sammartini material.

We are indebted to the following persons who have helped and encouraged us in a multitude of ways: Professor Barry S. Brook for help with French manuscripts; Herman Baron and Cecil Hopkinson for obtaining some early prints; Professor Dénes Bartha for information about Hungarian sources; the late Count Guido Chigi-Saracini for arranging the first all-Sammartini concert in modern times in Siena, 1952; Professor Gerhard Croll for information about Viennese performances of Sammartini's instrumental music; Professor Filippo Donini for acting as liaison between ourselves and Italian libraries; Mrs. Key Gervasi for having made the first typescript of a large part of this catalogue; Professor Christa Fuhrmann-Landon for obtaining the microfilm of *Memet*; Ortrun Landmann for information about the *Memet* libretto in Meiningen; Dr. Lucia Pallavicini for information on Italian libraries; Matthew Raimondi for the loan of microfilms of Sammartini symphonies and chamber music; Richard Wadleigh for research in Venice; Professor Eugene K. Wolf for information about the Egk catalogue; Marita McClymonds for information about the Jommelli cantatas she discovered; Dr. Stanley Sadie for notifying us of her discovery; and Hannah Abrahamson, Marie Pierce, and Jean Settin for help with proofreading.

Our deepest thanks go to Julia Hanes Hurley, our patient and indefatigable typist, to John L. Hurley, Jr., for organizing the index, and to Elvidio Surian for checking the manuscript. We extend warm thanks to the Ford Foundation for a two-year travel grant to Newell Jenkins; Vassar College for a faculty fellowship and a research grant-in-aid to Bathia Churgin; the Martha Baird Rockefeller Fund in Music, Inc., for a grant to cover the final expenses of preparing the catalogue; and to Professor Giuseppe Cardillo and the Istituto Italiano di Cultura in New York for the gift of xerox copies of all the Sammartini manuscripts in Bergamo.

Finally, we wish to express our profound gratitude to the American Musicological Society for sponsoring this publication; to the Society's Publication Committee, headed by Professors Gustave Reese and James Haar for its sympathetic and helpful counsel; and to Professor John Ward for recommending the catalogue to the Harvard University Press.

CONTENTS

ILLUSTRATIONS

Frontispiece

Giovanni Battista Sammartini. Copy by Domenico Riccardi, 1778, after an anonymous portrait. Oil painting on paper. Bologna, Cirico Museo Bibliografico Musicale.

INTRODUCTION

The Milanese composer Giovanni Battista Sammartini (1700/01-1775) was one of the leading composers of the early Classic period, and a key figure in the development of the Classic style. Active as a composer for some fifty years, Sammartini produced a large body of music in the major instrumental and vocal forms of his time—symphony, concerto, concertino, ensemble and solo sonata, dance, opera, cantata, ballet, glee, Mass, oratorio, psalm setting, canticle, hymn, and litany. He was described by a contemporary as a composer "of great reputation,"[1] and his music was known throughout Europe, as indicated by the widespread manuscript copies of his works and the many printed collections.

Sammartini's instrumental works, especially the sixty-eight symphonies and some two hundred ensemble sonatas, have survived in greatest number and appear to have been his most influential compositions.[2] Equal in quality are Sammartini's comparatively few extant sacred compositions, the product of his lifelong occupation as a church musician. Many of these have only recently come to light. In every form and medium in which he worked, Sammartini composed music of high artistic merit as well as historical interest.

Like many of his contemporaries, Sammartini was soon forgotten after his death, and was generally ignored throughout the nineteenth century. It was only in the period around the First World War, with the revival of interest in Classic music and the Mannheim School, that scholars started intensive research on Sammartini, the facts of his biography, and the chronology and style of his music. The most important of these scholars were Georges de Saint-Foix, Fausto Torrefranca, and Gaetano Cesari, and they effectively laid the foundation for future Sammartini studies. It was not until after the Second World War, however, that further, large-scale research was undertaken. In what may justly be termed a Sammartini revival, significant biographical studies have been published by Guglielmo Barblan and Claudio Sartori, and intensive efforts made by the present writers and Professor Jan LaRue to locate, authenticate, analyze, publish, perform, and record Sammartini's music. The studies thus far have confirmed Torrefranca's high estimate of Sammartini's work and his view of the composer's pioneering role in the development of the Classic symphony.

---

[1]La BordeE, III, 233. Citations are to author and initial letter or letters of the first key word in the title; for full references see the bibliography.

[2]A detailed analysis of all the symphonies is included in ChurginS, from which many portions of the introduction have been drawn as well. For a full listing of eighteenth-century prints of chamber music and solo sonatas, see our article on Sammartini in *MGG,* vol. XI.

Before discussing the organization of this catalogue, we have decided to append a biographical sketch of Sammartini. This seems appropriate since much new biographical information has been uncovered, most of it published in Italian and German articles that remain largely unknown to American and English musicians. Further, the biography reveals a figure of far more impressive dimensions than has been generally recognized. It details Sammartini's rich musical environment, the nature and scope of his activities and contacts with leading patrons and composers of the period, and the growth of his fame abroad. Without this frame of reference, we believe, much information in the catalogue would not be as comprehensible and meaningful as it should be.

BIOGRAPHY

Giovanni Battista Sammartini was probably born in Milan, but the precise date of his birth is unknown. Since, in his death certificate, he was said to be seventy-four at the time of his death on 15 January 1775,[3] he should have been born in 1700 or between 1 and 15 January 1701. His father, Alexis Saint-Martin, a French oboist who probably settled in Milan in the 1690's, and his older brother, the oboist and composer Giuseppe Sammartini (probably born in the early 1690's), were listed among the oboists of a special orchestra brought together in Novara on 14 June 1711 for the solemnities accompanying the translation of the relics of S. Gaudenzio to the cathedral. This is the only mention yet discovered of Sammartini's father and the earliest mention of Giuseppe.[4]

Nothing is known of Sammartini's musical education, but it is unlikely that he was self-taught as asserted by Giuseppe Carpani.[5] His first musical instruction must have been given by his father and perhaps even by his brother; later, Sammartini may have been a chorister at the Cathedral of Milan. Like his brother, he started his career as a professional oboist; both brothers were listed as oboists in 1720 among the thirty musicians in the opera orchestra of the Regio Ducal Teatro, at the salary of 17 Milanese lire for each performance.[6] There is no evidence that Sammartini played the violin professionally despite his profound knowledge of string instruments,[7] but he did become a skillful organist. Burney,

---

[3] See Saint-FoixH, p. 317.

[4] They are identified as "Alessio S. Martino francese" and "Giuseppe suo figlio milanese." The information about Alexis Saint-Martin and the festivities in Novara was first published by Vito Fedeli in his preface to vol. III of *Istituzioni e Monumenti dell'Arte Musicale in Italia* (Milan: Ricordi, 1933), p. 30. It is further elaborated in SartoriG, pp. 3-6. For a detailed description of musical life in Milan during the eighteenth century, see BarblanM, BurneyD, and CesariG. See also note 124.

[5] CarpaniH, p. 58. For information about Carpani see note 95.

[6] BarblanC, p. 16. See also note 124.

[7] CarpaniH, p. 58, said that Sammartini first played the oboe and then the violin, but BurneyG, II, 454, wrote that "the violin does not seem to have been his instrument." It is probable, however, that Sammartini had a working knowledge of the violin, as did most composers of his time.

who heard him play the organ in 1770, praised him for having "a way peculiar to himself of touching that instrument, which is truly masterly and pleasing."[8]

The music of Sammartini's first vocal works has disappeared, but librettos have survived documenting his musical activities in the 1720's. The earliest mention of his music occurs when he contributed the first aria to the oratorio *La Calunnia delusa,* performed in Milan on 23 May 1724 in the Regia ed Imperiale Cappella di Santa Maria della Scala. The oratorio was the collective effort of ten composers, among them Giuseppe Sammartini and the leading church composers of the city (see App. C 18). In the libretto Sammartini is given the honorable title of "maestro di cappella" although he was probably not yet attached to a church or congregation, perhaps indicating that he conducted the performance.

It was in this period that Sammartini established himself as a church musician. His first complete vocal works of which we know are five Lenten cantatas written in 1725 for the old Milanese congregation of Santissimo Entierro (founded 1633), which met in the Jesuit church of S. Fedele, not far from the present La Scala Opera. Sartori believes the cantatas were written in the hope of obtaining the position of *maestro di cappella* to the congregation. A second set of cantatas was presented in 1727, but Sammartini did not win the appointment until 1728.[9] He continued in this post almost to the end of his life, the last extant librettos of the Lenten cantatas for the congregation being dated 1773.[10]

Sammartini received his first church appointment on 23 February 1726, when he contracted to carry out, without payment, the duties of Ambrogio Bramanti, the *maestro di cappella* and organist of S. Ambrogio, who had become too old and infirm to fulfill his office. In the contract Sammartini is described as "molto celebre in simile professione," and is promised the position upon Bramanti's death.[11] The official appointment came after Bramanti died on 29 February 1728. The church of S. Ambrogio boasted both a choir and a permanent orchestra. From 1720 to 1724 Bramanti had the assistance of the organist Carlo Borroni, who was dismissed in 1724 for neglecting his duties. Sammartini, in applying for the post, equipped himself with recommendations from such figures as Otto Ferdinand, Count Traun (the son of the governor of Milan), General Vasmetotti, and Monsignor Proposto, showing that he already enjoyed the esteem of people of influence and position in the city. Also in 1726 Sammartini composed his most ambitious work up to that time, a Christmas oratorio entitled *Gesù bambino adorato dalli pastori* (see No. 116), performed 8 December in S. Fedele.[12] In that year, Johann Joachim Quantz (1697-1773), who trav-

---

[8]BurneyD I, 236.

[9]SartoriG, pp. 8-10.

[10]S. Fedele, being under the administration of the Jesuits, was suppressed by Pope Clement XIV in 1773, under the decree suppressing the entire Jesuit order. This explains the absence of cantata texts for the year 1774.

[11]BarblanC, pp. 17-18.

[12]SartoriG, p. 9. The performance took place under the patronage of the Congregazione dell'Immacolata Concezione. The oratorio was revived in Bologna in 1734, and in Forlì in 1754.

elled in Italy from 1724 to 1726, visited Milan and singled out Sammartini and Fiorino as the leading church composers of the city, dryly commenting that their music was "nicht übel" ("not bad").[13] Quantz was impressed with the excellence of the orchestra of the Regio Ducal Teatro, especially the violins, though he noted the lack of wind players (with the exception of Giuseppe Sammartini) and bass players.[14] His comments indicate how early a high standard of orchestral performance was established in the city.

As Sammartini's fame increased, his professional activities expanded. By the 1760's he was the leading church musician of Milan. The almanac *Milano Sacro* for the years 1761 (when it was first issued) to 1775 lists Sammartini as *maestro di cappella* of a total of eight churches; some time earlier he had also become organist of the ducal chapel of S. Gottardo.[15] In 1767 Sammartini's name appears among those attached to the court of the wife of Archduke Leopold, Beatrice d'Este, with a monthly salary of eight "zecchini gigliati,"[16] becoming in 1768 *maestro di cappella* of S. Gottardo.[17]

No matter how probable it may have been that Sammartini worked in the convent of S. Maria Maddalena, as Burney claimed,[18] there is no documentary proof that he did so. The church was destroyed by fire in 1798 and nothing has survived that refers to Sammartini.[19] However, not far from the place where S. Maria Maddalena once stood is the parish church of S. Alessandro, to which was attached a college for noblemen administered by the Barnabite Fathers; Sammartini was appointed a teacher there in 1730. Annual performances were presented at the college in which music played an important role. On 6 June 1730 a performance of *Didone,* written by the professor of rhetoric, P. Pietro Grazioli, was given at which (according to the *Acta Collegii D. Alexandri*) a "Concentus musicus a Domino Joanne Baptista Martini ingeniosissime variatus" was heard. No doubt this reference is to Sammartini. The same *Acta* mention

---

[13]QuantzL, p. 235. Francesco Fiorino was *maestro di cappella* of the Reale Castello (Sforza castle) and was mentioned as *maestro di cappella* of the congregation Santissimo Entierro that year (see SartoriG, pp. 7-9).

[14]QuantzL, pp. 235-236.

[15]The churches are listed in BarblanC, p. 24. They are: S. Ambrogio, S. Alessandro, S. Dionigi dei Servi di Maria, S. Maria del Carmine, S. Maria delle Grazie convento ducale dei PP. Domenicani, S. Maria della Passione, S. Sebastiano, and S. Francesco. SartoriG, p. 13, points out that Sammartini was probably not the *maestro di cappella* of each church, but of a number of congregations that met in different churches where he would conduct.

[16]CesariG, p. 24n.

[17]BarblanC, p. 25.

[18]BurneyD, I, 77. For the origin of the erroneous statement that Sammartini became *maestro di cappella* of that convent in 1730, see BarblanC, p. 20, n. 18. Burney's remark (p. 73) that Sammartini was *maestro di cappella* "to half the churches in Milan" is obviously an exaggeration.

[19]Information from Professor Barblan.

Sammartini once again: the entry for 1 July 1737 refers to a performance of a "concentus novus et suavissimus, et dignus communi approvatione auctore Joa. Batt. Martini."[20]

Sammartini's earliest instrumental compositions probably date from the 1720's, including some concertos and symphonies. The decade of the 1730's saw a notable stream of sonatas, concertos, and symphonies from his pen as well as the composition of two of his three known operas.

Sammartini's first opera, *Memet,* was performed in Lodi in 1732 and possibly also in Vienna the same year (see No. 88). His Milanese debut as an opera composer took place in the Regio Ducal Teatro on 26 December 1734 with a performance of his second opera, *L'Ambizione superata dalla virtù* (see No. 89).[21] The impressive cast included Vittoria Tesi, contralto, one of the greatest dramatic singers of the eighteenth century; Angelo Maria Monticelli, a leading soprano in Dresden, Naples, Venice, and London; Antonia Carminati, a Milanese soprano; Giuseppe Appiani, a Milanese contralto and pupil of Nicola Porpora; and Angelo Amorevoli, tenor, who sang the principal roles in Hasse's operas in Dresden.

It was in this decade that Sammartini began his career as a teacher. Of his undoubtedly numerous pupils, only two can be identified with certainty: Count Giorgio Giulini (1716-1780) and Christoph Willibald Gluck (1714-1787). Giulini, a poet and author of a valuable history of Milan in the Middle Ages, was a dilettante symphony composer of some renown. In his youth he studied with some of the leading performers of Milan, and Sammartini taught him composition.[22] His style, like that of other Milanese composers, was strongly influenced by Sammartini.

Gluck, having come to Milan to serve as chamber musician to Prince Francesco Saverio Melzi, Administrator-General of Lombardy, probably studied with Sammartini from 1737 to 1741. Melzi had met Gluck in Vienna while visiting Gluck's patron, the young Prince Ferdinand Philipp Lobkowitz, and had induced Lobkowitz to release him in order to continue his studies in Italy. Sammartini exercised considerable influence over Gluck's early compositions, not only in the eight trio sonatas he must have written under Sammartini's tutelage, but in the orchestral style of his early operas and overtures.[23] Gluck also paid homage to Sammartini in the manner of the age by borrowing movements from two of Sammartini's symphonies for two dramatic works written in 1747 and

---

[20]BarblanC, pp. 20-21.

[21]Paglicci-BrozziR, p. 118. For further information about opera in the ducal theater in the 1730's, see CambiasiN. We are grateful to Mr. Elvidio Surian for this reference.

[22]The information is given in the earliest biographical notice of Giulini in FabronioV, XII, 324. Fabronio states that Giulini studied string instruments with Milan's best violinist, Carlo Zuccari, winds with Antonio Sammartini, cembalo with Carlo Borroni, and psaltery with Antonio Antoniani (see also CesariG, pp. 14-15). See also note 124.

The only study of Giulini's music was made by CesariG.

[23]See Saint-FoixD.

1749.[24] In turn Gluck may have influenced Sammartini's last operatic effort, *L'Agrippina, moglie di Tiberio* (see No. 90), performed in the Regio Ducal Teatro in January 1743.[25]

Many other composers were active in Milan during this period and later in the century, providing a vigorous musical environment for Sammartini's creative efforts. Prominent among the composers of instrumental music were Antonio Brioschi (active c. 1730-1750 perhaps near rather than in Milan), the most prolific symphonist of the group besides Sammartini; the violinist Ferdinando Galimberti (active c. 1730-1750); G. B. Lampugnani (1706-1784), also a well-known opera composer in Milan and London; Melchiorre Chiesa (died c. 1783); and Count Giorgio Giulini. Some members of the ducal orchestra were also composers, the most important being Angelo Maria Scaccia, a violinist and violist (active c. 1710-1750), and Carlo Zuccari, Milan's leading violinist (active c. 1730-1780). Most of these composers, and several others not mentioned here, wrote symphonies as well as other kinds of instrumental music. Together with Sammartini, they formed the earliest school of symphonists in Europe, and the only school of its kind in Italy. Most significant among the many composers of sacred and operatic music were the church composers Giuseppe Paladino (died c. 1760) and Giovanni Andrea Fioroni (1704-1778), *maestro di cappella* of the Cathedral of Milan 1747-1778, and the opera composer Carlo Monza (c. 1735-1801), who became *maestro di cappella* of the Cathedral in 1787.

Sammartini married Rosalinda Acquania probably in the 1720's. The only information we have about his family is the name of his wife, given in Sammartini's death certificate, and two references to his daughter. One is an anecdote dating from the year 1762, in which the famous Milanese poet Giuseppe Parini (1729-1799) took the part of Sammartini's daughter in an argument with the Duchess Maria Vittoria Ottoboni Serbelloni. The only other reference occurs in a letter from the Duchess Serbelloni to Count Giulini on the occasion of an *accademia* which she organized: "La duchessa Serbelloni rende avvisato il Sig. Conte Giulini che le è riuscito di indurre la figlia Sammartino a prendere la parte nella Cantata . . . ." From these references we learn that Sammartini's daughter was a singer, and it is probable that Parini and Sammartini knew each other well.[26]

By the late 1730's Sammartini's fame had begun to spread beyond the borders of Italy, and he was becoming recognized as one of the leading Italian masters. The first known performance of his music abroad occurred in Amsterdam on 7 January 1738, when Antonio Vivaldi conducted one of his symphonies during the dramatic spectacle given in celebration of the centennial of the Theater of Amsterdam (see No. 65). This performance also establishes at least a musical contact between Sammartini and his illustrious older contemporary. In June

---

[24]The Gluck borrowings were discovered by Saint-Foix, *ibid.,* pp. 43-45. For further details, see Nos. 44 and 57.

[25]Paglicci-BrozziR, p. 118. See also p. 10.

[26]BarblanC, pp. 24-25.

1738 a notice in the *Mercure de France,* which has hitherto escaped attention, lists Sammartini with Solarini (Paolo Salulini?), Francesco Veracini, and Vivaldi among Italy's most able composers of string music.[27] The Paris musicians may have become familiar with Sammartini's music through Carlo Zuccari, who performed with great success at the Concert Spirituel on Easter of 1737.[28]

By whatever means, Sammartini's music became well known in Paris and London in the 1740's. It was given large representation in the manuscript collection known as the Fonds Blancheton (dated c. 1740-c. 1744; see pp. 24-25). His sonatas and symphonies were published for the first time by LeClerc, Huë, Giannotti, Estien, and Boivin in Paris, and by Simpson and J. Walsh in London. New prints continued to appear in the 1750's and 1760's, while, in addition, many works were widely circulated in manuscript.

Sammartini achieved unusual popularity in England. More than twenty-five different prints partly or totally devoted to his compositions or arrangements thereof were published in London. His music became so familiar in English circles that Laurence Sterne could refer as a matter of course to a Sammartini concert in Milan in his novel *A Sentimental Journey* (1768).[29] The library of Robert Clive (1725-1774) contained a copy of his trio sonatas, Op. 1,[30] and in America various prints of Sammartini's music were included in the library of Thomas Jefferson.[31]

In Paris, over twenty prints appeared, including many of Sammartini's finest symphonies and chamber works. His music was performed by a number of private orchestras: those of Pierre Philibert de Blancheton (1697-1756), the Marquis Adrien-Nicolas de Lasalle d'Offement (1735-1818; see No. 33), and the Fermier-général Alexandre Jean Joseph Le Riche de La Pouplinière (1693-1762; see No. 73). The orchestra of the Concert Spirituel is reported to have performed a "Concerto de Martini" in 1749[32] and "une belle symphonie" by Sammartini at the beginning of its concert on All Saints' Day 1751.[33] Another Sammartini

[27]The reference occurs in an article entitled "Memoires pour servir à l'Histoire de la Musique Vocale et Instrumentale," under the heading "Violon": "Il est vrai qu'en Italie, outre les trois plus fameux que nous avons nommés, et qui peuvent le disputer à nos trois célèbres Violons, ils ont encore comme nous très habiles Maîtres, comme *Solarini, Veracini, San Martini, Vivaldi,* Prêtre, Chanoine Vénitien, plus sçavant dans la Composition, que pour l'execution; et encore *Bononcini, Indel* en Angleterre, &c.," I, 1117.

[28]BrenetC, p. 195; La LaurencieE, II, 47.

[29]The reference is found in the chapter entitled "The Translation," in the sentence beginning, "I was going one evening to Martini's concert in Milan, and was just entering the door of the hall." See BarblanC, p. 25.

[30]The copy is now in the Music Library of the University of California at Berkeley, and is of the Bremner edition, c. 1765. Lord Clive was famous in the mid-eighteenth century for his military exploits in India, especially for the conquest of Bengal.

[31]NewmanS, p. 804.

[32]Saint-FoixC, p. 315.

[33]*Mercure de France,* Dec. 1751, p. 157.

symphony was heard as the overture to the spurious Pergolesi opera (by Pietro Auletta) *Il Maestro di Musica,* performed in the Académie Royale de Musique on 19 September 1752. The *Mercure* reported what was evidently a poor performance: "On a mis à la tête de cet Intermède une ouverture de *San Martini,* dont la composition & le chant indiquent un grand Maître, mais dont l'effet a été médiocre."[34]

Sammartini's music appears to have reached German audiences by the late 1740's since a lost symphony (App. C 3) formerly in Darmstadt was copied c. 1747-1750.[35] A possible allusion to a performance of Sammartini's symphonies in Frankfurt occurs in an advertisement of 30 July 1751 for a concert by Milanese and Florentine singers which would also include a group of the newest Milanese symphonies.[36]

According to Carpani, Sammartini's music was introduced to Viennese audiences by Count Harrach, governor of Lombardy from 1747 to 1750. It immediately became the vogue and was sought after for the private concerts given by other Viennese noblemen, such as Counts Pálffy and Schönborn, and Haydn's first patron, Count Morzin. Through these performances, Carpani suggests, Haydn became familiar with Sammartini's music for the first time.[37] Haydn heard more of it, Carpani maintains, when he entered the services of Prince Esterházy, because the Prince had commissioned from Sammartini at least two compositions a month, for which the composer was paid eight gold zecchini by the banker Castelli in Milan.[38] So far, no evidence has been found in support of this claim,[39] but Sammartini's works were unquestionably known in Esterháza since

---

[34]*Mercure de France,* Nov. 1752, pp. 166, 169.

[35]Information from Herr Koch, librarian of the Hessische Landes- und Hochschulbibliothek, Darmstadt.

[36]The advertisement, quoted in IsraëlF, p. 37, runs as follows: "Signor Bartolomeo Tedeschini nebst zwey Italiänischen Sängerinnen: Signora Angiola Tedeschini aus Mayland und Signora Dionisia Lepri aus Florenz führen im Schärffischen Saal ein Concert auf mit Arien, Duetten; man wird auch mit den neusten Milanesischen Symphonien dabey aufwarten."

[37]CarpaniH, pp. 61-62: "Prima del *Pallavicini,* era stato governatore della Lombardia Austriaca il conte d'*Harrach.* Questi aveva il primo portata a Vienna la musica del *Sammartini,* la quale subito ottenne applausi e voga in quella gran capitale così amante d'un tal genere di passatempi. Il conte *Palfi* gran cancelliere d'Ungheria; il conte *Schönborn* e il conte di *Mortzin,* facevano a gara in procurarsene della nuova, e si sfoggiavano in que' loro concerti quasi giornalieri. L'*Haydn,* giovinetto e studioso pote e dovette udirla piu volte." For information about a performance of a Sammartini concerto in Vienna in 1758, see No. 73.

[38]*Ibid.,* p. 62. Carpani does not specify which Prince Esterházy, Paul Anton or Nicolaus, commissioned Sammartini. At the same time, Carpani noted that Count Pálffy had also commissioned Sammartini, adding that the Pálffy archives contained more than a thousand of his compositions. The present writers have attempted to trace the Pálffy collection, but unfortunately the portions of it in the Bratislava University Library as well as the Bratislava Slovak Academy of Sciences do not appear to contain any works by Sammartini.

[39]In a letter to Jan LaRue, Dénes Bartha wrote that there is no indication in the Esterházy Archives in Budapest that Sammartini had ever composed music for the Prince.

an inventory of the music in Eisenstadt made in 1759-1761 includes two of his symphonies.[40]

According to Eduard Hanslick, Sammartini's symphonies also reached Salzburg: "Die Musiken beim Grafen Firmian in Salzburg dauerten von 5 bis 11 Uhr,— es wurden unter Anderem an Einem Abend 4 Sinfonien von Martini und einige Sinfonien von Em. Bach gespielt."[41] Hanslick gives no date for the occasion, but it is probable that through such performances Mozart became acquainted with Sammartini's compositions before his visit to Milan in 1770.

Sammartini's music was probably introduced in Prague through the influence of the Bohemian nobility associated with the Viennese court or their Milanese counterparts. The first reference to Sammartini in Prague is found in the inventory of the Kreuzherren (Crusaders') Archives for the years 1737-1738 (see App. C 17) in which a lost Magnificat "a 2 Chori" is mentioned. Three Lenten cantatas by Sammartini were performed in the church of St. Francis, near the famed Charles Bridge, on Good Friday 1753; two others were heard in the same church on Good Friday 1754. Later in the century the monks at Osacky (Osek) monastery also performed Mass sections and Latin translations of some Sammartini cantatas (see Nos. 100, 120 and 121).

For many years Sammartini was associated peripherally with the Cathedral of Milan. He served at various times as a judge in the auditions for those seeking employment in the chapel of the Cathedral. He is first mentioned in February 1733 in connection with the competition to select a bass. The decision was signed by the *maestro di cappella* of the Cathedral, Carlo Baliani (d. 1747), by Giuseppe Paladino, the *maestro di cappella* of S. Simpliciano, both also contributing composers to *La Calunnia delusa* (see p. 3 and App. C 18), and by Sammartini.[42] He is next mentioned in December of 1740 in connection with the commission to select a second organist and two basses. On this occasion the other judges were Carlo Baliani and Antonio Francesco Messi, a teacher at the school of the Barnabites of Casale.[43] In June of 1741 Sammartini sat again with Baliani and Messi to judge a contralto, and in April of 1743 to judge Pietro Valle, aspirant to the post of coadjutor to Baliani (a post that Valle did not receive).[44] He was called near the end of his life to examine candidates for the important position of organist at the Cathedral on 6 May 1773, when he sat on the jury with

---

[40]The symphonies are ascribed to "Martino," a typical shortened form of Sammartini's name, and they appear on the list of symphonies from the inventory given in LarsenH, p. 115. Dénes Bartha informed Jan LaRue that no works of Sammartini are found in the present Esterházy Archives.

[41]HanslickG, I, 40.

[42]BarblanC, p. 21.

[43]*Ibid.* Messi had competed against Baliani for the post of organist to the Cathedral in 1714, at which time Baliani was elected. Messi then became *maestro di cappella* to the church of S. Maria della Rosa. He was known principally as a composer of oratorios. The page inscribed with the opinions of Sammartini and his colleagues is reproduced in BarblanM, p. 639.

[44]BarblanC, p. 22.

Carlo Monza and G. B. Zucchinetti, a pupil of Fioroni.[45] Sammartini was also a judge in such competitions elsewhere. A connection between Sammartini and the famous teacher, theorist, and composer Padre Giovanni Battista Martini of Bologna (1707-1784) has been recently established by a letter from Sammartini to the Padre, dated 8 September 1762, which refers to a competition for the post of *maestro di cappella* at the church of S. Maria della Scala.[46]

Sammartini participated in a number of important and solemn religious occasions in and near Milan. On 18 January 1741 he conducted a Mass of his own composition at the basilica of S. Ambrogio in memory of Cardinal Benedetto Odelscalchi.[47] In 1742 he travelled with his own orchestra to Vigevano, a small cathedral town some fifty miles southwest of Milan, to conduct a concert in the church of S. Paolo de' Barnabiti.[48] One can conjecture that there might well have been some connection between the Barnabite college associated with S. Alessandro in Milan and the church in Vigevano. On 23 September 1743 at S. Maria delle Grazie, he conducted a *Gran Messa di ringraziamento* "a più cori di scelta musica e sinfonie" to celebrate the elevation to Cardinal of P. Maestro Luigi Maria Lucini; five days later at S. Ambrogio he led another Mass "con musica sceltissima e sinfonia" for the feast of S. Bernardo.[49]

Sammartini's last known opera, *L'Agrippina, moglie di Tiberio* (see No. 90), was produced in January 1743 at the Regio Ducal Teatro. Saint-Foix believed that the opera might have been written in artistic competition with Gluck, whose *Artaserse* and *Demofoonte* had been performed in Milan in 1741 and 1742 respectively. He pointed out the musical resemblance between *Demofoonte* and *L'Agrippina*, and also suggested that Sammartini's opera itself might have influenced Gluck's *Ipermestra*, performed in Venice in October 1744.[50] Like Sammartini's previous opera, *L'Agrippina* had a fine cast of singers, with a famous castrato, Giovanni Carestini, in the role of Tiberio. Though Sammartini wrote no more operas to the best of our knowledge, he continued to compose minor dramatic works, the music of which has unfortunately not survived except for one aria from *La Gara dei geni*, an "introduzione e festa da ballo," written to celebrate the birth of Archduke Peter Leopold, the third child of Maria Theresa, and performed in the Regio Ducal Teatro on 28 May 1747 (see No. 91).[51]

[45]*Ibid.*, p. 26.

[46]This letter, not in Sammartini's hand, is the only letter by the composer found thus far. It was discovered by Howard Brofsky and will be published by him in a forthcoming article. We are most grateful to Professor Brofsky for sharing this information with us.

[47]CesariG, p. 22, note 2.

[48]*Ibid.*, p. 19.

[49]*Ibid.*, p. 22, note 2.

[50]Saint-FoixD, pp. 32-39.

[51]SartoriG, p. 12. Sammartini's interest in opera continued after the composition of his last known work in this form. His attendance at the opera performances in the Regio Ducal Teatro is documented for the years 1748 and 1749 and we may assume continued throughout his later years (see BarblanC, p. 23, note 31, and CesariG, p. 23, note 1). Cesari remarks that while Giulini had to pay 75 Milanese lire for his opera subscription, Sammartini paid only 40.

In 1748 Sammartini conducted an *accademia* "di suoni e canti de'piú celebrati professori," organized in the palace of the Marchese di Caravaggio, Don Filippo Sforza Visconti, in honor of Count Gian Luca Pallavicini, the Lieutenant-Governor of Austrian Lombardy.[52] That same year he also took an orchestra to Orta, in the lake district northwest of Milan, for the celebrations connected with the canonization of two Capuchins, Fidelis of Sigmaringen and Joseph of Lyoness.[53]

We find in 1749 the first documentation concerning the outdoor symphony concerts which were presented three times weekly on the banks of the moat of the Castello Sforzesco, sometimes under the direction of Sammartini (see figure 4). This series of concerts was organized by Count Pallavicini. The orchestra was described as being "a piú ordini, per vari cori di sinfonia da arco e da fiato" in the *Ragguagli di varj paesi* published in Milan on 8 October 1749. The programs consisted of new symphonies by Sammartini and other Milanese composers.[54] Carpani described one of these outdoor performances in which he said that Sammartini emerged victorious over his Milanese rivals by virtue of the "abundance, fire, and novelty" of his style, though "he remained much below Paladino and the others in the science of harmony." In these symphonies one heard for the first time the "separate play of the violas . . . and the continual movement of the second violins, which flowed with a beautiful novelty in a completely different way from that of the first violins."[55]

The Barnabite Fathers of S. Paolo associated with the parish church of S. Alessandro, commissioned Sammartini in 1750 to compose a cantata, *Paride riconosciuto* (see App. C 13), to be performed by their students at the Collegio Longone.[56] In September 1751 Sammartini took part in the festivities connected with the translation of the remains of S. Carlo Borromeo to the Cathedral by directing concerts both at the Castello Sforzesco and in the Palazzo Ducale.[57] The remarks on the engraving referring to this event mention an "exquisite" *accademia* on 19 and 21 September given outdoors near the Castello Sforzesco by over sixty of the "best players" (see figure 3).

In 1753 Sammartini collaborated with Niccolò Jommelli (1714-1774) in two

[52]BarblanC, p. 23.

[53]CesariG, p. 20.

[54]*Ibid.*, p. 18; BarblanC, p. 23.

[55]CarpaniH, p. 59. It must be admitted, however, that the circumstances of the performance described by Carpani are in doubt. Carpani wrote (p. 58) that Sammartini's first symphonies for large orchestra were commissioned by Count Pallavicini, and were first performed in these outdoor concerts. Although it is true that Count Pallavicini sponsored such concerts, he was governor of Milan only in 1746-1747, and 1750-1753, long after Sammartini had started composing symphonies. Records of these outdoor concerts have so far been discovered only for the period 1749-1752 (CesariG, pp. 18-19). Carpani's account implies that the qualities of Sammartini's music were unknown until this performance. Yet, by the 1740's, Sammartini's style must have been quite familiar. We cannot be sure what Carpani meant by the phrase "large orchestra," but he must have been referring to symphonies with winds and brass, in contrast to Sammartini's earlier symphonies for strings.

[56]SartoriG, p. 12.

[57]BarblanC, p. 23.

cantatas, *La Regia de'fati* and *La Pastorale offerta* (see Nos. 91.1 and 91.2), commissioned by Count Pallavicini and performed in the Regia Ducal Corte on the birthday of Archduke Joseph of Austria.[58] It is probable that during the 1750's Sammartini became acquainted with some of the Mannheim composers traveling in Italy, such as Christian Cannabich (1731-1798), who was probably in Milan early in 1754, and Ignaz Holzbauer (1711-1783), who had been in Milan sometime between 1744 and 1746, and returned there in 1759 for the performance of his opera *Alessandro nell' Indie*. Johann Christian Bach (1735-1782) arrived in Milan about 1754 under the patronage of the Milanese nobleman Count Agostino Litta, remaining until the spring of 1762.[59] While in Milan Bach composed sacred, instrumental, and dramatic works (including three operas), and on 12 June 1760 he became the organist of the Milan Cathedral. It is inconceivable that during his long sojourn in Milan he did not meet Sammartini or hear his music. How greatly Sammartini influenced Bach's style is a subject yet to be investigated.

In 1760 Sammartini published one of his finest sets of chamber works, the six string trios later reprinted in the Le Clerc edition as Op. 7.[60] This is the only authentic print of his music that we know. The print contains a long dedication to Duke Don Filippo of Parma (1721-1765), who is revealed to have been one of Sammartini's most important patrons. Sammartini's musical development may have been significantly affected by his contact with the remarkable renaissance of musical life in Parma that occurred during the Duke's reign. Guided by the Duke's French minister, Guillaume du Tillot, the Francophile court heard operas by Jean-Philippe Rameau, François Rebel, François Francoeur, and Jean-Joseph Cassanéa de Mondonville, and two reform operas by Tommaso Traetta, the *maestro di cappella* of Parma from 1758 to 1765 and one of Italy's best opera composers of the period. Of potential importance, too, is the possibility of a fruitful exchange between Sammartini and Traetta during Traetta's stay in Parma.

Also dating from 1760 is evidence of Sammartini's association with the ducal chapel. The organist Giovanni Lorenzo Fascetti[61] wrote a plea to the court on 16 May that he aspired "all'impiego di organista nella R. D. Cappella al caso che per la morte del Vignati, attuale Maestro di cappella . . . venisse a tale impiego l'attuale Organista S. Martino."[62] From this document it is clear that Sammartini

---

[58]SartoriG, p. 12. Jommelli may have visited Milan that year for the performance of his opera *Demofoonte*.

[59]The usual date given for Bach's departure for Italy is 1756, but DownesO, II, 9, gives cogent reasons for moving the date back to 1754.

[60]Copies of the print are in the library of the Institut de Musicologie of the University of Strasbourg, and in the Archivio di Stato, Verona (Violin I only). For further information see ChurginN.

[61]Fascetti (born in Lucca c. 1700) came to Milan about 1757 and became *maestro di cappella* of S. Maria presso S. Celso, where he remained until 1775. He was still composing in 1779.

[62]BarblanC, p. 24. Giuseppe Vignati became *maestro di cappella* of the ducal chapel in 1737 (BarblanM, p. 657). He died in 1768.

had held the post of organist for some time and was expected to become *maestro di cappella* of the court in the event of Vignati's death.

On 10 April 1758 Sammartini became one of the founders of an "Accademia Filarmonica," an orchestra of amateur players (see figure 10 showing the petition for the Accademia signed by Sammartini).[63] This unusual emphasis on orchestral music in Milan is further illustrated by the lavish entertainments that took place in July 1765 to celebrate the visit to Pavia and Cremona of Beatrice d'Este, the wife of Archduke Leopold. The expense accounts that have survived give us a most detailed picture of such Milanese entertainments.[64] A large and expert group of performers was employed, consisting of two singers and fifty-nine instrumentalists. The two "virtuosi di Canto" were Caterina (or Cattarina) Pilaj[65] and Antonio Priori; the "flutta di concerto" was Mattia Stabingher;[66] the two "violini di concerto" were Luca Felice Roscio[67] and Giuseppe Boroni. The only composer mentioned in the documents is Sammartini, who was paid "per direzione e composizione d'alcune sinfonie, servite per entrambe le accademie."[68] On the evenings of 24 and 25 July, an orchestra of thirty-six performed in two *accademie* and *feste di ballo* which took place in the Casa Botta in Pavia. On the next evening an orchestra of thirty-eight performed in the home of the Marchese Rodeschini in Cremona.[69] The orchestras were drawn from local musicians: eleven from Pavia, fourteen from Cremona, two from Lucca, and a large contingent of thirty-two from Milan.

The occasion had particular significance because the two instrumentalists from Lucca who performed in both Pavia and Cremona were Luigi Boccherini (1743-1805), who played cello, and his father Leopoldo, who played double bass. This is the only known meeting between Sammartini and Boccherini, and it provided an opportunity for the younger composer to become acquainted with

---

[63] BarblanM, pp. 634-635, which gives further details about the organization of the orchestra.

[64] CesariG, pp. 24-25; SartoriG, pp. 17-18; BarblanS, pp. 31-32, and BarblanB. The documents, entitled "Registro delle spese occorse in Cremona ed in Milano . . . ," are found in the Archivio di Stato, Milan, P. S. n. 89, Registro del 1765.

[65] Pilaj is described in GerberH, II, 146, as "eine vortreffliche Sängerin in Königl. Pohlnischen Diensten zu Dressden in den Jahren 1750 bis 1760, hatte sich während dem siebenjährigen Kriege von Dressden wieder nach ihrem Vaterlande begeben, und ist daselbst um 1762 gestorben." However, she was clearly alive and performing in 1765.

[66] "Registro," f. 74. Mattia Stabingher (also spelled Stabinger), c. 1740-1815, also gained fame as a composer of operas and ballets as well as instrumental music. His opera buffa *Le Astuzie di Bettina* was conducted by Haydn at Esterháza in October 1785, and won such acclaim that it was revived for nine performances in 1786. See Dénes Bartha and László SomfaiH, pp. 126-127, 296-297.

[67] Roscio was the concertmaster of the orchestra in Pavia, while Carlo Zuccari held that position in Cremona. Roscio was a member of the orchestra of La Scala after 1778 (SartoriG, p. 18). Two of his violin concertos can be found in the Library of Congress, Washington.

[68] "Registro," f. 68.

[69] The figures include the soloists.

Sammartini's latest and most sophisticated symphonies as well as his general musical taste and point of view.

Though Sammartini received the large sum of 40 zecchini for his efforts, Pilaj, evidently the main performer, was given 60; Priori obtained 24, the flutist about 19, and the solo violins 15 each. Special payment was made to the Milanese violist Giovanni Battista Fiamenghino (a member of the ducal orchestra of 1748) for copying "tutti le Sinfonie, Concerti, Arie, Duetti, etc."[70] All the manuscripts were returned to Sammartini, which may indicate that he composed more of the music for the festivities than just the symphonies.

Other small details in the accounts may be of interest. The rehearsals for the concerts took place in Milan in the homes of Don Giuseppe Casati and Pilaj herself, and a *spinetta* was lent for the rehearsals by the noble Trotti family, who were among the sponsors of the entertainment. Refreshments, consisting of lemonade and bread, were supplied for the musicians rehearsing in the Casa Casati. Another entry reveals that Sammartini traveled to and from the concerts in a special carriage, which he shared with the violinist Roscio.[71]

On 8 November 1768 Sammartini was appointed to succeed Vignati as *maestro di cappella* of the Regia Ducal Corte, the final step in official recognition. The post of organist that he had left vacant went to Carlo Monza (despite Fascetti's letter).[72]

The well-known contact between Sammartini and the Mozarts is documented for the first two of their four visits to Milan in January-March 1770, and October 1770-January 1771. The references, however, are meager and contain no comments regarding Sammartini's music. Arriving in Milan at the end of January, the Mozarts were quickly introduced to the leading aristocrats and musicians of the city, including Sammartini. On 7 February 1770 Sammartini attended a reception given by Count Carl Joseph Firmian, Governor-General of Austrian Lombardy, at which the young Mozart performed.[73] Leopold Mozart mentioned the occasion to his wife in a letter dated 10 February: "It would take too long to describe in detail the evidence of his knowledge which Wolfgang has given in the presence of Maestro Sammartini and of a number of the most brilliant people, and of how he has amazed them."[74] In his second visit to Milan, Mozart composed his first opera seria, *Mitridate, Rè di Ponto* (K. 87), which was performed in the Regio Ducal Teatro on 26 December 1770. Though intrigues were raised against the opera, partly because of the composer's youth (he was fourteen), Sammartini and other important Milanese composers rallied to Mozart's support. This is revealed in Leopold's letter dated 22 December 1770: "Meanwhile we hear that our good friends are hopeful and delighted and indeed they congratulate my son with genuine pleasure; on the other hand the malevolent are now silent.

---

[70]"Registro," f. 74.

[71]"Registro," ff. 73, 74.

[72]BarblanC, p. 25.

[73]DeutschM, p. 100.

[74]AndersonL, I, 112.

The greatest and most distinguished Kappellmeisters of this town, Fioroni and Sammartini, are our true friends; and so are Lampugnani, Piazza, Colombo and others. Thus the envy, or rather distrust and the wicked prejudices which some cherished in regard to our son's composition, will not be able to injure him very much."[75] How much of Sammartini's music the Mozarts heard is unknown, but from the evidence, there apparently was little contact with Sammartini since his name is absent from the Mozart correspondence for the visits later in 1771 and in 1772-1773, when Mozart composed two more dramatic works for Milan.

A few months after Mozart's initial visit to Milan, Charles Burney came to the city. He met Sammartini and other leading musicians and wrote an invaluable account of Milanese musical life, including the only description we have of a performance (a Mass) conducted by Sammartini (see below, pp. 18-19 for an extended discussion of Burney's comments).

Also in 1770 Sammartini appeared as conductor of a cantata at the congregation of Santissimo Entierro at S. Fedele. The work was not his own but by the *maestro di cappella* of the Cathedral, Giovanni Andrea Fioroni. Two years later we find him again composing for the Collegio Longone of the Barnabite Fathers, this time the cantata *Iride,* which made up part of a *rappresentazione accademica* entitled *Ciro in Media* (see App. C 16).[76] These last years of Sammartini's life were so active that they fully substantiate Burney's remark that, despite his age, Sammartini's "fire and invention still remain in their utmost vigour."[77] What a contrast to Carpani's statement that Sammartini had become "vecchio e pigro," and that to all requests to send new compositions to Vienna, urged on by the Milanese banker Castelli, he could only answer "farò, farò; ma il cembalo m'ammazza."[78] On 13 and 14 May 1773 four of his cantatas were performed in the aula of the school in S. Alessandro.[79] In August the musicians of the Ducal Chapel turned to the Archduke to request a raise in salary, but only for themselves, since Sammartini was "provvisto di altre risorse."[80] Sammartini was also busy composing a cycle of six quintets for three violins, viola, and bass, one each in the months of April to September.[81] In the autumn the Duke of Cumberland, brother of George III of England, visited Milan and was given a grand reception by Count Alberico Balbiano di Belgioioso to which Sammartini was also invited. The Duke himself performed for more than an hour, and Belgioioso commented

---

[75]AndersonL, I, 175. Gaetano Piazza was *maestro di cappella* of S. Maria di Caravaggio and S. Fedele in the period 1760-1770 and a composer of operas and instrumental music. In the same decade Giovanni Colombo was *maestro di cappella* of S. Barnaba, S. Antonio, and S. Carlo (CesariG, p. 24).

[76]SartoriG, p. 13.

[77]BurneyD, I, 73.

[78]CarpaniH, p. 62.

[79]BarblanC, p. 26.

[80]*Ibid.*

[81]The dated MS parts are in the Bibliothèque Nationale, Paris, D. 11. 622.

about the Duke in a letter "che ama passionatamente la composizione dell'arte di quell'autore [that is, Sammartini]."[82] At the end of the year, on 29 December, the *Gazzetta di Milano* reported a performance in the Regio Ducal Teatro of a *ballo* by Sammartini entitled *Il Trionfo d'amore* (see App. C 12).[83]

Nothing is known of Sammartini's activities in the last year of his life. From the death certificate issued 17 January 1775 by D. Enrico Magnocavallo, the curate of S. Alessandro in Zebedia, we learn that he died on 15 January 1775 in that parish after receiving the last rites of the church and a special papal blessing with plenary indulgence, a mark of the great esteem in which he was held.[84] He was buried in the church of S. Alessandro the evening of 16 January, and on 17 January the musicians of S. Fedele, the church of one of his earliest congregations, Santissimo Entierro, petitioned Count Durini for a fund to celebrate a "solenne uffizio con cui intendono suffragare il defunto Maestro S. Martino."[85] The death certificate movingly describes the final homage paid to Sammartini's memory: "La mattina del giorno dieciotto gli fù cantata, con apparato funebre, da tutta la Cappella musicale del Duomo, ed altri Musici coll'accompagnamento di copiosa scelta sinfonia, l'Ufficio e Messa solenne. Il qual onorevole Suffragio gli fu fatto sì per essere socio della Congregazione dei Musici, quanto perchè nella Sua professione di Musico fu eccellentissimo Maestro e celebre per chiarissima fama. A sì strepitosa funzione intervenne gran concorso di persone, alla quale fù dato fine coll'intervento di tutti li nostri Religiosi, Sacerdoti, e Chierici con gestatoria all'assoluzione del feretro."[86] ("On the morning of the eighteenth, with funeral panoply, the Office and Solemn Mass was sung for him by all the musicians of the Chapel of the Cathedral and other musicians, with the accompaniment of a number of select symphonies. This honorable memorial was thus rendered him not only as a member of the Congregation of Musicians, but also because he was in his musical profession a most excellent master and celebrated by a most brilliant renown. A great gathering of people took part in this imposing ceremony, which was terminated by the participation of all our monks, priests, and clerics with the gestatorial chair at the absolution of the bier.")

But the story does not end here. The library of the Brera in Milan possesses an almanac for the year 1775, entitled *La Galleria delle Stelle*,[87] which contains a list of the projected activities of Sammartini in his role as church musician for the year of his death. As the almanac was probably printed at the end of 1774 and it can be assumed that Sammartini had agreed to the schedule set down therein, it can be supposed that the composer's death was sudden and unexpected. Here is the impressive list of his planned activities had he lived throughout 1775:

[82]SartoriG, p. 14.

[83]BarblanC, p. 27.

[84]The death certificate was discovered by Saint-Foix (see Saint-FoixH).

[85]BarblanS, p. 33.

[86]Saint-FoixH, p. 318.

[87]This and the following information comes from SartoriS.

Sunday, 15 January (the day of his death	Music in S. Ambrogio by Sig. Sammartino.
Wednesday, 25 January	Music in S. Michele al Gallo for St. Anthony the Abbot.
Friday, Saturday, and Sunday, 3-5 March	Music for three days in S. Alessandro for the Forty Hours' Devotion.
Monday, 13 March	Music in S. Dionigi.
Saturday, 25 March	Music for the first Vespers in S. Giuseppe.
Sunday, 2 April	Music in S. Maria della Passione (perhaps for the whole week).
Sunday, 23 April	Music in S. Alessandro for the Blessed Alessandro Sauli, Confessor of S. Carlo Borromeo.
Tuesday, 13 June	Music in S. Francesco for the whole Octave.
Monday, 19 June	Music in S. Ambrogio.
Sunday, 25 June	Music in S. Michele al Gallo.
Friday, 30 June	Music in S. Alessandro.
Sunday, 16 July	Music in S. Maria del Carmine.
Wednesday, 26 July	Music in S. Maria del Carmine.
Friday, 4 August	Music in S. Maria delle Grazie.
Sunday, 20 August	Music in S. Ambrogio.
Saturday, 26 August	Music in S. Alessandro.
Sunday, 27 August	Music in S. Teresa.
Saturday, 16 September	Music for the first Vespers in S. Satiro, sung by the monks of S. Ambrogio.
Sunday, 17 September	Music in S. Satiro: Mass sung by the monks of S. Ambrogio.
Wednesday, 4 October	Music in S. Francesco.
Sunday, 15 October	Music in S. Teresa.
Thursday, 28 December	Music in S. Francesco.

Thus in the year of his death Sammartini was *maestro di cappella* of eleven churches in Milan, a record hardly surpassed by any other composer. The churches were: S. Alessandro, S. Ambrogio, S. Dionigi, S. Francesco, S. Giuseppe, S. Maria del Carmine, S. Maria delle Grazie, S. Maria della Passione, S. Michele al Gallo, S. Satiro, and S. Teresa. In comparison with the list of churches in which Sammartini was active in 1761 (see note 15), four new ones appear: S. Giuseppe, S. Michele al Gallo, S. Satiro, and S. Teresa, while S. Sebastiano is omitted. *La Galleria delle Stelle* lists nine other composers active in twenty-four churches, not including the Cathedral. This vividly illustrates the intensive musical activity in the churches of Milan at the end of Sammartini's career.

It seems appropriate to close this biographical summary with reference to the more important remarks about Sammartini's music by J. B. de La Borde, Charles Burney, and Giuseppe Carpani. These comments offer a valuable perspective on the contemporary and near-contemporary view of Sammartini's style and the significance of his music.

Though little was written about Sammartini during his lifetime, his music was well known and respected, especially during the latter part of his life. La Borde, as noted earlier, called him a "composer of great reputation," whose "instrumental music is valued and widely known, even in Germany."[88]

Substantial contemporary criticism of Sammartini's work, however, appeared only in the writings of Charles Burney. He remarked that Sammartini had produced for string instruments "an incredible number of spirited and agreeable compositions between the years 1740 and 1770,"[89] and that he had composed an "almost infinite" number of Masses.[90] In his discussion of Pergolesi's trios, Burney named Sammartini as one of the founders of the early Classic style: "If the SONATAS ascribed to Pergolesi, for two violins and a base, are genuine, which is much to be doubted, it will not enhance their worth sufficiently to make them interesting to modern ears, accustomed to the bold and varied compositions of Boccherini, Haydn, Vanhal, &c. They are composed in a style that was worn out when Pergolesi began to write; at which time another was forming by Tartini, Veracini, and Martini of Milan, which has been since polished, refined, and enriched with new melodies, harmonies, modulation, and effects."[91]

Burney discussed Sammartini's music in some detail only in the chapter describing his visit to Milan 16-24 July 1770. In that period, he heard a Mass, a motet, and an "excellent" symphony by Sammartini, the latter performed at an *accademia* which Burney attended.[92]

Of the Mass, Burney thought the instrumental portions skillfully written and organized, the music displaying Sammartini's characteristic energy. But he criticized the excessive number of fast movements and what he felt was an overly active instrumental accompaniment: "The second mass which I heard to-day was composed by Battista San Martini, and performed under his direction at the church of the Carmini; the symphonies were very ingenious, and full of the spirit and fire peculiar to that author. The instrumental parts in his compositions

---

[88]La BordeE, III, 233. The full entry runs as follows: Sammartino, Maître de chapelle au service de l'Archiduc de Milan, Compositeur d'une grand réputation. Sa Musique instrumentale est estimée & répandu, même en Allemagne. Il a composé des opera autrefois: actuellement il ne travaille que pour l'église." It is the only biographical notice before the twentieth century that is wholly accurate.

[89]BurneyG, II, 454.

[90]BurneyD, I, 73.

[91]BurneyG, II, 924.

[92]BurneyD, I, 74.

are well written; he lets none of the performers be long idle; and the violins, especially, are never suffered to sleep. It might, however, sometimes be wished that he would ride his *Pegasus* with a curb-bridle; for he seems absolutely to run away with him. Without metaphor, his music would please more if there were fewer notes, and fewer *Allegros* in it: but the impetuosity of his genius impels him, in his vocal compositions, to run on in a succession of rapid movements, which in the end fatigue both the performer and the hearers."[93] The following Sunday, however, Burney heard a "motet" by Sammartini sung in the Convent of Santa Maria Maddalena, which was described as making "ample amends for the want of slow movements in his mass on Friday, by an *adagio* . . . which was truly divine."[94] The adagio was written for solo voice with organ accompaniment. Burney so liked the beautiful singing that he rushed back to hear the afternoon service in which the same motet was repeated, to his great delight.

The critical comments by Giuseppe Carpani are far more extensive than Burney's, and of great interest and importance.[95] He stated that Sammartini was a better instrumental than vocal composer, and that he devoted himself especially to the composition of trios and symphonies.[96] Sammartini is credited with having introduced the "mordente," "note sincopate," "contro arcate," and "punteggiature continuate," "graces which, if they were known, were not in great use."[97]

---

[93]*Ibid.*, p. 73.

[94]*Ibid.*, p. 77.

[95]CarpaniH, pp. 56-62, 141. Carpani's biography of Haydn is arranged as a series of letters, the discussion of Sammartini occurring in Letter Four, dated 18 July 1808, and Letter Nine, 28 February 1809. Carpani was born in Vill'Albese in Lombardy on 28 January 1752, and spent more than half his life in Milan. He studied in the Brera College and the University of Pavia, and was active in Milan as a man of letters. He left the city in 1796 to escape the French invasion of Italy (having written anti-French articles for the *Gazzetta di Milano*), and moved to Vienna where he remained until his death in 1825. Carpani made an Italian translation for Haydn's *Creation*, and his biography of Haydn is one of the three earliest, the others being by G. A. Griesinger and A. C. Dies. The biography has been criticized as "the least reliable and least necessary of the three, although it is the most entertaining to read" in GotwalsE, p. 459. Nevertheless Carpani's remarks about Sammartini should be given serious consideration, since he probably heard many performances of Sammartini's music during his stay in Milan, and may have collected biographical details and anecdotes from those who were acquainted with Sammartini or his circle of friends. Some of his critical remarks may also reflect the opinions of the Milanese. At the end of his discussion, Carpani cites a reference to Sammartini in Rousseau's *Dictionnaire de musique* (in the article "Adagio"), and quotes in full the passages given above from Burney's *Tours*. He uses the good opinion of Burney to support his own high estimate of Sammartini's music.

[96]CarpaniH, pp. 58-59.

[97]*Ibid.*, p. 58. In Tartini's treatise on ornamentation, the term "mordente" refers to both the modern mordent and the three-note turn. The former is characteristic of Sammartini's middle period style, the latter, of his late style. See TartiniT, pp. 88-91. The term "contro arcate" (also spelled "contr'arco") refers to string figuration involving the motion of the bow from higher to lower strings, rather than the reverse. The definition, with examples, is given in GaleazziE, I, 155, tables VII and VIII. Such figuration was also common in late Baroque music.

Carpani stressed the indebtedness of Gluck and Haydn to Sammartini. He pointed out that Gluck had studied with Sammartini for a number of years, and that his knowledge of instruments and his instrumental style owed much to his teacher.[98]

The most famous of Carpani's comments refer to the possible influence of Sammartini on the early works of Haydn. He remarked that Sammartini's sacred music had preceded Haydn's in adopting a symphonic approach and creating a style at once brilliant and dignified.[99] He recounted how thirty years before (c. 1780) the Bohemian composer Joseph Mysliveček (1737-1781) had attended an *accademia* in Milan at which Carpani and another Bohemian composer, Wenzel Pichl (1741-1804), were also present. When Mysliveček heard some old symphonies by Sammartini, whose music he had not known, he exclaimed, "I have found the father of Haydn's style," an opinion with which Pichl concurred.[100] Carpani, however, did not fully agree, noting that Haydn's style was far more complex and original than Sammartini's.[101] Yet, he did feel that Haydn's early compositions were influenced, if only unconsciously, by the performances he heard of Sammartini's music, that Haydn "could easily contract Sammartini's taste and imitate its gestures, fire, vivacity, and certain beautiful eccentricities which reigned in that rich and inventive music."[102] As an example of Sammartini's influence, he pointed specifically to the independent second violin and viola parts at the beginning of the development in the first movement of Haydn's first quartet.[103]

Carpani added, however, that Haydn was too good a contrapuntist and too rational a composer to be deeply influenced by "the most capricious" Sammartini who, on the contrary, had "rashly followed the impulses of his fervid imagination."[104] He presents an image of Sammartini as a self-taught and undisciplined genius, expressing the conviction that if Sammartini had combined his

---

[98]CarpaniH, pp. 59-60. Carpani exaggerated the length of time Gluck spent as Sammartini's student, saying that it was ten years, though it was probably four.

[99]*Ibid.*, p. 141.

[100]*Ibid.*, p. 57: "Io non dimenticherò mai che 30 anni sono, trovandosi il *Myslivicek* in Milano ad una accademia, e sentendovi alcune vecchie sinfonie del *Sammartini,* della di cui musica non aveva in prima contezza quel valente Boemo, proruppe, me presente, in questa esclamazione - ho trovato il padre dello stile d'Haydn!-"
It is known that Mysliveček was in Milan about this time, perhaps for the performance of his opera *Armida,* first given on 26 December 1779 in the Teatro alla Scala. Pichl came to Milan in 1775 as the director of music and chamber composer to Archduke Ferdinand, governor of the city.

[101]CarpaniH, p. 57.

[102]*Ibid.*: "L'Haydn potè contrarre facilmente il gusto del *Sammartini* ed imitarne le mosse, il fuoco, il brio e certe belle stravaganze che regnano in quella musica piena d'idee e d'invenzioni."

[103]*Ibid.*

[104]*Ibid.*, pp. 58: "ma seguitava all'impazzata gli impeti della sua fervida fantasía."

excellent qualities with "a more grounded theory and a greater diligence, Italy would have had its Haydn before Germany."[105]

Carpani frankly reported that although Haydn had acknowledged the influence of C. P. E. Bach, he told Carpani many times that he "owed nothing" to Sammartini, adding that Sammartini was "a faker" ("un imbroglione").[106] Haydn's reaction was even more vehement when another of his biographers, Griesinger, mentioned the Mysliveček anecdote. Though Haydn admitted having heard Sammartini's music, he said that he had never prized it "because Sammartini was a scribbler" ("denn Sammartini sey ein Schmierer").[107] Haydn's uncharacteristic attack may have been due to the generally low opinion of Italian music held by German musicians at the beginning of the nineteenth century, and also to the natural inability to understand one's youthful enthusiasms when they have long since been extinguished. Whatever the reasons, a close study of Sammartini's music tends to support Carpani's point of view, revealing an affinity between Sammartini and Haydn, especially in aspects of rhythm and structure.

STYLE

Sammartini's compositions fall into three defined stylistic periods:[108] an early period from about 1724 to about 1739, showing a hybrid Baroque-Classic style; a middle period, from about 1740 to about 1758, in the early Classic style; and a late period, from about 1759 to 1774, embodying many features of the later Classic idiom. Thus he appears as the archetype of the transitional composer, his music displaying the traits of three distinct musical epochs in all genres of composition. Sammartini had a deep capacity for change and growth, and a sensibility that was ever alert, curious, and flexible, while maintaining a strong and consistent individuality. Though it would be neither appropriate nor fully possible to include in this volume a detailed discussion of his style, it seems useful to give a brief stylistic survey of his compositions since his music is still so little known.

Sammartini's early orchestral works reflect the influence of the north Italian concerto tradition, especially of Vivaldi. Though the style is predominantly homophonic, it already shows a special sensitivity to textural contrasts and new uses of counterpoint. Many symphony allegro movements are in sonata form, while binary designs are preferred for slow movements and minuets. In the

[105]*Ibid.*, p. 59: "Se a questi pregi unito avesse il *Sammartini* una più fondata teoria, e una maggiore applicazione, avrebbe avuto l'Italia il suo *Haydn*, prima che lo avesse l'Alemagna." Modern scholarship does not share these views of Carpani.

[106]*Ibid.*, p. 56.

[107]GriesingerB, pp. 14-15.

[108]The dates of the three stylistic periods have been slightly modified from those given in *MGG* and ChurginE. This discussion is drawn from the section on style in our *MGG* article on Sammartini, with several changes and additions.

middle period, most Baroque traits disappear, and sonata form characterizes all movements, even the minuets. Movements become longer, richer in thematic material, and more varied in texture. The late style is marked by more extensive periods, more complex harmony, and a more intense lyricism, which invades even the symphonic first movements. An even more varied and contrapuntal texture appears in which themes are imitated, combined, or distributed in dialogue fashion among the various instrumental parts. Throughout his life, a fundamental aspect of Sammartini's style is his mastery of rhythmic organization and his ability to maintain an intense musical flow in his compositions.

The symphonies of Sammartini are the earliest dated symphonies we know: movements of two of them were used in 1732 as introductions to Acts II and III of his first opera *Memet*. There is no evidence, however, for the statement in SchmidlD that Sammartini composed a four-movement symphony in 1734. The only extant four-movement symphony (see No. 39) comprises three movements with an appended minuet borrowed from a popular trio. The early symphonies are scored for strings *a 3* or *a 4*, and have three movements, some with minuet finales. Nearly all the first movements, some slow movements, and most finales are organized in a clear sonata form, with differentiated themes, long developments, and well-defined recapitulations almost always beginning with the primary theme. Sammartini transferred to the symphony the lyrical slow movement of the concerto and the moderate 3/4 rather than 3/8 minuet. He particularly favored the 2/4 andante, which became the standard Classic type of slow movement, and 2/4 and 3/8 final movements also occur frequently. The formal variety and imagination, the expressive slow movements, and the frequent textural interest contrast markedly with the Italian overtures of the period. The main influences on the early symphonies are to be found rather in the concerto and the trio sonata.

Most of the symphonies from the middle period call for strings and two horns or trumpets; the late symphonies add independent oboe parts and often separate cello and bass. Sammartini brought textural vitality to the symphony, as Carpani noted, by giving greater independence to the second violin and viola. Especially characteristic is his use of voice-exchange between the violins, and non-imitative counterpoint in which contrasting motives often appear in the second violin, though coordinated with the first-violin phrasing. The three-movement symphony with minuet finale is typical, but in the middle period two-movement symphonies (fast-minuet) also appear. The first movements evolve through energetic rhythmic figures and an intensive continuity of structure. A great number of themes are well integrated in a flexible sonata form in which themes may return in a different order or as variants. The recapitulation is thus usually reformulated and functions as a continuing development. As in Haydn, each movement creates a new formal solution and presents an unpredictable succession of regular and irregular phrase lengths that enhances the rhythmic drive. In many ways, Sammartini's slow movements are his finest creations of this period, the best of them achieving a perfect balance between a delicately wrought form and varying degrees of lyric intensity. Many are in minor, and though concise, they favor rich harmony, and full, varied texture. The melodic lines display a refined balance of contours, utilizing sigh motives, affective intervals, and sensitive chromatic alterations.

Since most of the remaining instrumental and vocal works have not yet been carefully studied, only more general aspects of their style can be mentioned. Of the ten concertos, most are written for solo violin or flute, accompanied by string orchestra. The three-movement plan prevails except for two middle-period works in two movements (fast-minuet), which call for a group of soloists and anticipate the style of the later *symphonie concertante* (Nos. 73 and 76). The concertos display a variety of formal solutions. In one early and one late work, the violin solos are confined to the cadential or development sections of otherwise symphonic fast movements. Other concertos use ritornello structure, but with no uniform plan. In some movements the final ritornello is a da capo of the first. The opening ritornellos present a great many contrasting ideas, often arranged in two-part form, or in some cases even sonata form. The later concertos incorporate more thematic interplay between the solo and orchestra, and more closely integrate the thematic material of the solo sections. One late concerto (No. 78) joins ritornello with sonata form in each movement, the tutti and solo sharing the principal ideas as in the later Classic style.

Sammartini's orchestral concertinos fall into two groups of four early and three later concertinos. The early works, scored for strings *a 4,* have three movements and achieve a unique synthesis of symphony, concerto, and chamber traits. The later concertinos call for a larger orchestra of two flutes or oboes, two horns, two violins, and bass (omitting violas), and consist of only two movements. These works resemble the divertimento in style and feature solo passages for the wind instruments.

The remaining instrumental works include many solo keyboard sonatas and a vast quantity of chamber music: solo sonatas for flute, violin, and cello; duos for harpsichord and violin, and for two flutes; trios for two violins and bass, or flute, violin, and bass; quartets for three violins and bass, or flute, two violins, and cello or bass, or two violins, viola, and cello; and quintets for three violins, viola, and bass. Chamber works, in two or three movements, often open with a slow or moderately fast movement and conclude with a minuet. They place unusual emphasis on sound structure, and feature a more ornamental melody and intricate rhythm. Trios for two violins and bass form the largest group, and they show a wide range of type and interplay between the violins. In some compositions the first violin dominates in the manner of the solo sonata. The late *sonate notturne,* Op. 7 (1760), which rank among Sammartini's best works, reflect the trend in his later style toward climinating the basso continuo and achieving an equality of parts within a homophonic framework. The late solo concertinos for two violins, viola, and cello (1763-1767) may be considered early examples of the string quartet. Together with the quintets, they are Sammartini's most complex chamber works in harmony and texture.

Sammartini's three operas adhere to the conventions of *opera seria,* including the nearly exclusive use of the da capo aria. Nevertheless, the two operas of the 1730's, *Memet* and *L'Ambizione superata dalla virtù,* exhibit unexpected dramatic power and contain many elaborate and expressive settings. The orchestra is given considerable prominence in both operatic and sacred works, the energetic, often sophisticated orchestral part reflecting the composer's skill in the symphonic idiom.

In his religious works, Sammartini is revealed as a great master of the sacred style. In the eight cantatas for the Fridays in Lent, the recitatives exploit chromatic and dissonant chords, especially the diminished seventh, and the da capo arias have a great lyric beauty, with a fine feeling for the inner meaning of the poetry. In general, Sammartini is fundamentally concerned with projecting the moods and accents of the text. Larger works, such as the Mass sections, Magnificats, and psalm settings, fuse the *galant* and learned styles. They incorporate broadly planned movements in various sonata-form designs, operatic arias and accompanied recitatives, imitative choral and instrumental passages, and complete fugues for concluding sections. It is in Sammartini's sacred music that we find many of his most dramatic, complex, and imaginative pages, and a grandeur of expression and effect that has no parallel in his other compositions.

Sammartini's music played a significant role in the transition from the Baroque to the Classic style. From the earliest period, he utilized a complex, multithematic structure and a complete, integrated sonata form. His originality lies particularly in the manipulation of rhythm, texture, and structure. He was the first great master of the symphony, and he maintained his originality despite the rise and dominance of the Mannheim and Viennese schools.

The symphonies have little in common with the early Classic Italian overture beyond the use of minuet finales and subsidiary themes in reduced texture. The Parisian prints and performances of Sammartini's music helped introduce the early Classic style in France. In comparison with the early Viennese school, his music is more *galant* and more tightly knit. Such special qualities as the rhythmic drive, the experimental attitude toward structure, and the exploitation of phrase asymmetries could not have failed to impress Haydn. The full extent of Sammartini's influence, however, cannot yet be ascertained. At the present time, his greatest importance appears to lie in the development of the Classic symphony, sacred style, and ensemble idiom.

SOURCES AND AUTHENTICITY

The largest sources of Sammartini's orchestral and vocal music are the Fonds Blancheton in the Paris Conservatoire; the Waldstein Collection in the Národní Muzeum, Prague; the Abbey of Einsiedeln; the Badische Landesbibliothek, Karlsruhe; the Kungl. Musikaliska Akademiens Bibliotek, Stockholm; and the Paris Conservatoire and Bibliothèque Nationale, Paris.

The Fonds Blancheton,[109] which has been dated by Lionel de La Laurencie c. 1740–c. 1744, is one of the earliest collections of Classic symphonies, concertos, concertinos, and chamber works, and it also contains some Baroque

---

[109]See La LaurencieI, which is a thematic catalogue of the entire collection. For further remarks about the dating of the collection, see No. 7 and ChurginE. All numerical references in this section are to authentic works only.

compositions. It includes the greatest number of early Sammartini symphonies (17) and orchestral concertinos (4) as well as 2 violin concertos, and otherwise gives a large representation to Milanese composers. The collection consists of three hundred instrumental works, copied for the French magistrate and music patron Pierre Philibert de Blancheton (1697-1756). The compositions are arranged in seven volumes. The first six volumes have opus numbers from I to VI (Op. IV is lost), and the seventh volume, of concertos only, is also labeled Op. I. Each volume contains fifty pieces, and works in the first six volumes are numbered consecutively from 1 to 300. All of Sammartini's orchestral music appears in Opp. I-III and the concerto volume.

The Waldstein Collection belonged to the Waldstein family, descendants of the famous General Wallenstein of the Thirty Years War.[110] It was housed in Schloss Hirschberg am See, the family seat in Doksy (also spelled Dux), until 1949, when it was moved to the Národní Muzeum in Prague. The greater part of the collection consists of manuscript copies of works dating back to the middle of the eighteenth century.[111] It would thus seem to have been formed under the direction of Count Emanuel Philipp von Waldstein (1731-1775) and his eldest son, Joseph (1755-1814). Some of Sammartini's manuscripts bear the initials of Emanuel Waldstein, inscribed by the keeper of the Waldstein archive. The Waldstein name is best remembered through Emanuel's youngest son, Ferdinand (1762-1823), an early friend of Beethoven and recipient of the dedication to Beethoven's piano sonata Op. 53. The collection, which is one of the largest and most important of the earlier Classic period, contains the most substantial group of Sammartini's middle-period symphonies (32), in addition to two early symphonies, and a host of chamber and keyboard works. It also includes many valuable copies of works in Milanese hands which we have designated as Hands A, B, and C.

Other large collections of Sammartini's instrumental music include more chamber works than symphonies. Of the some seventy works in Karlsruhe, thirteen are symphonies, two are concertos, three are concertinos, and one is an aria. The collection, together with Einsiedeln, is the most reliable of the major sources, only two compositions bearing incorrect attributions. Recently discovered catalogues (mostly thematic) of the eighteenth-century collection show that it once contained an even greater number of Sammartini's works, including five additional symphonies and an aria from L'Agrippina. These catalogues list many works by other Milanese composers, particularly sacred compositions, suggesting a special musical connection between Karlsruhe and Milan in the mid-eighteenth century.[112] As in Prague, the collection has several manuscripts in the Milanese Hands A, B, and C, in addition to autograph scores of three flute quartets.

[110]See NettlM, pp. 95-98, and HeerG, p. 62. The librarian of the collection from 1785 to 1798 was the famous Casanova.

[111]Information from Dr. Alexander Buchner of the Národní Muzeum. LandonSu, p. 19, also lists eight Haydn symphonies of the 1760's which are found in the collection.

[112]The catalogues were discovered by Klaus Häfner, music librarian of Karlsruhe. He suggests that the Catholic church music was probably intended for Rastatt, the Catholic residence of Baden-Baden, since Karlsruhe was Protestant.

Sammartini's great popularity in Sweden is attested by the large number of his works in Stockholm, which possesses over sixty different compositions, many in duplicate copies. Much of this music was acquired by Swedish businessmen and music patrons during their travels on the continent. The most important sources of the collection are the manuscripts once belonging to the eighteenth-century literary society Utile Dulci and the music patron Patrik Alströmer (1733-1804).[113] Though chamber works form the largest group of manuscripts, the library contains thirteen symphonies and one concerto in manuscript, and several symphonies and concertos in English and French prints. Especially helpful to the scholar are the many eighteenth-century scores of works by Sammartini and other composers.

The heterogeneous collections in Paris are rich in prints, and notable for the autographs of Sammartini's opera *L'Agrippina* (see No. 90) and fragments of four early symphonies (see No. 23). The Conservatoire library also preserves twelve symphonies in modern score, eight of which are unique copies of late symphonies whose original versions have disappeared (see No. 11).

The most extensive collection of Sammartini's church music is located in the great Baroque Benedictine abbey at Einsiedeln in Switzerland, famous for its performances of concerted sacred music in the eighteenth and nineteenth centuries.[114] Sammartini's compositions were apparently obtained for the abbey by Marianus Müller von Aesch (1724-1780), who studied with Paladino in Milan, December 1751 to September 1755, and later became the Prince Abbot of Einsiedeln, 1773-1780.[115] According to a report of P. Sigismund Keller (1803-1882),[116] Müller probably met Sammartini, and it is likely that the greater part of the sacred works in the collection was copied in Milan during Sammartini's lifetime. The majority of the large vocal works are actually in Milanese hands, including Hands A and D. The collection also includes a number of symphonies and chamber works. Many sacred and chamber works were copied in score by Keller, an early devotee of Sammartini's music and Regens Chori (choirmaster) in Einsiedeln at various times between 1846 and 1881.[117] Some of the Einsiedeln collection was probably first located in the Gymnasium of Bellinzona (1675-1852), which was under the direction of the Benedictine Fathers of Einsiedeln, and which had close contact with such cities as Milan and Como.

The absence of important collections of Sammartini's music in Italy is striking. Perhaps further research will uncover new sources there, but at present the only known collection of substance is located in the Milan Conservatory, which has many chamber works in the Noseda Collection. The conquest of Milan by Napoleon in 1796 may account in part for the loss of many Sammartini manu-

---

[113]See JohanssonS.

[114]See KellerM.

[115]See HenggelerM.

[116]See KellerM.

[117]Keller, who was also in Bellinzona and St. Peter's in Salzburg, came to the United States and died in Wapakoneta, Ohio, on 21 February 1882 (see HenggelerM).

scripts in the city, and also for the transference of some autographs to Paris. It would appear that, because of the overwhelming emphasis on opera in most of Italy during Sammartini's lifetime, his music won greater appreciation abroad than in his native land.

The problem of authenticity is one of the most difficult facing scholars of this period, and is a major concern with relation to Sammartini's music because so few autographs and authentic copies (works copied or published under the composer's direction or with his approval) have survived. The problem even occurs where, from available evidence, the authenticity of some lost symphonies is in question. Since final decisions can have little reliability without an examination of the music, we have not placed such works with the doubtful and spurious symphonies.

The greatest confusion in attribution occurs with Milanese composers—especially with the little-known Antonio Brioschi and Count Giorgio Giulini, Sammartini's pupil. As Sammartini's style was imitated by these and other Milanese composers, confusions were bound to occur. Sammartini is also mistaken for his brother Giuseppe in several Parisian prints (see No. 33). Saint-Foix[118] points out that the shortened form of Sammartini's name, "Martini," could lead to confusion with two other composers: Padre Martini, whose first and middle names are also Giovanni Battista, and Jean Paul Martini (1741-1816), called "il Tedesco," since he was of German origin though active in Paris.[119] Possible confusion might arise too with Pietro Sammartini, a late seventeenth-century Tuscan composer, with Giuseppe and Melchiorre Sammartini, south Italian composers resident in Malta (1752–c. 1796), and with Vincente Martin y Soler (1754-1806), the noted Spanish composer (see No. 90).

Most conflicts of attribution occur with the symphonies. When sources have different attributions for the same work, style has been the determining factor in deciding authenticity, though all objective data has been taken into account. Consequently a number of symphonies with conflicting attributions have nevertheless been included in this volume as authentic works because in rhythm, melody, texture, and structure they are thoroughly characteristic of Sammartini. Several works listed as doubtful or spurious (Appendix D) exist in only one source, and decisions regarding authenticity had to be made entirely on the basis of style. In many of these works, single movements or sections appear to be authentic, but uncharacteristic features in the remaining portions make the work suspect. Such features can be any one or a combination of the following: awkward harmony or rhythm; Baroque contrapuntal texture, especially with regular imitation and a motivic bass; thin texture, especially in works *a 4* or *a 6,* with excessive unison doubling of the violins; frequent phrase repetitions and cadences; an excess of stereotyped figuration; little modulation; loose formal structure; and uncharacteristic stylistic idioms. The same features mark doubtful instrumental works in other forms, and the doubtful vocal works, which may also contain examples of poor text setting.

[118]Saint-FoixC, pp. 308-309.

[119]Martini was also known as Schwartzendorf.

The number of sources attributing a work to Sammartini was found to be inconclusive as a criterion for attribution. Thus, for example, symphony Number 18 is ascribed to Sammartini in two sources, to Jommelli in two others, to Galuppi in one, and is anonymous in yet another. Still, the work is so true to Sammartini's style that it has been accepted as genuine. Another symphony, Appendix D 33, is ascribed to Sammartini in three sources, and to Galimberti and Giulini in two others, but the style has too many doubtful features to be judged authentic. Two symphonies (App. D 13 and 45) are such borderline cases that the remarks for these works give a detailed summary of the conflicting features of style. Most of the doubtful works are in the style of Sammartini's early and middle periods.

Sammartini's autographs also pose certain problems (for examples of characteristic pages, see figures 7, 8, and 9).[120] The only certain examples we know of Sammartini's handwriting are his written opinion for the organ competition at the Duomo in December 1740, and his signature on the Philharmonic petition of April 1758 (see figure 10). Using these examples and a detailed comparison of musical handwriting characteristics, we have confirmed the authenticity of a small group of autographs. These include the fragmentary autograph of four early symphonies, dated c. 1732 or earlier (see No. 23), most of the opera *L'Agrippina,* probably composed in 1742 (see No. 90), and three solo concertinos in Karlsruhe (Mus. Hs. 795-797; not listed in this volume); all these works are in score and clearly identical in handwriting. The symphony and opera autographs are unsigned; the concertino autographs are dated October 1750, and the title page is inscribed "originale." The many revisions in *L'Agrippina* confirm the authenticity of the score. Most of the recitatives, however, are written in a second hand which we call Hand A (see figure 11). This hand must have belonged to a copyist who worked closely with Sammartini, and it recurs on copies of his music in Bergamo, Brussels, Einsiedeln, Karlsruhe, Paris, and Prague. An autograph alto aria is also found in the *Magnificat* in Einsiedeln (No. 111) and five autograph pages in a litany at Bergamo (No. 110).

Copies of the solo string concertinos in the Paris Conservatoire, dated 1763-1767 (Mss 1217, 1219-1221; not listed in this volume), have been thought to be examples of late autographs. Many other dated and undated chamber works as well as vocal and instrumental parts of sacred works in Einsiedeln are also written in this hand. Yet a careful comparison of the handwriting with the authentic Sammartini examples of 1740, 1758, and the score of *L'Agrippina* reveals too many differences and errors for the hand to be considered autograph. It must have belonged, rather, to a copyist who worked regularly for Sammartini in the last years of his life. We have therefore called it Hand D (see figure 14; for Hands B and C, see below). That Sammartini's late hand hardly differs from earlier examples is proven by the autograph part in the *Magnificat,* a work probably composed in the late 1750's or the 1760's. The same work contains

---

[120]Bengtsson and DanielsonH provide a very detailed and useful study of the problems in identifying musical handwriting. Our work on Sammartini's autographs was greatly aided by the suggestions and comments of Jan LaRue.

pages copied in Hand D, conclusive evidence that this hand belonged to a different person.

Sammartini's autographs often use the abbreviations *fe* and *po* for the indications *forte* and *piano*. These abbreviations rarely occur together except on Milanese manuscripts, or manuscripts copied from Milanese sources. In addition, other handwriting characteristics help determine whether a manuscript is possibly Milanese. These include the reversed bass clef (drawn counterclockwise); a squeezed, sometimes elliptical "C" for common time, placed between lines two and four of the staff; the numbers 2 and 3 with a long left loop; an open natural sign (♮); and a mordent-like wavy line (actually like a written "i" in Sammartini's autographs) as a trill sign. Many of these characteristics can be seen in the reproductions of pages from Sammartini's autographs, figures 7-9. Though some of these features are typically Italian, together with the abbreviations for *forte* and *piano* and the watermarks mentioned below, they offer convincing proof of Milanese provenance. Consequently, manuscripts with these Milanese traits have been given precedence in the catalogue.

In addition to Hands A and D, two other hands recur so often in copies of Sammartini's music that they have been designated Hand B and Hand C (see figures 12 and 13). These hands have typical Milanese characteristics and occur on paper with Milanese watermarks. Two works copied by Hand B, however, are doubtful (see App. D 8, 87). The copies in Hand C thus far discovered are all instrumental works, especially symphonies. Works by the Milanese composers Antonio Brioschi, Melchiorre Chiesa, and Ferdinando Galimberti (manuscripts in Einsiedeln and Prague) were also copied by these hands, as well as by Hand A.

Watermark studies made by Bathia Churgin in 1964 and 1969 have yielded some useful information about Milanese watermarks during Sammartini's lifetime. Autograph and Milanese manuscripts were examined in Einsiedeln, Karlsruhe, Milan, Paris, Prague, Vienna, and Zürich. Though many watermarks were unclear or entirely lacking, the general types can be described, some in complete detail. The watermarks most frequently found consist of a circle or double circle enclosing small circles or initials. Sometimes the initials appear below the circle. A stem with three-leaf clover (hereafter called a trefoil) is usually attached above the circle. The fleur-de-lys, found in many Milanese copies, occurs infrequently in the autographs.

In the symphony autograph (c. 1732 or before) we find a circle containing indistinct initials, with a fleur-de-lys placed above the circle. The clearest watermark in the autograph score of *L'Agrippina* (c. 1742) is a circle enclosing the number and initials 3 B / C, with stem and trefoil. The letter C probably stands for *cartiera,* the Italian word for papermill.[121] Watermarks that faintly appear in the autograph Karlsruhe concertinos (October 1750) show a circle containing indistinct initials, with stem and trefoil. A fleur-de-lys also occurs in a page of the third concertino.

Since only two autograph pages have thus far been found in a late work (the *Magnificat*, No. 111), and no watermark appears in these pages, we are forced to

---

[121]LaRueW, p. 139.

rely on dated manuscripts copied by Hand D for Milanese watermarks of the 1760's. The works in question are the concertinos dated 1763-1767 cited above, and a string trio dated 1764 (D.11.621) in the Paris Conservatoire. Most important of the watermarks in these manuscripts is the circle enclosing three small circles (arranged 0 0 / 0), with stem and trefoil. The watermark appears in the concertino dated October 1766, and is faintly outlined in the 1764 trio and concertino dated July 1767. This "three-circle" watermark recurs in pages of several undated manuscripts copied partly by Hand D: the *Beatus vir* (No. 104), *Dixit Dominus* (No. 105), and *Magnificat* (No. 111) in Einsiedeln.

The fact that some manuscripts copied by Hands B and C contain the three-circle watermark confirms the Milanese origin of these hands. Even more convincing evidence is provided by another watermark, which can definitely be identified as Milanese. It consists of a fleur-de-lys flanked by the initials M C. Besides appearing in many manuscripts copied by Hands B and C, as well as other Milanese hands, it also occurs in the Prague score of Sammartini's *Miserere*, composed in 1750 and copied by Hand A (see No. 112). The paper was probably manufactured in Vaprio d'Adda, a small town near Milan that produced non-music paper with a similar watermark that can be documented for the years 1780 and 1781.[122] Also probably Milanese is the watermark that has the initial A (15 millimeters high) in a baroque frame, which occurs most often in paper copied by Hand C.

EDITORIAL PROCEDURES

Authentic works of Sammartini are listed in the main body of the thematic catalogue that follows. There are five appendices, dealing with arrangements (A), contrafacta (B), lost works (C), doubtful and spurious works (D), and a general chronology of the symphonies (E).

The instrumental music is catalogued according to type and key. Since many of the works are undated, and most of the dates available for the remaining compositions come from secondary sources, a chronological order is impossible. Consequently we have chosen to organize the instrumental part of the catalogue according to key in ascending chromatic order, first major and then minor: C major, C minor, D major, D minor, etc. Within each key, the order of the compositions is determined by the initial notes of the incipits of the first movements. The first works are those starting on the tonic note, with the most repetitions of that note. The works proceed in order to the fewest repetitions of the tonic note and then to those with incipits first ascending, then descending from the

---

[122]EinederA, exx. 631 and 632. Bartha and SomfaiH cite a similar watermark (no. 28 on their list) with the initials M G rather than M C, and the word VAP???0 (which would seem to be the name Vaprio). The watermark is one of three in the paper of a fragmentary score of Mattia Stabingher's *Le Astuzie di Bettina,* conducted by Haydn at Esterháza in October 1785. The score is Milanese and signed "Giovanni Procolo Preta Copista dell' Archivio in Milano."

tonic note by progressively larger intervals—seconds, thirds, fourths, etc. The same procedure is then applied to works beginning on other degrees of the scale, starting with the second and ending with the seventh degree.[123]

The vocal music is divided into two sections, secular and sacred, arranged according to type within each section. Since we have many more specific performance dates for vocal works, a chronological order has been used wherever possible, in particular for operas and dated cantatas. The psalm settings and canticles are listed together alphabetically, but when there is more than one setting of the same text, they are ordered according to the modified LaRue system explained above. All other types of vocal compositions are ordered according to the same system.

Dates, when given, are the earliest known for each work. They indicate that a work cannot have been composed later than that year, but do not indicate the actual date of composition. The only exceptions are the few entries dated, for example, "1732 or before," (see No. 23), and the dated operas, oratorios, cantatas, and arias. For the first, the date is given because the style of the work and facts concerning the dating suggest it was probably composed in that year or just a few years earlier. For the second, exact performance dates or apparent dates of composition, appear on manuscripts or printed librettos, or may be ascertained by consulting the church calendar for the year in question (see Nos. 117-121, for example). In general it may be assumed that a work was composed shortly before the date of the first performance.

The date given for a printed source is the date of its announcement in a Paris or London newspaper or periodical. If no announcement has been found, but an approximate dating of the print is possible, the date has been taken from LesureR or SchnapperB. Other dated sources consist of dated manuscripts (see No. 88), manuscript collections, borrowings (see No. 44), and eighteenth-century catalogues (see No. 69).

For all works found in manuscript sources and catalogues, a short title is provided, consisting of the original title and last name of the composer, both in the original spelling (except for some minor changes, such as the omission of abbreviation signs, and the normal placement of "t" in St.).

Sammartini's name appeared in various forms in the eighteenth century, but rarely in the modern spelling. In the two autograph signatures, Sammartini spelled his last name "St. Martino" (1740) and "S. Martino" (1758; see figure 10). However, his name most frequently appears in one of the following forms: S., St. or San Martino(i) or simply Martino(i). The reader will also find other interesting and even amusing spellings in this catalogue.

As most of the works exist in manuscript parts, special indication is given in parentheses only for scores whenever found. According to present knowledge the best sources for Sammartini's music (listed alphabetically) seem to be Einsiedeln, Karlsruhe, Paris, Prague, and Zürich. These collections contain autograph or Milanese copies, or preserve the most convincing versions of Sammartini's works.

---

[123]This system follows the basic arrangement developed by Jan LaRue for his union thematic catalogue of eighteenth-century symphonies (see LaRueU).

With further research and study, it is possible that other sources may be given preference in certain cases. There is no evidence at present that Sammartini had any connection with the many printed editions of his music issued in England and France, except possibly the works published with the music or the "approval" of Felice Giardini, a Milanese composer active in London (see Nos. 22 and 73). In general, the prints examined so far offer unsatisfactory musical texts.

In the listing of manuscript sources, the most reliable one appears first, followed by all other sources arranged alphabetically according to city. The autograph or first source listed is the one from which the incipits have been taken, unless otherwise indicated in the remarks about the work. In Appendix D, incipits are taken from the manuscript or print ascribed to Sammartini unless otherwise noted. Library numbers for manuscripts and prints have been included whenever available. It was necessary to indicate the origin of the incipits because the sources, both manuscript and printed, often differ in instrumentation, tempo, rhythmic details, and even notes.

The incipits come from the first violin part or leading melodic voice. For vocal works, both the instrumental and vocal incipits are given. The original vocal clefs for the source of the incipits are indicated in parentheses. Some slight editing of the incipits has occasionally been necessary—for example, the correction of wrong notes and rhythms, the addition of triplet indications, and the substitution of the "tr" sign for the French + sign. All editorial ties are indicated by dotted lines; other editorial additions are placed in brackets. Editorial accidentals appear above the notes and remain in effect throughout the measure unless canceled. The spelling of tempo indications has been modernized.

After much thought and lengthy discussion, we have reluctantly and regretfully decided to omit almost all articulation and dynamic marks, since a reliable selection and placement of such indications depend on a detailed editing of the sources that has not been possible in most cases. These omissions do not essentially alter the incipits and therefore do not diminish the value of the catalogue, which is primarily a locator index and not a text for performance. We have made one exception in retaining dynamic indications that affect an entire movement: *sempre piano* or *sempre pianissimo*, or simply *pp*, *p*, and *mf* appearing in the first measure with the same meaning. No doubt arises regarding the placement of these indications and they represent an important practice of the period.

Appoggiaturas are notated as unslurred eighths, and three-note turns as unslurred thirty-seconds, since they appear this way in Sammartini's autographs and the authentic print of the *Sonate notturne,* Op. 7. The only exceptions occur in a few incipits in Appendix D of autograph or late sources, where the appoggiaturas are sixteenths. The original beaming has been followed throughout, but multiple stemming of chords has been replaced by single stemming. Original key signatures have been retained. For vocal works, the text of the printed libretto has been used whenever possible.

The instrumentation indicated is that of the first source. If it differs in a second source, the new instrumentation appears in parentheses with the source listing. When the only difference is the addition of woodwind and brass parts, reference is made only to these parts.

The "Remarks" contain information and explanations about the dating, special collections, handwriting, origin of text, performance dates, inscriptions on manuscripts, names of copyists and scene designers, biographical information about singers, and the like. The entries include full references to modern editions. Bibliographical references appear in shortened form representing the last name of the author and the initial letter or letters of the first key word in the title; for complete references, the reader should consult the bibliography. Entries under "Literature" have been limited to studies containing pertinent information about the work in question rather than stylistic analyses. In Appendix D, brief identifications are provided for obscure composers whose works are confused with Sammartini's. A question mark after "Possible Author" means that the available sources do not indicate a possible composer, or else they are so confused that no one composer can be selected.

While both authors have worked on all parts of the catalogue, Bathia Churgin is primarily responsible for the symphony sections, and Newell Jenkins for the remaining musical sections. This catalogue embodies the results of only the first stage of Sammartini research. Further work on the edition of the complete symphonies now underway, on editions of other compositions, and continuing research on Sammartini problems will surely expand and refine the material here presented.[124]

---

[124] Just before this catalogue was published, an article appeared, DonàN, that provides important information about Sammartini's father and family contained in Alessio's recently discovered will and death certificate. Alessio was probably born in 1664 and died in Milan on 5 September 1724. His wife, Gerolama Federici (or Federicis), may have been related to the Federici family of oboists in Milan (see also App. D 4). Alessio mentions seven children: Giuseppe, Giovanni Battista, Antonio, Carlo, Francesca, Maddalena, and Rosa (the order of names follows that of the will for the sons and daughters). It is possible that Antonio was a composer and oboist: that the ascriptions of three symphonies listed in this catalogue referred to him (see No. 68, App. D 67 and 68), and that he, not Giuseppe, was Giulini's wind teacher (see footnote 22). It is also possible that the reference in 1720 to the "Fratelli Martini" as oboe players in the orchestra of the Regio Ducal Teatro does not apply to Giovanni Battista in addition to Giuseppe but to Antonio or even Carlo.

Further recent information concerning the portrait of Sammartini (see frontispiece) in possession of the Civico Museo Bibliografico Musicale of Bologna has been received from Sergio Paganelli, who writes that Anne Schnoebelen of Rice University, Houston, Texas, had discovered the information below in the correspondence to Padre Martini. The painting is a copy of a lost original by an unknown artist of the first half of the 18th century, painted in 1778 by Domenico (Donino) Riccardi, painter and scenographer, active in the second half of the eighteenth century. The copy is documented in a letter from Giovenale Sacchi (1726-1789) addressed to a close collaborator of Padre Martini (see Epistolario Martiniano 1 10 26), but the name and address of the addressee has been cut from the body of the letter, dated 11 April 1778. Sacchi writes "at the postoffice you will find the portrait of Sig. San Martino. The portrait is by Sig. Riccardi who has also painted mine, and the original from which it is taken was done many years ago. I can testify that it is an extremely good likeness. If the Padre Maestro (meaning Martini) wishes, he may add the name and age 'Sig. Gio. Battista S. Martino (for thus he wrote his name himself) Milanese, died in the year 1775, 17 January at the age of 74'." For additional biographical information that appeared too late for inclusion in this catalogue, see InzaghiN.

1 Interior view of the courtyard of the Palazzo Ducale, Milan. The spire belongs to the ducal chapel of San Gottardo. The tower and roof in the background belong to the Regio Ducal Teatro

2 A prospect of the Regio Ducal Teatro, Milan, for the performance of *La Gara dei Geni* on 28 May 1747 (see No. 91)

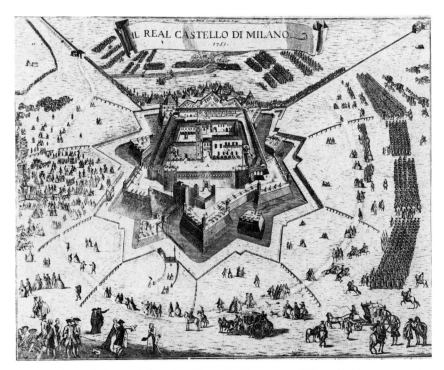

3   A view of the Real Castello (Castello Sforzesco), Milan, 1751, showing the
procession on the occasion of the translation of the body of S. Carlo
Borromeo

4   Detail of figure 3, showing the orchestral shell used for outdoor concerts
in mid-eighteenth century Milan

5 A view of the Piazza San Fedele with the facade of the church and of Palazzo Marino, Milan

6 A page from the opera *Memet*, 1732 (see No. 88). Act III, aria of Irene

7   An autograph page of Symphony No. 59, c. 1732, fol. 10r, third movement

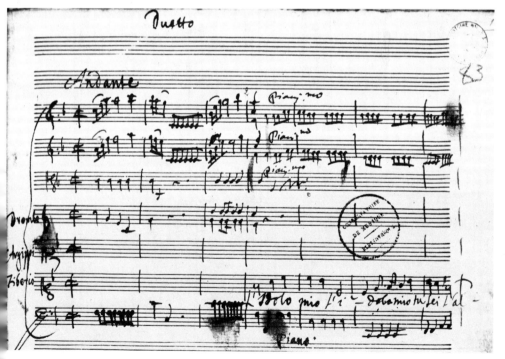

8   An autograph page from the opera *L'Agrippina*, performed in January 1743
      (see No. 90). Act II, duet of Agrippina and Tiberio

9   Another page from the duet of Agrippina and Tiberio, fol. 88v

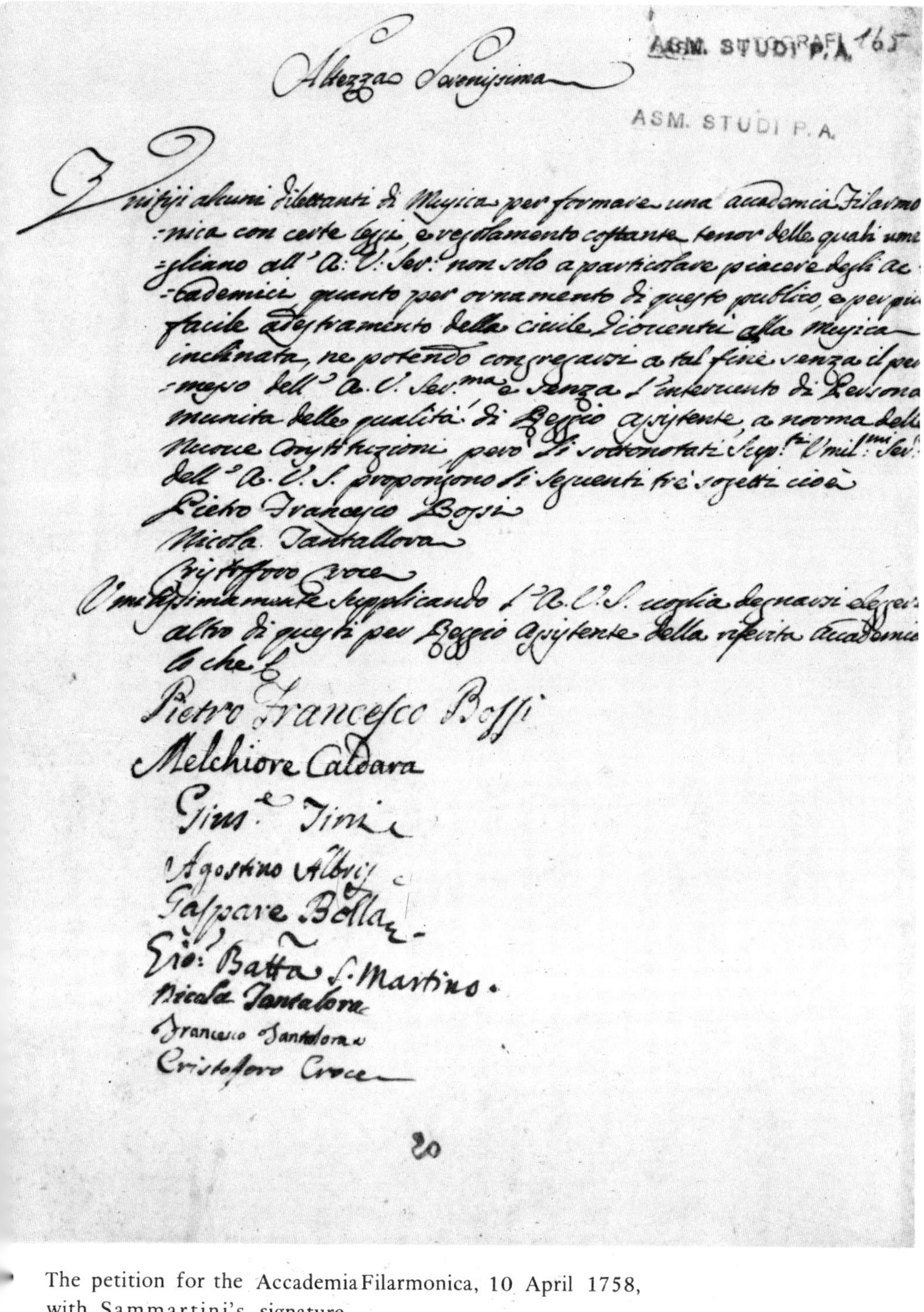

Altezza Serenissima

[petition text in Italian cursive]

Pietro Francesco Bossi
Nicola Tantallova
Cristoforo Croce

Pietro Francesco Bossi

Melchiore Caldara

Gius.e Timi

Agostino Albici

Gaspare Bolla

Giò: Batta S. Martino

Nicola Tantalora

Francesco Santalora

Cristoforo Croce

The petition for the Accademia Filarmonica, 10 April 1758, with Sammartini's signature

11   A sample of Hand A, from the opera *L'Agrippina,* Act I, fol. 1v

12   A sample of Hand B, from symphony No. 62a, first violin part

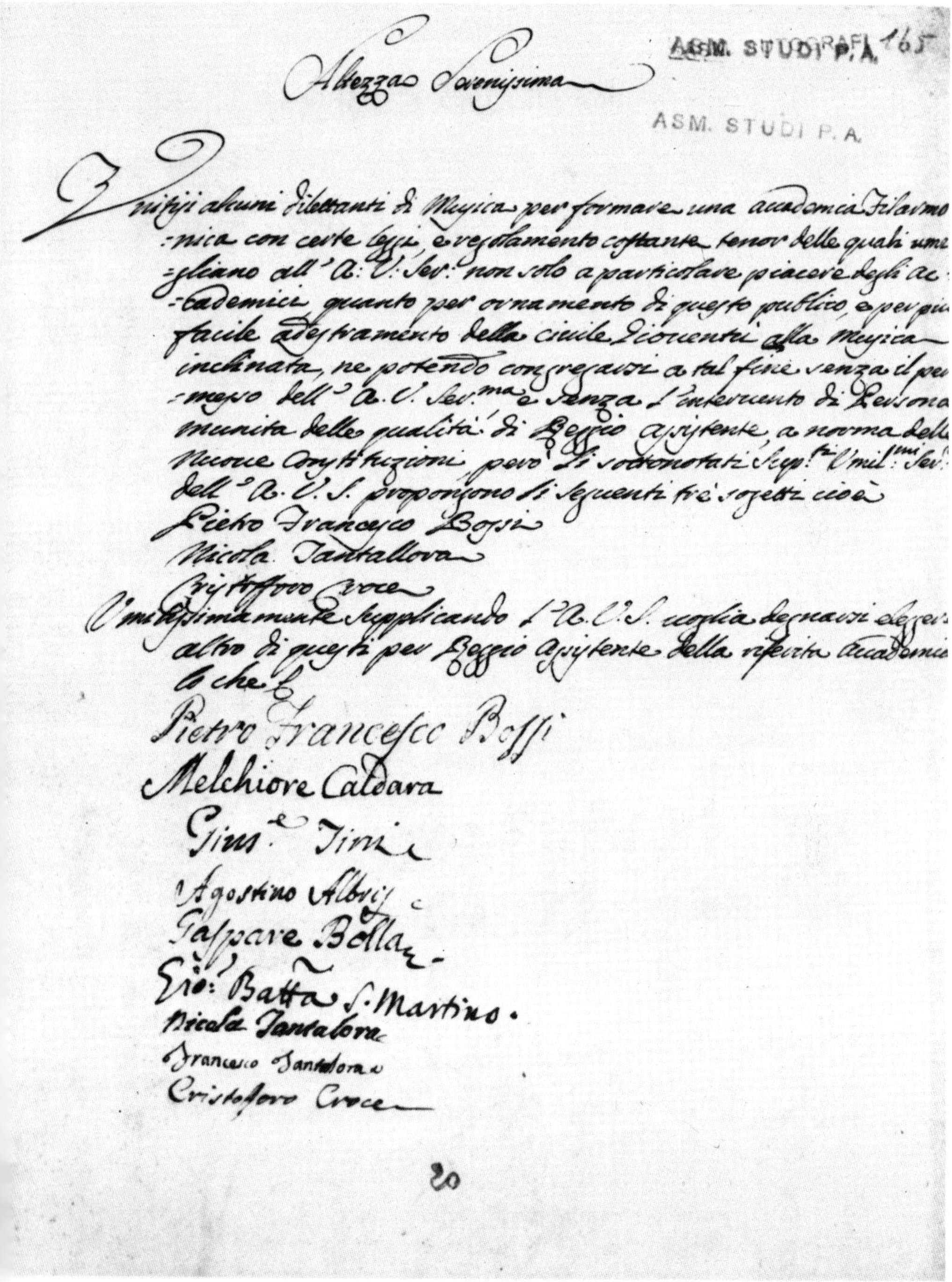

Altezza Serenissima

Unitisi alcuni dilettanti di Musica per formare una accademia Filarmo-
-nica con certe leggi, e regolamento costante tenor delle quali umi-
-gliano all'A: V: Ser: non solo a particolare piacere degli ac-
-cademici quanto per ornamento di questo publico, e per più
facile addestramento della civile Gioventù alla Musica
inclinata, ne potendo congregarsi a tal fine senza il per-
-messo dell'A. V. Ser.ma e senza l'intervento di Persona
munita delle qualità di Regio assistente, a norma delle
Recenti Constituzioni, però li sottonotati Supp.ti Umil.mi Ser.i
dell'A. V. S. propongono li seguenti tre sogetti cioè
Pietro Francesco Bossi
Nicola Tantallora
Cristoffero Croce
Umilissimamente supplicando l'A. V. S. voglia degnarsi elegger
altro di questi per Regio assistente della riferita Accademia
lo che &c.

Pietro Francesco Bossi
Melchiore Caldara
Giuse. Tirri
Agostino Albrici
Gaspare Bollazzi
Gio: Batta S. Martino.
Nicola Tantalora
Francesco Tantalora
Cristoforo Croce

20

0 The petition for the Accademia Filarmonica, 10 April 1758, with Sammartini's signatur

11   A sample of Hand A, from the opera *L'Agrippina*, Act I, fol. 1v

12   A sample of Hand B, from symphony No. 62a, first violin part

13 A sample of Hand C, from symphony No. 44, first violin part

14 A sample of Hand D, canto part, *Beatus Vir*, No. 104

15 Title page, Venier print Op. IX, 1757 (see No. 8)

VI
SINFONIE
A Più Stromenti
Composte
DA VARI AUTORI

I. Dell. Sig.r Beck. & IV. Dell Sig.r Reluzi.
II. Dell. Sig.r Priali. & V. Dell Sig.r Jomelli. Nel Teatro O di Roma l'ano 1757.
III. Dell. Sig.r Martini. & VI. Dell Sig.r Stamitz.

Opera IX
Prix 9ᵗ

Fait Graver par Mr. Venier
A PARIS

Chez { Mr. Bayard rue St Honoré à la Regle d'Or.
Mr. le Clerc rue du Roule à la Croix d'Or.
Mᵉˡˡᵉ Castagnerie ruë des Prouvaurs à la Musique
Royale.

On vend la Partie de Cor de chasse Séparément.
Avec Privilege du Roi.

H 113, a Gravée par Mᵉˡˡᵉ Vandôme.

16 Title page, Bremner print, 1766 (see Nos. 21, 70, and 78)

An
OVERTURE
and
TWO GRAND
CONCERTOS
Composed by
SIG.R GIO: BATTISTA ST MARTINI
of MILAN:
Approved and Recommended
by
SIG.R F. GIARDINI.
Opera 4.

LONDON.

Printed and Sold by R. BREMNER, facing Somerset-house in the STRAND,
of whom may be had for Concerts

The Earl of Kelly's Overtures | Periodical Overtures 2 Sets
Giardini's Overtures | Martini of Milan's 3 F. Horn Concertos. Op. 2.
Abel's Overtures. Op: 1. | Zannetti's Quintettos
Ditto Op: 4. | Stamitz's Quartettos
The Operas Cleonice, Siroe, Leucippo & Zenocrita, with the Instrumental parts printed separately.

Four
Overtures & one Quattro Compos'd by
Sig.r Felice Degiardino
and one Concerto with two Violins & two Hautboys Obligato
Compos'd by Sig.r Gio Batta S.t Martini Dedicated to the
Hon.ble HARRIOTT LANE by her most Oblig'd and
Very Hum.ble Servant
Felice Degiardino

Printed for Jn.o Cox at Simpson's Musick Shop in Sweetings Alley Royal Exchange.

17   Title page, Cox print, 1756 (see No. 73)

ABBREVIATIONS
USED IN CITING LIBRARIES, COLLECTIONS,
CATALOGUES, AND NEWSPAPERS

For abbreviations used in citing books and journals see the Selected Bibliography.

LIBRARIES

AGEN   Agen, Archives départementales

AMS   Amsterdam, Universiteits-Bibliotheek

ANC   Ancona, Biblioteca Comunale "Benincasa"

BAS   Basel, Universitätsbibliothek

BER   Berlin, Staatsbibliothek der Stiftung Preussischer Kultur-besitz

BERG   Bergamo, Biblioteca Civica

BERK   Berkeley, University of California at Berkeley Library

BOL   Bologna, Civico Museo Bibliografico Musicale

BPL   Boston Public Library

BRAT   Bratislava, Slovenskej Akadémie Vied, Ústav Hudobrej Vedy [Music Division of the Slovak Academy of Sciences]

BRNO   Brno, Moravské (Moravian) Muzeum

BRUS   Brussels, Bibliothèque du Conservatoire royale de musique

CARD   Cardiff Public Library

CKC   Cambridge University, King's College Library

CNL   Chicago, Newberry Library

COP   Copenhagen, Det Kongelige Bibliotek

CU   Cambridge University, University Library

DARM   Darmstadt, Hessische Landes- und Hochschulbibliothek

DONAU   Donaueschingen, Fürstlich Fürstenbergische Hofbibliothek

DRES   Dresden, Sächsische Landesbibliothek

EDIN   Edinburgh, Reid Library

EINS   Einsiedeln (Switzerland), Stiftsbibliothek

ENG   Engelberg (Switzerland), Stiftsbibliothek

FAE   Faenza, Biblioteca Comunale

GEN   Genoa, Biblioteca del Liceo Musicale "N. Paganini"

GENF   Genoa, Biblioteca Franzoniana

GLAS   Glasgow, Mitchell Library

GRAZ   Graz, Diözesenarchiv

GYÖR   Györ (Hungary), Cathedral Archive

HAR   Harburg, Fürstlich Oettingen-Wallerstein'sche Bibliothek

HEIL   Heiligenkreuz (Lower Austria), Stiftsbibliothek

HERZ   Herzogenburg (Lower Austria), Stiftsbibliothek

KARL   Karlsruhe, Badische Landesbibliothek

KÖNIG   Königsberg, Stadt-und Universitätsbibliothek

KREMS   Kremsmünster (Upper Austria), Stiftsbibliothek

LAM   Lambach (Upper Austria), Stiftsbibliothek

LBM   London, British Museum

LBMQ   London, British Museum, Queen's Library

LEI   Leiden, Universiteits-Bibliotheek

LOAM   London, Royal Academy of Music

LORC   London, Royal College of Music

LUND   Lund, Universitetsbiblioteket

MAD   Madrid, Biblioteca Nacional

MAN   Manchester Public Library

MELK   Melk (Lower Austria), Stiftsbibliothek

MILA   Milan, Biblioteca Ambrosiana

MILB   Milan, Biblioteca Nazionale di Brera

MILC   Milan, Biblioteca del Conservatorio "Giuseppe Verdi"

MILS   Milan, Museo della Scala

MILT   Milan, Biblioteca Trivulziana

MOD   Modena, Biblioteca Estense

MOG   Mogiła (Poland), monastery library

MUN   Munich, Bayerische Staatsbibliothek

MÜNS   Münster, Universitätsbibliothek

NAP   Naples, Biblioteca del Conservatorio

NH   New Haven, School of Music Library, Yale University

NYPL   New York Public Library

OOC	Oxford, Oriel College
OTTO	Ottobeuren, Bibliothek der Benediktiner-Abtei
OXBOD	Oxford, Bodleian Library
PARP	Parma, Biblioteca del Conservatorio (with the Biblioteca Palatina)
PBA	Paris, Bibliothèque de l'Arsenal
PBN	Paris, Bibliothèque nationale
PC	Paris, Bibliothèque nationale, fonds du Conservatoire
PIST	Pistoia, Biblioteca Capitolare del Duomo
PM	Paris, Bibliothèque Mazarine
PRA	Prague, Department of Music, Národní (National) Muzeum
PSG	Paris, Bibliothèque Sainte-Geneviève
REG	Regensburg, Fürstlich Thurn-und-Taxissche Hofbibliothek
ROCH	Rochester (New York), Sibley Music Library, Eastman
ROMC	Rome, Biblioteca S. Cecilia (Conservatorio)
SCHW	Schwerin, Mecklenburgische Landesbibliothek
STAMS	Stams (Tyrol, Austria), Stiftsbibliothek
STOCK	Stockholm, Kungl. Musikaliska Akademiens Bibliotek
TEN	Tenbury Wells, St. Michael's College
TOR	Toronto, University of Toronto Library
UPP	Uppsala, Universitetsbiblioteket
URB	Urbana, University of Illinois Library
VENC	Venice, Biblioteca del Conservatorio (Fondo Correr e Fondo Giustiniani)
VENL	Venice, Fondazione Levi, Biblioteca del Palazzo Giustinian Lolin a San Vidal
VENM	Venice, Biblioteca Nazionale Marciana
VGM	Vienna, Gesellschaft der Musikfreunde
VNB	Vienna, Österreichische Nationalbibliothek
WIL	Wilhering (Upper Austria), Stiftsbibliothek
WLC	Washington (D.C.), Library of Congress
WOLF	Wolfenbüttel, Herzog-August-Bibliothek
ZÜR	Zürich, Zentralbibliothek (Collection of the Allgemeine Musikgesellschaft)

SPECIAL COLLECTIONS

Aiguillon	Fonds des ducs d'Aiguillon (largely formed c. 1770-1788), Agen.
Alstr.	Collection of Patrick Alströmer (1733-1804) and his brothers, Stockholm.
AMG	Allgemeine Musikgesellschaft (founded 1812), Zürich.
Canal	Collection of Pietro Canal (1807-1883), Venice, Biblioteca Nazionale Marciana.
Carminati	Collection of the Carminati family, Venice, until 1918; deposited in the Museo Correr and in 1939 in the Biblioteca del Conservatorio, Venice.
Clam-Gallas	Collection of Count Christian Philipp Clam-Gallas (1748-1805), Vienna, Gesellschaft der Musikfreunde.
Crusaders' archives	Crusaders' archives (inventory dated 1737-1759), Prague.
Drexel	Collection of Joseph W. Drexel (1833-1888), New York.
Eng.	Collection of H. C. Engelhart, b. 1694 (dated before 1780), Lund.
F. Bl.	Fonds Blancheton (Rés. F. 441-446, dated c. 1740-c. 1744), Paris Conservatoire.
Hirsch	Paul Hirsch Library (formed 1896-1936), London, British Museum.
Kraus	Collection of Friedrich Kraus (largely formed c. 1745-c. 1780), Lund.
Mayr	Collection of Simone Mayr (1763-1845), Bergamo.
Mazer	Collection of Johan Mazer (1790-1847), Stockholm.
Noseda	Collection of Gustavo Adolfo Noseda (1837-1866), Milan Conservatorio.
Osacky	Collection of the Osacky (Osek) monastery (c. 1760–after 1800), Prague.
Pachta	Collection formed by Count Filip Pachta (d. c. 1760) and expanded by his nephew Count Jan Josef Pachta (1756-1834), Prague.
Rosp.	Collection of Don Clemente Rospigliosi (donated to PIST c. 1972).
Saras.	Collection of Lucas Sarasin (1730-1802), Basel.
Utile Dulci	Collection of the Stockholm literary society Utile Dulci, founded 1766, which was donated in the 1790's to the Royal Academy of Music, Stockholm.

Wagener	Collection of Guido Richard Wagener (1822-1896), Berlin and Brussels.
Waldst.	Collection formed by Count Emanuel Philipp von Wald-stein (1731-1775) and his eldest son, Joseph (1755-1814), Prague.
Wens.	Collection of the Wenster family of musicians connected with Lund Cathedral and University (eighteenth and nineteenth centuries), Lund.

EIGHTEENTH-CENTURY THEMATIC CATALOGUES

Br. 62, 66, 72	Breitkopf catalogue of 1762, 1766, 1772: *Catalogo delle Sinfonie, che si trovano in Manuscritto nella Officina Musica di Giovanni Gottlob Immanuel Breitkopf, in Lipsia.* Parte I^ma-VI^ta 1762-1765; Supplemento I-XVI, 1766-1787. Modern edition: Barry S. Brook, ed. *The Breitkopf Thematic Catalogue.* New York: Dover, 1966.
Brtnice	MS catalogue in Brno of the music collection formerly in Brtnice [Pirnitz] castle (see StrakováH). The catalogue is entitled *Inventario per la musica* and is dated c. 1752-1769.
Egk	MS catalogue in the Státní Archiv, Olomouc (Olmütz), Czechoslovakia, sign. C, k. 504, fol. 61-74, of the music collection once belonging to the chapel of the Bishop of Olmütz, Leopold II. Friedrich Graf Egk von Hungers-bach (1696-1760), *Cathallogus über die Hochfürstl. Musicalia und Instrumenta.* The music, now lost, was ob-tained in the period 1759-1760 (see No. 4).
Freising	MS catalogue in the Kreisarchiv, Munich, of music, for-merly at the court of the Prince-Bishop of Freising. The catalogue is entitled: *Themata Von allen vorhandenen Kirchen und Kammer Musicalien welche in der den I. Setpber [September] 1796 neu verfassten Designation enthalten sind.*
Hund	MS catalogue of Joanes Hund: *Catallogus Symphonarium et Triosonatium,* 1753, 1754. LBM Add. MSS 31994.
Karl.	Five MS catalogues of the Karlsruhe collection, identified in this volume by the letters A-E. All the catalogues except D are thematic, and many of the works listed have disappeared. Catalogue A is in the hand of J. M. Molter (c. 1695-12 Jan. 1765), *Kapellmeister* in Karls-

ruhe 1722-1733 and 1743-1765. His catalogue probably dates from the period c. 1755-c. 1762.

Lam.   MS catalogue in Lambach, Stiftsbibliothek: *Catalogus Musicalium et Instrumentorum ad Chorum Lambacensem pertinentium conscriptge MDCCLXIIX [sic] 1768.*

Sig.   MS catalogue in the Fürstlich Hohenzollernsche Hofbibliothek, Sigmaringen, Germany, of music formerly in the Sigmaringen Castle: *Catalogus Über die Sämtliche Musikalische Werck, und derselben Authora, nach Alphabetischer Ordnung; welche von Ihro Hochfürst: Durchlaucht dem Durchlauchtigsten Fürsten und Herrn, Herrn Carl Friedrich Erbprinzen zu Hohenzollern [etc.] consignitt von mir dem Expeditions Rath, und Music: Directore Schindele aᵒ. 1766* (completed c. 1770).

EIGHTEENTH-CENTURY PARTLY THEMATIC CATALOGUE

Sharp   *Catalogue of the Manuscript and Instrumental Music in the joint Collection of Messʳˢ: William, James, [and] Granville Sharp. London 1759* (probably completed in the 1790's). NYPL Drexel 1022 (see No. 102).

EIGHTEENTH-CENTURY NEWSPAPERS AND PERIODICALS

An.   *Annonces, affiches et avis divers,* Paris.

Gen. Adv.   *The General Advertiser,* London.

Gen. Ev. Post   *General Evening Post,* London.

Lon. Ev.-Post   *London Evening-Post,* London.

M. de Fr.   *Mercure de France,* Paris.

Pub. Adv.   *The Public Advertiser,* London.

GENERAL ABBREVIATIONS

A	Alto
anon.	anonymous
App.	Appendix
arr.	arrangement
b	bass (cello, contrabass and, excepting late works, harpsichord/organ)
B	Bass (voice)
bn	bassoon
cat. ref.	catalogue reference(s)
cb	contrabass
cemb	cembalo
cl	clarinet(s)
dev.	development
ed(s).	edition(s)
expos.	exposition
fl	flute(s)
hn	horn(s)
imperf.	imperfect copy
m (mm)	measure(s)
mod.	modern
mvt(s).	movement(s)
no.	number
ob	oboe(s)
obbl.	obbligato
Op. II/5	Opus II No. V
org	organ
pt(s).	part(s)
pub.	published
Racc. I/2	Raccolta I No. II
recap.	recapitulation
S	Soprano
str	strings (2 vn, va, b)
T	Tenor
tbn	trombone(s)
timp	timpani
tr	trumpet(s)
tr da c	tromba (trombe) da caccia
va	viola(s)
vc	violoncello(s)
vc picc	violoncello piccolo
vn	violin(s)
I, II, III (alone)	first mvt., second mvt., third mvt.

THEMATIC CATALOGUE

ORCHESTRAL WORKS

SYMPHONIES

C MAJOR

NO. 1*
2 hn, 2 vn, va, b

Cat. ref.   Karl. cat. E, Overteur, Martino.

MS sources   PRA Waldst. XXXIV C 312, Overteur, St. Martino (hn pts. missing); COP Sammlung C, Sinfonia 21, Anon. (2 ob, 2 hn, bn); STAMS K IIb, Sonata, St. Mart⁰.

Remarks   The oboes in COP are omitted in the second movement. In STAMS the title page bears the inscription "ad Chorum Stamsensam," and oboes are specified in the second violin part at the beginning of part II of the Andante.

NO. 2
2 ob, 2 hn, 2 vn, 2 va, b

*Five symphonies formerly considered authentic have been transferred to Appendix D. Therefore the numbers of the symphonies after No. 13 do not correspond with the catalogue numbers given in ChurginE.

Date	1772?
MS source	DARM 198/b, Sinfonia, Sammartini (destroyed in World War II).
Remarks	For explanation of the date, see No. 60.
Mod. ed.	Fausto Torrefranca (Milan: Carisch, 1936), heavily edited, with added bassoon and timpani parts in I and III, and 2 flutes in II.

NO. 3

2 tr, 2 vn, va, b

MS source	PRA Waldst. XXXIV C 322, Overteur, St. Martino.
Remarks	The title page bears the name of J. Slama, the probable copyist.

NO. 4

2 hn, 2 vn, va, b

Date	before 1760.
Cat. ref.	Egk No. 89, 1760, Sinfonia, St. Martino; Br. 62, Racc. II/2, Sinfonia, Martino; Karl. cat. A, Sinfonia, St. Martino.
MS sources	PRA Waldst. XXXIV C 412, Sonata, St. Martino; KARL Mus. Hs. 812, Sonata, St. Martino (str only); LUND Kraus 170, Concerto, Martino (2 ob or 2 fl, 2 tr, timp); STOCK O-R, 3 copies: (1) Sinfonia, Martini, mvts. I, II (str only); (2) Sinfonia, Anon.; (3) Sinfonia, Anon. (2 vn, b); another copy: Alstr., Sÿnphonia, Martino; VENC Fondo Carminati-Museo Correr, Busta 9-20, No. 18, Sinfonia, Sammartino (2 tr da c); VGM XIII 23566, Sinfonia, St. Martino (2 ob, 2 hn, cemb; 2 hn, va pts. missing).
Remarks	Egk became Bishop of Olmütz 25 May 1758 and died 15 December 1760. The catalogue lists 226 compositions by genre, and includes 123 symphonies and 56 trios. Much of the music was purchased in Vienna. An annotation after symphony No. 50 states that the music up to that point was paid for on 25 November 1759. The date 1759 also appears at the beginning of the list of symphonies with the indication "Von Wien mitgebracht." Symphonies 1-50 can therefore be dated in the year 1759, with 25 November being the *terminus ad quem* for that group. Since a second annotation next to symphony No. 51 states that it was obtained on 14 February 1760, it seems safe to assume that all the symphonies after No. 50 were obtained in 1760.

The PRA and KARL MSS are copied in Hand C, and the PRA title page bears the initials E. W. (referring to Emanuel Waldstein, 1731-1775). In LUND the MS is dated 1762 and has four movements. The original first and third movements are transposed to the key of D. A second Andante in C (incipit below) precedes the original Andante in G, and is doubtful in style.

Though trumpets are indicated on the title page, the word "cornu" (horn) appears on the parts. The oboe/flute parts are independent. Added parts like these, probably composed by local musicians, also occur in LUND copies of Nos. 34 and 37. The title page is inscribed "Academia Carolina," which was the name given to Lund University on ceremonial occasions; "Carolina" refers to Charles IX (1550-1611).

The STOCK copies belonged to the literary society Utile Dulci. In VGM oboes are not mentioned on the title page and are probably later additions. The parts are copied by a different hand on different paper and double the violins.

Mod. eds.   1) With 2 hn: Ettore Bonelli (Padua: Zanibon, 1956), heavily edited. 2) In Ursula Lehmann, *Deutsches und italienisches Wesen in der Vorgeschichte des klassischen Streichquartetts* (Würzburg: Triltsch Verlag, 1939), Notenbeilage, pp. 10-14 (expos. and dev. of I, KARL version).

Literature   SehnalK.

NO. 5

2 hn, 2 vn, va, b

MS sources   PRA Waldst. XXXIV C 390, Sinfonia, S. Martini; another copy XXXIV C 391, Sinfonia, St. Martino; GYÖR M. 3., Sinfonia, Martino (2 tr, timp); MELK V/1425, Simfonia, S. Martino; MÜNS MS 1462, Sinphonia, S. Martino.

NO. 6

2 vn, va, b

MS source   PRA Waldst. XXXIV C 331, Overteur, Martino.

NO. 7

2 vn, va, b

Date   before c. 1742.

MS sources   PC F. Bl. Op. II/87, Sonata, St. Martino; DRES Mus. 2/N/24,5, Sinfonia, Anon. (18th-century score; III missing); LUND Wens. Litt. C 4, Sinfonia, San Martini; another copy Wens. Litt. L 50, Sonata, Anon. (2 vn, b).

Remarks   This work has been dated before c. 1742 because it appears in the Op. II of the F. Bl. The Op. I (non-concerto) and Op. II of this collection were probably in existence by 1742, since nine works from these volumes were published in Le Clerc's print of Sammartini's sonatas and symphonies, Op. II, of that year (see No. 33). Works by Sammartini in the other volumes of the F. Bl. have been dated "before c. 1744" (if no earlier date was available), which is the latest date for the collection suggested in La LaurencieI.

The name "Christ: Wenster Senior" appears on the lower right-hand corner of the title page of Wens. Litt. C 4. The inscription probably refers to the second of three musicians in the Wenster family line with this name (1704-1779) rather than the first (d. 1727). This source and the score in DRES contain a viola part that differs in many details from the PC part and is inferior to it. The second LUND copy is the poorest version of the symphony and is found in a collection of trio sonatas.

Mod. ed.   ChurginE.

C MINOR

NO. 8

2 hn, 2 vn, va, b

Date	c. 1750 to 5 March 1751.

MS sources   EINS 543/16, Introduzione, cantata No. IV (see No. 117; I only; 2 ob; mod. score); PRA XXXII A 331, Sinfonia, Anon. (I only; str only).

Print   Venier, July 1757 (M. de Fr.): VI / SINFONIE / A Più Stromenti / Composte / DA VARI AUTORI / I. Dell. Sig^r. Beck. / II. Dell. Sig^r. Priali. / III. Dell. Sig^r. Martini. / IV. Dell Sig^r. Reluzi. / V. Dell Sig^r. Iomelli. / Nel Teatro di Roma Lano 1757 / VI. Dell Sig^r. Stamitz. / Opera IX / Prix 9£. / fait Graver par M^r. Venier A PARIS / Chez M^r. Bayard rue St Honoré à la Regle d'Or. / M^r. le Clerc rue du Roule à la Croix d'Or. / Melle Castagnerie rüe des Prouvairs à la Musique / Royale. / On vend la Partie de Cor de chasse Séparêment. / Avec Privilege du Roi. / Gravée par Melle. Vendôme. PC H. 113; MUN (2 hn only).

Remarks   Each of the eight cantatas for the Fridays in Lent in EINS contains a one-movement overture, five of which are found elsewhere as parts of complete symphonies: the overtures to Nos. 117 (No. 8/I), 118 (No. 58b/III), 120 (No. 29/I), 121 (No. 25/I), and 122 (No. 56/I). For further information about these cantatas and their librettos, see Nos. 117-124. It is likely that the original versions of the cantatas employed the same overtures as in EINS, thus allowing us to date the overture movements and the symphonies from which they came. Sammartini probably borrowed these movements from previously existing works, adding wind parts for the cantata versions. Cantata No. 117 was performed at S. Fedele in Milan on 5 March 1751, thereby providing a terminal date for this symphony, whose first movement appears as the overture to the cantata. Pater Sigismund Keller made the scores in EINS and MUN in 1875 and 1880 respectively. The first-movement incipit is taken from EINS as the more reliable source. The PRA copy belonged to the Osacky (Osek) monastery.

NO. 9

2 vn, va, b

Date	before c. 1742.
MS source	PC F. Bl. Op. I/24, Overtura, St. Martino.
Remarks	For explanation of the date, see No. 7.
Mod. ed.	ChurginE.

D MAJOR

NO. 10

2 hn, 2 vn, va, b

Date	before c. 1747.
Cat. ref.	Br. 62, Racc. II/1, Sinfonia, Martino.
MS sources	BERK (uncatalogued), Overteur, Anon.; COP Sammlung L, Sinfonia 16, Martino (with bn; hn II pt. missing);

KÖNIG Sammlung 516a, Anon. No. 4 (destroyed in World War II); PRA Waldst. XXXIV C 23, Overtura, Anon.

Prints   1) Simpson, c. 1747: THREE / CONCERTOS / FOR / Violins French Horns etc. / Compos'd by / Sig^r. Gio. Battista S^t. Martini / of MILAN / Opera II^da / NB. These Concertos may be play'd as Sonatas / by leaving out the French Horn Parts / LONDON. Printed for J. Simpson at the Bass Viol and Flute in Sweeting's / Alley opposite the East Door of the Royal Exchange; Concerto II. Concertos I and III doubtful, and probably by Melchiorre Chiesa (see App. D 17 and 39). Copies in URB and in the possession of Newell Jenkins (2 hn, va pts. missing).

2) Bremner: reprint of Simpson ed. c. 1765–c. 1766, title as above; LBM g. 1780. q. (11.), STOCK VO-R.

Remarks   No announcement of the Simpson print has been found. Since it is called Op. II, it must have appeared after Simpson's print of Sammartini's trio sonatas Op. I, announced 3 July 1744 in the *General Advertiser.* Six other Simpson prints advertised on the title page of the Op. II have been dated 1744-1746 in the *British Union-Catalogue,* one, containing six trio sonatas by Gluck, appearing in November 1746. The Sammartini print, or issue of the print, thus appeared after November 1746 and probably in 1747. Simpson died c. 1749, which is the latest possible date for the print. Robert Bremner announced his acquisition of the plates of part of Simpson's stock in trade in the *Public Advertiser* 10 October 1764, listing this collection and Sammartini's trios Op. I among the works purchased. Bremner's reprint was probably published 1765-1766, since the advertisement of this work appears on Bremner's edition of Sammartini's Op. 4 (see No. 21), which was announced 27 November 1766.

    The BERK copy is probably north Italian. The STOCK print belonged to the literary society Utile Dulci.

NO. 11

2 ob, 2 hn, 2 vn, va, vc, cb

Presto

MS source	PC D.13.662, Sinfonia per Camera, St. Martino (mod. score).
Remarks	The score is one of eight made in 1882 for J. B. Weckerlin, librarian of the Paris Conservatoire, from parts once in the Conservatoire and now lost. All these symphonies are late works and unique copies. They include Nos. 11, 22, 26, 28, 31, 40, 60, and 63.
Literature	Weckerlin J.

NO. 12
2 hn, 2 vn, va, b

Allegro staccato

Andante

Spiritoso

Date	before 1760.
Cat. ref.	Egk No. 123, 1760, Sinfonia, S. Martino.
MS source	PRA Waldst. XXXIV C 317, Overteur, St. Martino.

NO. 13
2 tr, 2 vn, va, b

Spiritoso e sciolto

Minuetto. Allegro moderato

Trio

| Cat. ref. | Karl. cat. E, Overteur, Martino. |

MS sources	PRA Waldst. XXXIV C 301, Sonata, St. Martino; COP Sammlung L, Sinfonia 20, Martino (2 hn, bn); GEN N.1.6.6. (Sc. 17), Avertura, San Martino (2 hn; I only; see App. D 13); ZÜR AMG XIII 7043 a-e, Overtura [No. 5], St. Martino.
Remarks	The PRA title page bears the initials E. W. (referring to Emanuel Waldstein, 1731-1775), and the MS is copied in Hand C. The ZÜR collection contains six symphonies bound in the following order: Nos. 16, 44, 57, 54, 13, and 56. Four symphonies—Nos. 16, 44, 13, and 56—are copied in Hand B, the incipits written in Hand C. Two symphonies—Nos. 57 and 54—are copied in two other Milanese hands on Milanese paper. The full title of the collection on the cover of the first violin part reads: "6 Sinfonie ó sia overture di St Martino." The initials H. M. appear on the cover of each part.

NO. 14

2 vn, va, b

Date	before c. 1742.
MS source	PC F. Bl. Op. I/50, Avertura, Martini.
Remarks	For explanation of the date, see No. 7.
Mod. ed.	ChurginE.

NO. 15

vn, va, b

MS source	BER Mus. ms. 19396/3, Sinfonia, San Martino; BRUS Wagener V. 13.449, Sinfonia, San Martini (mod. score of BER copy).
Remarks	The BER scoring is uncharacteristic of the trio symphony, and is probably not authentic. A second violin part may have been lost or adapted for the viola since the existing violin part is headed "Violino Primo." In BRUS the symphony is the first in a collection of seven Sammartini trios, Nos. 2-7 being trio sonatas.
Mod. eds.	1) ChurginE. 2) Sammlung Sondheimer No. 49 (Berlin: Edition Bernoulli, 1937). Unreliable: vn II part added by Sondheimer; all parts altered; harmonies, motives changed. In I, the recapitulation is altered; in II, the tempo is changed, con sordino added, and a da capo of I after II specified; in III, the tempo is changed, the movement lengthened, and repeat marks inserted after bar 10 and omitted for part II. 3) HAM, Vol. II, No. 283 (I only; Sondheimer version). 4) Louis Scarmolin (Cleveland; Ludwig Publishing Co., 1955), arranged for full symphony orchestra. Unreliable: I and III based on Sondheimer; II spurious.

NO. 16

2 tr, 2 vn, va, b

Date	before 1762.
Cat. ref.	Br. 62, Racc. II/6, Sinfonia, Martino; Karl. cat. E, Overteur, Martino.

MS sources	ZÜR (see No. 13), Overtura (No. 1), St. Martino; PRA Waldst. XXXIV C 314, Overteur, St. Martino; STOCK Alstr., Synphonia, S. Martini (str only).
Remarks	The ZÜR MS is copied in Hand B and omits the slow movement. In STOCK the first movement is headed "Overteur" on the first page of the violin and bass parts.

NO. 17

2 ob, 2 hn, 2 vn, va, b

Date	1759 or before.
Cat. ref.	Egk No. 18, 1759, Sinfonia, S. Martino.
MS sources	PRA Waldst. XXXIV B 314, Sinfonia, St. Martino; VGM XIII 1318, Sinfonia, St. Martino; PC D.13.659, Sinfonia, San Martino (mod. score).
Remarks	The MS listed in the Egk catalogue was obtained in Vienna before 25 November 1759 (see No. 4). The PC score is one of four Sammartini symphonies purchased in 1880 from the library of Otto Jahn (1813-1869) (see also Nos. 49, 52, and 62a). This excellent collection was probably made from the MS copies in VGM in relation to Jahn's monumental biography of Mozart, which appeared 1856-1859.

NO. 18

2 tr, 2 vn, va, b

Date   1747 or before.

MS sources   PRA Waldst. XXXIV C 311, Overtura, S. Martino (tr II
                missing); DONAU Mus. Ms. 1791, Sinfonia, Anon. (2 hn);
                MELK V/1426, Simfonia, St. Martino (2 ob, 2 hn);
                MILC Fondo Noseda G-99, Sinfonia, Galuppi (overture
                to *L'Olimpiade*); STOCK Od-R, Simphonie, Jomelli (str
                only).

Print   Attributed to Jommelli. Boivin, c. 1748: SIMPHONIE /
                NOVELLE / A QUATRO. / del Signor / NICOLÒ
                JOMELLI / Maestro di Musica / in Napoli. / Gravées par
                Mme. Leclair. / Prix 7^£. 4^s. [6^£. on vn II, va, b] / A
                PARIS / Chez / La Ve. Boivin, rue S^t. Honoré à la Régle
                d'Or. / Le S^r. Leclerc, rue du Roule à la Croix d'Or. /
                Melle. Castagnery, rue des Prouvaires à la musique Roy-
                al. / Avex Privilége [sic] du Roy; PC H.215 a-d, Simpho-
                nia III (str only).

Remarks   Galuppi's opera was performed in the Regio Ducal Teatro
                in Milan on 26 December 1747, thereby dating the sym-
                phony borrowed for the opera. Despite the conflicting
                attributions there can be no doubt that this work was
                composed by Sammartini, for it is unquestionably in
                his style.

                It is possible that the print was published c. 1748
                since the symphony is called "new," and the indication
                "Veuve" is rarely attached to Boivin's name after 1748.
                The viola part in the print and STOCK MS differs from
                the part in the other sources, doubling the bass at the
                octave above rather than filling in the harmonies. The
                STOCK version was copied by Johan Gustaf Psilander-
                hielm (1723-1782), an amateur musician and a copyist
                of the literary society Utile Dulci (to which this MS
                belonged), who was active especially in the 1770's and
                1780's. The symphony was probably copied from the
                Paris print, which it follows in title, ascription, scoring,
                and many musical details. In DONAU the title page is
                inscribed "Chori Zering: 175[?]3." The added oboes in
                MELK play only in the outer movements, and they
                double or outline the violins.

Mod. ed.   Ascribed to Galuppi (with newly composed oboe parts
                in I and III, and the 2 trumpets exchanged for 2 horns):

Roberto Lupi (Milan: Carisch, 1956), heavily edited,
with spurious alterations in the second movement: bars
11 and 14 are repeated, the repeat of bars 14-15 omitted,
and the final tonic chord is embellished with appoggiaturas in the violins.

NO. 19

2 ob, 2 hn, 2 vn, va, vc, cb

MS source   DONAU Mus. Ms. 1286, Sinfonia, S. Martino.

Remarks   The MS contains a probably spurious timpani part, not
mentioned on the title page, which is written on different
paper in a different hand.

NO. 20

2 ob?, 2 hn, 2 vn, va, b

MS sources   PRA Waldst. XXXIV C 410, Sonata, St. Martino; BAS
Saras. 39, Overtura, St. Martino (2 hn).

Remarks   The PRA title page bears the initials E. W. (referring to Emanuel Waldstein, 1731-1775), and the BAS MS is probably north Italian. In PRA, the viola parts of movements II and III and the complete two horn parts are copied in Hand C. It is difficult to determine whether the oboes are original or added parts. Though they double the violins extensively, even in the second movement, they also play independent motives in the first movement and skillfully arranged solos after the double bar in the first and second movements.

Mod. ed.   The exposition of the first movement is arranged for keyboard in Robert Sondheimer, "Die formale Entwicklung der vorklassischen Sinfonie," *AfMw*, IV (January 1922), 125-126.

NO. 21

2 ob, 2 hn, 2 vn, va, vc, b; solo vn in II.

Date   1766 or before.

Print   R. Bremner, 27 Nov. 1766 (Pub. Adv.): An / OVERTURE / and / TWO GRAND / CONCERTOS / Composed by / SIG^R: GIO: BATTISTA S^T. MARTINI / of MILAN. / Approved and Recommended / by / SIG^R: F. GIARDINI. / Opera 4. / LONDON. / Printed and Sold by R: BREMNER, facing Somerset-house in the STRAND. LBM h.57.h.; STOCK VO-R (2 hn pts missing); WLC M 1004.A2S19 (hn II pt. missing).

Remarks   The symphony is a composite work, containing a concerto-like second movement for solo violin which may have been written specifically for Giardini or taken from a now lost violin concerto. Felice Giardini (1716-1796) studied in Milan and knew Sammartini. One of the leading violinists of his time, Giardini resided in England from 1750 until his death and was also active as a composer and conductor.

The STOCK copy belonged to the literary society Utile Dulci.

NO. 22

2 ob, 2 hn, 2 vn, va, b

MS source   PC D.13.664, Sinfonia Per Camera, St. Martino (mod. score; see No. 11).

D MINOR

NO. 23

2 vn, b

Date   c. 1732 or before.

Autograph   Mvts. II and III in score (undated and unsigned), PBN Vm^7. 7708, ff. 5r-8r.

MS source   PC F. Bl. Op. I/30, Avertura, St. Martino.

Remarks   The MS in PBN is the only known autograph of Sammartini's symphonies, containing in score the latter two movements of four early trio symphonies in

the following order: Nos. 38, 23, 59, and 66a. All but
No. 59 are also found in copies in the F. Bl. The sixteen-
page MS is in oblong format and measures 210 x 283
millimeters, each page containing ten staves, characteristic of Italian music paper in this period. The binding is
old and has the title "Airs." It is not known when the
library obtained the MS. It bears the stamp of the Second Empire, but may have been in the library long before without having been stamped. Since the first movements of Nos. 38 and 66a were used in Sammartini's
opera *Memet* in 1732 (see No. 88), it is probable that
all the works in the MS were composed in or before
that year.

In the F. Bl. the viola part, though not mentioned in
the title, contains a copy of the bass part, probably to be
doubled at the higher octave. This type of doubling,
which was apparently optional, is found in the F. Bl. for
all works *a 3*—symphonies, concertinos, and even trio
sonatas.

Mod. ed.   ChurginE.

E-FLAT MAJOR

NO. 24

2 hn, 2 vn, va, b

MS source   PRA Waldst. XXXIV B 24, Sinfonia, S. Martino.

NO. 25

2 tr, 2 vn, va, b

Date	c. 1750 to 2 April 1751.
Cat. ref.	Karl. cat. E, Overteur, S. Martino.
MS sources	EINS 12/11, Overtur, San Martini; EINS 109/1, Introduzione, cantata No. VI (see No. 121; I only; 2 ob; pts. and mod. score); PRA Waldst. XXXIV C 324, Overtura, St. Martino (2 hn).
Remarks	For explanation of the date, see Nos. 8 and 121.

NO. 26

2 ob, 2 hn, 2 vn, va, b

MS source	PC D.13.666, Sinfonia per Camera, St. Martino (mod. score; see No. 11).

NO. 27

2 vn, va, b

Date	before 12 January 1765.
Cat. ref.	Karl. cat. A, Sinfonia, St. Martino.
MS sources	PRA Waldst. XXXIV C 385, Sinfonia, St. Martino; KARL Mus. Hs. 811, Sinfonia, St. Martino.
Remarks	The Karl. catalogue provides an ultimate date for this work, since it was compiled by J. M. Molter who died 12 January 1765. This movement is probably an overture to a lost vocal work, or the first movement of a symphony whose succeeding movements are lost. In PRA the first violin part is inscribed "Sonata." The title page bears the initials E. W. (referring to Emanuel Waldstein, 1731-1775), and the MS is copied in Hand C. The KARL MS is copied in Hand B, the incipits on the title page written in Hand C.

NO. 28

2 ob, 2 hn, 2 vn, va, vc, cb

MS source   PC D.13.668, Sinfonia Con più Istromenti, St. Martino (mod. score; see No. 11).

NO. 29

2 hn, 2 vn, va, b

Date   c. 1750 to 26 March 1751.

MS source   EINS 543/16, overture to cantata No. VII (see No. 120; I only; 2 ob, 2 hn; mod. score).

Print   Hummel, 10 May 1761 (Pub. Adv.): Six Favourite / OVERTURES / in Six Parts, / for / Two Violins, Two French-Horns, / A Tenor and Bass. / Composed by Different Authors, / Viz^t: / Galuppi, S^t. Martini & Jomelli. / LONDON: / Printed for A: HUMMEL at his Musick Shop facing Nassau Street in King Street / S^t. Anns Soho; Overture VI. Nos. III and VI are by Sammartini; No. IV is probably by Galimberti or Giulini (see App. D 33). LBM g. 474.a. (8), GLAS (imperf.), both copies c. 1770.

Remarks   For explanation of the date see Nos. 8 and 117. The incipit of the first movement comes from EINS. The second
movement, which is also in E-flat, appears in No. 57 in
all other sources and undoubtedly belongs to that symphony. It seems probable that No. 29 originated as a
two-movement symphony (fast-minuet), or contained a
slow movement that was lost, the movement from No.
57 inserted, perhaps, to make a longer and more characteristic cycle. The use of the same key for all three
movements does not otherwise occur in Sammartini's
symphonies dating after c. 1740.

NO. 30
2 ob, 2 hn, 2 vn, va, b

MS source   PRA Waldst. XXXIV B 23, Sinfonia, St. Martino.

E MAJOR

NO. 31
2 ob, 2 hn, 2 vn, va, b

MS source   PC D.13.661, Sinfonia per Camera, St. Martino (mod. score; see No. 11).

F MAJOR

NO. 32
2 vn, va, b

Date   before c. 1744.

MS source   PC F. Bl. Op. III/144, Sinfonia, St. Martini.

Remarks   For explanation of the date, see No. 7.

Mod. eds.   1) ChurginE.
2) Newell Jenkins ("Grahl's Orchester-Serie" No. 1. Frankfurt am Main: H. L. Grahl, 1953).

NO. 33
2 vn, va, b

Date   before c. 1733-c. 1738.

Cat. ref.   Egk No. 116, 1760, Sinfonia, S. Martino; Br. 62, Racc. VII/6 (2 ob, 2 hn), Sinfonia, Hasse; Karl. cat. E, Overteur St. Martino.

MS sources   PC F. Bl. 6, Avertura, Martini (3 vn, b); BAS kr IV.285, Saras. 21, Overtura, Martino (2 hn); PC D.11.182, Sonata, Martini (3 vn, b); WLC M 1104.S2O8 Case, Concerto, Martino.

Prints   1) Ascribed to Giuseppe Sammartini. Le Clerc, 1742: XII / SONATE / a Due è Tre Violini / Col Basso. / Del Signor / GIUSEPPE SAN MARTINI / Milanese / OPERA SECONDA / Gravé par Labassée / Prix 9£. / A PARIS / Chez / Mr. le Clerc C. rue St. Honoré vis à vis l'Oratoire chés le Bonnetier. / Le S. le Clerc Md. rue du Roule a la Croix d'Or. / La Ve. Boivin Mde. rue St. Honoré a la Regle d'Or. / AVEC PRIVILEGE DU ROI; Sonata XI (3 vn, b). Later issues of the print are in LBM g.86.a. (1), PBA M. 439¹, PC K.5511 (3 other copies PC, PBN). Another copy TOR.
2) I. Walsh, 23-26 Nov. 1751 (Lon. Ev.-Post): SIX / CONCERTOS / in 8 Parts, / For / VIOLINS, FRENCH HORNS, HOBOYS, & c. / with a Bass for the / VIOLON-CELLO and HARPSICORD. / Compos'd by / Sigr. GIO: BAT: St. MARTINI of Milan. / and / Sigr. HASSE. / London. Printed for I. Walsh in Catharine Street in the Strand; Concerto I, with the march from Handel's *Judas Maccabaeus,* Act III, added as a fourth movement (2 hn). LBMQ R. M. 17.d.4.(5.), and a second copy. Also BOL KK. 412.

Remarks   The minuet of this symphony appears in a "Receüil de plrs. Menuets de Cremône et de Milan et autres," scored for violin and bass, in PSG Ms. 2366-2367. The movement is entitled "Menuet" and ascribed to "Martini Milano." This French MS contains five suites of minuets, each comprising 8-33 minuets arranged by key, followed by two smaller groups of minuets, the first entitled "menuets allemds." The first suite is dated "de l'année 1733 et suive. [suivante]," the fifth suite "de l'année 1738," and the last group "de 1739." The Sammartini minuet occurs as No. 10 in the second suite, and would thus be dated probably between 1733 and 1738. Since it is likely that the minuet was taken from the symphony, the dating can be applied to the symphony as a whole.

The Le Clerc print is the first printed collection of symphonies and trios by Sammartini. Though published under the name of his brother, it contains no music by Giuseppe. Eight sonatas are by G. B. Sammartini, four of them, Nos. I, V, VII, and XI, actually being symphonies (see also Nos. 35, 37, and 38). Four symphonies, Nos. II,

VI, X, and XII, are by Antonio Brioschi (see App. D 15). The print is listed in a catalogue issued by the publishers Boivin and Ballard in Paris, 1742 (PBN Rés. Vmd. 35), and was presumably published in that year or slightly earlier. It appears under "SAN-MARTINI" as his "Deuxième Livre Trio." The PC copy D. 11.182 is inscribed "a M^r. le Mis. de la Salle," indicating it was probably intended for Adrien-Nicolas Marquis de Lasalle d'Offement (1735-1818), a Parisian music patron and minor literary figure (see also Nos. 35 and 38). The horn parts of the Walsh print and BAS are identical and probably not authentic; the print itself contains no other works by Sammartini. It is likely that the erroneous ascription of this work to Hasse in the Breitkopf catalogue stems from the presence of the symphony in the Sammartini-Hasse print. This would also explain the instrumentation with oboes, specified for most of the works in the print but not for this symphony. The instrumentation with three violins reflects French rather than Italian practice of this period, and it does not recur in the best sources of other Sammartini symphonies.

The minuet of this symphony became very popular, especially in France, and was arranged for several different combinations: (1) for keyboard, with a variation, in Michel Corrette, *Les Amusemens du Parnasse*, vol. II, Paris (PC); (2) for keyboard, in a MS "Recueil de Sonates et autres Pièces," in BRUS V. 6327, ff. 44-45; (3) for violin alone in L'Abbé le Fils, *Principes du violon*, Paris 1761, p. 12 [Anon.] ; (4) for two violins, with two variations, in T. J. Tarade, *Premier Recueil Des plus beaux Airs*, Paris, 1773 (PC); (5) for two flutes (the minuet transposed to G major), in Michel Blavet, *IIe. Recueil de Pièces, petits Airs, Brunettes, Menuets &c.*, Paris, c. 1755 (copies in PBN and elsewhere); and (6) for string trio in *2^d. Sett Flores Musicae Being twelve Sonatinas For Two Violins and a Violoncello With a Thorough Bass for the Harpsichord Taken from the Works of the best English and Italian Authors by C. A. Esqr.*, London, c. 1758; Sonatina 3/III [Anon.], NYPL (vn I pt only).

Mod. eds.

1) ChurginE.

2) Karl Nef, *Geschichte der Sinfonie und Suite* (Leipzig: Breitkopf & Härtel, 1921), pp. 318-332 (based on BAS, with some changes and uncorrected errors).

3) The minuet as arranged by Corrette. Paul Brunold, ed., *Les Maîtres français du clavecin des XVIIme et XVIIIme siècles* (Paris: Senart, n.d.).

NO. 34

2 vn, va, b

Date	before c. 1742.
MS sources	PC F. Bl. Op. I/22, Overtura, St. Martini (2 vn, b); LUND Kraus 77, Sinphonia [Prima], Kellerij [Fortunato Chelleri] (2 ob, 2 hn); UPP Instr. mus. i hs. 55:3c, Sinphonia, Martino (va pt. only).
Remarks	For explanation of the date, see No. 7. The LUND MS can be dated 1753, since it is the last entry for that year in the Kraus Inventarium of the collection. While the viola part in PC merely doubles the bass an octave higher (see No. 23), the part in LUND and UPP is a harmonic filler. This part may not be authentic (as suggested by some awkward passages), but it is indispensable for the outer movements. The second violin and bass parts in LUND also differ in some details from PC, while the oboe and horn parts are not authentic but added parts, typical of LUND and also found in the LUND versions of Nos. 4 and 37. The LUND title page bears the inscription "Academia Carolina" (see No. 4).
Mod. ed.	ChurginE.

NO. 35

2 vn, va, b

Date	before 1742.
MS sources	PC F. Bl. Op. I/45, Overtura, Martini; DONAU Mus. Ms. 2076, Symphonia, Zani (mvts. I and III only); PC D.11.183 and D.11.184, Sonata, Martini (3 vn, b).
Print	Paris, Le Clerc, 1742 (for the title and sources see No. 33); Op. II/5 (3 vn, b).
Remarks	The viola part in DONAU differs considerably from the part as found elsewhere, and may have been recomposed by a local musician. The name "Ser: Maria Hildegardis Fuchsin" appears on the title pages of this symphony and No. 65, together with the reference "chor Ambtenhausen 1769" on No. 65. Since the DONAU copies of both symphonies are in the same hand, it is likely that both copies date from the 1760's.
	The two PC copies probably constitute one set of performance parts, and each part is inscribed "a Mr. le Mis. de la Salle" (see No. 33). All the hands or the main hands of these copies recur in the PC copies (not in the Fonds Blancheton) of Nos. 33 and 38.
Mod. ed.	ChurginE.

NO. 36

2 vn, va, b

Date	before c. 1742.
MS source	PC F. Bl. Op. II/69, Overtura, St. Martino.
Remarks	For explanation of the date, see No. 7.
Mod. ed.	ChurginE.

NO. 37

2 vn, va?, b

Date	before 1742.
Cat. ref.	Br. 62, Racc. I/3, Sonata, Martino (2 vn, b).
MS sources	PC F. Bl. Op. I/46, Overtura, Martini; AGEN II. 111, Sonata [No. VI], St. Martino (2 vn, b; vn II missing); DARM 169/c, Sinfonia, Sammartini (destroyed in World War II); LUND Eng. 137, Sinfonia, Martino (3 copies): (1) with 2 hn; (2) for str; (3) an 18th-century score, with hn); PRA Waldst. XXXIV C 16, Overtura, Anon.; SCHW Mus. 3569, Overteure, St. Martino; STOCK, 5 copies: copies 1-3 0d-R, Sinfonia or Sinphonia, Martini (copy 3, no ascription), and copies 4-5, Sinfonia, Martini (copy 5, 18th-century score); UPP Instr. mus. i hs. 55:3a, Sinfonia, Martini.
Prints	1) Paris, Le Clerc, 1742 (for the title and sources, see No. 33); Op. II/8 (3 vn, b).
	2) I. Walsh, 14-16 Nov. 1745 (Gen. Ev.-Post): Six / SONATAS / FOR TWO / VIOLINS / with a Thorough-Bass for the / Harpsicord or Violoncello. / Compos'd By / Sig^r. GIO. BATISTA LAMPUGNANI / AND / S^t. MARTINI of Milan. / Opera Seconda / London. Printed for and Sold by I. Walsh, in Catharine Street in y^e. Strand; Sonata III, Martino. Defective copies, without opus number, in CARD and CU. Copies with opus number, dated c. 1748, in LBM g. 480. (2.), LBMQ, LOAM, LORC, OOC Vc 30-32, and ROCH.
	Another edition c. 1750: A Second Set of Six / SONATAS . . . (wording as in the original print). Copies in BRUS V 13, 445, LOAM, LORC, NYPL (vn I only), PC K.4133, WLC, and several other sources.
Remarks	Three sonatas in the Walsh print—Nos. I, III, and V—are ascribed to Sammartini, all of them actually symphonies

(for sonata V, see No. 66b). Sonata I, however, was probably composed by Antonio Brioschi (see App. D 15). Smith and HumphriesB does not distinguish between the 1745 and c. 1748 issues of this print.

Copies 1 and 2 of this symphony in LUND probably constitute one set of performance parts; the score (copy 3) is based on copy 1. The horn parts are not authentic but added parts, typical of other LUND copies of Sammartini symphonies (see Nos. 4 and 34). All the Swedish copies are nearly identical, indicating that they must stem from the same source. Copies 1 and 2 in STOCK belonged to the literary society Utile Dulci, and copies 4 and 5 to the large collection formed by the Swedish businessman Johan Mazer (1790-1847). Copy 4 is in the hand of Per Brant (1713-1767). The cembalo part of copy 2 contains revisions of the original bass line of the first and second movements. Many notes are placed an octave lower, several leaps eliminated, and some rhythmic patterns simplified. The name J. G. Sander, inscribed on the UPP title page, probably refers to Johan Gotthard Zander, a member of the Royal Chapel in Stockholm, 1740-1748. This copy must have been made or obtained before 1748, the year of Zander's death. The DARM MS was copied by Christoph Graupner (1683-1760), the *Kapellmeister* at Darmstadt, 1712-1760; its title comes from the library catalogue.

Although the symphony exists *a 4* in most sources, the viola has all the earmarks of an added part, which may have been composed by Sammartini. The symphony thus probably originated as a trio symphony, but gained greatest popularity in its four-part setting.

Mod. ed.   ChurginE.

NO. 38
2 vn, b

Date	1732 or before.
Autograph	Mvts. II, III in score (undated and unsigned), PBN Vm7. 7708, ff. 1r-3r (see No. 23).
MS sources	HEIL IVb, *Memet*, St. Martino, Act III, Introdutione (I only; score; 2 vn, va, b); PC F. Bl. Op. I/17, Sinfonia, Martini (see No. 23 regarding va pt.); PC D.11.180, Sonata, Martino.
Print	Paris, Le Clerc, 1742 (for the title and sources, see No. 33); Op. II/1.
Remarks	The score of *Memet* is probably of north Italian origin and is dated 1732 (see No. 88). The first movement of this symphony, which was incorporated in the opera, appears on ff. 139-142 and contains an added viola part probably composed by Sammartini. The date of the opera provides a terminal date for this symphony and No. 66a, the earliest known dated symphonies by Sammartini (see also No. 66a).
	The second PC copy is inscribed "Overtura" on the inside pages of each part. Since the handwriting matches the main hand of PC copies of Nos. 33 and 35 made for the Marquis de Lasalle, it is likely that this copy, too, was intended for the marquis (see No. 33).
Mod. ed.	ChurginE.

G MAJOR

NO. 39

2 vn, va, b

Date	before c. 1744.
MS source	PC F. Bl. Op. III/150, Sinfonia, St. Martini.
Remarks	For explanation of the date, see No. 7. The minuet comes from Sammartini's trio sonata in E-flat major, PC F. Bl. Op. III/121, also published by John Simpson as the second of six trio sonatas Op. I, announced 3 July 1744 in the Gen. Adv. (copies in LBM, WLC, and elsewhere). A variation of the minuet follows the minuet proper, a procedure found in many chamber minuets but absent from Sammartini's symphonic minuets. It is likely that Blancheton's musicians borrowed the minuet to provide some lyrical interest otherwise lacking from the symphony because of the transitional slow movement. They transposed the movement, and added a viola part that doubles the bass an octave higher. The symphony is thus a three-movement cycle with an appended minuet, and not an early example of a four-movement symphony. The minuet also appears as an aria in D major, with the text "Who upon the Oozy beach," in Act III of the English comic opera *The Maid of the Mill*, 1765 (copies of the Bremner edition are in BRUS, LBM, WLC, and elsewhere); and as an Andante in G major, for two flutes, in a print of J. and J. Simpson entitled *Duetts for two German Flutes Collected from the Favourite Operas Entertainments &c.*, London, c. 1775 (LBM).
Mod. eds.	1) ChurginE.
	2) Newell Jenkins (London: Eulenburg No. 540, 1956).
	3) La LaurencieI, II, with several uncorrected errors.

NO. 40

2 ob, 2 hn, 2 vn, va, vc, cb

MS source	PC D.13.665, Sinfonia Per Camera, St. Martino (mod. score; see No. 11).

NO. 41

2 tr, 2 ob added in II, 2 vn, va, b

Date	before 1762.
Cat. ref.	Br. 62, Racc. III/1, Sinfonia, Martino; Karl. cat. A, Sinfonia, St. Martino; Karl. cat. E, Sonata, St. Martino.
MS sources	ZÜR AMG XIII 7042 a-i, Overtur, S. Martino (ob II pt. missing); EINS 12/12, Overteure, San Martino (2 ob or 2 fl in II); KARL Mus. Hs. 809, Sinfonia, S. Martto (2 ob and 2 fl in II); REG, Sinfonia, Pichl (2 vn, b).
Remarks	The ZÜR copy is probably Milanese. In KARL/II flutes double the oboes at the unison. Though 2 horns are specified in the KARL title, 2 trumpets are used instead. In AGEN II.142, only the title page of this symphony survives, in a version for strings alone attributed to "St. Martiny."
Mod. eds.	1) Second movement of the KARL version in Lothar Hoffmann-Erbrecht, *Die Sinfonie.* ("Das Musikwerk," vol. 29. Cologne: Arno Volk Verlag, 1967). 2) Norbert Zimpel (Zürich: Eulenburg No. 10057, 1973). Not a critical edition; unreliable.

NO. 42

2 vn, va, b

Date	before 12 January 1765.

Cat. ref.	Karl. cat. A, Concerti e quatri concertanti, St. Martino.
MS source	PRA Waldst. XXXIV C 328, Overteur, St. Martino.
Remarks	The finale appears in KARL Mus. Hs. 806 as the first movement of a "Partia" for flute, violin, viola, and bass which is listed in Karl. cat. A compiled by J. M. Molter (d. 12 January 1765).

NO. 43

2 vn, va, b

Date	before 1772.
Cat. ref.	Br. 72, Sinfonia, Zimmermann (2 ob, 2 hn).
MS sources	PRA Waldst. XXXIV C 383, Sinfonia, S. Martino; MILT MS 98, Sonata notturna No. 6, Sammartino (2 vn, b; b missing), I and III only.
Remarks	The trio sonata in MILT is one of six *sonate notturne* originally in possession of Sammartini's pupil Count Giorgio Giulini (see App. D 2). In the first movement incipit, the trill figures in small notes appear in MILT.
Literature	CesariS.

NO. 44

2 tr, 2 vn, va, b

Date	before June 1747.

Cat. ref.	Br. 66, Sinfonia, Gluck (2 ob, 2 hn); Karl. cat. E, Overteur, Martino.
MS sources	KARL Mus. Hs. 846, Sonata, St. Martino; DRES (1) Musica 2763, N. 1, Sonata, Martini (2 fl, 2 ob, 2 hn, bn, cemb); and (2) Sinfonia, St. Martino (18th-century score); MELK V/1423, Sinfonia, St. Martino (2 hn); PRA Waldst. XXXIV C 303, Sonata, St. Martino; STOCK O-R, Sinfonia, San Martino; ZÜR (see No. 13), Overtura (No. 2), St. Martino.
Remarks	The KARL and PRA MSS are copied in Hand C, and the PRA title page bears the initials E. W. (referring to Emanuel Waldstein, 1731-1775). In ZÜR the MS is copied in Hand B, the incipit on the title page written in Hand C.

Gluck used the first movement in the overture to his serenata *Le Nozze d'Ercole e d'Ebe*, performed in Pillnitz, near Dresden, on 29 June 1747 (for another Gluck borrowing see No. 57). The music was written for the festivities connected with the double wedding of the Elector Max Joseph of Bavaria with Princess Maria Anna of Saxony, and the Electoral Prince Friedrich Christian of Saxony with Princess Maria Antonia Walpurga of Bavaria. Since Gluck probably left Milan at the end of the summer of 1745, it is possible that both Sammartini symphonies he borrowed had been composed by that time and he was able to take copies with him.

In his three-movement overture, Gluck retains Sammartini's larger formal plan. He follows Sammartini's movement with a corresponding slow movement in the tonic minor and duple meter (cut time), and ends with a minuet finale. However, in the borrowed movement, he shortens the primary theme by two measures, destroying its balance, and omits the final two-measure link to the slow movement, ending instead on a firm half cadence. He also omits the coda-like return of the Allegro after the slow movement. Thus, in Gluck's version, the slow movement is not enclosed within the first movement as in the Sammartini symphony, a procedure that became popular in the opera overture in the second half of the eighteenth century.

Gluck uses Sammartini's horn parts but his oboe parts differ from the Sammartini parts in DRES (which are probably not authentic; see the remarks below). The viola part in Gluck's movement is a harmonic filler, and it occurs in all the Sammartini MSS except those in Hand C, in which the viola doubles the bass at the octave above most of the time. It is likely that this simpler part is the authentic one. The filler part continues in the second and third movements of Sammartini's symphony, the third movement identical with the part in Hand C.

In DRES the flutes double the first violins, but the oboes are more independent. Both the oboes and the bassoon, which doubles the bass line, are omitted in the slow movement. These wind parts were probably added by musicians in DRES, where similar wind parts were added to No. 65 and the second (fast) movement of Sammartini's trio sonata in A, F. Bl. Op. I/1 (published by Le Clerc in 1742 as Op. II/7, and by Simpson in 1744 as Op. I/1). The STOCK MS belonged to the literary society Utile Dulci, and it replaces the original minuet with the longer minuet and trio of No. 41.

Mod. eds.	1) Gluck's overture is reprinted in *DTB*, II Folge, Jg. 14, Bd. 2. The introduction by H. Abert includes a reprint of the Sammartini DRES flute, oboe, and horn parts.
	2) Norbert Zimpel (Zürich: Eulenburg No. 10058, 1973). Based on DRES; unreliable.
Literature	Saint-FoixD, pp. 43-44; WotquenneT, No. 12.

NO. 45

Date	before c. 1757-c. 1759.
MS sources	STOCK O-R, Sinfonia, Giulini (18th-century score and parts; 2 hn); PRA Waldst. XXXIV C 381, Sinfonia, St. Martino.
Print	Attributed to Stalder, c. 1757-c. 1759: SEI / SINFONIE / A due Violini Alto Viola e Basso / DEDICATE / All' Jllma. Sra. Contessa di Belzunce / Dama D'Onore della Real / Principessa Di Francia / Madame Adelaide / COMPOSTE / DA GIUSEPPE STALDÊRO / Prix 7£. 4s. /

A PARIS / aux adresses ordinaires / Avec privilege du Roi. / Gravée par Melle. Vendôme; Sinfonia III (source of incipits). BRUS 7895 (va pt. missing); ENG (vn I pt. missing).

Remarks   Joseph Stalder (1725-1765) was born and died in Lucerne, and was also active as a composer in Italy, England, and France. He may have obtained this symphony during his visit to Milan in c. 1746, where he continued his theological and musical studies. Since other Parisian prints of Stalder's music appeared 1757-1759, with dedications to various members of the French nobility, it is likely that this print was also published in the same period. The minuet in the print contains an inserted trio-like episode between the end of the development and the beginning of the recapitulation that was undoubtedly composed by Stalder.

The STOCK score is copied on Italian paper in an Italian hand, and is bound together with a symphony by Giulini (see App. D 2). Both score and parts belonged to the literary society Utile Dulci, the parts copied from the score in Sweden. The rudimentary horn parts found in STOCK could not have been composed by Sammartini. Stalder's version and the STOCK MS correspond in most essential details, but the print contains more performance indications than the casually marked STOCK copy.

NO. 46

2 vn, va, b

MS source   PRA Waldst. XXXIV C 382, Sinfonia, St. Martino.

NO. 47

2 hn, 2 vn, va, b

Date	before 1761.
Cat. ref.	Karl. cat. A, Sinfonia, St. Martino.
MS sources	KARL Mus. Hs. 803, Overteur, St. Martino (2 hn or tr, va pts. missing); PRA Waldst. XXXIV C 392, Sinfonia, S. Martino; REG 2, Sinfonia, St. Martino; STOCK Alstr., Sinfonia In Milano, S. Martini (2 tr).
Print	London, Hummel, 1761 (for the title and sources, see No. 29); Overture III.
Remarks	The KARL MS is copied in Hand C. Most of the STOCK parts are written on the same paper and in the same hand as most of the STOCK parts of No. 62a, and are probably north Italian. The minuet is also found as the finale of *A Favourite Lesson for the Harpsichord or Piano Forte Composed by the Celebrated St. Martini of Milan*, published in London by John Preston c. 1775; LBM g.443.y.(27.).
Mod. ed.	Fausto Torrefranca (Milan: Carisch, 1931), heavily edited, with added flutes and oboes in I and III.

NO. 48
2 hn, 2 vn, va, b

Date	before 1762.
Cat. ref.	Br. 62, Racc. II/3, Sinfonia, Martino; Karl. cat. A, Sinfonia, St. Martino.
MS sources	PRA Waldst. XXXIV C 413, Sonata, St. Martino; KARL Mus. Hs. 816, Sonata, St. Martino; STOCK O-R, Overteur, St. Martino.
Remarks	The PRA and KARL MSS are copied in Hand C, and the PRA title page bears the initials E. W. (referring to Emanuel Waldstein, 1731-1775). The STOCK MS belonged to the literary society Utile Dulci.
Mod. ed.	Norbert Zimpel (Zürich: Eulenburg No. 10059, 1973). Not a critical edition; unreliable.

NO. 49

2 hn, 2 vn, va, b

MS sources	VGM XIII 8567/99, Sinfonia, S. Martino; PC D.13.660, Sinfonia, San Martino (mod. score; see No. 17).

NO. 50

2 hn, 2 vn, va, b

MS source	PRA Waldst. XXXIV C 386, Sinfonia, St. Martino.

NO. 51

2 hn, 2 vn, va, b

Date	before 1753.
Cat. ref.	Hund 1753 (No. 12), Sinfonia, St. Martino (*a 6;* pts. unspecified); Karl. cat. E, Overteur, Martino.
MS sources	AGEN II. 112, Sonata, St. Martino (2 vn, b); KARL Mus. Hs. 248, Sinfonia, Lampugnani; STOCK Alstr., Sinfonia, Martini (hn pts. missing).
Print	I. Walsh, 7 October 1757 (Pub. Adv.): CONCERTI GROSSI / Con due Violini Viola e Violoncello / obligati con due altri Violini e Basso / di Ripieno. / Opera Sesta / DI / GIO: BATTA St. MARTINI. / Questi Concerti sono composti da diversi / Notturni del St. Martini / DA / FRANCESCO BARSANTI. / London. Printed for I. Walsh in Catharine Street in the Strand; Concerto I. BERK (org/b pt. missing), BPL, LBM, LORC, PBN, ROCH, STOCK VO-R, WLC 2 copies: M 1040.A2S2 Case; M 1040.S21 Case.
Remarks	In AGEN the parts are copied in Hand C. The title page of the STOCK MS is dated 1764, and it bears the name of Johan Wellander (1735-1783), "a very well-known poet in the society of Stockholm in the 1760's and 70's, and for some time the 'director' of the 'Musical Areopagus' of the Utile Dulci" (Bengtsson and DanielsonH, p. 55). Also on the title page, written in another hand, is the comment "god paisabel" (good, passable). The Walsh print in STOCK belonged to the Utile Dulci.
	In Barsanti's arrangement, the viola part is new, and the other string parts (excluding Vn I obbligato) are occasionally altered, mostly in the accompaniment of the solo sections. For information about Barsanti and the sources of the remaining concertos, see App. A 1.

NO. 52

2 ob?, 2 hn, 2 vn, va, b

Date	before 1762.
Cat. ref.	Br. 62, Racc. III/2, Sinfonia, Martino.
MS sources	PRA Waldst. XXXIV C 404, Sonata, St. Martino; KARL Mus. Hs. 807, Sinfonia, S. Martino (2 tr da c); MAD Obertura, San Martino (2 hn; va pt. only); VGM XIII 8568/99, Sinfonia, S. Martino; PC D.13.658, Sinfonia, San Martino (mod. score; see No. 17).
Remarks	The PRA title page bears the initials E. W. (referring to Emanuel Waldstein, 1731-1775), and the MS is copied in Hand C. The oboes in PRA and VGM double the violins except for a solo passage in mm. 44-52 of the first movement.

NO. 53

2 tr, 2 vn, va, b

Date	before 12 January 1765.
Cat. ref.	Karl. cat. A, Sinfonia, St. Martino; cat. E, Overteur, without ascription but in a group of symphonies ascribed to "Martino."

MS sources	PRA Waldst. XXXIV C 414, Sonata, St. Martino; AGEN II.86, Ouverteur, San Martino (b only); KARL Mus. Hs. 805, Overteur, St. Martino; MELK V/1424, Sinfonia, St. Martino (2 hn).
Remarks	The Karl. catalogue provides an ultimate date for this work, since it was compiled by J. M. Molter who died 12 January 1765. The PRA title page bears the initials E. W. (referring to Emanuel Waldstein, 1731-1775), and the MS is copied in Hand C. The suggested trill in the incipit of the Minuetto appears in KARL, which is copied in Hand B.

NO. 54

2 hn, 2 vn, va, b

MS source	ZÜR (see No. 13), Overtura (No. 4), St. Martino.
Remarks	The MS is Milanese (see also No. 13 and No. 62b).

NO. 55

2 hn, 2 vn, va, b

Date	before 1762.
Cat. ref.	Br. 62, Racc. I/2, Sinfonia, Martino (str only).
MS sources	PRA Waldst. XXXIV C 315, Overteur, St. Martino; VGM XIII 53379, Sinfonia, Martini (str only).

G MINOR

NO. 56

2 vn, va, b

Date	before 16 March 1759.
Cat. ref.	Karl. cat. E, two entries: Overteur, Martino; Overteur, St. Martino.
MS sources	EINS 109/1, Sinfonia, cantata No. II (see No. 122; I only; 2 ob, 2 hn; pts. and mod. score); ZÜR (see No. 13). Overteur (No. 6), St. Martino.
Remarks	The EINS copy is Milanese, but contains duplicate first and second violin parts in a hand that is probably not Milanese. The ZÜR copy is written in Hand B. Its title comes from the bass part; all other parts are marked *Overtura*. The tempo mark of the first movement is taken from ZÜR, since it is missing in EINS. Only the viola and bass parts contain the dynamic indication of the second movement. In EINS the development section differs in several details from ZÜR, the overture version clearly being a revision of the symphonic original. For explanation of the date, see Nos. 8 and 122.

NO. 57

2 hn, 2 vn, va, b

Date	before 1749.
Cat. ref.	Karl. cat. A, Sinfonia, St. Martino; Karl. cat. E, Overteur, Martino.
MS sources	KARL Mus. Hs. 802, Overteur, St. Martino (str only); PRA Waldst. XXXIV C 411, Sonata, St. Martino, and another copy, XXXIV C 319, Overteur, St. Martino; REG 6, Overteur, St. Martino; STOCK O-R, Ouverteur, St. Martino; ZÜR (see No. 13), Sonata (No. 3), St. Martino.
Remarks	Gluck borrowed the finale, omitting the horns and making some minor alterations, as the introduction to the second part of his serenata *La Contesa dei numi.* The work was performed in Copenhagen 9 April 1749 (a copy of the score is in BER), the performance date providing a *terminus ad quem* for the symphony. For additional remarks about the dating, see No. 44, another borrowed work. The second movement also appears in No. 29, published by Hummel in London in 1761.

The sources divide into two groups according to common variants, the first and better version comprising KARL, PRA copy 1, and STOCK, the second version found in the remaining copies. The KARL and first PRA MSS are copied in Hand C, the PRA title page bearing the initials E. W. (referring to Emanuel Waldstein, 1731-1775). Also of Milanese origin is the ZÜR copy, whose *basso* title page is written in Hand C. The STOCK MS belonged to the literary society Utile Dulci. The title on the cover was written by Pehr Frigel (1750-1842), a member of the Royal Swedish Academy of Music from 1778 and its secretary from 1796 to 1841. Duplicate horn parts in STOCK are entitled "Sinfonia," and were copied by Per Brant (1713-1767), who was "hovkapellmästare" of the Royal Court Orchestra, and a very active copyist.

NO. 58—Version A

2 vn, va, b

Date   before 1758.

Cat. ref.   Egk No. 106, 1760, Sinfonia, Martini; Br. 62, Racc. I/3, Sinfonia, Martino; Karl. cat. A, Sinfonia, St. Martino; Karl. cat. E, Overteur, Martino.

MS sources   PRA Waldst. XXXIV C 302, Sonata, St. Martino; KARL Mus. Hs. 804, Overteur, St. Martino; MELK V/1428, Sinfonia, St. Martino; STOCK O-R, Sinfonia, St. Martini (eighteenth-century score).

Print   La Chevardière, 11 September 1758 (An.): SEI / OVERTURE / a Più Stromenti. / Composte / DA / VARI AUTORI. / Dédiées / A Son Altesse / MONSEIGNEUR DIMITRY / PRINCE GALLITZIN. / 1ª. del Sigr. Olxbaurg. / 2ª. del Sigr. Stamitz. / 3ª. del Sigr. Olxbaurg. / 4ª. del Sigr. Martini. / 5ª. del Sigr. Jomelly. / 6ª. del Sigr. Stamitz. / Prix 9£. / Les 2 Simphonies de Stamitz sont avec des Hautbois. / A PARIS / Chez M. de la Chevardière, rue du Roule a la Croix d'Or. / & aux Adresses Ordinaires / A LYON / Chez Mrs. Les freres Legoux place des Cordeliers. / Avec Privilege du Roy; Sinfonia IV. STOCK OB-R; PBN Vma. 1621 (1), va only.

Remarks   The PRA title page bears the initials E. W. (referring to Emanuel Waldstein, 1731-1775), and the MS is copied in Hand C. The KARL MS is copied in Hand B. In STOCK the score is found in a volume containing scores of all the symphonies in the La Chevardière collection listed above. This volume belonged to Johan Fredrik Hallardt (1726-1794), an amateur musician and member of the Royal Academy of Music.

     The symphony ascribed to "S. Martini" that was advertised in the La Chevardière catalogue of 1763 as No. 55 of his "Sinfonies Périodiques" was probably a reprint of the 1758 edition. This is suggested by the fact that when the periodical symphony was listed, the *vari autori* collection containing Sammartini's symphony was dropped from the catalogue. Unfortunately, no copy of this later print has yet been located.

NO. 58—Version B
2 ob, 2 hn, 2 vn, va, b

I, II the same as A

III   Presto

Date	c. 1750 to 12 March 1751 (of III only).
MS sources	EINS 543/16, Introduzione, cantata V (see No. 118; III only; mod. score); STOCK O-R, Sinfonia, San Martini (2 ob, 2 tr).
Remarks	For explanation of the date of Version B, see Nos. 8 and 118. The oboe and horn parts in EINS differ from those in STOCK. The STOCK MS belonged to the literary society Utile Dulci and is copied in the same hand as No. 61. It is probable that the overture was used in place of the original finale because it is a far more powerful movement. A similar substitution was made in the STOCK copy of No. 44.

NO. 59

2 vn, b

I missing

Date	c. 1732 or before.
Autograph	In score (unsigned and undated), PBN Vm^7. 7708, ff. 9r-12r (see No. 23).
Mod. ed.	ChurginE.

A MAJOR

NO. 60

2 ob, 2 hn, 2 vn, 2 va, b

Date	September 1772.
MS sources	PC D.13.663, Sinfonia per Camera Concertata, St. Martino (mod. score; see No. 11); PBN Vma. ms. 373 (same title as PC; mod. score); DARM 198/a, Sinfonia, Sammartini (with 2 va; destroyed in World War II).
Remarks	The date appears on the PBN copy, made for G. de Saint-Foix. No. 2, also with two violas, was probably composed about the same time.
Literature	TorrefrancaO, *RMI,* XX (1913), 301-303; XXI (1914), 278-287.

NO. 61

2 vn, va, b

Date	before c. 1755.
MS sources	PRA Waldst. XXXIV C 384, Sinfonia, St. Martino; STAMS K I 30, Synfonia, Giulino (2 hn); STOCK O-R, Sinfonia, Stalder (2 hn).
Prints	1) Venier, c. 1755: SEI / OUVERTURE / a Piu Stromenti, / COMPOSTE / Da Varri / AUTORI, / 1º. dell Sig^r. ANDREI. / 2º. dell Sig^r. GALINBERTI. / 3º. dell Sig^r. JOMELLI. / 4º. dell Sig^r. MARTINI. / 5º. dell Sig^r. PERETZ. / 6º. dell Sig^r. ROSSETTI. / OPERA QUARTA. / Prix 9£. / Gravé Par Ceron. / Fait Gravé A PARIS, par Venier. / Chez / M^r. Vernadé M^d. rüe du Roule, á la Croix d'Or, M^r. Bayard, M^d. rüe St. Honoré á la régle d'Or. / Melle. Castagnery, rüe des Provaires á la Musique Royale. / AVEC PRIVILEGE DU ROY / On vend les parties de Cors de Chasse Séparement. PC H. 108.
	2) Bremner, c. 1765: Six / SYMPHONIES. / In four Parts. / Proper for small or great CONCERTS / Composed by / J: STAMITZ; / his Pupil the EARL of KELLY, / and Others. / Opera Seconda. / LONDON. / Printed by R: BREMNER, at the Harp and Hautboy, / Opposite Somerset-House / in the STRAND; Quartetto

II, without ascription. LORC; WLC M 100.S6P case;
STOCK OB-R.

Remarks   On the STAMS title page: "ad Chorum Stamsensam."
The STOCK MS and print belonged to the literary society Utile Dulci, and the MS is copied in the same hand
as the STOCK copy of No. 58b.

NO. 62—Version A

2 tr, 2 vn, va, b

Date   before c. 1756-1757.

Cat. ref.   Br. 62, Racc. II/4, Sinfonia, Martino; Lam. 1768, Sinfonia, Martino; Karl. cat. A, Sinfonia, St. Martino; Karl.
cat. E, Overteur, Martino.

MS sources   PRA Waldst. XXXIV C 299, Sonata, St. Martino, and
another copy XXXIV C 387, Sinfonia, S. Martino; BOL
KK 373, Sinfonia, San Martino (2 hn; mod. score);
KARL Mus. Hs. 801, Overteur, St. Martino (str only);
LAM, Sinfonia, S. Martino (str only); PC D.13.657,
Sinfonia, San Martino (2 hn; mod. score; see No. 17);
PARP 61683 T-11-10, Sinfonia, Sammartini (str only;
mod. score based on Venier print); STOCK Alstr., Sin-
fonia In Milano, S. Martino; VGM XIII 8566/99, Sinfonia,
S. Martino (2 hn).

Print   Venier, c. 1756-1757: SEI / OVERTURE / A Più Stro-
menti. / COMPOSTE / Da Vari / AUTORI. / 1ª. Dell Sigr.
MARTINI. / 2ª. Dell Sigr. GALLUPPI / 3ª. Dell Sigr.
WAGENSEIL. / 4ª. Dell Sigr. RAINA. / 5ª. Dell Sigr.
JOMELLI. / 6ª. Dell Sigr. WAGENSEIL. / OPERA, VII. /
Prix 9£. / Gravé Par Ceron. / Fait Graver A PARIS. Par
Venier. / Chez / Mr. Bayard rüe St. Honoré á la régle
D'Or. / Mr. Vernadé rüe du roule á la Croix D'Or. / Melle.
Castagnery rüe des Prouvaires á la Musique royale. /
AVEC PRIVILEGE DU ROY. / On Vend les parties des
Cors de Chasse Séparement. PC H.111, dated c. 1760;
MUN (2 hn pts. only).

Remarks   The first PRA title page bears the initials E.W. (referring to Emanuel Waldstein, 1731-1775), and the MS is copied in Hand C. The KARL MS is copied in Hand B. Most of the STOCK parts are probably north Italian (see also No. 47).

Mod. ed.   Walter Lebermann (Mainz: Edition Schott 6176, "Concertino" series, 1970), for strings only, with several errors in notes, dynamics, and bowings (unreliable).

NO. 62—Version B

2 hn, 2 vn, va, b

I, II same as A

III

MS source   GEN N.1.6.6 (Sc. 17), Overteur, St. Martino.

Remarks   This MS is copied in the same hand as the Milanese copy of No. 54.

NO. 63

2 ob, 2 hn, 2 vn, va, vc, b

MS source   PC D.13.667, Sinfonia per Camera, St. Martino (mod. score; see No. 11).

NO. 64

2 vn, b

Date	before c. 1744.
Cat. ref.	Br. 62, Racc. V/4, Sonata, Martino.
MS sources	PC F. Bl. Op. III/113, Overtura, St. Martino (see No. 23 regarding va pt.); STOCK Alstr., Sonata, Martini (mvts. I and III only); UPP Instr. mus. i hs. 55:5, Sonata, Martini (mvts. I and III only).
Print	Paris, Estien, 2 March 1747 (An.): SINFONIE / A DUE VIOLINI / E BASSO / Dei piu Celebri Autori / d'Italia / Receüillis par M^r. / ESTIEN / PREMIER RECEÜIL. / Prix 6$^£$. / Chez M^r. Estien, rüe Montmar^{tre}. / au coin de la rüe Neuve S^t. Eustache / chez M^r. Touvenot Notaire. / Aux adresses Ordinaires. / Et chez Melle. Castagniery, a l'Hotel de Soissons; Sinfonia V [Anon.]. NYPL Drexel 5831, PBN Vm^7. 1199, PC (vn II only).
Remarks	The STOCK and UPP MSS are nearly identical, the STOCK copy being more accurate. In this version, many added trills and appoggiaturas, especially in the first violin part, produce a more chamber-like effect. The UPP copy is No. 4 in a collection of forty trio sonatas ascribed to Sammartini. The title page of the first violin part is dated 1772, and it shows traces of a name that may have been Dahlbeck, perhaps the original owner or copyist of the music. For explanation of the date, see No. 7.
Mod. ed.	ChurginE.

NO. 65

2 vn, va, b

Date	before January 1738.
MS sources	PC F. Bl. 88, Sonata, St. Martino; AMS Kamer I 22, Sonata, Anon.; DONAU Mus. Ms. 1804, Synphonia, Anon. (mvts. I and III only; 2 vn, b); DRES Musica 2763 N/3, Sinfonia, Martini (2 fl, 2 ob, bn); MILC, Ouvertur, St. Martino.

Remarks   This symphony was conducted by Vivaldi in Amsterdam
               on 7 January 1738 for the centennial of the Theater of
               Amsterdam. In AMS a MS copy of the symphony is
               found as Sonata IX in the collection entitled "DE
               SCHOUWBURG / van / AMSTELDAM / en zyn / OUDE
               EN NIEUWE TOONEELEN / BESCHREEVEN; / met
               Desselfs / EEUWGETYDE / Geviert den 7. van Louw-
               maand des Jaars 1738." In DRES, the added wind parts
               are of the *colla parte* type. Oboes are omitted in II and,
               with the bassoon, in the trio-like sections of I and III.
               The DONAU title page is inscribed "In usum: M: Hilde-
               gardis Fuchsin, chor Ambtenhausen 1769," and is copied
               in the same hand as the DONAU version of No. 35,
               whose title page also bears the name of Fuchsin. The
               many similarities between this symphony and the over-
               ture to *Memet* (see No. 88) suggest an earlier date for the
               symphony, closer to 1730 than 1737.

Mod. ed.   ChurginE.

Literature   PincherleA, I, 24-25, II, Addenda P. 447; PincherleV,
               p. 67.

B-FLAT MAJOR

NO. 66—Version A
2 vn, b

Date   1732 or before.

Autograph   Mvts. II, III in score (undated and unsigned), PBN Vm^7.
               7708, ff. 13r-16v (see No. 23).

MS sources   HEIL IVb, *Memet*, St. Martino, Act II, Introduzione
               (I only; score; 2 vn, va, b); PC F. Bl. Op. I/7, Trio, G. B.
               Somis (see No. 23 regarding va pt.); PC L.2609 (1-3),
               Sonata [V], San Martino.

Remarks   The score of *Memet* is probably of north Italian origin and is dated 1732 (see No. 88). The date of the opera provides a terminal date for this symphony and No. 38, the earliest known dated symphonies by Sammartini (see also No. 38).

                  No. 66a/I (ff. 58-61) differs in numerous small details from No. 66b/I, which is probably a later revision. The viola part in *Memet* is a harmonic filler probably composed by Sammartini. A short cadenza for the first violin appears in the F. Bl. copy of No. 66a/II.

Mod. ed.   ChurginE.

NO. 66—Version B

2 vn, b

Date   before 1745.

MS source   SCHW Mus. 3563, Sonata, St. Martino (2 vn, va, b).

Print   London, I. Walsh, 14-16 Nov. 1745 (for the title and sources, see No. 37); Op. II/5.

Remarks   The second and third movements of Version B are later in style than the corresponding movements of Version A. The viola in SCHW merely doubles the bass at the octave above.

Mod. ed.   ChurginE.

NO. 67

2 vn, va, b

Date	before c. 1744.
MS source	PC F. Bl. Op. III/145, Sinfonia, St. Martini.
Remarks	For explanation of the date, see No. 7.
Mod. ed.	ChurginE.

NO. 68

2 vn, va, b

Date	before c. 1744.
MS sources	PRA Waldst. XXXIV C 341, Sonatta, Gio. Batta. S. Martino (2 vn, b); PC F. Bl. Op. III/149, Sinfonia, Antonio St. Martino.
Remarks	Two other symphonies in the F. Bl., Op. III/146 and 148, ascribed to "Antonio" St. Martino or St. Martini, were probably composed by Antonio Brioschi (see App. D 15). This symphony, however, is clearly in Sammartini's style. Though the texture of the symphony requires a viola, the part as found in PC is so awkward that it must be considered spurious. For explanation of the date, see No. 7. See also Introduction, note 124.
Mod. ed.	ChurginE.

CONCERTOS

C MAJOR

NO. 69

Solo vc picc (or vn), 2 vn, va, b

Date	before 1762.
Cat. ref.	Br. 62 II, Racc. I/2, Concerto, Martino.
MS source	BER Mus. ms. 19396/30, Concerto a Cello Piccolo Concertato o Violino Concertato, Martino.
Mod. ed.	Newell Jenkins (London: Eulenburg 1211, 1956).

D MAJOR

NO. 70

Solo vn, 2 ob, 2 hn, 2 vn, va, vc, b

Date	before November 1766.
Print	Bremner Op. IV/3. For full title, see No. 21.

NO. 71—Version A

Solo fl, 2 vn, va, b

Date	before 1765.
Cat. ref.	Karl. cat. A, Concerto, St. Martino; Karl. cat. B, Concerto, Martino.
MS source	KARL Mus. Hs. 780, Concerto, St. Martino.
Remarks	For explanation of the date, see p. 83. The MS is copied in Hand C.

NO. 71—Version B

I, II the same as A.

III

MS source	SCHW 3558, Concerto, Martini.
Remarks	The second movement of the SCHW version contains eleven bars (from bar 45 on) which differ from the KARL version, and is four bars shorter. The SCHW last movement is in Sammartini's style but is not as good as the KARL finale. The different spelling of Sammartini's name on both MSS does not indicate a conflict in attribution, as Meylan surmises.
Literature	MeylanD, pp. 54, 60.

NO. 72

Solo fl, 3 [4] vn, [va], b

MS source KARL Mus. Hs. 790, Concerto, S. Martino.

Remarks The only extant violin parts are *violino primo obbligato*, *violino primo ripieno*, and *violino secondo obbligato*. As the two first violin parts almost always duplicate each other except in certain passages for the solo flute, it is to be assumed that a missing *violino secondo ripieno* would fulfill a similar function to the other second violin part. Possibly a viola part is also missing.

E-FLAT MAJOR

NO. 73
2 solo vn, 2 solo ob, 2 tr, 2 vn, va, b

Date before 1756.

Cat. ref. Br. 62 II, Racc. II/3, Martino.

MS sources PC D.11.187, Concerto à più Stromenti, St. Martino (2 ob, 2 tr, 2 hn; 2 vn pr. pts. missing); BER Mus. ms. 19396/15, Sonata, St. Martino.

Prints 1) Cox, 18 March 1756 (Pub. Adv.): Four / Overtures & one Quattro Compos'd by / Sig^r. Felice Degiardino / and one Concerto with two Violins & two Hautboys Obligato / Compos'd by Sig^r. Gio Batta S^t. Martini Dedicated to the / HON^{BLE}. HARRIOTT LANE by her most Oblig'd and / Very Hum^{ble}. Servant / Felice Degiardino / Printed for Jno. Cox at Simpson's Musick Shop, in Sweetings Alley, Royal Exchange. LBM g. 246; STOCK O-R; UPP Utl. instr. i tr. 57.

2) Bremner, c. 1765: Five / OVERTURES / Composed by / Sig^r: Felice Giardini, / and a / GRAND CONCERTO / by / Sig^r: Gio: Battista S^t: Martini, / of MILAN. / LONDON. / Printed for R: Bremner, opposite Somerset-House, in the STRAND. LOAM; LUND Wens. Litt. B 7; OXBOD (inc.) MUS. 221 c. 284 (3); STOCK O-R. Another issue c. 1770, MAN B. R. 580 Gk 21.

Remarks   All but the oboe and horn parts in PC are copied in Hand A. The two horn parts, which duplicate the trumpet parts, appear on a single staff and are in a different hand, probably a later addition. An inscription in another hand appears on the upper left-hand corner of the title page reading "a mr de la popliniere [sic]." This indicates that the concerto was performed by the famed private orchestra of the Parisian music patron Alexandre Jean Joseph Le Riche de La Pouplinière (1693-1762). The first movement employs two solo violins and one solo oboe, whereas the second movement uses two solo violins and two solo oboes. The engraving on the title page of the Cox print is by J. Cobb. This print contains a copy of the Royal Privilege granted to Giardini 27 September 1751. For biographical facts about Giardini see No. 21. This concerto may have been performed in Vienna. We are grateful to Gerhard Croll for information concerning performances on 19 and 28 February 1758 of a "Concert à plusieurs instruments" in the Burgtheater during a series of 15 Lenten concerts. This information is to be published in the series *Museion.* The source is the *Répertoire des toutes les Spéctacles à Vienne* by Philipp Gumpenhuber (1758-1763) from the collection of Count Durazzo in VNB and in the Harvard Theater Collection, Cambridge, Mass.

Literature   CucuelP, p. 374.

F MAJOR

NO. 74

Solo vn, 2 vn, va, b

Date   before c. 1750.

Cat. ref.   Br. 62 II, Racc. II/1, Martino; Brtnice, c. 1752-1769, Concerto, Martini.

MS sources   BER Mus. ms. 19396/20, Concerto, St. Martino; SCHW, C c12, Concerto, Anon.

Remarks   In SCHW, this concerto is ascribed to Antonio Vivaldi in a MS catalogue acquired c. 1750 (Mus. 3065/10).

G MAJOR

NO. 75
Solo vn, 2 vn, va, b

Date   before c. 1744.

Cat. ref.   Br. 62 II, Racc. I/1, Martino.

MS sources   BER Mus. ms. 19396/21, Concerto, Martino (duplicate copy Mus. ms. 19396/22, Concerto, Martino); PC F. Bl. 44, Concerto, St. Martino.

Remarks   The violin parts in the F. Bl. are entitled *Violino Principale*, *Violino Secondo*, *Violino Terzo*, and *Violino Quarto*. The third violin part corresponds to the first violin part of BER, while the second and fourth violin parts are duplicates and correspond to the second violin part of BER. The solo violin part in the F. Bl. contains a cadenza entitled "Capricio" [sic], to be performed before the final ritornello of the last movement. For explanation of the date, see No. 7.

A MAJOR

NO. 76

4 solo vn, 2 vn, va, b

MS source   PRA XXII E 42, Concerto a piu Istromi Obligati, Sancto Martino.

Remarks   The MS comes from the Pachta archives. Violin III is incomplete. There are 2 copies of the bass part.

NO. 77

Solo vn, 2 vn, va, vc, [b], org

Date   before c. 1744.

MS sources   PC F. Bl. 48, Concerto, St. Martino; STOCK VO-R, Concerto, S. Martino.

Remarks   The STOCK MS belonged originally to the collection of the literary society Utile Dulci and was incorporated into the Library of the Royal Music Academy by Pehr Frigel (see No. 57). For the other concertos in this collection, see App. D 76 and 80. For explanation of the date, see No. 7.

NO. 77.1

Solo vn, 2 vn, b

MS source   ANC Ms. M. 38, Concerto, S. Martini.

Remarks   There are double parts for vn I, II and b. The second movement is marked affetuoso (sic) in the solo vn part, adagio affetuoso (sic) in the vn I parts, and adagio in all others. All three movements are in *da capo* form, which may indicate that this concerto is an early work. Although the tutti sections are somewhat commonplace and the second movement stands in the dominant (highly untypical for Sammartini) we have decided to place this work in the authentic section because of the treatment of the solo passages.

B-FLAT MAJOR

NO. 78

Solo vn, 2 hn, 2 vn, va, vc, b

Date   before November 1766.

Print   Bremner, Op. IV/2. For the full title, see No. 21.

CONCERTINOS

C MAJOR

NO. 79

[2 ob], 2 hn, 2 vn, b

MS sources   EINS 84/11, 34 and 35, Concertino, S. Martino; KARL Mus. Hs. 792, Concertino, San Martino (2 ob, 2 hn, bn; eighteenth-century score); PRA Waldst. XXXIV C 332, Concertino, St. Martino.

Remarks   In EINS oboes are specified on the first page of the violin parts (see No. 86).

NO. 80

2 fl, 2 hn, 2 vn, b

Date   before 1765.

Cat. ref.   Karl. cat. A, Concerto, St. Martino; Br. 66 (listed under "Sinfon. Cassat. etc. a Flauto Traverso"), "dell Academia" (sic) [No. 2], Martino; Karl. cat. E, Marche e Minuetto, S. Martino.

MS sources   KARL Mus. Hs. 794, Concertino, San Martino; another copy of the first movement alone, KARL Mus. Hs. 783, St. Martino (eighteenth-century score for 2 fl, 2 ob, 2 hn, 2 tr, b); another copy of the second movement alone, KARL Mus. Hs. 782, St. Martino (eighteenth-century score for 2 fl, 2 ob, 2 hn, 2 tr, b).

Remarks   For explanation of the date, see p. 83. In Karl. cat. A
the two movements are listed separately in inverse order.
This may account for the numberings of the two single
movements. It seems that Sammartini liked the juxta-
position of march and minuet. See Nos. 84 and 86.

F MAJOR

NO. 81
2 vn, va (or vn III), b

Date   before c. 1744.

MS source   PC F. Bl. 107, Concertino, St. Martino.

Remarks   The viola part in the F. Bl. is given to a third violin, for
Violino 3o per Viola is written over the part. Although
this practice was favored by the French, it is uncharacteristic of Sammartini. For explanation of the date,
see No. 7.

G MAJOR

NO. 82
2 vn, va, b

Date	before c. 1744.
MS source	PC F. Bl. 103, Concertino, St. Martino.
Remarks	For explanation of the date, see No. 7.

NO. 83

2 vn, va, b

Date	before c. 1744.
MS source	PC F. Bl. 106, Concertino, St. Martino.
Remarks	For explanation of the date, see No. 7.
Mod. ed.	Newell Jenkins ("Grahl's Orchester-Serie," No. 4, Frankfurt am Main: H. L. Grahl, 1953).

NO. 84

2 fl, 2 hn, 2 vn, b

Date	before 1765.
Cat. ref.	Karl. cat. A, Concerto, St. Martino; Br. 66 (listed under "Sinfon. Cassat. etc. a Flauto Traverso"), "dell' Academia" (sic) [No. 1], Martino.
MS sources	KARL Mus. Hs. 793, Concertino, San Martino (eighteenth-century score); another copy of the second movement alone, KARL Mus. Hs. 788 (2 fl, 2 ob, 2 hn, b); BRAT XIV. 60, Notturno, S. Martino; PIST Rosp. B 247, 10, Sonata, S. Martino (2 hn pts. missing).

Remarks   For explanation of the date, see p. 83. In Karl. cat. A the
two movements are listed separately in inverse order. The
PIST MS gives the tempo markings as Spiritoso Moderato
and Menuetto, and there are numerous slight rhythmic
differences in the musical text.

B-FLAT MAJOR

NO. 85

2 vn, va, [vc], b

Date   before c. 1744.

MS source   PC F. Bl. 100, Concertino, St. Martino.

Remarks   For explanation of the date, see No. 7. In movements I
and III the presence of thematic and figural passages in
the tenor clef indicate a division between cello and bass,
and also suggest the possibility that these passages were
intended for solo cello.

MARCHES and MINUETS

NO. 86

[2 ob] , 2 hn, 2 vn, b

(no tempo mark)

MS sources	EINS 84/11, San Martino; EINS 200/26, Marcia, S. Martino.
Remarks	The first MS, dated 1784, consists of thirty-nine numbers and is entitled "Marcie e Minuetti del Sig. Paladino e San Martino." The violin I and II parts carry the indications "oboe primo" and "oboe secondo" on the first inside pages. This march is number 27. Of the second MS, which bears the title "Maestosi Quidam Minuetti," only the first violin part is extant. The collection consists of thirteen numbers, duplicating the first collection as follows:

200/26	84/11
1	3
2	4
3	5
4	7
5	12
6	13
7	29
8	30
9	39
10	19
11	14
12	16
13	27

(See also No. 87.)

NO. 87

2 vn, (2 ob), 2 hn, b

(no tempo mark)

MS source   EINS 84/11 (see No. 86).

Remarks   This collection has ascriptions over the first work of each
               composer, later ascriptions appearing only with the
               change of composer. With this series of three movements
               under the number 36 there has been a change in ascrip-
               tion from San Martino to Paladino in the second horn
               part only. As the second horn part of 36 and 37 start in
               much the same way, it is possible that the ascription is
               the copyist's error. There is no change in ascription in
               the other parts until number 37, except in the first violin,
               which lacks any further ascription.

VOCAL WORKS

OPERAS

NO. 88 MEMET
Tragedia

Text: Author unknown

Performed: Lodi, 1732

Cast: Solimano   *Soprano*
      Memet   *Tenor*
      Irene   *Soprano*
      Demetrio   *Alto*
      Zaide   *Soprano*

Instrumentation: 2 tr, 2 vn, va, vc, b

ACT I

1   Introdutione
    2 vn, va, b

2   Aria: *Guerra, guerra, voglio guerra*
    Memet—2 tr, 2 vn, va, b (without cemb)

3   Aria: *S'amai se sospirai*
Solimano—2 vn, va, b (without cemb during vocal pt.)

4   Aria: *Pensa che tua son io*
Irene—2 vn, va, b

5   Recitativo: *Anime disperate*
Demetrio—2 vn, va, b

6   Aria: *Venite o Furie*
Demetrio—2 vn, va, vc, b

7   Aria: *Se vuoi che serva*
Solimano—2 vn, va, b

Se vuoi che ser - va al - men   la - scia-mi

8 Aria: *Non è pena in amor più crudele*
Zaide—2 vn, va, b (without cemb during vocal pt.)

Non   è   pe-na in   a - mor   più cru - de - - - [le]

ACT II

1 Introduzione
2 vn, va, b

2 Aria: *Si ti conosco Amor*
Irene—2 vn, va, b

Si   ti co-nos-co A - mor   tu   sei so - lo Sig - nor

3 Aria: *Non sa chi ben non ama*
Memet—2 vn, va, b

Non   sa   chi ben non a - ma

4 Duetto: *Se ben amano due cori*
Irene, Demetrio—2 vn, va, b

Se ben a - ma - no du - e co - ri

5 Aria: *Sù di metalli e sonore trombe*
Solimano—2 tr, 2 vn, va, b

Sù di me - tal - li e di so - no - re trom - be

6 Aria: *Misero amante core*
Irene—2 vn, va, b (without cemb)

Mi - se - ro A-man - te co - re pre-pa - ra pur so - spi - ri

7 Terzetto: *A me sarò crudele*
Irene, Demetrio, Zaide—2 vn, va, b

A me sa - rò cru - de - le cru - de - le

8 Aria: *Si pur fedele a me*
Zaide—2 vn, va, b

Si   pur fe - de - le a   me   fe - de   -   le a   me

ACT III

1 Introdutione
2 vn, va, b

2 Aria: *Presto a godere*
Memet—2 vn, va, b

Pres - to a go - de - re   chi   tar - da il   pia - ce - re

3 Aria: *Se mai dolce se mai grato*
Irene—2 vn, va, b (without cemb during vocal pt.)

Se   mai   dol - ce   se   mai gra - to   se   mai   gra - to

4   Aria: *Palpito, sudo, tremo*
     Demetrio—2 vn, va, b

5   Aria: *Si viva si more in grazia d'amore*
     Zaide—2 vn, va, b

6   Aria: *Il mio amor ti fa regina*
     Memet—2 vn, va, b

7   Aria: *Son vendicato*
     Memet—2 vn, va, b

8   Coro (quintet of soloists): *Guerra, strage, Ruine*
     2 tr, 2 vn, va, b

(Solimano)

Guer - - - - - ra

MS source	HEIL IVb, St. Martino (eighteenth-century score).
Libretto	VNB has a catalogue reference to a libretto perhaps of this work that was once in Meiningen, East Germany. The libretto belonged to a collection of librettos in the possession of the former Herzogliche Bibliothek, part of which was auctioned c. 1930, and part of which remained in Meiningen (die Staatlichen Museen) until 1945 when it disappeared. The VNB reference reads as follows: Memette. / DA / CANTARSI / NEL / TEATRO / PRIVI-LEGGIATO / DA / S. M. C. C. CATT. / IN VIENNA / NELL' ANNO MDCCXXXII. / VIENNA / GIO. PIETRO VAN GHELEN. 31 pp. Meiningen Di / II, 3c 220.
Remarks	The title page of the score is dated 1732. Information about the opera has been found only in Franz Stieger's manuscript "Opernlexikon," II, 572 (VNB, S. M. 8960), which contains the following entry: "Memet op. 3 Giamb. Sammartini. Lodi 1732 (Uraufführung)." The opera MS is probably of north Italian origin and is written in two hands except for Act III, recitative 6, which is in a third hand. The overture to Act I also appears as a symphony in SCHW Mus. 2142 ascribed to J. G. Graun, in LUND Eng. 243 ascribed to J. A. Hasse, and in Br. 62, Racc. I/5, ascribed to Pietro Conti. Number 66a/I is used as the Introduction to Act II and No. 38/I as the Introduction to Act III. The date of the opera thus dates these symphonies, which are the earliest known dated symphonies by Sammartini. Aria 6 in Act II has a key signature of three flats.
	A performance of *Memet* in Vienna is suggested by the fact that the score of *Memet* belongs to a collection of primarily Viennese compositions once in the possession of the Austrian composer Georg von Reutter the younger (1708-1772), the *Kapellmeister* of St. Stephen's Cathedral from 1736 and of the Viennese court from 1751. The collection was inherited by his only son, Karl (d. 1805), who was Abbot of Heiligenkreuz and bequeathed the collection to the Abbey on his death.
Mod. ed.	Overture to Act I and Introductions to Acts II and III: ChurginE.

NO. 89 L'AMBIZIONE SUPERATA DALLA VIRTÙ
Drama

Text: Author unknown

Performed: Regio Ducal Teatro, Milan, 26 December 1734

Cast: Giulia Mammea   *Alto*
        Alessandro   *Soprano*
        Salustia   *Soprano*
        Claudio   *Alto*
        Marziano   *Tenor*
        Albina   *Alto*

Instrumentation: 2 ob, 2 hn, [bn], 2 vn, va, b

ACT I

1 Overture (missing)

2 Coro (missing)
Viva viva il nostro Augusto

3 Aria: *Guida il tuo Nome in Campo*
Marziano—2 hn, 2 vn, va, b

Gui - da il tuo no - me in   cam - - - po

4 Aria: *Parto Amante*
Alessandro—2 vn, va, b

Par - to   par - to A - man - te

5 Aria: *Sdegno, indegno, Affetti, inganni*
Giulia—2 vn, va, b

Sdeg - no, in - deg - no,   Af - fet - ti,   in - gan - ni

6 Aria: *Non vò che un infedele*
Albina—2 vn, va, b

Non   vò   che un in-fe - de - le   si   van - ti   de' miei pian - ti

7 Aria: *L'onor del tuo comando*
Claudio—2 vn, va, b

L'o - nor   del   tuo   co - man - - - - - do

8 Aria: *Querele non sento*
Giulia—2 vn, va, b

Que - re - le   non   sen - to   In - ten - do   l'af - fan - no

9 Aria (missing): *Dirò . . . la Madre . . . il foglio*
Alessandro

10 Aria: *Chi sà dir qual pena sia*
Salustia—2 vn, va, b

Chi sà dir qual pe - - na si - a

11 Aria: *Lascio di sospirar*
Claudio—2 vn, va, b

La - scio, la - scio di so - spi - rar

12 Aria: *Padre addio. Dammi un amplesso*
Salustia—2 vn, va, b

Pa - dre ad - di - o. Dam - mi un am - ples - so

13 Aria: *Anche a costo del mio sangue*
Marziano—2 vn, va, b

An - che a co - sto del mio san - - - gue

ACT II

1 Aria: *Vuò morir. Sazia il tuo sdegno*
Alessandro—2 vn, va, b

2 Aria (missing): *Non ho in petto un'alma ingrata*
Giulia

3 Aria: *Dell'infido a te s'aspetta*
Albina—2 vn, va, b

4 Aria: *Se parlo, e ti salvo*
Salustia—2 vn, va, b

5 Aria: *In sì torbida procella*
Giulia—2 vn, va, b

6 Aria: *Al calor di primo Sole*
Alessandro—2 vn, va, b

Al ca - lor di pri - mo So - le

7 Aria: *In cuor di Padre amante*
Marziano—2 vn, va, b

In cuor di Pa - dre, di Pa - dre - man - te

8 Aria: *Sù quelle luci istesse*
Claudio—2 vn, va, b

Sù quel - le lu - ci i - stes - se

9 Quartetto: *Non hò voci che di sdegno*
Giulia, Alessandro, Salustia, Marziano—2 vn, va, b

(*Giulia*)

Non hò vo - ci che di sde - gno

ACT III

1 Aria: *Raggio di speme*
Alessandro—2 vn, va, b

(no tempo mark)

Rag - gio di spe - me

2 Aria: *Voglio dal tuo dolore*
Albina—2 vn, va, b

Affettuoso ma non tanto

Vo - glio dal tuo do - lo - re

3 Aria: *Vanne alla bella sfera*
Claudio—2 vn, va, b

Andante

Van - ne van - ne alla bel - la sfe - ra

4 Aria: *Infedel, dell'alta impresa*
Marziano—2 vn, va, b

Presto

In - fe - del, in - fe - del, dell' al - ta im - pres - sa

5 Aria: *Dirò che sei dei giorni miei*
Giulia— 2 ob, 2 hn, 2 vn, va, b

6 Aria: *Affetti di Padre, affetti di Sposo*
Salustia—2 vn, va, b

7 Coro (missing): *Alle palme, ed a gli allori*

MS source   BRUS, a series of arias: Nos. 4784, 4794, 4797, 4792, 4789, 4795, 4781, 4788, 4793, 4779, 4803, 4782, 4798, 4787, 4778, 4785, 4800, 4791, 4796, 4802, 4801, 4786, 4783, 4777; St. Martini (eighteenth-century scores).

Libretto   L'AMBIZIONE / SUPERATA / DALLA VIRTU' / DRA-MA / Da rappresentarsi nel Regio-Ducal Teatro / di Milano / Sotto il Clementissimo Patrocinio / DELLA / SACRA REAL MAESTA' / DI / CARLO EMANUELE / RE DI SARDEGNA, DI CIPRO / DI GERUSALEMME, / E DUCA Ecc Ecc. / Nel Carnevale dell'Anno 1735. / IN MILANO, MDCCXXXIV. / Nella Reg. Duc. Corte, per Giuseppe Richino Malatesta / Stampatore Regio Camerale / con licenza de'Superiori. MILB RACC. DRAMM. 6048/1; MILS MUS. S. XIV. 1; BOL 4987; DRES Lit. Ital. D. 525 (destroyed in World War II).

Remarks   The arias and ensembles are not bound in order. The numbering listed above corresponds to the correct sequence in the opera. Although no bassoons are mentioned in the BRUS scores, we have added them to the instrumentation because the work was performed in the Teatro Ducal, whose orchestra contained two bassoons. They most probably doubled the bass part, particularly in those arias which had other winds in the instrumentation. This is also true of L'Agrippina (see No. 90).

There are two copies of the aria Act III, no. 6, "Affetti di Padre." The aria "Care Pupille" (4780) is not in the printed libretto, but comes from Sammartini's oratorio Gesù Bambino Adorato dalli Pastori (see No. 116). From the libretto we learn that the music was by Giovanni Battista San Martini, the scenery by Pietro Righino of Parma, the costumes by Giovanni Mainino, and the choreography and ballet by Gaetano Grossatesta. The singers were: Giulia Mammea, Vittoria Tesi Tramontini; Alessandro, Angelo Maria Monticelli; Salustia, Antonia Carminati; Claudio, Giuseppe Appiani; Marziano, Angelo Amorevoli; Albina, Eleanora Sermantini. According to Paglicci-BrozziR, Pinacci sang in the Milan performance in place of Sermantini (mentioned in the libretto). The singers mentioned in the BRUS MS are the same as those in the printed libretto with the exception of Carlo Salvioni who replaced Sermantini. These changes in cast may indicate three different performances. (For further information about the singers, see the introduction, page 5.) There are occasional slight differences in punctuation and text between the printed libretto and the MS copy. In such cases the printed version has been followed. The same libretto, entitled La Giulia, was set as a pasticcio by G. B. Lampugnani and others, performed in Milan during carnival 1761 (two copies of the score are in the Biblioteca da Ajuda, Lisbon).

Literature   Paglicci-BrozziR, p. 118; Saint-FoixS, pp. 358-361.

NO. 90   L'AGRIPPINA, MOGLIE DI TIBERIO
Dramma per Musica

Text: Guido Riviera (d. 1755)

Performed: Regio Ducal Teatro, Milan, January 1743

Cast:

Augusto	Tenor	
Agrippina	Soprano	
Tiberio	Soprano	
Livia	Soprano	
Agrippa	Alto	
Emilio	Soprano	
Sejano	Tenor	

Instrumentation: 2 ob, [bn], 2 tr, 2 tr da c, timp, 2 vn, va, b

ACT I

1   Overture (missing)

2   Coro di popolo Romano: *Viva Augusto, e viva Roma*
Chorus—S, T, T, B; 2 ob, 2 tr, 2 tr da c, timp, 2 vn, va, b

3   Aria: *Vanne, trionfa*
Augusto—2 tr da c, 2 vn, va, b

4   Aria: *Dirò, che ognora*
Emilio—2 tr, 2 vn, va, b

5   Aria: *Son passaggier, che in mare*
Agrippina—2 vn, va, b

6 Aria: *A un labbro mentitor*
Livia—2 tr, 2 vn, va, b

A un lab - bro men - ti - tor

7 Aria: *Torbida notte intorno*
Tiberio—2 tr, 2 vn, va, b

Tor - bi - da not - - - te in - tor - no

8 Aria: *Deh lasciami in pace*
Agrippina—2 vn, va, b

Deh la - scia - mi in pa - ce

9 Aria: *So che ad un altro oggetto*
Tiberio—2 vn, va, b

So che ad un al - tro og - get - to

10 Aria: *Al ciglio oscuro, e torbido*
Agrippina—2 tr da c, 2 vn, va, b

Al ci - glio o - scu - ro,e tor - - - bi - do

11   Aria: *Se questi affetti miei*
     Sejano—2 vn, va, b

Se ques-ti af – fet – ti miei in sen d'a- mor mi ac - ce – se

12   Aria: *Non ho più vele*
     Agrippina—2 tr, 2 vn, va, b

Non ho più ve - le, non ho più ve - le, non ho più sar - te

ACT II

1   Aria: *Quel rio velen, che in petto*
     Agrippa—2 vn, va, b

Quel rio ve - len, che in pet - to

2   Aria: *Saggio fra noi si tiene*
     Livia—2 tr, 2 vn, va, b

Sag – – – – gio fra noi si tie – ne

3 Aria: *Di regnar già sazio io sono*
Augusto—2 tr, 2 vn, va, b

Di re - gnar già sa - zio io so - no

4 Aria: *Sento già l'alma mia*
Tiberio—2 tr, 2 vn, va, b

Sen - to, sen - to quest' al - ma mi - a, quest' al - ma mi - a
[già l'al - ma] [già l'al - ma]

5 Aria: *Dal mio ben, dall'idol mio*
Agrippina—2 tr, 2 vn, va, b

Dal mio ben, dall' i - dol mi - o

6 Coro: *E in questo giorno ammiratore*
Chorus—S, T, T, B; 2 tr da c, timp, 2 vn, va, b

E in ques - to gior - no am - mi - ra - to - re

7 Aria: *Quel foco tuo primiero*
Augusto—2 tr, 2 vn, va, b

Quel fo - co tuo pri - mie - ro

8 Aria: *Lungi da lei, che adora*
Livia—2 tr, 2 vn, va, b

Lun - gi da lei, che a - do - ra

9 Aria: *Con quell'onda, che bagna l'arena*
Sejano—2 vn, va, b

Con quell' on - da, che ba - gna l'a - re - na

10 Duetto: *L'Idolo mio tu sei*
Agrippina, Tiberio—2 tr, 2 vn, va, b

(Tiberio)

L'I - do - lo mi - o, l'i - do - lo mio tu sei

ACT III

1   Aria: *Chi di fierezza ha il vanto*
Agrippa—2 tr, 2 vn, va, b

2   Aria: *Giunge il tuo orgoglio a segno*
Augusto—2 vn, va, b

3   Aria: *Madre la Sposa o Dio!*
Tiberio—2 vn, va, b

4   Aria: *Se tal dolore, Tanto cordoglio*
Emilio—2 tr da c, 2 vn, va, b

5   Aria: *Perfidi m'ingannate*
Agrippina—2 vn, va, b

Per - fi - di,   per - fi - di   m'in-gan - na - te

6   Aria: *Le tue virtudi impresse*
Livia—2 tr, 2 vn, va, b

Le   tue   vir - tu - di im - pres - se

7   Aria: *Nel loro instabil core*
Sejano—2 vn, va, b

Nel   lo - ro in - sta - bil   co - re

8   Coro (soloists): *Se di piacer si amabile*
2 tr, timp, 2 vn, va, b

Se   di   pia - cer si a - ma - bi - le

Cat. ref.   Br. 65, Aria "Torbida Notte," Act I, no. 7 (in A), S, 2 vn, va, b, Martino; Karl. cat. E, Aria "Le tue virtudi impresse," Act III, no. 6, S. Martino.

Autograph   PC ms 1224-26, Martino (score).

MS source   EINS 543/6, Beatus vir ["Non ho più vele," Act I, no. 12], St. Martino (Solo B; see App. B 2); PARP 35622 CF 1-2, "Torbida Notte," Act I, no. 7, S. Martino (eighteenth-century score).

Libretto   L'AGRIPPINA / MOGLIE DI TIBERIO / DRAMMA PER MUSICA / DI GUIDO RIVIERA PIACENTINO / Da rappresentarsi nel Regio-Ducal Teatro / di Milano nel Carnovale dell'Anno 1743. / DEDICATO / A SUA ECCELLENZA / IL SIGNOR / OTO FERDINANDO / CONTE D'ABENSPERG, / E TRAUN / CONFALO-NIERE DELL'AUSTRIA / SUPERIORE DE INFERI-ORE, / COLONNELLO D'UN REGIMENTO / DI / FANTERIA, / CONSIGLIERE INTIMO DI STATO / DI SUA MAESTA', / MARESCIALLO DI CAMPO GENE-RALE / DE' SUOI ESERCITI, / COMANDANTE GE-NERALE DELLE TRUPPE / ESISTENTI IN ITALIA, / GOVERNATORE, E CAPITANO GENERALE / DELLO STATO DI MILANO, / MANTOVA, PARMA, E PIA-CENZA, ec. / IN MILANO, MDCCXLIII. / Nella Regia Ducal Corte, per Giuseppe Richino / Malatesta Stampa-tore Regio Camerale. / Con lic. de'Superiori. BOL 4988; DRES Lit. Ital. D. 1577 (destroyed in World War II); MILB RACC. DRAMM. 6018/2; WLC ML 48. A5, Vol. 18, Item 4.

Remarks   The score in PC is autograph in part only, and is in three volumes, one for each act. The ten-stave music paper, in oblong format, measures 305 x 255 milli-meters. The score was probably acquired by PC between 1810 and 1825, and is inscribed under the entry num-bers 2875, 2876, and 2877. Its origin is unknown. Act I contains 88 pages; Act II, 93 pages; and Act III, 64 pages. On the spine of each volume the last letter of the composer's name has been deleted, and below the first name "Vincent" has been added in ink, in the mis-taken impression that the opera was by Martin y Soler. The title page is lacking. While all the arias are auto-graph, most of the recitatives are written in Hand A. The autograph is notable for the many revisions it contains in Sammartini's hand.

In Act I, Scene IV (p. 7 of the MS), two references are found to "fagotti" in a passage that Sammartini crossed out. The passage is scored for two oboes, two trombe da caccia, timpani and chorus. The "fagotti" play mostly an octave below the vocal bass line. This is the only mention of bassoons in Sammartini's operas, and it suggests that bassoons as well as oboes may have been automatically included in all tutti passages, a practice common in the period. This possibility is strengthened by the fact that the list of performers in the Ducal orchestra of 1748 includes two bassoonists (CesariG, p. 21).

A dedication by the *Cavalieri delegati* follows the title page of the printed libretto. From this libretto we learn that the music was by Gio. Battista San Martino, the scenery by the brothers Galliari, the costumes by Francesco Mainini, and the choreography and ballet by Andrea Cattaneo. The singers were: *Augusto*, Cristoforo del Rosso; *Agrippina*, Barbara Stabili; *Tiberio*, Giovanni Carestini; *Livia*, Domenica Casarini; *Agrippa*, Agata Elmi; *Sejano*, Felice Novelli; *Emilio*, Giuseppe Useda. According to the libretto the role of Emilio was added for the Milan performance, but could be omitted at will. There are occasional slight differences in punctuation and text between the published libretto and the autograph. In such cases the published libretto has been followed. The aria "So che ad un altro oggetto," Act I, no. 8, is also found as a contrafactum (see App. B 3), as is the aria "Non ho più vele," Act I, no. 11 (see App. B 2).

The Count Abensberg and Traun mentioned on the title page of the libretto is the same Count Traun who wrote a letter of recommendation for Sammartini (see p. 3).

Literature   Paglicci-BrozziR, p. 118; Saint-FoixD, pp. 34-40.

OTHER SECULAR VOCAL WORKS

NO. 91   LA GARA DEI GENI
Componimento Drammatico

Text: Guido Riviera (d. 1755)

Performed: Regio Ducal Teatro, Milan, 28 May 1747

Cast: Gloria
Fama
Genio della Germania
Genio dell'Italia

Aria: *V'è chi per suo diletto*
Fama—S, 2 tr, 2 vn, va, b

V'è chi per suo di - let - to   si   fà   dal cor   ti - ran - no, si   fà

MS source	PC D.7413(6), Aria con Sinfa:, S. Martino (eighteenth-century score).
Libretto	LA / GARA DEI GENJ / NEL FELICE NASCIMENTO / DEL / SERENISSIMO / ARCIDUCA D'AUSTRIA / PIETRO LEOPOLDO / COMPONIMENTO DRAMMATICO / [at the end of the text:] IN MILANO, MDCCXLVII / Nella Regia Ducal Corte, per Giuseppe Richino Malatesta / Stampatore Regio Camerale. / CON LICENZA DE' SUPERIORI. MILB XMX.IV.30/1 (duplicate copy XX.XII.9/3), ROMC Collezioni Speciali Lib. Governo Vol. 5.2.
Remarks	This is the only extant music from the Componimento and appears as the first aria. The PC score may be of Milanese origin, and bears the name of Gandini, who sang the role of *Fama* (see below). On the second page of the libretto the following information is found: Quest'Azione Drammatica fu rappresentata nel Regio Ducal Teatro di Milano la sera del giorno 28: di Maggio dell'Anno

MDCCXLVII per introduzione ad una pubblica solenne
Festa di Ballo, ordinata in testimonianza di giubilo da
S. E. il Signor Conte GIAN-LUCA PALLAVICINI."
From the libretto we learn that the music was by Giambattista Sammartino, the text by Guido Riviera, and the
architecture and decorations by Francesco Croce. The
scene was set "nel vasto Teatro di Milano," as is testified
by an engraving of Marc'Antonio Dal Rè, a print of which
is in the Museum of La Scala, Milan (see figure 2). The
singers were: *Gloria,* Caterina Visconti; *Fama,* Isabella
Gandini; *Genio della Germania,* Ottavio Albuzio; *Genio
dell'Italia,* Filippo Elisi.

Literature   Saint-FoixS, p. 363; SartoriG, p. 12.

NO. 91.1   LA REGGIA DE' FATI
Cantata

Text   Gaetano Eugenio Pascali

Performed   Milan, 13 March 1753

Cast   Il Destino
              Pallade
              Ebe Dea della Gioventù
              Il Genio Germanico
              Coro di Fati

1   Aria: *Farsi grande in quella mente*
Pallade—S, 2 ob, 2 tr, 2 vn, va, b

2   Aria: *Se in un solo oggetto istesso*
Ebe—S, 2 ob, 2 hn, 2 vn, va, b

Se in un so - lo og - get - - to is - tes - so

MS sources	PC D.6255, D.6256, St. Martino (eighteenth-century scores).
Remarks	These arias are the only two composed by Sammartini for the cantata *La Reggia de' Fati.* This cantata is found together with *La Pastorale Offerta* under Jommelli's name with the title "Serenata à Quatro Voci, con Sinfonia." Both works were hitherto presumed lost, but have been recently found by Marita McClymonds who has generously shared this information with us. The title page and ascriptions to the Sammartini arias are written in Hand A. For information about the librettos, see App. C 14 and 15. The first line of text in the libretto for aria 1 reads "Ingrandirsi in quella mente".

NO. 91.2 LA PASTORALE OFFERTA
Cantata

Text	Gaetano Eugenio Pascali
Performed	Milan, 19 March 1753
Cast	Nerina
	Silvia
	Alceste
	Montano
	Coro di Ninfe, e di Pastori

Aria: *La fama talora*
Alceste—S, 2 hn, 2 vn, va, solo vc, b

La fa - ma tal - o - ra d'in - co - gni - to og - get - to, d'in-[cognito oggetto]

MS source	PC D.6257, St. Martino (eighteenth-century score).

Remarks   This aria is the only one composed by Sammartini for the cantata *La Pastorale Offerta*. This cantata is found together with *La Reggia de' Fati* under Jommelli's name (see No. 91.1). For information about the librettos, see App. C 14 and 15.

NO. 92   ARIA

Aria: *Non così rapido scende dal Monte*
S, 2 tr, 2 vn, va, b

Non   co - sì   ra - pi - do   scen - de dal Mon - te,   scen - de dal Mon - te

MS source   PC D.7413$^{(4)}$ (eighteenth-century score).

Remarks   This aria has no title or ascription, but is found as a tenor aria "De torrente" (with 2 hn) in the *Dixit Dominus*, EINS 544/7 (see No. 106). This work has not been consigned to App. B (Contrafacta) because it seems possible that this version with Italian text may have preceded the Latin setting. All known contrafacta contain Latin texts of Italian settings, not the reverse. The score is possibly of Milanese origin.

NO. 93   ARIA

Aria: *Chiusi i lumi cheto giace*
S, [2 vn, va, b]

Chiu - si i   lu - mi   che - to   gia - ce

MS source   PC D.7413$^{(3)}$, Aria, St. Marto. (eighteenth-century score); PC D.7413$^{(7)}$, Aria, St. Martino (eighteenth-century score).

Remarks   The second PC score is in the key of D major. Both scores are possibly of Milanese origin. The instrumentation is not specified.

NO. 94   ARIA

Aria: *Deh spiegate quel affanno*
S, 2 tr, 2 vn, va, b

MS source   PC D.7413[2], Aria, S. Martino (eighteenth-century score).

Remarks   The score is possibly of Milanese origin.

NO. 95   ARIA

Aria: *Non hà dolor più rio*
[A], 2 vn, va, b

MS source   BRUS 4790, Sammartini (mod. score).

Remarks   The score was made by A. Wotquenne in 1900 from eighteenth-century parts now lost. In the score the voice part is not specified by clef, but the low tessitura indicates that it is an alto aria. On the title page: "per la Signora Stella Fortunata Cantelli."

NO. 96   ARIA

Aria: *Fieri venti già soffiano a gara*
S, 2 tr, 2 vn, va, b

MS source	KARL Mus. Hs. 808, Aria con Sinfonia, St. Martino (eighteenth-century score).
Remarks	The MS is copied by Hand A.

NO. 97   ARIA

Aria: *Se voi che serva almen*
[S] , 2 vn, va, b

Date	1733.
MS source	BRUS 4799, Sammartini (mod. score).
Remarks	The score was made by A. Wotquenne in 1899 from eighteenth-century parts now lost. In the score the voice part is not specified by clef, but the high tessitura indicates that it is a soprano aria. On the title page: "a Pavia, 1733. Signor Filippo Finassi." Finassi (also spelled Finazzi), b. Bergamo 1710, d. Hamburg 1776, was a soprano castrato and a composer. In 1728 he was a member of the Italian opera troupe in Breslau, and shortly thereafter entered the service of the Duke of Modena. He sang in Lampugnani's *Angelica* in September 1738 in the Regio Ducal Teatro, Milan. (See CambiasiN, pp. 462-468).

NO. 98   GLEE

Glee: *Campana che suona*
[S, A, B]

Date	before 1763.
MS source	BER Mus. ms. 19395, San Martino.
Prints	1) Thomas Warren, 1762: A COLLECTION OF / Catches Canons and Glees / FOR / Three, four, five, six and nine Voices / never before published / Selected by / Thomas Warren / London Printed for, & sold by the Editor at Mr^s. Burgess's in great / Queen Street Lincolns Inn Field, & at the Music Shops, MDCCLXIII. Vol. 1, pp. 27-28, Bapta. St. Martini. BPL, M 220.9; NAP 35.3.34.
	2) Thomas Warren, c. 1764: A collection of SONGS and GLEES / for two three and four voices / Composed for the / CATCH CLUB at ALMACK'S / by / Dr. ARNE, Dr. HAYES, Sig^r. GIARDINI, / Sig^r. COCCHI, Mr. BATTISHILL, St. MARTINI &c: / LONDON Printed by WELCKER in Gerrard Street St. Ann's Soho CNL VM 1503 A73c; NH Mr60/W25. Another edition 1767.
	3) Five editions of "catches, glees, canons, canzonets, madrigals, &c." published in London by John Bland (c. 1785, c. 1787, c. 1787-90), Longman & Broderip (c. 1796), and R. Birchall (c. 1800). The glee appears in Vol. I, p. 96, with the ascription "Sigr. Martini." The editions are identical with the exception of the Bland print of c. 1787.
Remarks	The BER copy originally belonged to Johann Gottlieb Naumann (1731-1801), and was acquired by the Prussian State Library in 1904 from the composer's grandson, Professor Ernst Naumann.
Literature	RubinE, II, 5.
Facsimile ed.	The Warren collection. Melifont Press, White Plains, N.Y., 1970 (a reprint of that published by the Irish University Press).

NO. 99   TERZETTO

Terzetto: *Perche si lento il giorno*
3 S, 2 tr, 2 vn, va, b

MS source	PC D.7413[5] (eighteenth-century score).
Remarks	This terzetto has no ascription, but can be assumed to be by Sammartini because of the style and because it is found in the PC collection of other Sammartini arias (see Nos. 91-94). The score is possibly of Milanese origin. The three characters represented are: Fede, Carità, and Amor.

SACRED VOCAL WORKS

MASS

NO. 100   MISSA SOLEMNIS

Instrumentation: Solo S, A, T, B; chorus S, A, T, B; 2 fl, 2 ob, 2 hn,
2 tr, 2 vn, va, b, org

Kyrie
Chorus; 2 fl, 2 tr, 2 vn, va, b, org

Christe
Solo S, A; chorus; 2 hn, 2 vn, va, b, org

Kyrie
Chorus; 2 tr, 2 vn, va, b, org

Gloria

Solo S, A, B; chorus; 2 fl, 2 ob, 2 tr, 2 vn, va, b, org

Laudamus te

Solo A; 2 vn, va, b, org

Gratias

Solo S, A, T, B; chorus; 2 ob, 2 vn, va, b, org

Domine Deus

Solo S; 2 ob, 2 hn, 2 vn, va, b, org

Qui tollis

Chorus; 2 ob, 2 tr, 2 vn, va, b, org

Qui sedes
Solo A; 2 vn, va, b, org

Qui se - des, qui se - des, qui se - des, qui se - des

Quoniam
Solo S, A; chorus; 2 fl, 2 ob, 2 tr, 2 vn, va, b, org

Quo - ni - am tu so - lus, tu so - lus, so - lus

Cum Sancto Spiritu
Solo S, A; 2 vn, va, b, org

Cum San-cto Spi - ri - tu in glo - ri - a De - i Pa - tris

Cum Sancto Spiritu
Chorus; 2 ob, 2 tr, 2 vn, va, b, org

Cum San - cto Spi - ri - tu in glo - ri - a De - i Pa - tris A - men

MS source   PRA XXXIII A 20, Missa Solennis, Martino.

Remarks   The inscription on the lower right-hand corner of the
title page states that the parts were copied by Pater
Eustachius Fischer for the collection formerly in the
Osacky (Osek) Monastery. The *Gratias* ends with a fugal
allegro on the text *Propter magnam gloriam tuam.* The
indications for the oboes appear in the flute parts, and
those for the horns in the trumpet parts. Tempo marks
when in brackets are taken from the vocal parts. The fact
that each section is in a different key (the *Kyrie* in C
and the *Gloria* in D) indicates that this is a composite
Mass using a variety of sources which may have been
single Mass sections or parts of complete Masses now
lost. Another version of dubious authorship exists (see
App. D 88).

MASS SECTIONS

NO. 101 KYRIE

Kyrie
Chorus S, A, T, B; 2 ob, 2 tr, 2 vn, va, vc, b, org

(no tempo mark)

Ky - ri - e   e - le - i - son

Cat. ref.	Karl. cat E, anon.
MS source	EINS 544/1, St. Martino.
Remarks	The MS is Milanese. In the soprano and alto parts the occasional notation "a 2" may mean that these sections could be sung by soloists.

NO. 102 GLORIA

Instrumentation: Solo S, S, A, A, T, B; chorus S, S, A, A, T, B; 2 ob, 2 vn, 2 va, vc, cb

Gloria
Solo S, S, A, A, T, B; chorus; orchestra

Allegro assai

Glo - - - - - ri - a in ex - cel - sis

Bone voluntatis
Chorus; orchestra

Largo
[with Vn I]

Bo - ne vo - lun - ta - - - - - - tis

Laudamus te
(voice parts missing), orchestra

Andante

Gratias
Chorus; orchestra

(text missing)
(voice parts missing); orchestra

(text missing)
(voice parts missing); orchestra

Domine Deus
Chorus; orchestra

Filius Patris
Chorus; orchestra

(text missing)
(voice parts missing); orchestra

Qui tollis
Chorus; orchestra

Suscipe
Chorus; orchestra

(text missing)
(voice parts missing); orchestra

(text missing)
(voice parts missing); orchestra

Cum Sancto Spiritu
Chorus; orchestra

MS source   TEN MS 1234, Gloria, St. Martino (score).

Remarks   This MS belonged to Sir Frederick Ouseley (1825-1869),
             who was the founder of St. Michael's College, Tenbury,
             and a scholar and composer.
                 It would seem to be identical with the Gloria listed in
             Part II, page 133, of the eighteenth-century MS catalogue
             of the Sharp music collection, in the section entitled
             "Compleat Scores of Oratorios and other Performances,
             the parts of which are not yet wrote [sic] out." The
             entry reads: "Gloria in excelsis. by Martini in a Large
             Folio half bound, containing two hundred and thirty
             pages, M. S." Tenbury's score contains 235 pages, nearly
             the same number as the Sharp *Gloria*. The Sharp collec-
             tion was probably begun by the Reverend Thomas Sharp

of Durham (d. 1758), father of the Sharp brothers, William, James, and Granville, who developed the collection. Granville Sharp, the most important of the three brothers, was a famous philanthropist and a leading figure in the anti-slavery movement. Though the title page of the catalogue is dated 1759, entries were made until the 1790's and possibly later. The latest date of the few dated items is 1783. Included in the catalogue are lists of musical instruments, compositions by some 350 composers, and books on music.

According to the Auction Sale Catalogue of the Granville Sharp Library (1814), Lot 89, "Martini *Gloria in Excelsis,* in Score MS" was sold to T. Jones for three shillings and six pence (information from Jeanette Holland). Jones came from Nottingham and collected several musical MSS now in the British Museum. He sold his collection on 13-15 February 1826. The ascription is to *Gio.* St. Martino, precluding any confusion with Giuseppe Sammartini.

Literature   Holland and LaRueS.

NO. 103   CREDO

Instrumentation: Chorus S, A, T, B; 2 hn, 2 vn, va, org

Patrem omnipotentem
Chorus; 2 hn, 2 vn, va, org

Et incarnatus est
Chorus; 2 hn, 2 vn, va, org

Crucifixus

Chorus; 2 hn, 2 vn, va, org

Cru - ci - fi - xus e - ti - am pro no - bis.

Et resurrexit

Chorus; 2 hn, 2 vn, va, org

Et re - sur - re - xit ter - ti - a di - e

MS source   PRA XXXV D 140, S. Martino.

Remarks   The MS parts belong to the Kreuzherren (Crusaders')
                   Archives in Prague. This organization was a prominent
                   and wealthy music center which sponsored annual can-
                   tata performances at the Church of St. Francis. An in-
                   ventory of the music performed in this church from
                   1738 to 1759 is to be found in the National Museum at
                   Prague. The music itself has been brought there from the
                   seat of the order in Znujmo Hradiště sv. Hipolyta (St.
                   Pölten). For other works mentioned in the inventory, see
                   No. 115, App. C 17 and App. D 88.

                       A second set of voice parts and a duplicate organ part
                   exist. These parts are not of Milanese origin. In the lower
                   right-hand corner of the title page just below the ascrip-
                   tion the following inscription is found: *prod. die 14
                   Sept. 1781*. This date refers to a performance.

OTHER SACRED VOCAL WORKS

NO. 104   BEATUS VIR

Instrumentation: Solo S, A, T, B; chorus S, A, T, B; 2 fl, 2 ob, 2 hn,
2 vn, va, vc, cb, org

Beatus vir
Solo S, A, T, B; chorus; 2 ob, 2 hn, 2 vn, va, vc, cb, org

Exortum est
Solo S; 2 fl, 2 hn, solo vn or vc, 2 vn, va, vc, cb, org

In memoria
Solo B; 2 ob, 2 hn, 2 vn, va, vc, cb, org

Gloria Patri
Solo A, T; 2 ob, 2 vn, va, vc, cb, org

Sicut erat
Chorus; 2 ob, 2 hn, 2 vn, va, vc, cb, org

MS sources   EINS 544/5, St. Martino; another copy EINS 544/6b (mod. score).

Remarks   All title pages and parts except the two *violino di concerto* parts are copied in Hand D, as is the violin obbligato part to the *Exortum est.* There is an alternate solo passage for violoncello in the vc part. The bass is figured. The two violin parts are in the same hand as hand II of the Nisi Dominus (see No. 113). An alternative simplified version of the tenor part to the *Gloria Patri* appears in another, probably later hand on a separate sheet. The score was made by Pater Sigismund Keller in 1873.

NO. 105   DIXIT DOMINUS

Instrumentation: Solo S, A, A, T, B; chorus S, A, T, B; 2 ob, 2 hn, 2 vn, va, b, org

Dixit Dominus
Chorus; 2 ob, 2 hn, 2 vn, va, b, org

Juravit Dominus
Solo S; 2 ob, 2 hn, org

Judicabit
Chorus; 2 ob, 2 hn, 2 vn, va, b, org

Implebit
Chorus; 2 ob, 2 hn, 2 vn, va, b, org

De torrente
Solo T; 2 hn, 2 vn, va, b, org

Gloria Patri
Solo A, A, B; 2 ob, 2 vn, va, b, org

Sicut erat
Chorus; 2 ob, 2 hn, 2 vn, va, b, org

MS sources	EINS 544/7, St. Martino; another copy EINS 544/6a (mod. score).
Remarks	The MS parts are copied by several hands: the va by Hand A; the choral T part and title pages of hn I and II by Hand D, and the remaining parts by other hands. The score was made by Pater Sigismund Keller in 1873. The tenor aria *De torrente* appears in PC as a soprano aria with 2 trumpets and strings, with the text "Non così rapido scende dal monte" (see No. 92).

NO. 106 DIXIT DOMINUS

Instrumentation: Solo S, A, T, B; chorus S, A, T, B; 2 vn, va, b, org

Dixit Dominus
Chorus; 2 vn, va, b, org

Tecum principium
Solo S; 2 vn, va, b, org

Dominus a dextris
Solo T, B; b, org

Judicabit
Chorus; 2 vn, va, b, org

Ju - di - ca [bit]

Implebit
Chorus; 2 vn, va, b, org

Im - ple - bit ru - i - nas: con - quas - sa - bit ca - pit - a in ter - ra mul - to - rum

De torrente
Solo T; 2 vn, va, b, org

De tor - ren - te in vi - a bi - bet

Gloria Patri
Solo S, A; 2 vn, va, b, org

Glo - ri - a Pa - tri, glo - ri - a Fi - li - o

Sicut erat
Chorus; 2 vn, va, b, org

Si - cut er - at in prin - ci - pi - o et nunc

Et in saecula
Chorus; 2 vn, va, b, org

Et in sae - cu - la sae - cu - lo - rum A - men

MS sources   EINS 543/12, S. Martino; another copy 543/16 (mod. score; last three mvts. only); WLC M 2020.S218 M2, San. Martino (mod. score).

Remarks   The EINS and WLC scores were copied by Pater Sigismund Keller. The WLC copy also contains a *Magnificat* (see No. 111) and a dubious *Credo* (see App. D 90).

NO. 107 LAUDATE PUERI

Instrumentation: Solo S, A, T, B; chorus S, A, T, B; 2 ob, 2 hn, 2 vn,
va, vc, cb, org

Laudate pueri

Solo S, A, B; chorus; 2 ob, 2 hn, 2 vn, va, vc, cb, org

Excelsus

Solo S, A, T, B; chorus; 2 ob, 2 hn, 2 vn, va, vc, cb, org

Quis sicut Dominus

Solo S; 2 ob, 2 vn, va, vc, cb, org

Suscitans

Solo S, A, T, B; chorus; 2 ob, 2 hn, 2 vn, va, vc, cb, org

Gloria Patri
Solo S; 2 ob, 2 hn, 2 vn, va, vc, cb, org

Sicut erat
Solo S, A, B; chorus; 2 ob, 2 hn, va, vc, cb, org

MS sources EINS 543/14, St. Martino; another copy EINS 544/6c, (mod. score).

Remarks The MS parts are copied by three hands: all title pages, S, A, T, B complete, ob I and II *Gloria Patri,* hn I and II except *Suscitans,* vn I complete, va except *Suscitans* and *Sicut erat,* vc except *Sicut erat,* and org complete are in Hand D; the rest of ob I and II, hn I and II *Suscitans* only, and vn II complete are in a second hand; va *Suscitans* and *Sicut erat* only, vc *Sicut erat* only, and cb complete are in a third hand.

The score was made by Pater Sigismund Keller in 1873.

NO. 108   LAUDATE PUERI

Instrumentation: Solo S; 2 tr, 2 ob, 2 vn, va, vc, cb, org obl.

Laudate pueri
Solo S; 2 ob, 2 tr, 2 vn, va, vc, b, org

Excelsus
Solo S; 2 ob, 2 vn, va, solo vc, cb, org

Quis sicut Dominus
Solo S; 2 ob, 2 tr, 2 vn, va, vc, cb, org obl.

Ut collocet
Solo S; 2 ob, 2 tr, 2 vn, va, vc, cb, org

Gloria Patri
Solo S; 2 ob, 2 vn, va, vc, cb, org

Sicut erat: identical with *Laudate.*

MS source   MOD E 210, St. Martino.

NO. 109 LITANY

Instrumentation: Chorus S, A, T, B; 2 vn, b

Kyrie

Agnus Dei

MS source
BERG Antisala B.7.12, Letanie della Bma. Vergine Maria, St. Martino (eighteenth-century score).

Remarks
This score, copied in Hand A, is found in a set of six liturgical compositions, five of which are ascribed to Sammartini. They consist of a Gloria, a Magnificat, and four Lauretan Litanies. Of this collection, only two litanies can be considered authentic. For the rest of the collection, see Nos. 110, App. D 87, 92, 93, and 94. The collection belonged to the music library of the opera composer Giovanni Simone Mayr (1763-1845), and was donated to BERG by the composer's son-in-law, Massinelli.

NO. 110 LITANY

Instrumentation: Solo S; chorus S, A, T, B; 2 hn, 2 vn, vc, cb, org

Kyrie

Agnus Dei

MS source	BERG Antisala B.7.12, Lettanie, S. Martino.
Remarks	The parts are written by 7 different hands. Among these are autograph pages of the *Agnus Dei* for the tenor, vn I (2 copies), vn II, and org. Another hand is the same as Hand A. A third hand is the same as Hand III of Litany App. D 92. There exist three copies of vn I and two copies of vn II. It is possible that the solo A, T, and B parts are lost. For the collection, see No. 109.

NO. 111   MAGNIFICAT

Instrumentation: Solo S, A, T, B; chorus S, A, T, B; 2 tr, 2 ob, 2 vn, va, vc, org

Magnificat
Chorus; 2 tr, 2 ob, 2 vn, va, vc, [cb] , org

Et exultavit
Solo S, A, T, B; chorus; 2 ob, 2 tr, 2 vn, va, vc, [cb] , org

Deposuit
Chorus; 2 ob, 2 tr, 2 vn, va, vc, [cb] , org

De - po - su - it   po - ten - tes   po - ten - tes   de   se - de

Gloria Patri
Solo A; 2 ob, 2 vn, va, vc, [cb], org

Glo - - - - - - ria   Pa - tri

Sicut erat
Chorus; 2 ob, 2 tr, 2 vn, va, vc, [cb], org

Si - cut   er - at   in   prin - ci - pi - o   et   nunc

MS sources	EINS 544/3, St. Martino; another copy EINS 544/6d (mod. score); WLC M2020. S218 M2 (mod. score).
Remarks	In EINS 544/3, one copy of the solo A aria *Gloria Patri* is autograph. The remaining parts are copied by several other hands. The choral S, A, B parts, the second copy of the solo A aria *Gloria Patri*, vn I, vn II page 1, and tr I and II are in Hand A; the solo S, A, B vocal parts and titles of the solo B and org are in Hand D. A simplified version of the first movement only of vn I, and cl I and II are in a hand which probably dates from the nineteenth century. The added clarinet parts are an arrangement of the oboe parts. The two scores were copied by Pater Sigismund Keller, the EINS score in 1874 and the WLC score dated 22 November 1880. For the WLC collection, see No. 106. Keller, in a written introduction to the scores of the eight cantatas, mentions that this Magnificat was still frequently performed at Einsiedeln in the 1830's.
Mod. ed.	1) Newell Jenkins (London; Eulenburg 985, 1956). 2) Piano-vocal reduction of the above edition. Michael R. Miller (New York; G. Schirmer 2676, 1967). 3) Piano-vocal score. Hans P. Keuning (Hilversum: Harmonia-Uitgave 1966). 4) Max Alberti (London; Eulenburg 10028, 1972).

NO. 112 MISERERE

Instrumentation: Solo S, S, A, T; chorus S, A, T, B; 2 fl, 2 ob, 2 tr, 2 tr da c, 2 vn, va, b, org

Miserere
Solo A; Chorus; 2 tr, 2 tr da c, 2 vn, va, b, org

Quoniam iniquitatem meam
Solo S; 2 vn, va, vc, b, org

Ecce enim
Solo S; 2 vn, va, b, org

Asperges me
Solo S, A, T; chorus; 2 ob, 2 tr, 2 vn, va, b, org

Libera me
Solo T; 2 fl, 2 vn, va, b, org

Li - be - ra me de san - gui - ni - bus De - us

Quoniam si voluisses
Solo S, A; 2 tr da c, 2 vn, va, b, org

Quo - ni - am si vo - lu - is - ses

Sacrificium
Solo A; chorus; 2 ob, 2 tr, 2 vn, va, b, org

Sa - cri - fi - ci - um De - o spi - ri - tus

Tunc imponent
Chorus; 2 tr, 2 vn, va, b, org

Tunc im - po - nent su - per al - ta - - - [re]

Date   1750.

MS sources   PRA XXXV D 13 (eighteenth-century score), S. Martino;
              EINS 543/11, Stº. Martino (2 hn, 2 vn, va, vc, b, org);
              KREMS F 24 30, Martino (2 ob, 2 vn, va, b, org); LAM
              1024, Martino (2 ob, 2 vn, va, b, org).

Remarks   The PRA score is copied in Hand A. Its title page is inscribed "Composto nell Anno 1750." The score belonged to the Kreuzherren (Crusaders') Archives (see No. 103). The complete *Miserere* is also found in LAM, while only the *Miserere, Quoniam, Ecce enim, Asperges me,* and *Tunc imponent* appear in EINS and KREMS. The MS in EINS was copied by Pater Bonaventura Beutler (1751-1813). Beutler entered the Abbey in 1769 and remained there until he was forced to flee during the French Revolution. He found refuge in German monasteries until 1803 when he returned to Einsiedeln. He copied much music for the library of the Abbey and was also its *Kapellmeister.* For other works by Sammartini copied by Beutler, see App. B 5, 6, 8, and 11.

In the *Miserere, Asperges me,* and *Sacrificium* Sammartini makes use of the plain chant *Miserere mei Deus,* sung at the Burial Service and at Lauds in the Office of the Dead (see the *Liber Usualis,* pp. 1763 and 1800). Despite the absence of documentary evidence, it is conceivable that this work, although composed in 1750, was performed in October 1751 in the Milan Cathedral during the ceremonies accompanying the translation of the remains of S. Carlo Borromeo (see figure 3).

NO. 113   NISI DOMINUS

Instrumentation: Solo S, A, T, B; chorus S, A, T, B; fl, 2 ob, 2 tr, 2 vn, va, vc, cb, org

Nisi Dominus
Solo S, A, T; chorus; 2 ob, 2 tr, 2 vn, va, vc, cb, org

Sicut sagittae
Solo B; 2 ob, 2 vn, va, vc, cb, org

Si - cut sa - git - tae

Beatus vir

Chorus; 2 ob, 2 tr, 2 vn, va, vc, cb, org

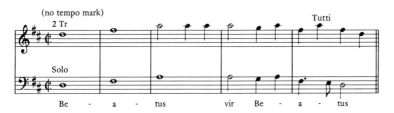

Be - a - tus vir Be - a - tus

Gloria Patri

Solo S; fl, 2 vn, va, vc, cb, org

Glo - ri - a Pa - tri Pa - tri et fi - li

Sicut erat

Chorus; 2 ob, 2 tr, 2 vn, va, vc, cb, org

Si - cut e - rat

MS sources   EINS 543/15, Martino; EINS 291/4 (mod. score).

Remarks   The ascription is written in pencil in another hand on the upper right-hand corner of the title page of each of the various parts. The MS is copied in one hand, which is similar to other Milanese hands, and the watermark is characteristically Milanese. Stylistically there is no reason to doubt the authenticity of this work. The score was made by Pater Sigismund Keller in 1874 and ascribed by him to Padre Martini. A flute is substituted for the first oboe in the Gloria Patri only. There are two copies of violins I and II. The title page of the cello part is inscribed "violoncello obligato che supplisce alla viola."

NO. 114 TE DEUM

Instrumentation: Solo S, A, T, B; chorus S, A, T, B; 2 ob, 2 hn, 2 vn, va, vc, cb, org

Te Deum

Solo S, A, [T], B; chorus; 2 ob, 2 hn, 2 vn, va, vc, cb, org

Te ergo

Chorus; 2 hn, 2 vn, va, vc, cb, org

Aeterna fac

Solo S, A, T, B; chorus; 2 ob, 2 hn, 2 vn, va, vc, cb, org

MS source   PC D.656, S. Martino (eighteenth-century score).

Remarks   The MS score is probably of Milanese origin. It comes from the collection of F. L. Henry, and was acquired by PC in 1877.

NO. 115 TE DEUM

Instrumentation: Solo S, A, T, B; chorus S, A, T, B; 2 fl, 2 ob, 2 tr, 2 vn, va, b, org

Te Deum

Solo S, A, T, B; chorus; 2 ob, 2 tr, 2 vn, va, b, org

Te De - um lau - da - mus, Te De - um lau - da - mus

Te ergo
Solo S, A, T, B; chorus; 2 ob, 2 tr, 2 vn, va, b, org

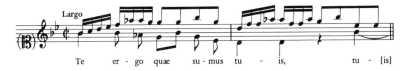

Te er - go quae su - mus tu - is, tu - [is]

Aeterna fac
Solo S, A, T, B; chorus; 2 ob, 2 tr, 2 vn, va, b, org

Ae - ter - na fac cum

Et rege eos
Solo S, A; 2 fl, 2 vn, va, b, org

Et re - ge, re - ge e - os

Dignare Domine
Solo S, A, T, B; chorus; 2 ob, 2 tr, 2 vn, va, b, org

Dig - na - re Do - mi - ne di - e

Date   1771.

MS source   PRA XXXV B 91, S. Martino.

Remarks   On the title page we find the inscription "posto in Musica d'aõ 1771." Also on the title page are noted two performances: one on 14 September 1781 (the Feast of the Cross), and the other in 1784 on the Saturday evening prior to the Feast of the Resurrection (31 March). The verse *Salvum fac populum* is indicated as *tacet* in all parts, suggesting that the music of this section may have been lost. A cadenza *a 2* for the solo soprano and alto in the *Et rege eos* appears at the end of each voice part, the soprano cadenza crossed out, however. The MS parts belonged to the Kreuzherren (Crusaders') Archives (see No. 103).

ORATORIO

NO. 116   GESÙ BAMBINO ADORATO DALLI PASTORI

Text: Author unknown.

Performed: Milan, 11 January 1726.

Cast: Tirsi Pastore
Elpino suo Figliolo
Giglia Pastorella
Angelo

Care pupille
S; 2 vn, va, b

MS source	BRUS 4780, St. Martino (eighteenth-century score).
Libretto	1) GESÙ BAMBINO / ADORATO / DALLI PASTORI. / ORATORIO / DA CANTARSI / NELLA CONGREGA- ZIONE / DELL'IMMACOLATA / CONCEZIONE / Eretta nella Casa Professa di S. Fedele de' RR. PP. / della Compagnia di GESÙ / Il giorno II. Gennajo 1726. / MUSICA / Del Sig. Gio. Battista S. Martini. / IN MI- LANO, MDCCXXVI. / Presso gli Eredi di Domenico Bellagatta. MILB ZCC. V. 17/13.

2) GESÙ BAMBINO / ADORATO / DA' PASTORI. / PASTORALE / DA CANTARSI NELL' ORATORIO / DE' P. P. DELLA CONGREGAZIONE / DI SAN FILIP- PO NERI / DETTI / DELLA MADONNA DI GALIERA. / MUSICA / Del Signor Giambattista San Martini. / IN BOLOGNA MDCCXXXIV. / Nella Stamperìa Bolognese di San Tommaso d'Acquino. / Con licenza de' Superiori. BOL 4986.

3) Gesù bambino adorato dai Pastori (full title not avail- able at this time). Forli 1754. FAE.

Remarks This score is found in a collection of arias and ensembles which makes up the greater part of the opera *L'Ambizione Superata dalla Virtù* (see No. 89). It is the earliest dated extant composition by Sammartini; the rest of the oratorio is lost. This is an aria for Elpino and appears as the third aria of the second part of the oratorio. The MS is copied in Hand A. According to a footnote on page 16 of the Bolognese libretto, the text was approved by the ecclesiastic authorities on 9 December 1734, so that one may assume the performance occurred during the Christmas season of that year. Another footnote on page 13 explains that although the text is printed in its entirety, a cut was made in the music at the Bolognese performance from the bottom of page 13 to the final chorus "Gran pietà del mio Signore!"

Literature SartoriG, p. 9.

CANTATAS

NO. 117   IL PIANTO DI S. PIETRO

Text: Author unknown.

Performed: San Fedele, Milan, 5 March 1751.

Cast: San Giovanni   *Soprano*
      San Giacomo   *Alto*
      San Pietro   *Tenor*

Instrumentation: 2 ob, 2 hn, 2 vn, va, b

1   Introduzione
    2 ob, 2 vn, va, b

2   Aria: *N'empie d'orrore*
    San Giacomo—A; 2 ob, 2 vn, va, b

N'em - pie   d'or - ro - re   ve - der - lo   op-pres - so

3   Aria: *Porto il rimorso*
    San Pietro—T; 2 vn, va, b

Por - to il   ri - mor - so a   fi - an - co

4 Aria: *Da tenebroso velo*
San Giovanni—S; 2 hn, 2 vn, va, b

5 Coro Finale: *Perchè buon Dio t'involi*
Solo S, A, T; 2 ob, 2 hn, 2 vn, va, b

MS sources   EINS 543/16, Cantata IV, S. Martino (mod. score); MUN 3641 (mod. score).

Librettos   1) Il pianto di S. Pietro. / CANTATA PER MUSICA / SOPRA LA PASSIONE DI NOSTRO / SIGNORE GESÙ CRISTO / Da recitarsi la sera del primo Venerdì di Quaresima / NELLA REGGIA, ED IMPERIALE / CONGREGAZIONE / DEL SS^MO. ENTIERRO / IN SAN FEDELE. / Musica del Sig. Gio. Battista Sammartino Maestro di Capella / di essa Congregazione. / IN MILANO)(MDCCLI. / Nella Stamperìa di Pietro Francesco Malatesta. / Con licenza de' Superiori. MILB 25. 5 F 24/10.

2) Lagrime di Pentimento, Tenerezza, e Compatimento. / O sia / Breve Dialogo Tragico-Sacro / . . . Diviso in trè Cantate ed in un Concerto / Musicale . . . / Nella Chiesa di S. Francesco del Sacro / Ordine Militare de' Crocigeri colla stella rossa, / presso il ponte di Praga, il giorno del Venerdì Santo, / a ore undeci della Mattina L'Anno MDCCLIII. Con licenza di Superiori. / Nella Stamperìa dell' Università Carol. Ferd. nel Colleg. della Compagnia di Giesù / à S. Clement; 1753. [Cantata Prima], S. Martino; PRA B 69.

Remarks   The introduction to this cantata is found as the first movement of a symphony (see No. 8). Both scores, each containing the same eight cantatas, were copied by Pater Sigismund Keller, the EINS score in 1875, the MUN score in 1880. The performance in Prague mentioned in libretto 2 took place on 20 April 1753 under the patronage of Count von Harteg (Hartig).

NO. 118   IL PIANTO DELLE PIE DONNE

Text: Author unknown.

Performed: San Fedele, Milan, 12 March 1751.

Cast: Veronica   *Soprano*
       Marta   *Alto*
       Angelo   *Tenor*

Instrumentation: 2 ob, 2 hn, 2 vn, va, b

1   Introduzione
    2 ob, 2 hn, 2 vn, va, b

2   Aria: *Da lungi miro*
    Marta—A; 2 ob, 2 vn, va, b

3   Aria: *Sembianza squallide*
    Veronica—S; 2 ob, 2 vn, va, b

4   Aria: *Stride l'arco*
    Angelo—T; 2 ob, 2 vn, va, b

5 Coro finale: *Fra 'l turbine fatale*
Solo S, A, T; 2 ob, 2 hn, 2 vn, va, b

Fra   'l tur - bi - ne   fa - ta - le

MS sources	EINS 543/16, V Cantata, S. Martino (mod. score); MUN 3641 (mod. score).
Librettos	1) Il pianto delle pie Donne. / CANTATA PER MUSICA / SOPRA LA PASSIONE DI NOSTRO / SIGNORE GESÙ CRISTO / Da recitarsi la sera del secondo Venerdì di Quaresima / NELLA REGGIA, ED IMPERIALE / CONGREGAZIONE / DEL SS^MO. ENTIERRO / IN SAN FEDELE. / Musica del Sig. Gio Battista Sammartino Maestro di Capella / di essa Congregazione. / IN MILANO)(MDCCLI. / Nella Stamperìa di Pietro Francesco Malatesta. / Con licenza de' Superiori. MILB 25.5 F.24/11.
	2) Della Passione / DI N. S. GESÙ CRISTO / CANTATA / Per il terzo Venerdì di Quaresima / NELLA REALE IMPERIALE / CONGREGAZIONE / DEL SS^MO. ENTIERRO / IN S. FEDELE. / MUSICA / Del Sig. Gio. Battista San-martino Maestro di Capella / di essa Congregazione. At the end of the libretto text: In Milano, per il Mazzucchelli successore del Malatesta. 1757. / Con licenza de' Superiori. GENF XXIX C 226.
	3) PRA B 69 (see No. 117), Cantata seconda.
	4) CANTATA PER MUSICA / . . . / Per la sera del terzo Venerdì di Quaresima / NELLA REGIA IMPERIALE / CONGREGAZIONE / DEL SS^MO. ENTIERRO / IN S. FEDELE. / La Musica è del Sig. Giambattista Sanmartino / Maestro di Capella della Regia Ducal Corte / e della suddetta Congregazione. / IN MILANO, MDCCLXXI. / Per Giuseppe Mazzucchelli nella Stamperìa Malatesta. . . . MILB VV.I.44/37.
Remarks	Both scores were copied by Pater Sigismund Keller (for dates of the scores, see No. 117). The introduction to this cantata is found as the third movement of a symphony (see No. 58b). The later performances in Milan took place on 11 March 1757 and 8 March 1771.

NO. 119   IL PIANTO DEGLI ANGELI DELLA PACE

Text: Author unknown.

Performed: San Fedele, Milan, 19 March 1751.

Cast: Angelo di Allianza   *Soprano*
      Angelo di Testamento   *Alto*
      Angelo di Grazia   *Tenor*

Instrumentation: 2 ob, 2 tr, 2 vn, va, vc obbl, b

1   Introduzione
    2 ob, 2 tr, 2 vn, va, b

2   Cor di tre Angeli: *Amare lagrime*
    Solo S, A, T; 2 ob, 2 vn, va, b

3   Recitativo accompagnato: *S'oscurino le stelle*
    Angelo di Grazia—T; 2 ob, 2 vn, va, b

4   Cor di tre Angeli: *Amare lagrime*
    (Same as no. 2 in a shortened version.)

5   Aria: *Oscurata, impallidita*
    Angelo di Testamento—A; 2 ob, 2 vn, va, b

6 Aria: *Rasserenate il ciglio*
Angelo di Allianza—S; 2 ob, 2 tr, 2 vn, va, vc obbl, b

Ras - se - re - na - te, ras - se - re - na - te il cig - lio

7 Aria: *Dal profondo di squallidi abissi*
Angelo di Grazia—T; 2 ob, 2 tr, 2 vn, va, b

Dal pro - fon - do di squal - li - di a - bis - si

8 Cor di tre Angeli: *Amare lagrime*
(Same as no. 4.)

MS sources   EINS 543/16, VIII Cantata, St. Martino (mod. score);
                  MUN 3641 (mod. score).

Librettos   1) Il pianto degli Angeli della Pace. / CANTATA PER
                  MUSICA / SOPRA LA PASSIONE DI NOSTRO /
                  SIGNORE GESÙ CRISTO / Da recitarsi la sera del
                  terzo Venerdì di Quaresima / NELLA REGIA, ED
                  IMPERIALE / CONGREGAZIONE / DEL SSMO. EN-
                  TIERRO / IN SAN FEDELE. / Musica del Sig. Gio.
                  Battista Sammartino Maestro di Capella / di essa Con-
                  gregazione. / IN MILANO)(MDCCLI. / Nella Stamperìa
                  di Pietro Francesco Malatesta. / Con licenza de' Superiori.
                  MILB 25.5 F.24/12.
                  2) LUTTO, e GIOJA. / Ciò è: / L'Amara Morte / DI /
                  GESÙ CRISTO / . . . In un brieve Dialogo Musicale,
                  diviso in due / Cantate, / . . . Nella Chiesa di S. Francesco
                  del Sacro, e Militare / Ordine de' Crociceri colla Stella
                  rossa presso 'l ponte di / Praga, il giorno del Venerdì
                  Santo, a Ore undeci della mattina, / L'Anno MDCCLIV. /
                  . . . Nella Stamperìa dell'Università Carol. Ferd. nell
                  Colleg. della Com- / pagnia di Gesù a S. Clemente 1754.
                  [Cantata prima *Tre Angeli che cantano*], S. Martino;
                  PRA B 70.

Remarks   Both scores were copied by Pater Sigismund Keller (for dates of the scores, see No. 117). The performance in Prague took place on 12 April 1754. Aria no. 6 is also found as a contrafactum (see App. B 4).

NO. 120   PIANTO DI MADDALENA AL SEPOLCRO

Text: Author unknown.

Performed: San Fedele, Milan, 26 March 1751.

Cast: Cleofe   *Soprano*
      Maddalena   *Alto*
      Angelo   *Tenor*

Instrumentation: 2 ob, 2 hn, 2 vn, va, b

1   [Overture]
      2 ob, 2 hn, 2 vn, va, b

2   Aria: *Vo pur fra pianti e gemiti*
      Cleofe—S; 2 ob, 2 vn, va, b

3   Aria: *Palpito, avvampo, e gelo*
      Maddalena—A; 2 ob, 2 vn, va, b

4 Aria: *Torva lo mira, e freme*
Angelo–T; 2 ob, 2 hn, 2 vn, va, b

5 Coro finale: *Porteran novelli allori*
Solo S, A, T; 2 ob, 2 hn, 2 vn, va, b

MS sources	EINS 543/16, VII Cantata, S. Martino (mod. score); MUN 3641 (mod. score); PRA XXXII E 186, Oratorium, Martino.
Librettos	1) Pianto di Maddalena al Sepolcro. / CANTATA PER MUSICA / SOPRA LA PASSIONE DI NOSTRO / SIGNORE GESÙ CRISTO / Da recitarsi la sera del quarto Venerdì di Quaresima / NELLA REGIA, ED IMPERIALE / CONGREGAZIONE / DEL SS^{MO}. ENTIERRO IN SAN FEDELE. / Musica del Sig. Gio. Battista Sammartino Maestro di Capella / di essa Congregazione. / IN MILANO)(MDCCLI. / Nella Stamperìa di Pietro Francesco Malatesta. / Con licenza de' Superiori. MILB 25.5 F.24/13.
	2) PRA B 70 (see No. 119), cantata seconda.
Remarks	Both scores were copied by Pater Sigismund Keller (for dates of the scores, see No. 117). The PRA MS came originally from the Osacky (Osek) Monastery in Czechoslovakia, and contains two cantatas with Latin text instead of the original Italian, of which this is the first, copied c. 1790 by Pater Eustachius Fischer. The introduction to this cantata is found as the first movement of a symphony (see No. 29). The performance in Prague took place on 12 April 1754. Aria no. 4 is also found as a contrafactum (see App. B 7).

NO. 121   MARIA ADDOLORATA

Text: Author unknown.

Performed: San Fedele, Milan, 2 April 1751.

Cast: Maria Vergine   *Soprano*
  Cleofe   *Alto*
  Giovanni   *Tenor*

Instrumentation: 2 ob, 2 vn, va, vc obbl, b

1   Introduzione
  2 ob, 2 vn, va, b

2   Aria: *Almen potesse chiudere*
  Cleofe—A; 2 ob, 2 vn, va, vc obbl, b

3   Aria: *Rupe in mar*
  Giovanni—T; 2 ob, 2 vn, va, b

4   Aria: *Il caro suo pegno*
  Maria—S; 2 vn, va, b

5   Coro finale: *Col magnanimo consiglio*
Solo S, A, T; 2 ob, 2 vn, va, b

Col   ma - gna - ni - mo con - si - glio

MS sources	EINS 109/1, Cantata VI, S. Martino; another copy EINS 543/16 (mod. score); MUN 3641 (mod. score); PRA XXXII E 186, Oratorium, Martino.
Librettos	1) Maria Addolorata. / CANTATA PER MUSICA / SOPRA LA PASSIONE DI NOSTRO / SIGNORE GESÙ CRISTO / Da recitarsi la sera del quinto Venerdì di Quaresima / NELLA REGIA, ED IMPERIALE / CONGREGAZIONE / DEL SS^{MO}. ENTIERRO / IN SAN FEDELE. / Musica del Sig. Gio. Battista Sammartino Maestro di Capella / di essa Congregazione. / IN MILANO)(MDCCLI. / Nella Stamperìa di Pietro Francesco Malestesta. / Con licenza de' Superiori. MILB 25.5 F.24/14. 2) PRA B 69 (see No. 117), Cantata terza.
Remarks	Both scores were copied by Pater Sigismund Keller (for dates of the scores, see No. 117). For information about the PRA MS, see No. 120. The introduction to this cantata is found as the first movement of a symphony (see No. 26).

NO. 122   GERUSALEMME SCONOSCENTE INGRATA

Text: Author unknown.

Performed: San Fedele, Milan, 9 March 1759.

Cast: Maria Maddalena   *Soprano*
        Cleofe   *Alto*
        Maria Salome   *Tenor*

Instrumentation: 2 ob, 2 hn, 2 vn, va, b

1   Sinfonia
2 ob, 2 hn, 2 vn, va, b

(no tempo mark)

2 Aria: *Lupo crudel, lupo rapace*
Maria Cleofe—A; 2 ob, 2 hn, 2 vn, va, b

Lu - po cru - del, cru - del ra - pa - ce

3 Aria: *Di Davidde il figlio*
Maria Salome—T; 2 hn, vn obbl, 2 vn, va, b

Di Da - vid - de il fi - glio

4 Aria: *Quel serto, quel manto*
Maria Maddalena—S; 2 ob, 2 vn, va, b

Quel ser - to, quel man - to

5 Coro Finale: *Forsennata Sione infedele*
Solo S, A, T; 2 ob, 2 hn, 2 vn, va, b

For - sen - na - ta Si - o - ne in - fe - de - le

MS sources   EINS 109/1 Cantata Sacra a Trè Voci con Sinfonia, St.
Martino; EINS 543/16 (mod. score); MUN 3641 (mod.
score); WLC M 2020. S22, Recitativo, Aria e Coro della
Cantata per il Venerdì nella Quaresima (mod. score);
BER Mus. ms. 19394, Rezitativo e Aria di Maria Mad-
dalena (mod. score).

Libretto   GERUSALEMME / SCONOSCENTE INGRATA / DIA-
LOGO PER MUSICA / DA RECITARSI / La sera del
primo Venerdì di Quaresima / NELLA REGIA, ED
IMPERIALE / CONGREGAZIONE / DEL / SS^MO. EN-
TIERRO / IN S. FEDELE. / La composizione della Mu-
sica è del Sig. Giambattista / Sammartino Maestro della
R. Imp. Capella / di essa Congregazione. / IN MILANO
MDCCLIX. / Nella Stamperìa di Giuseppe Mazzucchelli
Successore Malatesta. / Con licenza de' Superiori. GENF
XXIX C 266.

Remarks   All the parts in EINS except the duplicate Violins I and II
are written in one hand, probably Milanese, on Milanese
paper. All scores were made by Pater Sigismund Keller
(for the dates of the two complete scores, see No. 117).
The WLC score contains the recitative "Io stessa il vidi,"
and nos. 4 and 5, and the BER MS contains the same
recitative as WLC and no. 4. The introduction to this
cantata is found as the first movement of a symphony
(see No. 56). "De omni Tempore" is inscribed in another,
later hand on the bass part.

NO. 123 L'ADDOLORATA DIVINA MADRE

Text: Author unknown.

Performed: San Fedele, Milan, 6 April 1759.

Cast: Maria Cleofe   *Soprano*
      Maria Salome   *Alto*
      Maria Maddalena   *Tenor*

Instrumentation: 2 ob, 2 hn, 2 vn, va, b

1 [Overture]
   2 ob, 2 hn, 2 vn, va, b

(no tempo mark)

2 Aria: *Non bastò l'immenso affanno*
   Maria Maddalena—T; 2 vn, va, b

Allegro

Non bas - tò l'im - men - so af - fan - no

3 Aria: Ecce panis angelorum
Maria Cleofe—S; 2 ob, 2 vn, va, vc obbl, b

Ben lo pre - dis - se quel Ve - glio un gior - no
[Ec - ce pa - nis An - - ge - lo - rum]

4 Aria: *Non così d'alpi in cima*
Maria Salome—A; 2 vn, va, b

Non co - sì d'al - pi in ci - ma

5 Finale Coro a Tre: *Madre purissima*
Solo S, A, T; 2 ob, 2 hn, 2 vn, va, b

Ma - dre pu - ris - si - ma

MS sources   EINS 543/16, Cantata III, S. Martino (mod. score); MUN 3641 (mod. score).

Libretto   L'ADDOLORATA / DIVINA MADRE / E DESOLATIS-SIMA NELLA SOLEDAD / DIALOGO PER MUSICA / DA RECITARSI / La sera del quinto Venerdì di Quaresima / NELLA REGIA, ED IMPERIALE / CONGREGAZIONE / DEL / SS^MO. Entierro / IN S. FEDELE. / La composizione della Musica è del Sig. Giambattista / Sammartino Maestro della R. Imp. Capella / di essa Con-

gregazione. / IN MILANO MDCCLIX. / Nella Stamperìa
di Giuseppe Mazzucchelli Successore Malatesta. / Con
licenza de' Superiori. GENF XXIX C 266.

Remarks   Both scores were copied by Pater Sigismund Keller (for
dates of the scores, see No. 117). The introduction is
also found with a text as a terzetto, and rescored (see
App. B 9). The introduction to the aria "Non bastò
l'immenso affanno" is omitted in both scores, but appears
as the introduction to a *Confitebor* (see App. B 5).
The Italian text to aria no. 3 is found only in the libretto
and has been replaced with the "Ecce panis angelorum,"
probably by Pater Sigismund Keller. The aria "Non così
d'alpi in cima" is also found as a contrafactum (see
App. B 10).

NO. 124   DELLA PASSIONE DI GESÙ CRISTO

Text: Author unknown.

Performed: San Fedele, Milan, 14 March 1760.

Cast: Maria Salome   *Soprano*
        Maria Cleofe   *Alto*
        Maria Maddalena   *Tenor*

Instrumentation: 2 ob, 2 hn, 2 vn, va, b

1   Introduzione
     2 hn, 2 vn, va, b

2   Aria: *S'alma illustre si nasconde*
     Maria Salome—S; 2 hn, 2 vn, va, b

3   Aria: *Sò che nel cor volgea*
     Maria Cleofe—A; 2 vn, va, b

4   Aria: *D'iniqua mente e rio costume*
Maria Maddalena—T; 2 ob, 2 vn, va, b

D'i - ni - qua men - te, d'i - ni - qua   men - te

5   Terzetto finale: *Chi si colma il sen d'amore*
Solo S, A, T; 2 ob, 2 hn, 2 vn, va, b

Chi   si   col - ma il   sen   d'a - mo - re

Cat. ref.	Introduzione only: Karl. cat. A, Sinfonia, St. Martino.
MS sources	EINS 109/1, Venerdi Primo Cantata a Tre Voci con Sinfonia, St. Martino; EINS 543/16 (mod. score); MUN 3641 (mod. score). Sources for the Introduzione: KARL Mus. Hs. 810, Sinfonia, St. Martino (str only); PRA XXX C 378, Sonata, St. Martino (str only).
Libretto	DELLA PASSIONE / DI GESÙ CRISTO / SIGNOR NOS-TRO, / CANTATA / Nel terzo Venerdì della Quaresima. / PER LA REALE IMPERIALE / CONGREGAZIONE / DEL / SS^MO. ENTIERRO / IN S. FEDELE. / Musica del Sig. Giambattista San Martino, Maestro di Capella / di essa Imperiale Regia Congregazione. / IN MILANO, MDCCLX. / Nella Stamperìa di Giuseppe Mazzucchelli, Successore Malatesta. / Con licenza de' Superiori. GENF XXIX C 266.
Remarks	In EINS 109/1 only the Violin I—Oboe I and Violin II—Oboe II parts are extant. They are copied in Hand A. The aria "S'alma illustre" is also found as a contrafactum (see App. B 6), as is the aria "D'iniqua mente" (see App. B 8). The introduction to the aria "Sò che nel cor volgea" is missing in both scores, as is the introduction to the *terzetto finale.* This terzetto is also found as a contra-factum with the missing introduction (see App. B 11). Both scores were made by Pater Sigismund Keller (for

their dates, see No. 117). The KARL parts were copied by Hand B and the PRA parts by Hand C. The tempo mark for the incipit of this movement comes from these sources. The cast in the libretto differs from the score: S. Pietro, soprano; S. Giovanni, alto; Maria Maddelena, tenor.

Mod. ed.   KARL version of the *Introduzione* in Lothar Hoffmann-Erbrecht, *Die Sinfonie.* ("Das Musikwerk," vol. 29). Cologne: Arno Volk Verlag. 1967.

APPENDICES

APPENDIX A

ARRANGEMENTS

CONCERTOS IN PRINTED COLLECTION

2 solo vn, 2 vn, va, vc, b

A-1

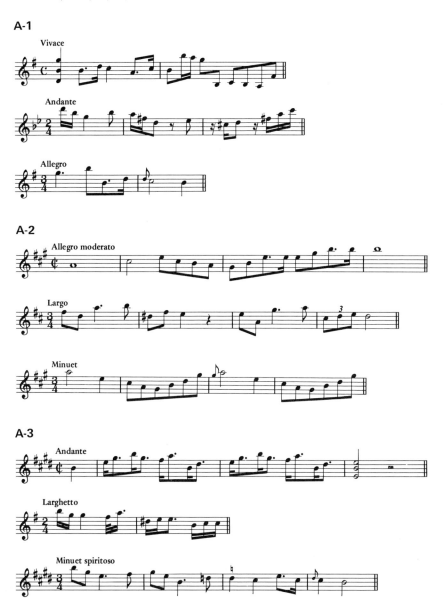

A-2

A-3

A-4

A-5

A-6

Date   before October 1757.

Print   I. Walsh. For full title and sources, see No. 51.

Remarks The concertos were arranged by Francesco Barsanti (c. 1690–before 1776), who came to London in 1714 and was active as a performer and composer. Concerto 1 is an arrangement of Symphony No. 51; the remaining concertos contain movements found in the following printed collections of chamber music: *XII Sonate* Op. V, for strings *a 3*, and flute, 2 violins, and bass, published in Paris by Le Clerc c. 1751 under the name of Giuseppe Sammartini; *Six Sonatas* Op. V, for strings *a 3*, published in London by I. Walsh, announced 4 December 1756; and *Six Sonatas call'd Notturni's* Op. IX, for flute, 2 violins, and bass, published in London by I. Walsh, announced 13 January 1762. The sources for concertos 2-6 are: concerto 2/I and III (Walsh Op. V/5), II (Walsh Op. IX); concerto 3/I and III (Le Clerc Op. V/5), II (Le Clerc Op. V/I0/II); concerto 4/I and III (Le Clerc Op. V/6), II (Le Clerc Op. V/9/II); concerto 5/I and II (Le Clerc Op. V/7), III (Le Clerc Op. V/11/II); concerto 6 (Le Clerc Op. V/1). The instrumental parts are entitled *violino primo, violino primo ripieno, violino secondo del concertino, violino secondo ripieno, viola, violoncello, organo o basso ripieno.*

The attribution of the Le Clerc print Op. V to Giuseppe Sammartini in MishkinP is incorrect in view of the *galant* style of the sonatas and the fact that they are found in three printed collections all ascribed to G. B. Sammartini. In addition, these sonatas exist in numerous eighteenth-century MS copies in collections of chamber works by G. B. Sammartini, often inscribed with the composer's full name. Four sonatas (nos. 1, 2, 4, 7) are also listed in collections of G. B. Sammartini's trios in the Breitkopf catalogue of 1762, and another sonata (no. 6) in the Breitkopf supplement of 1767.

Copies of the prints Le Clerc Op. V and Walsh Op. IX are in PBN, and Walsh Op. V in LBM and other sources.

APPENDIX B

CONTRAFACTA

B-1 AWAKE THOU LUTE AND HARP
Duetto
Solo S, S; 2 fl, 2 vn, va, b

(no tempo mark)

A - wake   thou Lute and Harp a - wake

Print   J. Corfe, c. 1800: SACRED MUSIC / Dedicated by Per-
mission to / The Right Honble. the / Earl of Malmesbury /
in TWO VOLUMES / Consisting of a Selection of the
most admired Pieces of / VOCAL MUSIC / from the / TE
DEUM / Jubilate, Anthems, & Milton's Hymn / adapted
to some of the / CHOICEST MUSIC / of the Greatest
Italian and other Foreign Composers, / JOMELLI, PER-
GOLESI, PEREZ, MARTINI, BERETTI, SCOLARI, &c
&c &c. / By the Late / James Harris, Esqr. / Arranged
and Published by / JOSEPH CORFE. / Gentleman of his
Majesty's Chapel & Organist of the Cathedral, Salisbury.
Vol. II, pp. 52-62, Martini of Milan; NYPL *MRHI +, an-
other copy Drexel 4709: CKC; LBM; LORC; WLC
M 2038.C8 Case.

B-2 BEATUS VIR
Solo B; 2 tr, 2 vn, va, b

Presto

Be - a - tus vir   qui   ti - met

Date   1743.

MS source   EINS 543/6, St. Martino.

Remarks   Same as soprano aria "Non ho piu vele," Act I no. 12
               from the opera *L'Agrippina* (see No. 90).

B-3   BEATUS VIR

Solo B; 2 vn, va, b

Be - a - tus   vir   qui   ti - met

Date   1743.

MS source   EINS 543/8, St. Martino.

Remarks   Same as soprano aria "So che ad un altro oggetto," Act I
               no. 9 from the opera *L'Agrippina* (see No. 90).

B-4   COMPUNCTO CORDE

Solo S; 2 ob, 2 vn, va, vc obbl, b

Com - punc - to   cor - de

Date   1751.

MS source   PRA XXXII E 129, St. Martino.

Remarks   This aria also appears as no. 6 in cantata No. 119, with
               the text "Rasserenate il ciglio." The MS belonged to the
               Osacky (Osek) Monastery in Czechoslovakia.

B-5   CONFITEBOR

Solo T; 2 vn, va, b

Con - fi - te - bor

Date   1759.

MS source   EINS 543/4, Sto. Martino.

Remarks   This aria also appears as no. 2 in cantata No. 123, with the text "Non bastò l'immenso affanno." It was copied by P. Bonaventura Beutler (1751-1813).

B-6   DE PROFUNDIS

Solo S; 2 hn, 2 vn, va, b

Date   1760.

MS source   EINS 700/15, St. Martino.

Remarks   This aria also appears as no. 2 in cantata No. 124, with the text "S'alma illustre." It was copied by P. Bonaventura Beutler (1751-1813).

B-7   IN ME SI FROMANT POENA

Solo T; 2 ob, 2 vn, va, b

Date   1751.

MS source   PRA XXXII E 129, St. Martino.

Remarks   This aria also appears as no. 4 in cantata No. 120, with the text "Torva lo mira, e freme." The MS belonged to the Osacky (Osek) Monastery in Czechoslovakia.

B-8   LAETATUS SUM

Solo T; 2 ob, 2 vn, va, b, org

Lae - ta - tus sum in his quae die - ta

Date	1760.
MS source	EINS 700/14, Sto. Martino.
Remarks	This aria also appears as no. 4 in cantata No. 124, with the text "D'iniqua mente." It was copied by P. Bonaventura Beutler (1751-1813).

B-9   LAETATUS SUM

Solo S, A, B; 2 cl, 2 hn, 2 vn, va, vc

Lae - ta - tus sum, lae - ta - tus sum

Date	1759.
MS source	EINS 544/2, St. Martino.
Remarks	This work also appears as the introduction to cantata No. 123, where it is found without voice parts, and with oboes instead of clarinets. Most probably this version is an arrangement by a later hand.

B-10   NISI DOMINUS

Iste quem loti colimus
Solo A; 2 vn, va, b

Is - te quem lo - ti   co - li - mus

Date	1759.
MS source	EINS 543/5, St. Martino.

Remarks A second text has been supplied under the first: Sumunt boni, sumunt mali. This work also appears as no. 4 in cantata No. 123, with the text "Non così d'alpi in cima."

B-11 OFFERTORIUM

Sub diversus speciebus
Chorus S, A, T, B; 2 hn, 2 vn, va, b, org

Date   1760.

MS source EINS 543/13, Offertorium de SSmo., Sto. Martino.

Remarks This work also appears as a terzetto, no. 5, in cantata No. 124, with the text "Chi si colma il sen d'amore." This arrangement, with the addition of the bass part, was copied by P. Bonaventura Beutler (1751-1813). The terzetto of cantata No. 124 lacks 33 bars of introduction which are present in this version.

APPENDIX C

LOST WORKS

SYMPHONIES

C MAJOR

C-1

2 vn, b

Date   before 1768.

Cat. ref.   Lam. cat. 1768, Sinfonia, Martino.

C-2

2 vn, b

Date   before 1762.

Cat. ref.   Br. 62, Racc. III/6, Sinfonia, Martini.

Remarks   The sequential style of the incipit is uncharacteristic of Sammartini. Two other symphonies in this group attributed to "Martini" are also doubtful (see App. D 56 and 57).

D MAJOR

C-3

2 hn, 2 vn, b

II Andante
III Presto

Date	before 1750.
MS source	DARM 169/a, Sinfonia, Sammartini (destroyed in World War II).
Remarks	The MS was copied c. 1747-1750 by Johann Samuel Endler (d. 1762), *Vize-Kapellmeister* at Darmstadt. Only the bass incipit of the first movement is available for this symphony and a second symphony in A (see App. C 6). According to HoferC, the symphony was concerto-like in style, the first movement ending on the dominant as in No. 33
Literature	HoferC, pp. 130-131.

C-3.1
2 vn, b ?

Date	before 1769.
Cat. ref.	Brtnice cat., c. 1752-1769, Sinfonia a tre, Martini.

G MAJOR

C-4
a 8

Date	before 1753.
Cat. ref.	Hund 1753 (No. 7), Sinfonia, Samartino (instrumental pts. not specified); Br. 62, Racc. III/4, Sinfonia, Martini (str only).
Remarks	Incipit from the Hund catalogue.

C-5	No incipit is available (MS destroyed in World War II). The work is listed in the KÖNIG catalogue as a sinfonia in G by San Martini, *a 3*, in two movements, Allegro

(4/4) and Menuetto (3/4). The trio scoring and two-movement scheme suggest that the work may have been a chamber sonata, not a symphony.

A MAJOR

C-6

2 vn, va, b

II Allegro
III Andante
IV Presto

MS source	DARM 169/d, Sinfonia, Sammartini (destroyed in World War II).
Remarks	Since this type of four-movement cycle is not found in Sammartini's extant authentic orchestral music, the attribution may be considered doubtful. The work may have been a concerto since Hofer writes that the first violin part contained tutti and solo indications.
Literature	HoferC, pp. 130-131.
C-7	A lost print: chez Moria, 27 Sept. 1756 (An.): Sei Sinfonie a piu Stromenti da Jomelli, Wagenseil, Flaminghino, San Martino. Prix 7 livres. (Cited in Saint-FoixC, p. 316.)
C-7.1	See App. C Addenda.

CONCERTOS

G MAJOR

C-8

Solo vn, orchestra

Date	before 1762.

Cat. ref. Br. 62 II, Racc. I/3, Concerto, Martino (source of incipit);
Brtnice cat., c. 1752-1769, Concerto a violino obligato,
Martini (source of tempo mark).

B-FLAT MAJOR

C-9

(instrumentation unknown)

(no tempo mark)

Date before 1762.

Cat. ref. Br. 62 II, Racc. II/2, Concerto, Martino.

C-9.1 See App. C Addenda.

C-10

MS source BRUS W. 13450 Receuil de 4 Morceaux divers
        a. Concerto pour Violon princ.
        b. Idem.
        c. Concerto pour 2 Violons
        d. Concerto pour Violoncello piccolo

Remarks These works may well have been copies of some of the
concertos in the former Wagener collection sold in part
to BRUS and in part to the Prussian State Library now
in BER. The concerto collection in BER parallels the
description of these BRUS concertos (See Nos. 69, 73-75).

CONCERTINO

C-11

(instrumentation unknown)

(no tempo mark)

Cat. ref. Karl cat. E, Concertino, S. Martino.

BALLET

C-12 IL TRIONFO D'AMORE
Ballo

Performed	Regio Ducal Teatro, Milan, 29 December 1773.
Literature	BarblanS, p. 32.

SECULAR CANTATAS

C-13 PARIDE RICONOSCIUTO
Azione Accademica

Text	Author unknown.
Performed	Milan, 1750.
Libretto	PARIDE RICONOSCIUTO / AZIONE ACCADEMICA / CONTENENTE / GLI ESERCIZJ / DI LETTERE E D'ARTI CAVALLERESCHE / SOSTENUTA / DA' SIGNORI CONVITTORI / DEL COLLEGIO NOBILE / REGIO IMPERIALE LONGONE / DIRETTO / DA' CHERICI REGOLARI DELLA CONGREGAZIONE / DI S PAOLO. On the last page: IN MILANO, nella Stamperìa di Pier Francesco Malatesta. 1750)(Con licenza de' Superiori. MILB ZCC V 5/18.
Remarks	The only two arias, "No, non temer, se il sonno" and "Qual Leon pien di dispetto" occur in the second of three parts; the music for these is ascribed to Giambattista San Martino. His contribution was a small part to a large and complex entertainment.

C-14 LA REGGIA DE' FATI

Text	Gaetano Eugenio Pascali.
Performed	Milan, 13 March 1753.
Cast	Il Destino
	Pallade
	Ebe Dea della Gioventù
	Il Genio Germanico
	Coro di Fati

Librettos

1) LA / REGGIA DE' FATI. / CANTATA / DA RECITARSI / NEL GIORNO NATALIZIO / DEL / SER^MO. REAL PRINCIPE / GIUSEPPE / ARCIDUCA D'AUSTRIA / PER COMANDAMENTO / DI SUA ECCELLENZA / IL SIGNOR GENERALE / CONTE GIANLUCA / PALLAVICINI / LUOGOTENENTE, GOVERNATORE / E CAPITANO GENERALE / DELLA LOMBARDIA AUSTRIACA ec. / IN MILANO)(MDCCLIII. / Nella Regia Ducal Corte, per Giuseppe Richino Malatesta / Stampatore Regio Camerale. Con Lic. de' Super. MILB XX. XIII. 29/3, ROMC Collezioni Speciali Lib. Governo Vol. 5. 11, another copy in VENC.
2) LA / REGGIA DE' FATI. / CANTATA / FATTA RAPPRESENTARE / DA SUA ECCELLENZA / IL SIG. MARESCIALLO / PALLAVICINI / IN QUESTO NUOVO PUBBLICO TEATRO / ALL' OCCASIONE DEL PASSAGGIO / DI SUA ALTEZZA / IL SIG. PRINCIPE / GIUSEPPE VINCISLAO / DI LIECHTENSTEIN / Cavaliere dell'Insigne Ordine del Toson d'Oro, Consigliere Intimo Attuale / di Stato, Supremo Commandante dell' Artiglieria, Colonnello di un / Reggimento di Dragoni, e Maresciallo nelle Armate di Sua Maestà / l'IMPERATRICE REGINA d'Ungheria, e Boemia ec. ec. ec. / IN BOLOGNA MDCCLXIII. / A S. Tommaso d'Acquino. CON LICENZA DE' SUPERIORI. BOL 2589.

Remarks

According to the MILB libretto the music was composed by Niccolō Jommelli and Gio. Battista Sammartino. No mention of Sammartini is made in the BOL libretto. For the Bolognese performance the cast was as follows.

Il Destino	Giuseppe Cicognani
Pallade	Rosa Tartaglini Tibaldi
Ebe	Caterina Flavis
Il Genio	Giuseppe Tibaldi

The costumes were by Pietro Antonio Biagi of Bologna. Three arias in the Bolognese libretto differ from those in the Milan libretto: "Ingrandirsi in quella Mente" is substituted for "Vi conosco, amiche stelle"; "Picciol Leon feroce" for "Così spaventa il tuono"; and "Più che nei Popoli" for "Agitata in van t'affanni." One may assume that arias originally composed by Sammartini were replaced for the Bolognese performance by Jommelli with arias of his own. The second of these substituted arias, "Così spaventa," appeared as aria no. 4 in *La Pastorale Offerta*, which identifies that aria as being by Jommelli.

Although both *La Reggia de' Fati* and *La Pastorale Offerta* were presented together in Milan, *La Reggia de' Fati* alone was given in Bologna. Marita McClymonds has recently discovered the music to these two works. For information, see Nos. 91.1-91.3.

Literature   AbertN, p. 55; SartoriG, p. 12.

C-15   LA PASTORALE OFFERTA

Text   Gaetano Eugenio Pascali.

Performed   Milan, 19 March 1753.

Cast   Nerina
Silvia
Alceste
Montano
Coro di Ninfe, e di Pastori.

Libretto   LA / PASTORALE OFFERTA. / CANTATA / PER IL GLORIOSO NOME / DEL / SER^MO. REAL PRINCIPE / GIUSEPPE / ARCIDUCA D'AUSTRIA. MILB XX. XIII. 29/4, ROMC Collezioni Speciali Lib. Governo Vol. 5. 11, another copy in VENC.

Remarks   This libretto is a companion piece to the *Reggia de' Fati*. In the introduction is found the author's apology: "Essendosi questo improvviso Drammatico Componimento prodotto nell' angusto intervallo di poche ore, siccome l'altro in quello di pochi giorni; l'Autore si richiama alla discretezza di chi legge per quelle debolezze, che per avventura possano esservi occorse." For the music, see No. 91.3.

Literature   AbertN, p. 55; SartoriG, p. 12.

C-16   IRIDE

Text   Francesco Antonio Mainoni.

Performed   Milan, 1772.

Libretto   CIRO IN MEDIA / RAPPRESENTAZIONE ACCADEMICA / DEDICATA / ALLE LL. AA. RR. / IL SERENISSIMO / FERDINANDO ARCIDUCA D'AUSTRIA / E / LA SERENISSIMA ARCIDUCHESSA /

MARIA BEATRICE D'ESTE / PRINCIPESSA DI MO-
DENA / DAI CONVITTORI DEL COLLEGIO DE'
NOBILI / REGIO IMPERIALE LONGONE / DIRET-
TO DA C. R. BERNABITI. On p. 47: IN MILANO
MDCCLXXII. / PER GIUSEPPE MAZZUCCHELLI,
NELLA STAMPERIA MALATESTA. / CON LICENZA
DE' SUPERIORI. MILB VV. III. 6/9; duplicate copies:
25. 8. H. 9/11; 25. 4. I. 16/6.

Remarks   This cantata appears at the end of the second part of the
             "rappresentazione accademica" *Ciro in Media.* From the
             libretto we learn that the composer of the cantata was
             Gio. Battista Sanmartino, Maestro di Capella (sic) della
             Regia Ducal Corte; the balletmaster, Antonio Porro; the
             composer of the arias, Carlo Sala; the architects and
             painters, Gio. Battista Riccardi and sons; and the cos-
             tume designer, Giovanni Mazza.

SACRED MUSIC

C-17 MAGNIFICAT

Date   1737 or before.

Remarks   A Magnificat "a 2 Chori 2 Oboë" ascribed to Sanmartino
             appears as the last work in the inventory of the years
             1737-1738 of the Kreuzherren (Crusaders') Archive in
             Prague (see No. 103).

ORATORIOS

C-18 LA CALUNNIA DELUSA

Aria: *Troppo s'avanza*

Text   Giacomo Machio.

Performed   Regia ed Imperiale Cappella di Santa Maria della Scala,
             Milan, 23 May 1724.

Cast   Wenceslao   Signor Ereditario
             Astasio   Consigliere, ed Accusatore
             Gismondo   Amministratore del Contado
             Bondimiro   Figlio di Gismondo

Libretto	LA CALUNNIA DELUSA. / ORATORIO / IN ONORE / DI S. GIOVANNI / NEPOMUCENO / TAUMATURGO DELLA BOEMIA, / DA RECITARSI / NELLA REGIA, ED IMPERIALE CAPPELLA / DI SANTA MARIA DELLA SCALA / Nell' ultimo giorno del di lui Ottavario, / che corre il dì 23 di Maggio. / IN MILANO, MDCCXXIV. / Nella Stamperìa di Giuseppe Pandolfo Malatesta. / Con licenza de' Superiori. MILB Misc. XMX V. 22/19.
Remarks	This is the earliest composition by Sammartini. The oratorio was a composite work, consisting of music by Milanese composers of the time: G. M. Marchi, F. Fiorino, Gius. Sammartini, G. Cozzi, D. I. Balbi, G. Paladino, A. M. Scaccia, C. Baliani, and G. Machio. Sammartini is mentioned in the libretto as "Maestro di Cappella," which may indicate that he conducted the performance. This aria is the first of the oratorio, and is sung by Gismondo.
Literature	SartoriG, pp. 6-8.

C-19 L'IMPEGNO DELLE VIRTÙ

Text	Tomaso Angelo Richini (or Ricchini)
Cast	Gloria
	Innocenza
	Amore
	Sapienza
	Umiltà
	Coro delle Virtù
MS libretto	BOL 4989, San Martini.
Remarks	The same libretto was set in 1718 by Giovanni Perroni, Maestro di Cappella of Santa Maria delle Grazie. The printed libretto of this earlier composition was published by Federico Bianchi, and is found in MILB VV. I. 44/10.

SACRED CANTATAS

C-20 LA PREGHIERA ET IL PERDONO DI GESÙ IN CROCE

Text	Author unknown.
Performed	San Fedele, Milan, 23 February 1725.

Libretto	LA PREGHIERA, ET IL PERDONO / DI GESÙ IN CROCE / CANTATA PRIMA / Da recitarsi alla sera il primo Venerdì / di Quaresima / Nella Reale, ed Imperiale Congregazione / DEL SS^{MO}. ENTIERRO / IN S. FEDELE. / IN MILANO, MDCCXXV. / Presso gli Eredi di Domenico Bellagatta. / Con licenza de' Superiori. MILB VV I.44/23.

Although the name of Sammartini does not appear in the title, it is probable that this cantata belongs to the series of Passion cantatas for the year 1725 because of the concordances in place of performance and publisher of libretto.

Literature	SartoriG, p. 9.

C-21 RISPOSTA DI GESÙ CROCIFISSO

Text	Author unknown.
Performed	San Fedele, Milan, 2 March 1725.
Libretto	RISPOSTA / DI GESÙ CROCIFISSO / AL LADRO IN CROCE. / CANTATA SECONDA / Da recitarsi alla sera il secondo Venerdì / di Quaresima / Nella Reale, ed Imperiale Congregazione / DEL SS^{MO}. ENTIERRO / IN S. FEDELE / Musica del Sig. Gio. Battista San Martino. / IN MILANO, MDCCXXV. / Presso gli Eredi di Domenico Bellagatta. / Con licenza de' Superiori. MILB VV. I. 44/24.
Literature	SartoriG, p. 9.

C-22 GESÙ SITIBONDO

Text	Author unknown.
Performed	San Fedele, Milan, 9 March 1725.
Libretto	GESÙ / SITIBONDO DI ANIME, / E DI PENE. / CANTATA TERZA / Da recitarsi alla sera il terzo Venerdì / di Quaresima / Nella Reale, ed Imperiale Congregazione / DEL SS^{MO}. ENTIERRO / IN S. FEDELE. / Musica del Sig. Gio. Battista San Martino. / IN MILANO, MDCCXXV. / Presso gli Eredi di Domenico Bellagatta. / Con licenza de' Superiori. MILB VV. I. 44/25.
Literature	SartoriG, p. 9.

C-23 MARIA SUL CALVARIO

Text   Author unknown.

Performed   San Fedele, Milan, 23 March 1725.

Libretto   MARIA / SUL CALVARIO. / CANTATA QUINTA /
Da recitarsi alla sera il quinto Venerdì di Quaresima /
Nella Reale, ed Imperiale Congregazione / DEL SS^MO.
ENTIERRO / IN S. FEDELE. / Musica del Sig. Gio.
Battista San Martino. / IN MILANO, MDCCXXV. /
Presso gli Eredi di Domenico Bellagatta. / Con licenza de'
Superiori. MILB VV. I. 44/26.

Literature SartoriG, p. 9.

C-24 GESÙ NELL' HORTO

Text   Author unknown.

Performed   San Fedele, Milan, 7 March 1727.

Libretto   GESÙ / NELL' HORTO. / CANTATA PRIMA / Da
recitarsi alla sera il primo Venerdì / di Quaresima / Nella
Reale, ed Imperiale Congregazione / DEL SS^MO. EN-
TIERRO / IN S. FEDELE. / Musica del Sig. Gio. Battista
San Martino. / IN MILANO, MDCCXXVII. / Presso gli
Eredi di Domenico Bellagatta. / Con licenza de' Superiori.
MILB VV. I. 44/19.

Literature SartoriG, pp. 9-10.

C-25 GESÙ TRADITO DA GIUDA

Text   Author unknown.

Performed   San Fedele, Milan, 14 March 1727.

Libretto   GESÙ / Tradito da Giuda, abandonato (sic) / da suoi,
negato da Pietro. / CANTATA SECONDA / Da recitarsi
alla sera il secondo Venerdì / di Quaresima / Nella Reale,
ed Imperiale Congregazione / DEL SS^MO. ENTIERRO /
IN S. FEDELE. / Musica del Sig. Gio. Battista San
Martino. / IN MILANO, MDCCXXVII. / Presso gli Eredi
di Domenico Bellagatta. / Con licenza de' Superiori.
MILB VV. I. 44/20.

Literature   SartoriG, pp. 9-10.

C-26 GESÙ FLAGELLATO

Text   Author unknown.

Performed   San Fedele, Milan, 21 March 1727.

Libretto   GESÙ / Flagellato, coronato di Spine, / esposto da Pilato. / CANTATA TERZA / Da recitarsi alla sera il terzo Venerdì / di Quaresima / Nella Reale, ed Imperiale Congregazione / DEL SS^{MO}. ENTIERRO / IN S. FEDELE. / Musica del Sig. Gio. Battista San Martino. / IN MILANO, MDCCXXVII. / Presso gli Eredi di Domenico Bellagatta. / Con licenza de' Superiori. MILB VV. I. 44/21.

Literature   SartoriG, pp. 9-10.

C-27 I PENSIERI DI MARIA

Text   Author unknown.

Performed   San Fedele, Milan, 4 April 1727.

Libretto   I PENSIERI DI MARIA / Nella sua Solitudine. / CANTATA QUINTA / Da recitarsi alla sera il quinto Venerdì / di Quaresima / Nella Reale, ed Imperiale Congregazione / DEL SS^{MO}. ENTIERRO / IN S. FEDELE. / Musica del Sig. Gio. Battista San Martino. / IN MILANO, MDCCXXVII. / Presso gli Eredi di Domenico Bellagatta. / Con licenza de' Superiori. MILB VV. I. 44/22.

Literature   SartoriG, pp. 9-10.

C-28 GLI AFFANNI DI GESÙ

Text   Author unknown.

Performed   San Fedele, Milan, c. 1728 (20 February).

Libretto   Gli Affanni di GESÙ orante / nel Getsemani. / CANTATA PRIMA / Da recitarsi alla sera il primo Venerdì / di Quaresima / NELLA REALE ED IMPERIALE / CONGREGAZIONE / DEL SS^{MO}. ENTIERRO / IN S. FEDELE. / Musica del Sig. Gio. Battista S. Martino

Maestro / di Capella del Santissimo Entierro. / In Milano, presso gli Eredi di Domenico Bellagatta. / Con licenza de' Superiori. MILB VV. I. 44/7.

Remarks   The date 1728 has been assigned by Sartori, although it does not appear on the libretto, because the printer of the cantatas dated 1725-27 and 1729-30 is the same. The cantatas for the year 1726 for the congregation Ss.mo Entierro were composed by Francesco Fiorino.

Literature   SartoriG, pp. 9-10.

C-29   L'ARCA DEL TESTAMENTO

Text   Author unknown.

Performed   San Fedele, Milan, 11 March 1729.

Libretto   L'Arca del Testamento presa / da Filistei / FIGURA / DI GESÙ PRIGIONIERO. / CANTATA PRIMA / Da recitarsi alla sera il primo Venerdì / di Quaresima / Nella Reale, ed Imperiale Congregazione / DEL SS^{MO}. ENTIERRO / IN S. FEDELE. / Musica del Sig. Gio. Battista S. Martino Maestro / di Capella del Santissimo Entierro. / IN MILANO, MDCCXXIX. / Nella Stampa degli Eredi di Domenico Bellagatta. / Con licenza de' Superiori. MILB VV. I. 44/32; MILB TT. IV. 79/4.

Literature   SartoriG, p. 10.

C-30   GIOBBE ULCERATO

Text   Author unknown.

Performed   San Fedele, Milan, 18 March 1729.

Libretto   Giobbe ulcerato / FIGURA / DI GESÙ FLAGELLATO / CANTATA SECONDA / Da recitarsi alla sera il secondo Venerdì / di Quaresima / Nella Reale, ed Imperiale Congregazione / DELL SS^{MO}. ENTIERRO / IN S. FEDELE. / Musica del Sig. Gio. Battista S. Martino Maestro / di Capella del Santissimo Entierro. / IN MILANO, MDCCXXIX. / Nella Stampa degli Eredi di Domenico Bellagatta. / Con licenza de' Superiori. MILB VV. I. 44/31; MILB TT. IV. 79/5.

Literature   SartoriG, p. 10.

C-31 IL SERPENTE DI MOSÈ

Text	Author unknown.
Performed	San Fedele, Milan, 25 March 1729.
Libretto	Il Serpente di Mosè / FIGURA / DI GESÙ CROCIFISSO / CANTATA TERZA / Da recitarsi alla sera il terzo Venerdì / di Quaresima / Nella Reale, ed Imperiale Congregazione / DEL SS^{MO}. ENTIERRO / IN S. FEDELE. / Musica del Sig. Gio. Battista S. Martino Maestro / di Capella del Santissimo Entierro. / IN MILANO, MDCCXXIX. / Nella Stampa degli Eredi di Domenico Bellagatta. / Con licenza de' Superiori. MILB TT. IV. 79/6.
Literature	SartoriG, p. 10.

C-32 IL SONNO DI ADAMO

Text	Author unknown.
Performed	San Fedele, Milan, 1 April 1729.
Libretto	Il Sonno di Adamo nel Paradiso / MISTERO / DI GESÙ CROCIFISSO, / E SUA CHIESA. / CANTATA QUARTA / Da recitarsi alla sera il quarto Venerdì / di Quaresima / Nella Reale, ed Imperiale Congregazione / DEL SS^{MO}. ENTIERRO / IN S. FEDELE. / Musica del Sig. Gio. Battista S. Martino Maestro / di Capella del Santissimo Entierro. / IN MILANO, MDCCXXIX. / Nella Stampa degli Eredi di Domenico Bellagatta. / Con licenza de' Superiori. MILB TT. IV. 79/7.
Literature	SartoriG, p. 10.

C-33 MARIA ADDOLORATA

Text	Author unknown.
Performed	San Fedele, Milan, 8 April 1729.
Libretto	MARIA ADDOLORATA / Abandona il Calvario, rivede il Getsemani, / comincia la / SOLITUDINE / DICENDO / CANTATA QUINTA / Da recitarsi alla sera il quinto Venerdì / di Quaresima / Nella Reale, ed Imperiale Congregazione / DEL SS^{MO}. ENTIERRO / IN S. FE-DELE. / Musica del Sig. Gio. Battista S. Martino Maestro / di Capella del Santissimo Entierro. / IN MILANO,

MDCCXXIX. / Nella Stampa degli Eredi di Domenico Bellagatta. / Con licenza de' Superiori. MILB TT. IV. 79/8.

Literature   SartoriG, p. 10.

C-34 L'ARCA NEL DILUVIO

Text   Author unknown.

Performed   San Fedele, Milan, 3 March 1730.

Libretto   L'ARCA NEL DILUVIO / L'Anima di GESÙ negli' Af-/ fanni dell' Horto. / CANTATA PRIMA / Da recitarsi alla sera il primo Venerdì / di Quaresima / Nella Reale, ed Imperiale Congregazione / DEL SS^{MO}. ENTIERRO / IN S. FEDELE. / Musica del Sig. Gio. Battista S. Martino Maestro / di Capella del Santissimo Entierro. / IN MI-LANO, MDCCXXX. / Nella Stamperìa degli Eredi di Domenico Bellagatta. / Con licenza de' Superiori. MILB VV. I. 44/34.

Literature   SartoriG, p. 10.

C-35 MATATIA, E SIMONE

Text   Domenico Balestreri.

Performed   S. Dalmazio, Milan, 7 February 1742.

Cast   Matatia
          Simone

Libretto   MATATIA, E SIMONE / CANTATE / PER INTER-MEDIO / ALLA DISPUTA GENERALE DELLA DOT-TRINA CRISTIANA / TENUTA / IN S. DALMAZIO / DAL SIG. GIUSEPPE BERSANI / DELLA SCUOLA DE' GIOVANI / DI S. MARIA DI CARUGATE / Il Giorno 7. febbrajo 1742. / Sotto gli Eccelsi Auspicj / DELL' EM^{MO}., E REV^{MO}. SIG. CARDINALE / CARLO GAE-TANO / STAMPA / ARCIVESCOVO DI MILANO. / Poesia / DEL SIG. DOMENICO BALESTRERI. / Musica / DEL SIG. GIO. BATTISTA SAN MARTINO / Maestro di Cappella dell' Insigne Imperiale Basilica di S. Ambrogio &c. / IN MILANO, Per Pietro Antonio Frigerio, Allievo del Gagliardi, e Nava. / Con licenza de' Superiori. MILA S. I. G. IV 7.

Remarks This work consists of three cantatas. This is the first group of cantatas giving a list of characters.

C-36 CRISTO COI DISCEPOLI

Text Guido Riviera.

Performed San Fedele, Milan, 8 March 1743.

Cast Cristo
Pietro
Angiolo
Coro d'Angioli

Libretto Cristo coi Discepoli nell' Orto / Agonizzante, conforta-to / dall' Angiolo. / CANTATA PRIMA / Da recitarsi alla sera del primo Venerdì di Quaresima / NELLA REALE CONGREGAZIONE / DEL SS^{MO}. ENTIERRO / IN S. / FEDELE. / Musica del Sig. GIO. BATTISTA SAN MAR-TINO / Maestro di Capella della suddetta Reale Congre-gazione. / IN MILANO)(MDCCXLIII. / Nella Stamperìa di Pietro Francesco Malatesta. / Con licenza de' Superiori. MILA S. I. G. V 20.

Remarks This libretto is one of a set of five with the covering title page LA PASSIONE / DI GESÙ CRISTO / E I DOLORI / DELLA VERGINE MADRE / IN CINQUE CANTATE / DEL SIG. DOTT. GUIDO RIVIERA. Only the librettos for the first, second, and third Fridays in Lent for the year 1743 are extant. We are grateful to Dottoressa Mariangela Donà for providing this information. See also App. C 37 and 38. These cantatas were repeated for the first three Fridays in Lent in the year 1773. See App. C 53-55.

C-37 CRISTO NELL' ORTO

Text Guido Riviera.

Performed San Fedele, Milan, 15 March 1743.

Cast Cristo
Pietro
Giuda coi Farisei
Coro dei Discepoli

Libretto Cristo nell' Orto Tradito / da Guida. / CANTATA SE-CONDA / Da recitarsi alla sera del secondo Venerdì / di

Quaresima / NELLA REALE CONGREGAZIONE / DEL SS^MO. ENTIERRO / IN S. FEDELE. / Musica del Sig. GIO. BATTISTA SAN MARTINO / Maestro di Capella della suddetta Reale Congregazione. IN MILANO)(MDCCXLIII. / Nella Stamperìa di Pietro Francesco Malatesta. / Con licenza de' Superiori. MILA S. I. G. V 20.

C-38   CRISTO GIUDICATO

Text   Guido Riviera.

Performed   San Fedele, Milan, 22 March 1743.

Cast   Cristo
            Ponzio Pilato Presidente della Guidea
            Claudia Procula sua Moglie
            Coro dei Giudei

Libretto   Cristo giudicato nel Pretorio / di Pilato. / CANTATA TERZA / Da recitarsi alla sera del terzo Venerdì / di Quaresima / NELLA REALE CONGREGAZIONE / DEL SS^MO. ENTIERRO / IN S. FEDELE. / Musica del Sig. GIO. BATTISTA SAN MARTINO / Maestro di Capella della suddetta Reale Congregazione. / IN MILANO)(MDCCXLIII. / Nella Stamperìa di Pietro Francesco Malatesta. / Con licenza de' Superiori. MILA S. I. G. V 20.

C-39   IL PERDONO DI DAVIDDE

Text   Author unknown.

Performed   S. Dalmazio, Milan, 7 February 1744.

Cast   Saulle
            Davidde

Libretto   IL PERDONO DI DAVIDDE. / CANTATE / PER INTERMEDIO / ALLA DISPUTA GENERALE / DELLA DOTTRINA CRISTIANA / TENUTA / IN SAN DALMAZIO / DAL CHIERICO SIG. ANTONIO CIPRIOTTO / DELLA SCUOLA DE' GIOVANI / DI SAN ROCCO / IN PORTA VERCELLINA / Il Giorno 7. Febbrajo 1744 / Poesia / DI UN ACCADEMICO AFFIDATO / Musica / DEL SIG. GIAMBATTISTA SANMARTINO / Maestro di Cappella dell' Insigne Imperiale Basilica di Sant'Ambrogio ec. / IN MILANO, Per Pietro Antonio Frigerio, Allievo del

Gagliardi, e Nava. / Con licenza de' Superiori. MILA S. I. G. IV 7.

Remarks   This work consists of three cantatas.

C-40 LE PAROLE DI GESÙ CROCIFISSO

Text   Author unknown.

Performed   San Fedele, Milan, 6 March 1744.

Cast   Gesù Cristo
San Disma
Gesma
Coro d'Angeli

Libretto   Le Parole di Gesù Crocifisso. / CANTATA SECONDA / Da recitarsi alla sera del secondo Venerdì / di Quaresima / NELLA REALE CONGREGAZIONE / DEL SS^{MO}. EN-TIERRO / IN S. FEDELE. / Musica del Sig. GIO. BATTISTA SAN MARTINO / Maestro di Capella della suddetta Reale Congregazione. / IN MILANO)(MDCCXLIV. / Nella Stamperìa di Pietro Francesco Malatesta. / Con licenza de' Superiori. MILB ZCC. V. 30/11.

C-41 LE PAROLE DI GESÙ CROCIFISSO

Text   Author unknown.

Performed   San Fedele, Milan, 27 March 1744.

Cast   Maria Vergine
S. Giovanni Evangelista
S. Maria Maddalena
Coro d'Angeli

Libretto   Le Parole di Gesù Crocifisso. / CANTATA QUINTA / Da recitarsi alla sera del quinto Venerdì / di Quaresima / NELLA REALE CONGREGAZIONE / DEL SS^{MO}. EN-TIERRO / IN S. FEDELE. / Musica del Sig. GIO. BATTISTA SAN MARTINO / Maestro di Capella della suddetta Reale Congregazione. / IN MILANO)(MDCCXLIV. / Nella Stamperìa di Pietro Francesco Malatesta. / Con licenza de' Superiori. MILB ZCC. V. 30/12.

C-42 LA GUERRA, E LA PACE

Text   Domenico Balestreri.

Performed   San Dalmazio, Milan, 7 February 1749.

Cast   La Guerra
La Pace

Libretto   LA GUERRA, E LA PACE. / CANTATE / PER INTRA-MEZZO / ALLA DISPUTA GENERALE / DELLA DOT-TRINA CRISTIANA, / CHE TIENE / IN SAN DALMA-ZIO / IL CHERICO SIG. AMBROGIO TREZZI / DELLA SCUOLA DE' GIOVANI / DI S. BERNARDINO IN P. TOSA / Nel Giorno 7 Febbrajo 1749. / Sotto gli Eccelsi Auspizj / . DELL' EM^{MO}., E REV^{MO}. SIG. CAR-DINALE / GIUSEPPE POZZOBONELLI / ARCIVES-COVO DI MILANO. / IN MILANO, Per Pietro Antonio Frigerio, Allievo del Gagliardi, e Nava; / Stampatore della Congregazione Generale della Dottrina Cristiana. / Con licenza de' Superiori. MILB XM. IV. 15/4.

Remarks   From the libretto we learn that the text was by Domenico Balestreri and the music by Giambattista Sammartino, "Maestro di Cappella dell' Insigne Imperiale Basilica di S. Ambrogio ec." The libretto contains three cantatas: the first entitled *La Guerra,* the second *La Pace,* and the third *La Guerra, e la Pace.*

C-43   DELLA PASSIONE DI N. S. GESÙ CRISTO

Text   Author unknown.

Performed   San Fedele, Milan, 9 March 1757.

Cast   Gesù
Angelo di Giustizia,
Angelo di Clemenza.
Coro d'Angeli

Libretto   Della Passione / DI N. S. GESÙ CRISTO / CANTATA / Per il Primo Venerdì di Quaresima / NELLA REALE IMPERIALE / CONGREGAZIONE / DEL SS^{MO}. EN-TIERRO / IN S. FEDELE. / MUSICA / Del Sig. Gio. Battista San-martino Maestro di Capella / di essa Con-gregazione. At end of libretto text: In Milano, per il Mazzucchelli successore del Malatesta. 1757. / Con licen-za de' Superiori. GENF XXIX C 266.

C-44   IL PIANTO DI EVA SUL MORTO ABELE

Text   Author unknown.

Performed	San Fedele, Milan, 1 April 1757.
Cast	Eva Adamo Angelo Coro
Libretto	Il Pianto di Eva / sul morto / Abele. / CANTATA / Per il Quinto Venerdì di Quaresima / NELLA REALE IMPE-RIALE/CONGREGAZIONE/DEL SS^{MO}. ENTIERRO / IN S. FEDELE / MUSICA / Del Sig. Gio. Battista Sanmartino Maestro di Capella / di essa Congregazione. At end of libretto text: In Milano, per il Mazzucchelli successore del Malatesta. 1757. / Con licenza de' Superiori. GENF XXIX C 266.

C-45 S. MARIA MADDALENA

Text	Author unknown.
Performed	San Fedele, Milan, 17 February 1758.
Cast	S. Maria Maddalena Giuda Iscariote Angelo Coro di Figlie di Sion
Libretto	S. Maria Maddalena / RAPPRESENTANTE / L'Anima divotissima verso / N. S. Gesù Cristo nella / sua SS. Passione / CANTATA / Per il primo Venerdì della Quaresima / NELLA CONGREGAZIONE / IMPERIALE REGIA / DEL SS^{MO}. ENTIERRO IN S. FEDELE. / La composizione della Musica è del Sig. Giambattista / Sammartino Maestro della R. Imp. Capella / di essa Congregazione. / In Milano, Nella Stamperìa di Giuseppe Mazzucchelli.)(1758. / Con licenza de' Superiori. MOD 70. I. 1/2.
Literature	SartoriG, p. 10.

C-46 SOPRA LA MORTE SANTISSIMA

Text	Author unknown.
Performed	San Fedele, Milan, 10 March 1758.

Cast	Angelo della Divina Giustizia Angelo della Divina Clemenza S. Maria Maddalena Coro d'Angeli
Libretto	Per il quarto Venerdì della Quaresima / SOPRA / LA MORTE SANTISSIMA / DI N. S. GESÙ IN CROCE / S. Maria Maddalena / in vista del Monte Calvario, / CANTA-TA / Da Recitarsi / NELLA CONGREGAZIONE / IM-PERIALE REGIA / DEL SS^{MO}. ENTIERRO / IN S. FEDELE. / La composizione della Musica è del Sig. Giambattista / Sammartino Maestro della R. Imp. Capella / di essa Congregazione. / In Milano. Nella Stamperìa di Giuseppe Mazzucchelli.)(1758. / Con licenza de' Superiori. MOD 70. I. 3/3.
Literature	SartoriG, p. 10.

C-47   LE FIGLIE DI SION

Text	Author unknown.
Performed	San Fedele, Milan, 17 March 1758.
Cast	La Prima La Seconda La Terza Coro
Libretto	Le Figlie di Sion / AL SEPOLCRO / DI GESÙ CRISTO / REDENTORE, / COMPONIMENTO / Per il quinto Venerdì di Quaresima / NELLA IMPERIALE REGIA / CONGREGAZIONE / DEL SS^{MO}. ENTIERRO / IN S. FEDELE. / La composizione della Musica è del Sig. Giambattista / Sammartino Maestro della R. Imp. Capella / di essa Congregazione. / In Milano. Nella Stamperìa di Giuseppe Mazzucchelli.)(1758. / Con licenza de' Superiori. MOD 70. I. 15/15.
Literature	SartoriG, p. 11.

C-48   LE INGIURIE DA GESÙ CRISTO, UOMO-DIO

Text	Author unknown.
Performed	San Fedele, Milan, 16 March 1759.

Cast　　　　　Maria Maddalena
　　　　　　　Maria Salome
　　　　　　　Marie Cleofe
　　　　　　　Coro delle Marie

Libretto　　　LE INGIURIE / DA GESÙ CRISTO, UOMO-DIO / Nella sua SS. Passione tollerate, / DIALOGO PER MUSICA / DA RECITARSI / La sera del secondo Venerdì di Quaresima / NELLA REGIA, ED IMPERIALE / CONGREGAZIONE / DEL / SS^{MO}. ENTIERRO / IN S. FEDELE. / La composizione della Musica è del Sig. Giambattista / Sammartino Maestro della R. Imp. Capella / di essa Congregazione. / IN MILANO MDCCLIX. / Nella Stamperìa di Giuseppe Mazzucchelli Successore Malatesta. / Con licenza de' Superiori. GENF XXIX C 266.

C-49　LA PERFIDIA GIUDAICA

Text　　　　　Author unknown.

Performed　　San Fedele, Milan, 23 March 1759.

Cast　　　　　S. Giovanni
　　　　　　　S. Pietro
　　　　　　　S. M. Maddalena
　　　　　　　Coro

Libretto　　　LA PERFIDIA GIUDAICA / Nella SS. Passione / DI GESÙ CRISTO, / DIALOGO PER MUSICA / DA RECITARSI / La sera del terzo Venerdì di Quaresima / NELLA REGIA, ED IMPERIALE / CONGREGAZIONE / DEL / SS^{MO}. ENTIERRO / IN S. FEDELE. / La composizione della Musica è del Sig. Giambattista / Sammartino Maestro della R. Imp. Capella / di essa Congregazione. / IN MILANO MDCCLIX. / Nella Stamperìa di Giuseppe Mazzucchelli Successore Malatesta. / Con licenza de' Superiori. GENF XXIX C 266.

C-50　STABAT MATER DOLOROSA

Performed　　San Fedele, Milan, 2 April 1762.

Libretto　　　STABAT MATER / DOLOROSA / DA CANTARSI / LA SERA DEL QUINTO VENERDÌ / DI QUARESIMA / NELLA REALE IMPERIALE / CONGREGAZIONE / DEL SS^{MO}. ENTIERRO / Maestro di Capella Sig. Giam-

battista San Martino. On the last page of the libretto: In
MILANO, per il Mazzuchelli, Successore Malatesta. 1762.
/ Con licenza de' Superiori. GENF XXIX C 266.

C-51   LA INVIDIA GIUDAICA

Text	Author unknown.
Performed	San Fedele, Milan, 11 March 1763.
Cast	Abele
	Adamo
	Caino
	Coro
Libretto	LA INVIDIA GIUDAICA / CONTRO / NOSTRO SI-GNOR / GESÙ CRISTO / In quella di Caino adombrata. / Aug. L. I. Doct. Chr. / DIALOGO PER MUSICA / Da recitarsi la sera del terzo Venerdì di Quaresima / NELLA REALE IMPERIALE / CONGREGAZIONE / DEL SS^{MO}. ENTIERRO / ERETTA IN S. FEDELE. / Maestro di Capella il Sig. Giambattista Sammartini. / IN MILANO)(MDCCLXIII / Nella Stamperìa di Giuseppe Mazzucchelli, successore Malatesta. / Con licenza de' Superiori. MILB VV. I. 44/36.
Literature	SartoriG, p. 11.

C-52   DELLA PASSIONE DI GESÙ CRISTO

Text	Author unknown.
Performed	San Fedele, Milan, 13 March 1767.
Cast	Maria Santissima
	S. Pietro
	S. Giovanni
	Coro
Libretto	DELLA PASSIONE / DI GESÙ CRISTO / SIGNOR NOSTRO / CANTATA / Nel primo Venerdì della Quaresima / PER LA REALE IMPERIALE / CONGREGAZIONE / DEL / SS^{MO}. ENTIERRO / IN S. FEDELE. / Musica del Sig. Giambattista San Martino, Maestro / di Capella di essa Imperiale Regia Congregazione. / IN MILANO)(MDCCLXVII. / Per il Mazzucchelli nella Stamperìa Malatesta / Con licenza de' Superiori. MILB VV. I. 44/35.

Remarks	There is another libretto of the same title but not the same text in MILB VV. I. 44/38, dated 1770, but with music by Giovanni Andrea Fioroni. The Fioroni cantata was composed for the congregation of Ss.mo Entierro, performed in San Fedele, and presumably conducted by Sammartini, who is mentioned in the libretto as *maestro di cappella* of the congregation.
Literature	SartoriG, p. 11.

C-53 CRISTO COI DISCEPOLI

Text	Guido Riviera.
Performed	San Fedele, Milan, 5 March 1773.
Cast	Cristo Pietro Angelo Coro d'Angeli
Libretto	CRISTO COI DISCEPOLI / NELL' ORTO AGONIZ-ZANTE / CONFORTATO DALL' ANGELO / CANTATA PRIMA / Da recitarsi alla sera del primo Venerdì di Quaresima / NELLA REALE IMPERIALE / CONGREG-AZIONE / DEL SS^{MO}. ENTIERRO / IN S. FEDELE. / La Musica è del Sig. Giambattista Sammartino Maestro / di Capella di S. A. R., e della suddetta / Congregazione. / IN MILANO. MDCCLXXIII. / Per Giuseppe Mazzuchelli nella Stamperia Malatesta. / Con licenza de' Superiori. MILB 25. 4. H. 3/19.
Remarks	The cantatas App. C 53-55 appear also for the year 1743. See App. C 36-38.

C-54 CRISTO NELL' ORTO

Text	Guido Riviera.
Performed	San Fedele, Milan, 12 March 1773.
Cast	Cristo Pietro Giuda con le Turbe Coro di Discepoli

Libretto   CRISTO NELL' ORTO / TRADITO DA GIUDA / CAN-
TATA SECONDA / Da recitarsi alla sera del secondo
Venerdì di Quaresima / NELLA REALE IMPERIALE /
CONGREGAZIONE / DEL SS^{MO}. ENTIERRO / IN S.
FEDELE. / La Musica è del Sig. Giambattista Sammartino
Maestro / di Capella di S. A. R., e della suddetta / Con-
gregazione. / IN MILANO, MDCCLXXIII. / Per Giuseppe
Mazzucchelli nella Stamperia Malatesta. / Con licenza de'
Superiori. MILB 25. 4. H. 3/20.

C-55   CRISTO GIUDICATO

Text   Guido Riviera.

Performed   San Fedele, Milan, 19 March 1773.

Cast   Cristo
Ponzio Pilato
Claudia Procula
Coro de' Giudei

Libretto   CRISTO / GIUDICATO NEL PRETORIO / DI PILATO /
CANTATA TERZA / Da recitarsi alla sera del terzo
Venerdì di Quaresima / NELLA REALE IMPERIALE /
CONGREGAZIONE / DEL SS^{MO}. ENTIERRO / IN S.
FEDELE. / La Musica è del Sig. Giambattista Sammartino
Maestro / di Capella di S. A. R., e della suddetta / Con-
gregazione. / IN MILANO, MDCCLXXIII. / Per Giuseppe
Mazzucchelli nella Stamperia Malatesta. / Con licenza de'
Superiori. MILB 25. 4. H. 3/18.

C-56   CRISTO COLLA CROCE

Text   Author unknown.

Performed   San Fedele, Milan, 26 March 1773.

Cast   Cristo
Maria Vergine Sua Madre
Simone Cireneo
Coro delle Donne

Libretto   CRISTO / COLLA CROCE SUL CAMMINO / DEL CAL-
VARIO / CANTATA QUARTA / Da recitarsi alla sera
del quarto Venerdì di Quaresima / NELLA REALE

IMPERIALE / CONGREGAZIONE / DEL SS^{MO}. EN-
TIERRO / IN S. FEDELE. / La Musica è del Sig. Giambat-
tista Sammartino Maestro / di Capella di S. A. R., e della
suddetta / Congregazione. / IN MILANO. MDCCLXXIII. /
Per Giuseppe Mazzucchelli nella Stamperia Malatesta. /
Con licenza de' Superiori. MILB 35. 4. H. 3/21.

ADDENDA

LISTINGS IN PUBLISHERS' CATALOGUES

C-7.1   I. Walsh, London: Six Overtures by Sig^r. St. Martini,
Galuppi, Jomelli [Second Collection], c. 1760 (cited in
Smith and HumphriesB, No. 1153).

C-9.1   J. P. LeClerc l'ainé, Paris: heading "Violons concerto,"
Martini, prix 2 liv. 8 s., c. 1742-1751, Paris, Bibliothèque
Mazarine (cited in DevriesE).

APPENDIX D

DOUBTFUL AND SPURIOUS WORKS

SYMPHONIES

C MAJOR

D-1

2 hn, 2 vn, va, b

Sammartini   PRA Waldst. XXXIV C 321, Overteur, St. Martino.

D-2

2 vn, va, b

Sammartini   PRA Waldst. XXXIV C 325, Overteur, Martini.

Possible
Author

Count Giorgio Giulini (1716-1780; Milanese dilettante
composer and Sammartini's pupil; author of numerous
symphonies; see CesariG): Br. 62, Sinfonia No. 4 (2 ob).
The Giulini incipit differs slightly from PRA as shown in
small notes.

D-3

2 vn, va, b

Sammartini	Br. 62, Racc. I/4, Sinfonia, Martino; PRA Waldst. XXXIV C 330, Overteur, St. Martino; another copy Waldst. XXXIV C 329.
Possible Author	Antonio Martinelli. Print: Paris, Chinzer: SIX / SIMPHONIES / En quatre Parties . . .; Sinfonia IV; PBN Vm^7. 1504.

D-4

[2 fl] , 2 vn, b

Sammartini	PC F. Bl. Op. III/126, Concertino, St. Martino (2 fl not indicated in title).
Possible Author	Frederici (probably either Baldassare or Francesco Federici, oboists in the orchestra of the Regio Ducal Teatro in Milan in 1748; see CesariG, p. 21): PC F. Bl. Op. I/4, Overtura (in G, without 2 fl).

D-5

2 vn, va, b

Sammartini	Br. 66, Racc. IV/2, Sinfonia, Martino (2 vn, b).
Probable Author	Anton Solnitz (c. 1708-1758; composer of symphonies and chamber music in Leiden): Sig. cat., Sinfonia; STOCK, Sinfonia (source of incipits); BAS Saras. 5, Trio; LUND Eng. 225, Sinfonia. Also ascribed to Pietro Locatelli in LUND Wens. Litt. C 9, Sinfonia; and Anon. in AMS, as a Concerto *a 4*, conducted by Vivaldi in Amsterdam on 7 January 1738 (see PincherleA, II, Addenda P. 446). For details of the performance and the title of the collection containing the symphony, see No. 65.

D MAJOR

D-6

2 ob, 2 tr, 2 tr da c (replaced by 2 hn in III), 2 vn, va, b

Sammartini	Br. 62, Racc. I/6, Sinfonia, Martino (str only).
Correct Author	Giovanni Battista Pergolesi: Overture to the oratorio *S. Guglielmo Duca d'Aquitania*, 1731 (2 ob, 2 hn, 2 tr); also the overture to his operas *Adriano in Siria*, 1734

(mvts. I and III only), and *L'Olimpiade,* 1735; ascribed to Pergolesi in Br. 66, Sinfonia (2 hn). The incipits come from the score of *L'Olimpiade* in WLC, where the overture is entitled *Introduzzione.*

D-7

2 fl, 2 ob, 2 hn, 2 tr, 2 vn, va, b

Sammartini	REG 3, Sinfonia, St. Martino.
Probable Author	Francis Xaver Pokorny (1728-1794; violinist and composer at REG). The style and four-movement cycle are thoroughly uncharacteristic of Sammartini. Pokorny copied the oboe and trumpet parts, and composed two other symphonies ascribed to Sammartini in REG (see App. D 21 and 54). Pokorny's symphonies also feature virtuoso horn parts of the type found in the trio of the minuet in this work. For a discussion of the numerous conflicting attributions in REG involving Pokorny, see BarbourP and LaRueM, pp. 188-196.

D-8

2 vn, b

| Sammartini | GEN N. 1. 6. 6 (Sc. 17), Overtur, S. Martino. |
| Remarks | The MS is copied in two hands, the second of which is Hand B. |

D-9
2 vn, va, b

| Sammartini | STOCK VO-R, Concerto, St. Martino (eighteenth-century score and pts.). |
| Remarks | This work is included in a group of four violin concertos ascribed to Sammartini (see No. 77 and App. D 76 and 80), despite its symphonic style and form. The score is copied in a different hand from the parts, which are attributed to "San Martini." Solo and tutti indications appear only in the score, where they are written in still another hand below the first violin and occasionally the second violin parts. The only soloistic passage occurs for 4½ measures in the second movement. The symphony was collected by Pehr Frigel (see No. 57). |

D-10
2 ob, 2 hn, 2 vn, va, b

Sammartini   GEN S.S.A. 1. 22 (G.8) (2 ob pts. missing), Sinfonia, Martini Gioabbo.

D-11

2 tr, 2 vn, va, b

Sammartini   Egk cat. No. 86, 1760, Sinfonia, S. Martino.

Correct   Melchiorre Chiesa (died c. 1783; Milanese composer of
Author   instrumental music and perhaps Sammartini's pupil):
               Lam. cat. 1768; MILC Fondo Noseda D 69-7, Overteur
               (source of incipits); STOCK, Sinfonia.

Remarks   The STOCK copy belonged to the literary society Utile
               Dulci.

D-12

2 vn, b

Sammartini   MÜNS, Sonata, Martino (3 vn, b).

Possible Author	Sommariva: PC F. Bl. Op. III/127, Sonata.
Print	Anon. Paris, Estien, 1747 (for the title and sources see No. 64); Sinfonia III.
Remarks	The third violin in MÜNS appears to be an added filler part. In the Fonds Blancheton and Estien print, the meter of the second movement is 12/8.

D-13

2 hn, 2 vn, va, b

III missing

Sammartini	GEN N.1.6.6. (Sc. 17), Avertura, San Martino.
Possible Author	? (1) Etienne Mangean: AGEN Fonds d'Aiguillon, Série II, No. 157 (va, 2 hn pts. missing); (2) Giuseppe Paladino: PRA Waldst. XXXIV B 241, Gloria Con Sinfonia (first mvt. of the symphony only; see *Remarks* below).
Remarks	The original finale of this symphony is lost. In GEN No. 13/I appears as the third movement, despite its first-movement style and later idiom. The title page bears the initials F. R., and the MS is probably north Italian.

The AGEN MS has no title page. Etienne Mangean (c. 1710–c. 1756), a well-known violinist active in Paris, copied and signed the parts in a clear attempt at plagiarism. He probably composed only the minuet (see the incipit below) that concludes the symphony.

The style of this symphony has little in common with Mangean's five trio symphonies in AGEN, which are small-scaled and conservative in idiom. Since Mangean may have been in the service of the Duc d'Aiguillon, as indicated by the presence of his symphonies in AGEN, he may have copied the music from a MS once in d'Aiguillon's collection and now lost. The date of Mangean's death establishes a *terminus ad quem* for the symphony.

An altered and extremely condensed version of the first movement appears as the opening sinfonia of a *Gloria* by Giuseppe Paladino (died c. 1760), a Milanese contemporary of Sammartini. The *Gloria* is scored for solo voices, chorus, 2 oboes, 2 *trombe da caccia*, strings, and organ (most of the vocal bass part is missing, as are the second violin, viola, and instrumental bass parts). The MS is Milanese. Paladino also derives the orchestra part of the first *Gloria* section from the first movement, and he includes ideas omitted from the sinfonia.

The symphony has many doubtful features, though the movements show considerable formal ingenuity. As in App. D 45, there is an unconvincing mixture of early and later style characteristics. The early features include a baroque-influenced idiom, with a concerto-like episode for the horns, and a unison arrangement of the violins throughout the second movement (found only in Sammartini's early symphonies Nos. 67 and 68). Later elements in the first movement include the scoring with horns, which first appears in Sammartini's middle period symphonies, the broader dimensions, the more specialized thematic functions, and the triad-stratified opening phrase, which recurs only in a late Sammartini symphony (No. 26). Some additional uncharacteristic details are the form of the primary theme, which modulates to the dominant key and then returns to the tonic for the horn solo; awkward melodic and harmonic tritones in the cadential and development sections; and imitation between the viola and bass. Even the tonic minor key relation of the second movement does not reflect Sammartini's usual choice in his D-major symphonies (only one further example exists in a late middle period work, No. 16). Sammartini prefers instead the relative minor in the early symphonies and the subdominant or dominant relation in the later symphonies. Also suspect in the slow movement are the many direct octaves between the viola or bass and the violins, and the harsh dissonance in m 6.

It would thus seem more likely that Paladino composed these movements rather than Sammartini. Yet the *Gloria* overture departs from the symphonic movement in several details, and is crudely written. The authorship of this work must therefore remain uncertain at the present time.

Literature   BrookS, II, 456-462.

D-14
2 vn, va, b

Sammartini   Br. 62, Racc. I/1, Sinfonia, Martino.

Possible   ? (1) G. B. Pergolesi: PRA Waldst. XXXIV B 237, Sym-
Author   phonia; (2) Anon.: SCHW, Synphonia (source of incipits).

D-15
2 vn, va, b

Sammartini   PC F. Bl. Op. III/147, Sinfonia, St. Martini.

Possible   Antonio Brioschi: Br. 62, Sonata 4 (2 vn, b). Brioschi
Author   (active c. 1730-c. 1750) was one of the earliest sympho-
nists and a north Italian contemporary of Sammartini. A composer of numerous symphonies and sonatas, his music was confused with Sammartini's early works more often than that of any other composer. His style resembles Sammartini's, but is more contrapuntal and repetitious.

D-16

2 vn, va, b

Sammartini   PRA Waldst. XXXIV C 327, Overteur, St. Martino.

Remarks   The fourth movement is not separate but inserted in the recapitulation of the third movement.

D-17

2 hn, 2 vn, va, b

Sammartini   Print (see below).

Probable   Melchiorre Chiesa (see App. D 11): BAS Saras. 10, Over-
Author   tura; PRA Waldst. XXXIV C 168, Overtura teatrali. Also
              ascribed to G. B. Lampugnani (1706-1784; Milanese com-
              poser of operas and instrumental music): Brtnice cat.,
              c. 1752-1769, Sinfonia.

Print   Ascribed to Sammartini. London, Simpson, c. 1747 (for title and sources, see No. 10); Op. II/3.

D-18
2 hn, 2 vn, va, b

Sammartini   PRA Waldst. XXXIV C 323, Overtura, St. Martino.

D-19
2 ob, 2 hn, 2 vn, va, b

Sammartini   SCHW 3559, Concerto, Martini.

Probable Author   Andrea Bernasconi (1706-1784; opera composer, born in Milan, active in Venice and Munich): Br. 62, Racc. I/6, Sinfonia; DRES Mus. 3017/N 12 (eighteenth-century score and pts.); GEN SS.B.110, Sinfonia; PC F. Bl. Op. VI/280, Sinfonia (2 hn). Also ascribed to Lampugnani as the overture to his opera *Fredegunda,* WOLF.

Remarks   In SCHW, the ascription on the title page is crossed out, and the parts are entitled "Ouvertur," not concerto. The DRES score is dated 1739.

D-20

2 hn, 2 vn, va, b

Sammartini   DONAU Mus. Ms. 1715, Sinfonia, Son [sic] Martino.

D-21

2 fl, 2 ob, 2 cl, 2 hn, 2 tr, timp, 2 vn, va, b

Sammartini   REG 4, Sinfonia, Martino.

Correct   F. X. Pokorny (see App. D 7): I from REG Pokorny 45;
Author   III from REG Pokorny 182; II probably by Pokorny
though no source has been found. The flute, trumpet,
and timpani parts were also copied by Pokorny.

D-22

2 vn, va, b

Sammartini	Lam. cat. 1768, Parthia, Battar; WLC M 1004.S2S5 Case, Sinfonia, S. Martino (2 vn, b); LAM, Parthia, Battar.
Possible Author	? Also ascribed to Pergolesi in Lam. cat. 1768, with the title Parthia.
Remarks	On the LAM title page: "A:A: / sub P. Antonio." The reference is to Pater Anton Kaserer (1719-1759), choir director (Regens Chori) of the monastery. In LAM, the first and second movements are several measures shorter than in WLC, ending on the dominant rather than the tonic. The tempo mark of the third movement comes from LAM.

D-23
2 hn, 2 vn, va, b

Sammartini	STOCK Alstr., Sinfonia, Martini.
Possible Author	Leopold Hofmann (1738-1793): COP Sammlung L, Sinfonia 29 (2 ob, 2 hn); PRA Waldst. XXXIV B 323, Sinfonia. Also attributed to Carlos d'Ordoñez (1734-1786): Br. 67, Racc. II/6 (2 ob, 2 hn).

E-FLAT MAJOR

D-24

2 vn, va, b

Sammartini	BER 19397/2, Sonate, San Martini (2 vn, b); UPP instr. i hs. 55:5, Sonata, Martini (2 vn, b; source of incipits).
Probable Author	Antonio Brioschi (see App. D 15): DARM Mus 121/7, Sinfonia; STOCK, Sinphonie; another copy, Sinphonia (fl, vn, va, vc or cemb; in G major).
Print	Ascribed to Sammartini. London, Simpson, 3 July 1744 (Gen. Adv.): SIX / SONATAS / for two / Violins and a Thorough Bass / Compos'd by / Sig^r. Gio: Battista S^t: Martini / Principal Composer in Milan / Opera Prima / LONDON / Printed for and sold by John Simpson at the Bass Viol and Flute in Sweeting's Alley / opposite the East Door of the Royal Exchange; Sonata III. A copy without opus number is in LBM. Copies with opus number, dated c. 1745 by the *British Union-Catalogue*, are in BERK, BRUS, DRES, VENM, WLC, and other sources.
Remarks	In BER the ascription "Giov. Batt. San" was added in a later hand. The DARM MS was copied by J. S. Endler (see App. C 3). The STOCK Brioschi copy in E-flat belonged to the literary society Utile Dulci. In UPP, the sonata is No. 24 of a collection of 40 trio sonatas ascribed to Sammartini, the first violin part dated 1772 (see also No. 64).
Mod. ed.	Ascribed to Sammartini. Hugo Riemann, ed. "Collegium Musicum" No. 28 (Leipzig: Breitkopf & Härtel, 1906).

D-25

2 vn, b

Sammartini	PC D.11.181, Overtura, Martino (2 vn, vc).
Probable Author	Antonio Brioschi (see App. D 15): Br. 62, Racc. III/6, Sinfonia (2 vn, va, b); PC F. Bl. Op. II/65, Concertino.
Prints	1) Attributed to G. Sammartini. Paris, Le Clerc, 1742 (for the title and sources see No. 33); Op. II/10.
	2) Anon. London (movement III only). *Flores Musicae* (same title as *2d. Sett;* see No. 33); Sonatina 5/II; NYPL (vn I only).
Remarks	The first movement incipit of the Le Clerc print differs slightly from the other sources as shown in small notes.

D-26

2 vn, b

Sammartini	LUND Eng. 129, Simphonia, Martino.
Possible Author	Antonio Brioschi (see App. D 15): LUND Kraus 23, Trio (dated 1749).

D-27

2 vn, b

Sammartini   PRA Waldst. XXXIV C 342, Trio, S. Martino.

D-28

2 vn, b

Sammartini   UPP Instr. mus. i hs. 55:6, Notturno, Martini.

Probable
Author

Antonio Brioschi (see App. D 15): Br. 62, Sonata VII;
LUND Wens. Litt. E 1 Trio; PC D.11.153, Sonata (2 vn,
vc); STOCK 149, Sinfonia (eighteenth-century score and
pts.; source of incipits). Also Anon. in AGEN No. 137.

Print

London, I. Walsh, 2-4 October 1744 (Lon. Ev.-Post):
SIX / SONATAS / FOR TWO / VIOLINS / with a Thor-
ough Bass for the / Harpsicord or Violoncello. / Compos'd
By / Sig^r. GIO. BATISTA LAMPUGNANI / AND / S^t.
MARTINI of Milan. / London. Printed for and Sold by
I. Walsh in Catharine Street, in the Strand. A later edi-
tion, ascribed only to G. B. Lampugnani as his "Opera
Prima," was announced 21-23 February 1745 (Gen. Ev.
Post). Another issue with the Lampugnani-Sammartini
attribution and "Opera Prima" added has been dated

c. 1748. Copies of the various editions and issues in
BRUS, LBM, LOAM, ROCH, UPP, and several other
sources; Sonata V.

Remarks   The STOCK copy belonged to the literary society Utile
Dulci. The UPP copy bears the name of Carl Daniel Burén
(1744-1838; the name is spelled "Bureen" on the MS), a
lawyer in the Supreme Court in Stockholm and probable
owner of the MS. It seems that the Walsh print ascribed
to Lampugnani alone omitted Sammartini's name when
the title page was re-engraved.

E MAJOR

D-29

2 vn, va, b

Sammartini   PRA Waldst. XXXIV B 25, Sinfonia, S. Martino.

F MAJOR

D-30

2 vn, va, b

Sammartini   STOCK, Sinfonia, Martino; another copy, Sinfonia, Martini (eighteenth-century score).

Possible   ? WIL, Sinfonia, Anon.
Author

Remarks   The STOCK score belongs to the Mazer collection.

D-31

2 vn, b

Sammartini   PRA Waldst. XXXIV C 400, Sonata, S. Martino.

Remarks   The first violin part of the minuet contains solo and tutti indications.

D-32

2 vn, va, b

Sammartini   STOCK O-R, Sinfonia, Martini (eighteenth-century score); UPP Instr. mus. i hs. 55:5, Sonata, Martini (2 vn, b).

Remarks   In STOCK the symphony is the eighth work in a MS collection of symphony scores labeled Op. VIII dating from the second half of the eighteenth century. The copy in

UPP is No. 35 of a collection of 40 trio sonatas ascribed to Sammartini, the first violin part dated 1772 (see also No. 64).

D-33
2 hn, 2 vn, va, b

Sammartini	Br. 66, Racc. IV/3, Sinfonia, Martino (1 fl, 2 hn); VGM XIII 23.557, Sinfonia, Martino (1 fl, 2 hn).
Possible Author	Either (1) Ferdinando Galimberti (active c. 1730-c. 1750; Milanese contemporary of Sammartini; violinist and composer): Venier print (see below); or (2) Giorgio Giulini (see App. D 2): BER Mus. ms. 7767/10.
Prints	1) Ascribed to Sammartini. London, Hummel, 1761 (for title and sources, see No. 29); Overture IV.
	2) Ascribed to Galimberti. Paris, Venier, c. 1755 (for the title and source, see No. 61); Op. IV/2.
Remarks	All movements in VGM differ in many details from the Hummel print. The first and third movements are longer, the second movement shorter, and the main themes in the finale return in reverse order.

D-34
2 vn, b

Sammartini	LUND Wens. Litt. Z:8, Sonata, San Martino (eighteenth-century score); UPP Instr. mus. i hs. 55:5, Sonata, Martini (source of incipits).
Possible Author	Giuseppe (?) Vaccari (active in the 1740's): STOCK Alstr., Synphonia.
Remarks	The sonata in UPP is No. 31 of a collection of 40 trio sonatas ascribed to Sammartini, the first violin part dated 1772 (see also No. 64).

D-35

2 vn, va, b

Sammartini	SCHW Mus. 3564, Sonata, St. Martino.

D-36

2 fl, 2 ob, 2 hn, 2 vn, va, b

Sammartini	STOCK Alstr., Overteur, S. Martini (str only).
Probable Author	Johann Adam (1725-1784, composer of ballets and instrumental music in Dresden): Br. 62, Sinfonia I; STOCK (2 fl, 2 hn); WLC M35 R Case; and other sources. Also ascribed to Graun (first name omitted) in MOG 928 (2 fl, 2 hn), and Anon. in BRAT.

D-37
2 hn, 2 vn, va, b

Sammartini	PRA Waldst. XXXIV C 313, Overteur, St. Martino; BERK, Sinfonia, San Martini.
Probable Author	Giorgio Giulini (see App. D 2): PC F. Bl. Op. V/228, Overtura (str only).
Print	Ascribed to Giulini. Paris, Venier, c. 1755: VI / OUVER-TURE / A PIU STROMENTI, / COMPOSTE / da varri / AUTORI, / . . . OPERA SECONDA . . .; Sinfonia V; PC H. 106; STOCK (2 hn, va pts. missing).

D-38
2 hn, 2 vn, va, b

Sammartini	VENL, Sinfonia, S. Martini.
Remarks	This work is listed in the catalogue of the Levi collection under item 62 (*Dono Bianchini,* Tomo VI, no. 3), where it is erroneously ascribed to Padre G. B. Martini. Since the writers were refused a microfilm of this work, authenticity was determined solely by the style of the incipits.

D-39

2 hn, 2 vn, va, b

Sammartini	Print (see below).
Probable Author	Melchiorre Chiesa (see App. D 11): Karl. cat. E, Overteur, Chiesa.
Print	Ascribed to Sammartini. London, Simpson, c. 1747 (for the title and sources, see No. 10); Op. II/1.

D-40

2 vn, b

Sammartini	LUND Kraus 208, Trio, Martini; UPP Instr. mus. i hs. 55:4, Sinfonia, Martini (source of incipits); another copy, Instr. mus. i hs. 55:5, Sonata, Martini.
Possible Author	? STOCK O-R, Sinfonia, Anon. (2 vn, va, b; eighteenth-century score).
Remarks	The LUND MS was copied in 1765. In STOCK the score is No. 5 in a collection of 12 symphony scores labeled Op. IX. The sonata in UPP is No. 34 of a collection of 40 trio sonatas ascribed to Sammartini, the first violin part dated 1772 (see also No. 64).

D-41

2 vn, va, b

Sammartini   PRA Waldst. XXXIV C 326, Overteur, St. Martino.

G MAJOR

D-42

2 vn, va, b

Sammartini   PRA Waldst. XXXIV C 380, Sinfonia, St. Martino.

Possible   Baldassare Galuppi: Br. 62, Racc. I/5, Sinfonia (2 hn).
Author

Remarks   The Galuppi incipit differs slightly from PRA as shown
              in small notes.

D-43

2 hn, 2 vn, va, b

Sammartini   Br. 62, Racc. II/5, Sinfonia, Martino; PRA Waldst. XXXIV
C 385, title unavailable (hn II, va pts. missing); another
copy XXXIV C 320, Overteur, St. Martino.

Remarks   While the symphony has Milanese traits, it contains a
primitive slow movement, with frequent two-part texture
(violins in unison, viola and bass in octaves), and simple
phrase repetitions. It does not seem likely that Sammartini could have composed this movement since his
slow movements are normally so finely made. Besides
some examples of parallel fifths and octaves in the first
and second movements, the symphony has simpler harmonies, often in root position, and more exact recapitulations than the authentic symphonies of Sammartini in
the middle period, which this symphony resembles. It is
also doubtful that Sammartini composed the simple horn
parts in this work, which produce some uncharacteristic
harmonic clashes in the minuet.

D-44
2 hn, 2 vn, va, b

Sammartini   PRA Waldst. XXXIV C 310, Overtura, S. Martini (2 hn,
va pts. missing).

D-45

2 vn, va, b

Sammartini	Karl. cat. E, Overteur, Martino; MELK V/1427, Sinfonia, S. Martino.
Possible Author	? (1) Leopold Hofmann: Br. 66, Racc. III/5, Sinfonia (2 hn); (2) Ignaz Holzbauer: PRA Waldst. XXXIV D 34, Overteur (2 hn); (3) G. C. Belletti: STOCK Alstr., Sinfonia (2 hn).
Remarks	The horns are added parts of a rudimentary character. STOCK follows the PRA version, the composer's name given in a corrupt form.

In addition to conflicting attributions, this symphony has several uncharacteristic features of style that place it in the doubtful category. In general, the symphony utilizes a more motivic language, and an early type of Andante, which would point to a date of composition c. 1740. However, its structure displays several advanced traits of a later period. Thus, the first movement contains long and defined primary, transitional, secondary, and closing sections, with a first closing theme in reduced texture, typical of Sammartini's writing in the later middle period. Small balanced arrangements of phrases occur in I/mm 1-3 and the Trio, mm 1-4. The minuet with trio itself appears otherwise only in the later middle period symphonies.

Other uncharacteristic aspects in the first movement include imitation between the viola and bass in the secondary theme, extended repetition of the second closing theme, return in the development of a phrase from the primary theme in the tonic key, and awkward harmony in the development, mm 52-53. The second movement makes far greater use of sequences than any other movement of this period, though Sammartini avoids extensive sequential writing after c. 1740. Sammartini similarly avoids using long sections in two-part texture (violins in unison, viola and bass in octaves), and melodies with tremolo accompaniment that we find in the minuet and trio respectively.

The two sources that ascribe this work to Sammartini are fairly reliable, however, making a final decision regarding authenticity especially difficult. Five remaining symphonies in MELK are all authentic, and the catalogues and collection in KARL form with EINS the most trustworthy of Sammartini sources. Nevertheless, the stylistic discrepancies remain too significant to ignore.

D-46

2 vn, va, b

Sammartini	MUN 1466, Sinfonia, S. Martino.
Probable Author	Giorgio Giulini (see App. D 2): PRA Waldst. XXXIV C 59, Overtura (in A major); STOCK, Sinfonia, Giulini (in A major; 2 hn).
Prints	1) Ascribed to Giulini. Paris, Venier, c. 1755: VI / SINFONIE / . . . COMPOSTE DA VARRI AUTORI / . . . OPERA . . . TERZA . . .; Trio I (2 vn, b); PC H.107. 2) Ascribed to Baldassare Galuppi. London, Hummel, 1761 (for the title and sources, see No. 29); Overture II (in A major; 2 hn).
Remarks	The STOCK MS belonged to the literary society Utile Dulci.

Mod. ed.   Arrangements ascribed to Sammartini:

1) *Quartetto Sinfonico,* arr. for str by Clementino de Macchi (New York, c. 1899).

2) *Quartetto Sinfonico,* arr. for band by Concetto Abate (Milan: Ricordi, c. 1900).

3) *Quartetto Sinfonico,* ed. R. Ferraguzzi (Milan: Zerboni, 1970).

D-47

2 hn, 2 vn, va, b

Sammartini   PRA Waldst. XXXIV C 389, Sinfonia, St. Martino.

D-48

2 hn, 2 vn, va, b

Sammartini   Br. 66, Racc. IV/I, Sinfonia, Martino (str only); REG 1, Sinfonia, Martino.

Probable   Giorgio Giulini (see App. D 2): (1) PRA Waldst. XXXIV
Author   C 50, Overteur (va pt. missing); (2) STOCK, Overtura (2 tr da c). Also ascribed to Niccolò Jommelli in BRAT and to Reluzzi (composer of instrumental music c. 1740-1760, active in Prague): GRAZ, Sinfonia (2 vn, b).

Remarks   The PRA MS is copied in Hand C.

D-49

2 vn, va, b

Sammartini	EINS 200/23 (no title), Martino (2 vn, b).
Probable Author	G. B. Lampugnani (see App. D 17): PRA Waldst. XXXIV B 212, Overteur; another copy XXXIV B 214.

D-50

2 hn, 2 vn, va, b

Sammartini	Lam. cat. 1768, Sinfonia, Martino (str only).
Possible Author	Antonio Gaetano Pampani (d. 1769; composer of operas and church music in Venice): STOCK, Sinfonie (eighteenth-century score).

D-51

2 vn, b

Sammartini	EDIN D 52-54, no. 42, Symphonia, Martini de Milano (vn I missing for II and III).
Possible Author	Ägidius Schenck (Styrian composer of sacred music): GRAZ Ms. 169, Sinfonia, A. Schenck.
Remarks	The GRAZ MS bears the date 1750. The EDIN MS is inscribed on the lower left-hand corner with the name Cyprian Calderon y Milan, the probable owner of the MS.

D-52

2 vn, va, b

| Sammartini | LUND Wens. Litt. C 8, Sinfonia, Martini. |

D-53

2 tr, 2 vn, va, b

Sammartini	PRA Waldst. XXXIV C 318, Overteur, St. Martino (2 hn); another copy XXXIV C 388, Sinfonia, St. Martino (2 hn).
Possible Author	Giuseppe Paladino (see App. D 13): PRA Waldst. XXXIV B 243, Overteur, Paladino.
Remarks	The viola part in the Sammartini copies is corrupt.

A MAJOR

D-54

2 fl, 2 hn, 2 vn, va, b

Sammartini	REG 5, Sinfonia, Martino.
Correct Author	F. X. Pokorny (see App. D 7).
Remarks	All the parts were copied by Pokorny.

D-55

2 vn, va, b

Sammartini	BOL KK 35 [no. 3], Sinfonia Teatrale, S. Martini (2 vn, b).
Probable Author	Reluzzi (see App. D 48): PC F. Bl. Op. V/227, Sinfonia.
Remarks	The slow introduction is found only in PC.

D-56
2 vn, va, b

Sammartini	Br. 62, Racc. III/3, Sinfonia, Martini.
Possible Author	? (1) Carassiè: STOCK Od-R, Sinfonia; (2) Giuseppe Tartini: STOCK O-R, Sinfonia.
Print	Anon. Paris, Le Clerc and Boivin, c. 1745: SINFONIE / ... DEI PIU CELEBRI AUTORI / d'Italia / Raccolte Da / PIETRO GIANNOTTI / DEUXIEME RECUEIL ...; Sinfonia VII (source of incipits); LBM Hirsch III 219a.

D-56.1
2 hn, 2 vn, va, b

See App. D-46.

D-57
2 vn, va, b

Sammartini	Br. 62, Racc. III/5, Sinfonia, Martini.
Possible Author	Either (1) Placidus von Camerloher (1718-1782; *Kapellmeister* in Freising): PC F. Bl. Op. VI/259, Sinfonia; STOCK, O-R, Sinfonia; or (2) Giorgio Giulini (see App. D 2): SCHW, Sinfonia; or (3) Bernardo Polazzi (or Polaci, composer of symphonies and concertos, c. 1720-c. 1750): Br. 66, Sinfonia. (4) Anon. 53, STOCK O-R.
Print	Ascribed to Camerloher. Paris, Le Clerc: XII / SINFONIE / a Quatro / . . . OPERA III . . .; Sinfonia X; PBN Vm^7. 1515; PC H. 213.
Remarks	In the Le Clerc version, the first movement has a different development section from the Fonds Blancheton copy. Both STOCK copies belonged to the literary society Utile Dulci. The STOCK MS ascribed to Camerloher was copied by Per Brant (1713-1767) (see No. 57).

D-58

2 vn, va, b

(no tempo mark)

Sammartini	Egk cat. No. 124, 1760, Sinfonia, S. Martino.
Possible Author	Adalbert Fauner (composer in Vienna c. 1760): Br. 66, Sinfonia 1.
Remarks	The appoggiaturas in brackets appear in the Breitkopf catalogue.

D-59

2 vn, va, b

Sammartini	PRA Waldst. XXXIV B 22, Sinfonia, St. Martino.

Possible Author	? Oberti (Galimberti?): PRA Waldst. XXXIV D 115, Overteur.

D-60

2 vn, va, b

Sammartini	PRA Waldst. XXXIV B 3, Symphonia, St. Martino; another copy XXXIV C 379.
Possible Author	Antonio Brioschi (see App. D 15): WLC, Overtur.
Remarks	The initials F. K. appear on the lower right-hand corner of the title page of the first PRA copy.

B-FLAT MAJOR

D-61

2 vn, va, b

Sammartini	BER Mus. ms. 19396/1, Sinfonia, Martino.
Probable Author	Melchiorre Chiesa (see App. D 11): EINS 199/47, Overtur (va pt missing; source of incipits).

D-62

2 vn, va, b

Sammartini	LUND Eng. 289, Sinfonia, Martino; UPP Instr. mus. i hs. 55:7, Sinfonia, Martino.
Possible Author	Either (1) Antonio Brioschi (see App. D 15): Br. 62, Racc. I/1, Sinfonia (*a 6*); LUND Wens. Litt i-12; or (2) Sirazi (Giuseppe Serassi, 1694-1760, composer in Bergamo): PC F. Bl. Op. II/93, Sonata.

D-63

2 vn, va, b

Sammartini	DARM 169/b, Sinfonia, Sammartini (destroyed in World War II).
Probable Author	Antonio Brioschi (see App. D 15): HERZ (bass incipit); PC F. Bl. 36, Sonata (2 vn, b); PC D.11.151 (duplicate copy D.11.152), Sonata (2 vn, b). Also anon. trio in WLC.
Prints	1) Ascribed to Giuseppe Sammartini. Paris, Le Clerc, 1742 (for the title and sources, see No. 33); Op. II/12 (3 vn, b; source of incipits).
	2) Ascribed to St. Martini, Brioschi, and other Masters. London, I. Walsh, 8 Nov. 1746 (Gen. Adv.): SIX / SO-

NATAS / . . . 3ᵈ. Set . . .; Sonata IV (without ascription; 2 vn, b); BRUS, LBM, ROCH, WLC, and several other sources.

Remarks The DARM MS was copied c. 1752 by Christoph Graupner (1683-1760), *Kapellmeister* at Darmstadt.

D-64
2 vn, va, b

Sammartini LUND Kraus 221, Trio, Martino (2 vn, b).

Correct Author Kaspar Fritz (1716-1783; Swiss violinist and composer): COP Sammlung C No. 3, Sinfonia (2 ob).

Prints Ascribed to Fritz.
1) London, printed for the author, 1742: Sei Sonate / . . . Opera Prima . . .; Sonata II (source of incipits); LBM and elsewhere. Other editions by Johnson and I. Walsh.
2) Paris, Le Clerc and Boivin: same title as above; PBN H.326. a-d.

D-65
2 vn, va, b

Sammartini BER Mus. ms. 19396/2, Sinfonia, Martino.

Probable Author	Johann Gottlieb Janitsch (1708-1763; composer of instrumental music in Berlin and member of the Royal Chapel of Frederick the Great): Br. 62, Racc. II/3, Sinfonia; STOCK.

D-66

2 vn, va, b

Sammartini	Br. 62, Racc. I/5, Sinfonia, Martino; PC F. Bl. Op. III/104, Overtura, St. Martino; VGM IX 23410, Sinfonia, Martino.
Possible Author	Antonio Brioschi (see App. D 15): Br. 62, Sonata III (2 vn, b). Also Anon. in Karl. cat. E.
Print	Ascribed to Sammartini. London, I. Walsh, 1745 (for the title and sources, see No. 37); Op. II/1, Martini.

D-67

2 vn, va, b

Sammartini	PC F. Bl. Op. III/148, Sinfonia, Antonio St. Martini.
Probable Author	Antonio Brioschi (see App. D 15): PRA XXII B 71, Concerto; STOCK, Sinfonia (eighteenth-century score); WLC, Overtur. Also ascribed to Franz Xaver Richter in Br. 66,

Racc. III/5, Sinfonia; and to Anton Laube (1718-1784; church composer in Prague) in BRNO Rajhrad A 12.769 L, Symphonia (2 vn, b).

Remarks   The PRA MS comes from the Pachta archive. The STOCK MS was copied by J. G. Psilanderhielm (see No. 18), whose name appears on the title page. See also Introduction, note 124.

D-68

2 vn, va, b

Sammartini   PC F. Bl. Op. III/146, Sinfonia, Antonio St. Martini.

Remarks   See also p. 33, note 124.

SYMPHONIES IN PRINTED COLLECTION

D-69

2 vn, va, b

D-70

2 vn, va, b

D-71

2 vn, va, vc

D-72

2 vn, va, b

D-73

2 vn, va, b

D-74

2 vn, va, b

Print	Mangean, c. 1750: SIX / SIMPHONIES / A 4 et 5 Parties / DEL Sig^nor. / SANS MARTINI / et BRIOCHI / Graves par Melle. Vendôme / Prix 9^£. / A PARIS / Ce vend / aux a=dresse Ordinaires / Et chez M^dme. Mangean a L'hotel de Soissons. / AVEC PRIVILEGE DU ROY; PC Ac.e^4. 164.
Remarks	This print contains no works by Sammartini. All symphonies are without ascription. The symphonies have been identified as follows: No. 69: Franz Xaver Richter, Karl. cat. E (No. 6), Sinfonia. No. 70: Blantini (perhaps Blanchini), PC F. Bl. Op. VI/295, Sinfonia; Antonio Brioschi (see App. D 15), Br. 62, Racc. II/6, Sinfonia; SCHW, Ouverture (2 vn, b); Paris print, Maupetit, 1745, Op. II/5, PBN. No. 71: Pietro Locatelli, VI Introduttioni Teatrali (1735), Op. IV/3, LEI. No. 72: J. G. Graun, Br. 62, Racc. III/6, Sinfonia (2 hn); DARM (2 fl, 2 hn); REG. No. 73: C. H. Graun, overture Adriano in Siria, 1746; Br. 62, Racc. II/7, Sinfonia (2 ob, 2 hn). No. 74: C. H. Graun, overture to Cajo Fabricio, 1746; Br. 62, Racc. II/9, Sinfonia (2 hn). The dating of the print is suggested by the dates of the Graun overtures and the date 1754 for Mangean at this address as given in HopkinsonS, p. 35. The bass is figured only in D 73.

CONCERTOS

C MAJOR

D-75

2 solo fl, 2 vn, b

| Sammartini | LUND Wens. Litt D-7, Concerto, Martini. |

D MAJOR

D-76

Solo vn, 2 vn, va, vc, b

Sammartini	STOCK VO-R, Concerto, San Martini (eighteenth-century score and parts).
Remarks	On all parts "Martini" is written in pencil (a twentieth-century attribution). "Dell Sign. Martini" is written in ink on the bass part in the same hand as the rest of the MS. This work was collected by Pehr Frigel (see No. 57).

D-77
2 solo ob, 2 vn, va, b

Sammartini   SCHW 3560, Concerto, Martini.

Mod. ed.   Ascribed to Sammartini; for 2 ob. and piano; ed. R. Lauschmann (Bonn-Bad Godesberg: R. Forberg, 1973). Heavily edited.

Remarks   The second movement is only a five-bar transition.

D-78
Solo fl, 2 vn, b

Sammartini   LUND Eng. 114, Concerto, Martini.

D-79

Solo vn, 2 vn, va, b

Sammartini	VGM IX 1428, Concerto, Martino.
Remarks	From the Clam-Gallas collection. This collection was originally housed in Friedland Castle, Czechoslovakia. The greater part is now in PRA.

E-FLAT MAJOR

D-80

Solo vn, 2 vn, va, b

Sammartini	STOCK VO-R, Concerto, Martini.
Remarks	This concerto was collected by Pehr Frigel (see No. 57).

G MAJOR

D-81

Fl, 2 solo vn, solo va, solo vc; 2 vn, va, b

Sammartini	KARL 791, Concerto, S. Martino.
Possible Author	Antoine Mahaut (active in Amsterdam c. 1737-1751): STOCK, Concerto a 5 (fl, 2 solo vn, 2 vn, va, vc, b).
Remarks	The first movement of the STOCK MS is written in half the time value of the KARL MS.
Literature	MeylanD, p. 54.

D-82

Solo ob, 2 vn, va, b

Sammartini   REG 9, Concerto, Samardino.

D-83

Solo fl, 2 vn, va, b

Sammartini   LUND Kraus 13, Concerto, Martino.

Remarks   The MS is dated 1748, and inscribed on the title page
               "Academia Carolina" (see No. 4).

D-84
2 hn, 2 vn, va, b

Sammartini   PRA Waldst. XXXIV B 26, Sinfonia, S. Martino.

Remarks   Though entitled Sinfonia, this work is a concerto for 2
               horns and strings.

OTHER ORCHESTRAL WORKS

G MAJOR

D-85
2 vn, va, b

Sammartini   PC F. Bl. 105, Concertino, St. Martino.

SACRED VOCAL WORKS

MASSES

D-86   MISSA SOLEMNIS

Instrumentation: Solo S, A, T, B; chorus S, A, T, B; 2 tr, timp, 2 vn, va,
b, org

Kyrie
Chorus; 2 tr, timp, 2 vn, va, b, org

Gloria
Chorus; 2 tr, timp, 2 vn, va, b, org

Domine Deus
Solo S; 2 vn, va, b, org

Qui tollis
Chorus; 2 tr, timp, 2 vn, b, org

Qui tollis
Chorus; 2 tr, timp, 2 vn, va, b, org

Cum Sancto Spiritu
Chorus; 2 tr, timp, 2 vn, va, b, org

In gloria Dei Patris
Chorus; 2 tr, timp, 2 vn, va, b, org

Credo
Chorus; 2 tr, timp, 2 vn, va, b, org

Et incarnatus est
Solo A, T; 2 vn, va, b, org

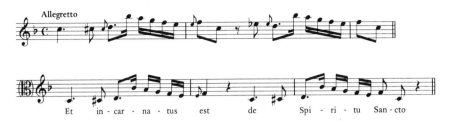

Et resurrexit
Chorus; 2 tr, timp, 2 vn, va, b, org

Sanctus
Chorus; 2 tr, timp, 2 vn, va, b, org

Benedictus
Solo S; 2 vn, va, b, org

Osanna
Chorus; 2 tr, timp, 2 vn, va, b, org

Page 269

Agnus Dei
Solo S; 2 vn, va, b, org

Agnus Dei
Chorus; 2 tr, timp, 2 vn, va, b, org

Dona nobis	same as Kyrie.
Sammartini	HAR III, 4 i/2, 2° fol. 115, Missa a IV. Vocibus, Martini.
Remarks	The date 1761 appears on the title page of the MS. On the inside cover: "In festo S. Scolasticae 1779, Solemnis." The date 1761 may be the date of composition or it may only refer to a performance; the date 1779 obviously refers to a specific performance. The Kyrie text of this MS omits the Christe and second Kyrie. There are further tempo changes within the main section, but they have not been indicated since they do not constitute separate movements. There are occasional differences of tempo indications among the parts. Those used are taken from the first violin part.

D-87   MASS

Instrumentation: Solo S, A, T, B; Chorus S, A, T, B; 2 fl, 2 ob, bn, 2 hn, 2 tr, timp, 2 vn, va, b, org

Kyrie	the same as No. 100.

Gloria
Chorus; 2 ob, bn, 2 hn, 2 tr, timp, 2 vn, va, b, org

Et in terra pax
Solo S, A; chorus; bn, 2 hn, 2 vn, va, b, org

Laudamus te
Solo S, A, T, B; 2 vn, va, b, org

Gratias
Chorus; 2 vn, va, b, org

Domine Deus
Solo S; 2 vn, va, b, org

Qui tollis
Solo S; chorus; 2 fl, 2 vn, va, b, org

Quoniam

Solo S, A; chorus; 2 fl, bn, 2 hn, 2 tr, timp, 2 vn, va, b, org

Cum sancto Spiritu

Chorus; 2 ob, bn, 2 hn, 2 tr, timp, 2 vn, va, b, org

Credo

Chorus; 2 ob, bn, 2 hn, 2 vn, va, b, org

Et incarnatus est

Chorus; bn, 2 vn, va, b, org

Et resurrexit

Solo S, A, T; chorus; 2 ob, bn, 2 hn, 2 vn, va, b, org

Et vitam venturi

Chorus; 2 ob, bn, 2 hn, 2 vn, va, b, org

Sammartini   Kyrie only: PRA XXXIII A 20, Missa Solennis, Martino; PRA XXXV A 238, Messa Solenne, S. Martino (eighteenth-century score); PRA XXXV B 160, Missa, Martino.

Remarks   The *Kyrie* is authentic, though altered (see below), but the *Gloria* and *Credo* are doubtful. The score and parts come from the Kreuzherren (Crusaders') Archives in Prague. For other works by Sammartini mentioned in the inventory of these Archives, see Nos. 103, 115, and App. C 17. The score of this Mass was copied at the end of the eighteenth century by either Wenzel or Johannes Praupner. The instrumentation includes bassoons and timpani, not found in version A.

After all subsections of the Mass a statement appears that the music of the original version has been shortened: the first *Kyrie* from 78 bars to 48 bars; the *Christe* from 154 bars to 113 bars; [the second *Kyrie* from 4 bars to 3 bars]; the third *Kyrie* from 68 bars to 61 bars; the *Gloria* from 99 bars to 88 bars; the *Et in terra pax* from 43 bars to 23 bars; the *Laudamus te* from 147 bars to 98 bars; the *Gratias* from 10 bars to 9 bars; the *Domine Deus* from 41 bars to 27 bars; the *Qui tollis* from 23 bars to 17 bars; the *Quoniam* from 148 bars to 113 bars; the *Cum Sancto Spiritu* from 123 bars to 102 bars; the *Credo* from 113 bars to 59 bars; the *Et incarnatus est* from 13 bars to 9 bars; the *Et resurrexit* from 80 bars to 36 bars; and the *Et vitam venturi* from 60 bars to 52 bars.

The *Kyrie* of Version B has not only been shortened, but has been partially recomposed, probably by a local musician. Since all the sections of the Mass have been shortened, it is probable that they have undergone the same kind of alterations. The fact that each section is in a different key indicates that this is a composite Mass, using a variety of sources, which may have been single Mass sections or parts of Masses now lost. There is no proof that the movements other than the first *Kyrie* were originally composed by Sammartini.

On page 66 of the score the copyist has noted the omission of a *Crucifixus* for solo duet, a fugal *Domine Deus* in the *Gloria,* and a *Qui sedes* for solo voice. The last page of the score contains an enumeration of 71 singers and instrumentalists used for a performance in the late eighteenth century: 4 sopranos and 3 ripieni; 4 altos and 3 ripieni; 4 tenors, 4 basses, a total of 6 oboes and flutes, 4 horns, 2 trumpets, timpani, 5 first violins and 5 ripieni; 5 second violins and 5 ripieni; 3

violas, a total of 4 cellos and bassoons, 4 double-basses
(violoni) and 5 organs.

D-88 MASS

Instrumentation: Solo S, S, A, T, T, B; chorus S, A, T, B; 2 ob, [2 hn or
tr], 2 vn, va, b, 2 org obbl

Kyrie
Chorus; 2 vn, va, b, org

Christe
Solo S; 2 vn, va, b, org

Kyrie
Chorus; 2 vn, va, b, org

Gloria
Solo S, A, T; chorus; 2 vn, va, b, org

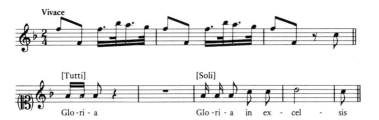

Laudamus te
Solo S; 2 vn, va, b, org

Gratias
Solo S, T, B; chorus; 2 vn, va, b, org

Domine Fili
Solo A; 2 org obbl. or vn obbl., 2 vn, va, b

Domine Deus
Solo S; chorus; 2 vn, va, b, org

Qui tollis
Solo S; chorus; 2 vn, va, b, org

Qui tollis
Chorus; 2 vn, va, b, org

Suscipe
Chorus; 2 vn, va, b, org

Qui sedes
Solo B; 2 vn, va, b, (senza org)

Quoniam
Solo T, T, or T, B; 2 vn, va, b, org

Cum Sancto Spiritu
Chorus; 2 vn, va, b, org

Credo
Chorus; 2 hn, 2 vn, va, b, org

Et incarnatus est
Chorus; 2 vn, va, b, org

Crucifixus
Solo S, S; 2 ob, 2 vn, va, b

Et resurrexit
Chorus; 2 hn, 2 vn, va, b, org

Et vitam venturi
Chorus; 2 hn, 2 vn, va, b, org

Et vi - tam ven - tu - ri sæ - cu - li a - - - men

Sammartini	Freising cat, Missa, Martino; SCHW 3565, St. Martino; BERG Antisala B. 6. 12, St. Martino (eighteenth-century score, *Gloria* only; 2 hn or tr); EINS 543/10, San Martino (*Credo* only; 2 ob, 2 hn).
Remarks	In EINS the date 1763 appears on the title page. In SCHW the ascription is found only on the organ part. The incipits for the *Kyrie* come from SCHW, for the *Gloria* from BERG, and for the *Credo* from EINS. For the BERG collection see No. 109. Only one organ part appears in SCHW. In the *Domini Fili* the organ obbligato corresponds to the violin alternative given in BERG. In SCHW the second solo soprano part in the *Crucifixus* is omitted. The order of the sections *Domine Deus* and *Domini Fili* have been reversed. The second *Qui tollis* is found in SCHW only. The fact that various sections are in different keys (the *Kyrie* in D, the *Gloria* in F, and the *Credo* in G) indicates that this is a composite Mass using a variety of sources which may have been single sections or parts of complete Masses now lost, possibly even by different composers.

D-89   MASS

Instrumentation: Solo S, A, T, B; chorus S, A, T, B; 2 trb, 2 vn, b

Kyrie
Chorus (solo B in Christe), 2 trb, 2 vn, b

Ky - ri - e   e - lei - - - son

Gloria
Chorus; 2 trb, 2 vn, b

Glo - ri - a glo - ri - a in ex cel - sis De - o

Laudamus te
Solo S, 2 vn, b

Lau -da - - - - - - - mus te

Gratias
Chorus; 2 vn, b

Gra - ti - as a - gi -mus ti - bi

Domine Deus
Solo A; 2 vn, b

Do - - - mi -ne De - us Rex cae - le - stis

Qui tollis
Chorus; 2 vn, b

Qui tol - lis

Quoniam
Solo T; 2 vn, b

Quo - ni - am tu so - lus, tu so - lus san - ctus

Cum Sancto Spiritu
Chorus; 2 trb, 2 vn, b

Cum San - cto Spi - ri - tu

Cum Sancto Spiritu
Chorus; 2 trb, 2 vn, b

Cum San - cto

Patrem omnipotentem
Chorus; 2 trb, 2 vn, b

Pa - trem om - ni - po - ten - tem

Et incarnatus est
Chorus; 2 trb, 2 vn, b

Et in - car - na - tus est

Crucifixus
Solo B; 2 vn, b

Cru - ci - fi - xus e - ti - am pro - no - bis

Et resurrexit
Chorus; 2 trb, 2 vn, b

Et re-sur-re-xit, re-sur-re-xit ter-ti-a di-e

Sanctus
Chorus; 2 trb, 2 vn, b

San-ctus, san - - - ctus, san - - - ctus

Benedictus
Solo S; 2 vn, b

Be - ne - di - ctus

Osanna
Chorus; 2 trb, 2 vn, b

O - san - na in ex - cel - sis

Agnus Dei
Chorus; 2 trb, 2 vn, b

A - gnus De - i qui tol - lis, qui tol - lis

Dona nobis pacem
Chorus; 2 trb, 2 vn, b

Do - na no - bis pa - cem

Sammartini   LAM, Missa, Martino.

Remarks   The *Christe* is not separated from the *Kyrie* by a double
                bar although it stands in C minor with the tempo mark
                Andante. The tempo marks in brackets are taken from
                parts other than the soprano. The trombone parts double
                the alto and tenor choral parts, a practice common in
                South Germany and Austria in the eighteenth century
                (see also App. D no. 96).

MASS SECTIONS

D-90 KYRIE

Instrumentation: Solo S, A, T, B; chorus S, A, T, B; 2 ob, 2 hn, 2 vn, va,
                 b, org

Kyrie

Kyrie

Ky - ri - e   e - le - i [son]

Kyrie

Ky - ri - e   e - le - i - son

MS source   VENM Marc. It. IV, 1787-1788 (= 11290-11291), San
                Martini (nineteenth-century score).

Remarks   This score is part of a collection belonging to Pietro
                Canal which was acquired by the Biblioteca Marciana
                in 1928.

D-91 CREDO

Instrumentation: S, T, B; 2 tr, 2 vn, vc, cb, org

Credo
S, T, B; 2 tr, 2 vn, vc, cb, org

Et incarnatus est
S, T, B; 2 tr, 2 vn, vc, cb, org

Crucifixus
S, B; 2 vn, vc, cb, org

Et resurrexit
S, solo T, B; 2 tr, 2 vn, vc, cb, org

Et vitam venturi

S, T, B; 2 tr, 2 vn, vc, cb, org

Sammartini	EINS 544/4, San Martino; BER Mus. ms. 19394, San Martino (mod. score; Et incarnatus and Crucifixus only); WLC M 2020.S218 M2, San Martino (mod. score; Et incarnatus and Crucifixus only).
Remarks	In EINS double violin parts are extant. There is no indication whether the voice parts are solo or choral, except for the indication of a short solo in the *Et resurrexit*. On the title page: "Ad Chorum Fabariensem p. m." indicating that this work was copied for Kloster Pfäffers. The BER and WLC scores were made by Pater Sigismund Keller of Einsiedeln. The WLC score is dated 22 November 1880.

D-92 CREDO

Instrumentation: S, A, T, B; 2 hn, 2 vn, va, b, org

Credo

Et incarnatus est

Et resurrexit

Et re - sur - re - xit ter - ti - a di - e

Sammartini ZÜR AMG XIII 7070 a-h, S. Martino.

Remarks In the soprano part certain bars are marked "solo," though similar sections in the other vocal parts are unmarked. On the title page of the first violin part is the ascription: "Auth. Martini."

OTHER SACRED VOCAL WORKS

D-93 LITANY

Instrumentation: Solo S, A, T, B; chorus S, A, T, B; 2 tr, 2 vn, b

Kyrie
Solo S, A, T, B; chorus; 2 tr, 2 vn, b

Ky - ri - e e - le - i - son

Agnus Dei
Solo S, A, T; chorus; 2 tr, 2 vn, b

A - gnus De - i qui tol - lis pec - ca - ta

Source BERG Antisala B. 7. 12, Letanie della B. V. (eighteenth-century score and parts).

Remarks The MS has no ascription. It is part of the Mayr collection (see No. 109). The score is copied in the same hand as the Litany App. D 94.

D-94 LITANY

Instrumentation: Solo S, A, T, B; chorus S, A, T, B; 2 tr, 2 vn obbl, 2 vn, vc, cb, org obbl

Kyrie
Solo S, A, T, B; chorus; 2 tr, 2 vn obbl., 2 vn, vc, cb, org obbl

Agnus Dei
Chorus; 2 tr, 2 vn, vc, cb

Sammartini   BERG Antisala B. 7. 12, Letanie della B. V., S. Martino (eighteenth-century score).

Remarks   The score is in the same hand as the score of Litany App. D-93, but the ascription is in another hand. The style of certain sections of the Kyrie implies solo treatment, although not indicated as such in the score.

D-95 MAGNIFICAT

Instrumentation: Solo S, A, T, B; Chorus S, A, T, B; 2 tr, 2 vn, va, vc, cb, org

Magnificat
Chorus; 2 tr, 2 vn, va, vc, cb, org

Gloria Patri

Chorus; 2 vn, va, vc, cb, org

Sicut erat

Chorus; 2 tr, 2 vn, va, vc, cb, org

Sammartini	BERG Antisala D. 9. 13, San Martino (eighteenth-century score and parts).
Remarks	Although both date (1751) and precise ascription are found on the title page of the MS score, it has been decided to place this work in this section of the catalogue on stylistic grounds. The work is given an incorrect number in the MS catalogue of BERG (Antisala B. 9. 13). For the collection see No. 109.

D-96 MISERERE

Instrumentation: Solo S, A, T, B; chorus S, A, T, B; 2 tbn, 2 vn, b, org

Miserere

Chorus; 2 tbn, 2 vn, b, org

Amplius lava

Solo S, A; 2 vn, b, org

Tibi soli peccavi
Chorus; 2 tbn, 2 vn, b, org

Ecce enim
Solo T, B, 2 vn, b, org

Asperges me
Chorus; 2 tbn, 2 vn, b, org

Averte
Solo A; 2 vn, b, org

Redde mihi laetitiam
Chorus; 2 tbn, 2 vn, b, org

Domine labia
Solo B; 2 vn, b, org

Do - - - mi - ne la - bi - a me - a a - pe - ri - es.

Sacrificium
Chorus; 2 tbn, 2 vn, b, org

Sa - cri - fi - ci - um De - o spi - ri - tus

Benigne fac Domine
Solo S; 2 vn, b, org

Be - ni - gne fac Do - mi - ne

Gloria Patris
Chorus; 2 tbn, 2 vn, b, org

Glo - - - - - - ri - a Pa - tris

Sicut erat
Chorus; 2 tbn, 2 vn, b, org

Si - cut e - rat in prin - ci - pi - o

Sammartini	OTTO MO 624, Martini Mediolanensi.
Remarks	The title page bears the following inscription in the lower right hand corner: "Auct: Sig Joanne Baptst Martini Mediolanensi. Comparavit P. Nicolaus Maichlbeck p. t. Chori Rgs. 1751." The parts are in three hands and were copied in 1751 in Ottobeuren. The names of the copyists, which are found on various parts, are: P. Nicolaus

Maichlbeck, Joannes Michael Haas and J. B. Lober. The trombone parts double the alto and tenor choral parts, a practice common in South Germany and Austria in the eighteenth century (see App. D 88). Verses 9, 14, and 15 of the psalm have not been set.

D-97   TANTUM ERGO

Instrumentation: Solo S; 2 vn, va, b, org

Tantum ergo

Tan - tum er - go sa - - - cra - men - tum

Genitori

Ge - ni - to - ri, ge - - - [nitori]

Amen

A - - - - - - - - [men]

Sammartini   EINS 543/7, S. Martino.

D-98

The Lord is righteous
Solo S, S; 2 vn, va, b

The   Lord   is   [righteous]

Sammartini   Print. London, J. Corfe, c. 1800 (for the title and sources, see App. B 1); Vol. I, pp. 44-51, Martini.

APPENDIX E

A SUGGESTED GENERAL CHRONOLOGY
OF THE SYMPHONIES, CONCERTOS, AND CONCERTINOS

Works arranged by key within each period.

Early Period, c. 1724–c. 1739

Nos. 7, 9, 14, 15, 23, 32-39, 59, 64-69, 72, 74, 75, 77, 77.1, 81-83, 85.

Middle Period, c. 1740–c. 1758

Nos. 1, 3-6, 8, 10, 12, 13, 16, 18, 20, 24, 25, 27, 29, 30, 41-58, 61, 62, 71, 73, 76, 79, 86, 87.

Late Period, c. 1759-1774

Nos. 2, 11, 17, 19, 21, 22, 26, 28, 31, 40, 60, 63, 70, 78, 80, 84.

BIBLIOGRAPHY

INDEXES

ABBREVIATIONS

AfMw   *Archiv für Musikwissenschaft*

AM   *Acta Musicologica*

DTB   *Denkmäler der Tonkunst in Bayern*

FAM   *Fontis Artis Musicae*

Grove   *Grove's Dictionary of Music and Musicians.* 5th ed. Ed. Eric Blom. 9 vols. London: Macmillan, 1954.

HAM   *Historical Anthology of Music.* Ed. Archibald Davison and Willi Apel. Vol. II. Cambridge, Mass.: Harvard University Press, 1950.

JAMS   *Journal of the American Musicological Society*

MfM   *Monatshefte für Musikgeschichte*

MGG   *Die Musik in Geschichte und Gegenwart.* Ed. Friedrich Blume. 14 vols. Kassel: Bärenreiter, 1949-1968.

MO   *Musica d'Oggi*

MQ   *Musical Quarterly*

RaM   *Rassegna Musicale*

RdM   *Revue de Musicologie*

RM   *Revue Musicale*

RMI   *Rivista Musicale Italiana*

SIMG   *Sammelbände der Internationalen Musikgesellschaft*

StMw   *Studien zur Musikwissenschaft*

SELECTED BIBLIOGRAPHY

For modern editions see in the catalogue numbers 2, 4, 7, 9, 14, 15, 18, 20, 23, 32—39, 41, 44, 47, 48, 59, 62a, 64—69, 83, 88, 98, 111, 124, and App. D 24, 46, 77.

CATALOGUES: GENERAL

Eitner, Robert. *Biographisch-bibliographisches Quellen—Lexikon der Musiker und Musikgelehrten.* 10 vols. Leipzig: Breitkop & Härtel, 1900-1904.

Lesure, François (ed.). *Recueils imprimés, XVIIIe siècle.* Répertoire international des sources musicales, B II. Munich: G. Henle, 1964.

Schnapper, Edith B. (ed.). *The British Union-Catalogue of Early Music Printed before the Year 1801.* 2 vols. London: Butterworths Scientific Publications, 1957.

CATALOGUES: THEMATIC (MODERN)

BASEL. Edgar Refardt. *Thematischer Katalog der Instrumentalmusik des 18. Jahrhunderts in den Handschriften der Universitätsbibliothek Basel.* (Publicationen der Schweitzerischen Musikforschenden Gesellschaft, Vol. VI.) Bern: Paul Haupt, 1957.

PARIS. Lionel de La Laurencie. *Inventaire critique du Fonds Blancheton de la bibliothèque du Conservatoire de Paris.* (Publications de la Société française de musicologie, ser. 2, vols. I and II.) Paris: E. Droz, 1930-31.

SCHWERIN. Otto Kade. *Die Musikalien-Sammlung des Grossherzoglich Mecklenburg-Schweriner Fürstenhauses aus den letzten zwei Jahrhunderten.* 2 vols. Schwerin: Druck der Sandmeyerschen Hofbuchdruckerei, 1893.

ZÜRICH. Georg Walter. *Katalog der gedruckten und handschriftlichen Musikalien des 17. bis 19. Jahrhunderts im Besitze der Allgemeinen Musikgesellschaft Zürich.* Zürich: Verlag der Allgemeinen Musikgesellschaft, 1960.

CATALOGUES: NONTHEMATIC (MODERN)

AGEN. *Département de Lot-et-Garonne. Ville d'Agen. Inventaire sommaire Des Archives Communales Anterieurs a 1790. Supplément à la Série II.* (Bibliothèque d'ouvrages de musique provenant du château des ducs d'Aiguillon.)

BOLOGNA. Gaetano Gaspari. *Catalogo della biblioteca del Liceo Musicale di Bologna.* Vol. IV, ed. Raffaele Cadolini; Vol. V, ed. Ugo Sesini. Bologna: Libreria Romagnoli dall'Acqua, 1905, 1943.

BOSTON. *Catalogue of the Allen A. Brown Collection of Music in the Public Library of the City of Boston.* Vol. III and the Supplement. Boston: Published by the Trustees, 1915, 1916.

BRUSSELS. Alfred Wotquenne. *Catalogue de la Bibliothèque du Conservatoire Royale de Musique de Bruxelles.* 4 vols. Brussels: Coosemans, 1898-1912.

EDINBURGH. Hans Gál. *Catalogue of Manuscripts, Printed Music and Books on Music up to 1850, in the Library of the Music Department at the University of Edinburgh (Reid Library).* Edinburgh: Oliver and Boyd, 1941.

GENOA. Salvatore Pintacuda. *Genova, Biblioteca dell'Istituto Musicale "Nicolò Paganini." Catalogo del Fondo Antico.* (Bibliotheca Musicae, IV.) Milan: Istituto Editoriale Italiano, 1966.

KÖNIGSBERG. Joseph Mueller. *Die musikalischen Schaetze der Koeniglichen- und Universitaets-Bibliothek zu Koenigsberg in Preussen.* Bonn: Marcus, 1870.

LONDON. Augustus Hughes-Hughes. *Catalogue of Manuscript Music in the British Museum. Vol. III: Instrumental Music, Treatises, etc.* London: Printed by Order of the Trustees, 1909.

LONDON. *Catalogue of Printed Music in the British Museum. Accessions. Part 53—Music in the Hirsch Library.* London: Published by the Trustees of the British Museum, 1951.

LONDON. William Barclay Squire. *Catalogue of the King's Music Library.* Vol. III. London: Printed by order of the Trustees, 1929.

MADRID. Higinio Anglés and José Subirá. *Catálogo Músical de la Biblioteca Nacional de Madrid.* Vol. I. Barcelona: Consejo Superior de Investigaciones Científicas, Instituto Español de Musicología, 1946.

MODENA. *Associazione dei Musicologi Italiani. Catalogo generale delle opere musicali, teoriche o pratiche, manoscritto o stampate.* Vol. VIII. *Città di Modena. R. Biblioteca Estense.* Compiled by Pio Lodi. Parma: Fresching, 1916-1924.

NAPLES. *Associazione dei Musicologi Italiani. Catalogo generale delle opere musicali, teoriche o pratiche, manoscritto o stampate.* Vol. X [2]. *Città di Napoli. Biblioteca del R. Conservatorio di Musica di S. Pietro a Majella.* Compiled by Guido Gasperini and Franco Gallo. Parma: Fresching, 1929-1934.

NEW YORK. *The New York Public Library Reference Department. Dictionary Catalog of the Music Collection.* 33 vols. and Supplement. Boston: G. K. Hall & Co., 1964.

PARIS. Madeleine Garros and Simone Wallon. *Catalogue du fonds musical de la Bibliothèque Sainte-Geneviève de Paris.* (Catalogus Musicus, IV.) Kassel: Internationale Vereinigung der Musikbibliotheken; Internationale Gesellschaft für Musikwissenschaft, 1967.

PARIS. Lionel de La Laurencie and Amédée Gastoué. *Catalogue des livres de musique (manuscrits et imprimés) de la Bibliothèque de l'Arsenal à Paris.* (Publications de la Société française de musicologie, ser. 2, vol. VII.) Paris: E. Droz, 1936.

PARMA. *Associazione dei Musicologi Italiani. Catalogo generale delle opere musicali, teoriche o pratiche, manoscritto o stampate.* Vol. I [1]. *Città di Parma.* Compiled by Guido Gasperini and Nestore Pellicelli. Parma: Fresching, 1909-1911.

TENBURY. E. H. Fellowes. *The Catalogue of Manuscripts in the Library of St. Michael's College, Tenbury.* Paris: Editions de l'Oiseau Lyre, 1934.

VENICE. *Associazione dei Musicologi Italiani. Catalogo generale delle opere musicali, teoriche o pratiche, manoscritto o stampate.* Vol. VI [1]. *Città di Venezia.* Compiled by Giovanni Concinna. Includes catalogues of the Museo Correr and the R. Biblioteca di S. Marco [now Biblioteca Nazionale Marciana], the latter compiled by Taddeo Wiel, A. d'Este, and R. Faustini. Parma: Fresching, [1913?]-1914.

VENICE. *Fondazione Ugo e Olga Levi, Centro di Cultura Musicale Superiore. Stampe e manoscritti preziosi e rari della Biblioteca del Palazzo Giustinian Lolin a San Vidal.* Compiled by Siro Cisilino. Venice: A cura del fondatore Dott. Ugo Levi sotto gli auspici dell'Ateneo Veneto, 1966.

WASHINGTON. Oscar Sonneck. *Catalogue of Opera Librettos Printed before 1800.* 2 vols. Washington, D. C.: Government Printing Office, 1914.

BOOKS AND ARTICLES

Abert, Hermann. "Einleitung," to C. W. Gluck, *Le Nozze d'Ercole e d'Ebe. DTB,* II. Folge, Jg. 14, Bd. II, vii-xxxvi.

_____ *Niccolò Jommelli als Opernkomponist.* Halle: Niemeyer, 1908.

Anderson, Emily (ed. and trans.). *The Letters of Mozart and His Family.* Vol. I. 2nd ed. prepared by A. Hyatt King and Monica Carolan. London: Macmillan, 1966.

Barblan, Guglielmo. "Boccheriniana," *RaM,* XXIX, No. 2 (1959), 123-128.

_____ "Contributo alla biografia di G. B. Sanmartini alla luce dei documenti," *Festschrift für Erich Schenk, StMw,* XXV (1962), 15-27.

_____ "La Musica strumentale e cameristica a Milano nel '700," in *Storia di Milano,* vol. XVI. Milan: Treccani, 1963, pp. 619-660.

_____ "Sanmartini e la scuolo sinfonica Milanese," in *Musicisti Lombardi ed Emiliani.* Siena: Accademia Musicale Chigiana, 1958, pp. 21-40.

Barbour, J. Murray. "Pokorny Vindicated," *MQ,* XLIX (January 1963), 38-58.

Bartha, Dénes, and László Somfai. *Haydn als Opernkapellmeister.* Budapest: Verlag der Ungarischen Akademie der Wissenschaften, and Mainz: Schott, 1960.

Bengtsson, Ingmar, and Ruben Danielson. *Handstilar och Notpikturer i Kungl. Musikaliska Akademiens Roman-Samling* [Handwriting and Musical Calligraphy in the J. II.-Roman-Collection of the Swedish Royal Academy of Music]. With an English Summary. (Studia Musicologica Upsaliensia.) Uppsala: Almqvist & Wiksells, 1955.

Blume, Friedrich (ed.). *MGG.* Articles in particular on Camerloher, Carpani, Chelleri, Darmstadt, Endler Giardini, Gluck, Graupner, Holzbauer, Janitsch, Karlsruhe, Lampugnani, Laube, J. P. Martini, Mysliveček, Molter, Monza, Pichl, Solnitz, and Stalder.

Borrel, Eugène. "La Strumentazione della sinfonia francese del sec. XVIII," *L'Orchestra.* Florence: G. Barbera, 1954, pp. 7-22.

Brenet, Michel (Marie Bobillier). *Les Concerts en France sous l'ancien régime.* Paris: Librairie Fischbacher, 1900.

Brook, Barry S. *La Symphonie française dans la seconde moitié du XVIIIe siècle.* 3 vols. Paris: Publications de l'institut de musicologie de l'université de Paris, 1962.

_____*Thematic Catalogues in Music: An Annotated Bibliography.* Hillsdale, N. Y.: Pendragon Press, 1972.

Burney, Charles. *Dr. Burney's Musical Tours in Europe.* Ed. Percy A. Scholes. Vol. I. London: Oxford University Press, 1959. An expanded edition of *The Present State of Music in France and Italy.* London: Becket, Robson, and Robinson, 1771.

_____*A General History of Music,* Vol. IV. London: Printed for the author, 1789. Modern edition, with critical and historical notes by Frank Mercer. Vol. II. New York: Dover Publications, 1935.

_____*Music, Men, and Manners in France and Italy, 1770. Being the Journal written by Charles Burney, Mus. D.* Edited with an Introduction by H. Edmund Poole. London: The Folio Society, 1969.

Cambiasi, Pompeo. "Note intorno all'esercizio del R. Ducal Teatro di Milano l'anno 1737-38." *Gazzetta musicale di Milano,* 52 (1897), 462-468.

Carpani, Giuseppe. *Le Haydine ovvero Lettere su la Vita e le Opere del celebre Maestro Giuseppe Haydn.* Milan: Buccinelli, 1812

Cesari, Gaetano. "Giorgio Giulini, musicista," *RMI,* XXIV (1917), 1-34, 210-271.

_____"Sei sonate notturne di G. B. Sanmartini," *RMI,* XXIV (1917), 479-482.

Churgin, Bathia. "G. B. Sammartini and the Symphony," *The Musical Times,* 116 (January 1975), 26-29.

_____"New Facts in Sammartini Biography: The Authentic Print of the String Trios, Op. 7," *JAMS,* XX (Spring 1967), 107-112.

_____(ed.). *The Symphonies of G. B. Sammartini. Vol. I: The Early Symphonies.* (Harvard Publications in Music, 2.) Cambridge, Mass.: Harvard University Press, 1968. (Cited throughout as ChurginE.)

_____"The Symphonies of G. B. Sammartini." 2 vols. Unpublished Ph. D. dissertation, Harvard University, 1963.

Churgin, Bathia, and Newell Jenkins. "Sammartini [G. B.]," *MGG,* XI, 1334, 1336-1343.

Cucuel, Georges. *La Pouplinière et la musique de chambre au XVIIIe siècle*. Paris: Librairie Fischbacher, 1913.

Deutsch, Otto Erich. *Mozart. Die Dokumente seines Lebens*. Kassel: Bärenreiter, 1961.

————"Thematische Kataloge," *FAM*, V (1958/2), 73-79.

Devries, Anik. *Edition et commerce de la musique gravée à Paris dans la première moitié du XVIIIme siècle*. Geneva: Minkoff, forthcoming.

Donà, Mariangela. "Notizie sulla famiglia Sammartini," *Nuova Rivista Musicale Italiana*, VIII (1974), 3-8.

Downes, Edward O. D. "The Operas of Johann Christian Bach as a Reflection of the Dominant Trends in *Opera Seria*, 1750-1780." 2 vols. Unpublished Ph.D. dissertation, Harvard University, 1958.

Eineder, Georg. *The Ancient Paper-Mills of the Former Austro-Hungarian Empire and Their Watermarks*. Hilversum: The Paper Publications Society, 1960.

Einstein, Alfred. *Gluck*. London: J. M. Dent & Sons, 1936.

Enciclopedia della Musica. Direttore: Claudio Sartori; Vice-direttore: Riccardo Allorto. 4 vols. Milan: Ricordi, 1963-1964.

Fabronio, Angelo. *Vitae italorum*. Vol. XII. Pisa: A. Rafaello, 1787.

Federhofer, Hellmut. "Alte Musikalien-Inventare der Klöster St. Paul (Kärnten) und Göss (Steiermark)," *Kirchenmusikalisches Jahrbuch*, Jahrg. 35 (1951), pp. 97-112.

Fétis, F. J. *Biographie universelle des musiciens*. 2d ed. 8 vols. Paris: Firmin Didot Frères, 1860-1865.

Galeazzi, Francesco. *Elementi teorico-pratici di musica con un saggio sopra l'arte di suonare il violino*. Vol. I, Rome: Cracas, 1791; Vol. II, Rome: Puccinelli, 1796.

Gerber, Ernst Ludwig. *Historisch-biographisches Lexicon der Tonkünstler*. 2 vols. Leipzig: Breitkopf, 1790-1792.

————*Neues historisch-biographisches Lexikon der Tonkünstler*. 4 vols. Leipzig: A. Kühnel, 1812-1814.

Gotwals, Vernon. "The Earliest Biographies of Haydn," *MQ*, XLV (October 1959), 439-459.

Griesinger, G. A. *Biographische Notizen über Joseph Haydn*. Leipzig: Breitkopf & Härtel, 1810.

Hanslick, Eduard. *Geschichte des Concertwesens in Wien*. Vol. I. Vienna: Braumüller, 1869.

Heawood, Edward. *Watermarks, Mainly of the 17th and 18th Centuries*. Hilversum: The Paper Publications Society, 1950; reprinted 1957.

Heer, Joseph. *Der Graf v. Waldstein und sein Verhältnis zu Beethoven*. (Veröffentlichungen des Beethovenhauses in Bonn, IX.) Leipzig: Quelle & Meyer, 1933.

Henggeler, P. Rudolph (cd.). *Monasticum-Benedictinum Helvetiae.* Vol. III: *Professbuch der Fürstl. Benedictinerabtei, Unser Lieben Frau zu Einsiedeln.* Einsiedeln: Fürstl. Benediktinerabtei, 1933.

Hofer, Heinrich. "Christian Cannabich." Unpublished Ph.D. dissertation, Munich University, 1921.

Holland, Jeannette B., and Jan LaRue. "The Sharp Manuscript, London 1759-c. 1793: A Uniquely Annotated Music Catalogue," *Bulletin of the New York Public Library,* 73 (March 1969), 147-166.

Hopkinson, Cecil. *A Dictionary of Parisian Music Publishers, 1700-1950.* London: Printed for the author, 1954.

Humphries, Charles, and William C. Smith. *Music Publishing in the British Isles.* London: Cassell, 1954.

Inzaghi, Luigi. "Nuova luce sulla biografia di G. B. Sammartini," *Nuova Rivista Musicale Italiana,* IX (April-June 1975), 267-271.

Israël, Carl. *Frankfurter Concert-Chronik von 1713-1780.* Frankfurt am Main: Verein für Geschichte und Alterthumskunde zu Frankfurt am Main, 1876.

Jenkins, Newell. "The Vocal Music of Giovanni Battista Sammartini," *Chigiana,* forthcoming.

Jenkins, Newell, and Bathia Churgin. "Giovanni Battista Sammartini," *Enciclopedia della musica,* IV, 105-106. Milan: G. Ricordi, 1964.

Johansson, Cari. *French Music Publishers' Catalogues of the Second Half of the Eighteenth Century.* Stockholm: Publications of the Library of the Royal Swedish Academy of Music, II, 1955.

_____"Studier kring Patrik Alströmers musiksamling," *Svensk Tidskrift för Musikforskning,* XLIII (1961), 195-207.

Keller, P. Sigismund. "Mittheilungen," *MfM,* VI (1874), 46-47.

King, A. Hyatt. *Some British Collectors of Music, c. 1600-1960.* Cambridge, Eng.: At the University Press, 1963.

La Borde, Jean Benjamin de. *Essai sur la musique ancienne et moderne.* Vol. III. Paris: E. Onfroy, 1780.

La Laurencie, Lionel de. *L'Ecole française de violon de Lully à Viotti.* 3 vols. Paris: Delagrave, 1922-1924.

Landon, H. C. Robbins. *The Symphonies of Joseph Haydn.* London: Universal Edition & Rockliff, 1955.

_____*Supplement to the Symphonies of Joseph Haydn.* London: Barrie and Rockliff, 1961.

Larsen, Jens Peter. "Haydn und das 'kleine Quartbuch,'" *AM,* VII (July-September 1935), 111-123.

LaRue, Jan. "Major and Minor Mysteries of Identification in the 18th-Century Symphony," *JAMS,* XIII (1960), 181-196.

_____"A Union Thematic Catalogue of 18th Century Symphonies," *FAM,* VI (January-June, 1959), 18-20.

_____"Wasserzeichen," *MGG*, XIV, 265-267.

_____"Watermarks and Musicology," *AM*, XXXIII (April-December 1961), 120-146.

Mendel, Hermann. *Musikalisches Conversations-Lexikon.* 3rd ed. 12 vols. Leipzig: List & Francke, 1890-1891 (started 1870, completed 1883).

Mennicke, Carl. *Hasse und die Brüder Graun als Symphoniker.* Leipzig: Breitkopf & Härtel, 1906.

Meylan, Raymond. "Documents douteux dans le domaine des concertos pour instruments à vent aux XVIIIe siècle," *RdM*, XLIX (July 1963), 47-60.

Mishkin, Henry. "The Published Instrumental Works of Giovanni Battista Sammartini: A Bibliographical Reappraisal," *MQ*, XLV (July 1959), 361-374.

Nettl, Paul. *Musik und Tanz bei Casanova.* Prague: Veröffentlichungen der Gesellschaft deutschen Bücherfreunde in Böhmen, VI, 1924.

Newman, William S. *The Sonata in the Classic Era.* Chapel Hill: The University of North Carolina Press, 1963.

Paglicci-Brozzi, Antonio. *Il Regio Ducal Teatro di Milano nel secolo XVIII.* Milan: G. Ricordi, 1894.

Pincherle, Marc. *Antonio Vivaldi et la musique instrumentale.* 2 vols. Paris: Floury, 1948.

_____*Vivaldi, Genius of the Baroque.* Trans. Christopher Hatch. New York: W. W. Norton, 1957.

Quantz, J. J. "Lebenslauf," in F. W. Marpurg, *Historisch-kritische Beyträge zur Aufnahme der Musik.* Berlin: Schützens Witwe, 1755, I, 197-250.

Rubin, Emanuel. "The English Glee from William Hayes to William Horsley." 2 vols. Unpublished Ph.D. dissertation, University of Pittsburgh, 1968.

Saint-Foix, Georges de. "La Chronologie de l'oeuvre instrumentale de Jean Baptiste Sammartini," *SIMG*, XV (1913-14), 308-324.

_____"Les Débuts Milanais de Gluck," *Gluck-Jahrbuch*, I (1913), 28-46.

_____"Découverte de l'acte de décès de Sammartini," *RM*, II (June 1921), 287-288.

_____"Histoire musicale: Une découverte," *RMI*, XXVIII (1921), 317-318.

_____"Sammartini et les chanteurs do son temps," *RMI*, XLIII (1939), 357-363.

Sartori, Claudio. "Giovanni Battista Sammartini e la sua corte," *MO*, III (March 1960), 3-18.

_____"Sammartini post-mortem," in *Hans Albrecht in Memoriam.* ed. Wilfried Brennecke and Hans Haase. Kassel: Bärenreiter, 1962.

Schmidl, Carlo. *Dizionario universale dei musicisti.* 2 vols. Milan: Sonzogno, 1928?-1929. *Supplemento*, 1938.

Sehnal, Jiří. "Kapela Olomouckého Biskupa Leopolda Egka (1758-1760) A Její Repertoár" [Die Kapella des Olmützer Bischofs Leopold Egk 1758-1760 und ihr Repertoire], with an English summary, *Acta Musei Moraviae*, L (1965), 203-230.

Smith, William C., and Charles Humphries. *A Bibliography of the Musical Works Published by the Firm of John Walsh during the years 1721-1766.* London: The Bibliographical Society, 1968.

Stieger, Franz. "Opernlexikon." Vol. II. MS in Vienna, Nationalbibliothek.

Straková, Theodora. "Hudba u brtnických Collaltů v 17. a 18. století." [A study of the thematic catalogue of the Pirnitz Schlosskapelle.] Ph. D. dissertation, Brno, 1967.

Tartini, Giuseppe. *Traité des Agrémênts de la Musique.* Paris: P. Denis, 1771. Mod. ed. by Erwin R. Jacobi. Celle, Germany: Moeck, 1961.

Torrefranca, Fausto. "Le Origini della sinfonia. Le Sinfonie dell' imbrattacarte (G. B. Sanmartini)," *RMI,* XX (1913), 291-346; XXI (1914), 97-121, 278-312; XXII (1915), 431-446.

Weckerlin, J. B. "J. B. Sammartini et Joseph Haydn," *Le Ménestrel,* LXI (January 1895), 3.

Wotquenne, Alfred. *Thematisches Verzeichnis der Werke von Chr. W. v. Gluck (1714-1787).* Leipzig: Breitkopf & Härtel, 1904.

INDEX OF TITLES AND FIRST LINES
OF NON-LATIN WORKS

References are to entry numbers

GENERAL INDEX

References are to page numbers